Augustus Craven, Henry James Coleridge

Life of Lady Georgiana Fullerton

Augustus Craven, Henry James Coleridge

Life of Lady Georgiana Fullerton

ISBN/EAN: 9783337331092

Printed in Europe, USA, Canada, Australia, Japan

Cover: Foto ©Raphael Reischuk / pixelio.de

More available books at **www.hansebooks.com**

LIFE OF
LADY GEORGIANA FULLERTON

FROM THE FRENCH OF

MRS. AUGUSTUS CRAVEN

BY

HENRY JAMES COLERIDGE
OF THE SOCIETY OF JESUS

(SECOND EDITION, REVISED)

LONDON

RICHARD BENTLEY & SON, NEW BURLINGTON STREET
Publishers in Ordinary to Her Majesty the Queen

1888

PREFACE.

On the decease of Lady Georgiana Fullerton, those whose right it was to have a voice in such a matter, agreed in wishing that a *Life* of her whom they had lost should be written by her dear and valued friend, Mrs. Augustus Craven, the well-known author of the beautiful *Récit d'une Sœur*. With some reluctance, Mrs. Craven kindly undertook the work. Having been one of those who urged it on her, I could not shrink from the endeavour to make it as light as possible, by taking on myself the responsibility of the English version, which, it was felt, ought to appear simultaneously with, or as soon as possible after, the *Life* in French. The result of that undertaking is the present volume, which cannot claim to be either a perfectly faithful translation, or an original work. It cannot claim to be a faithful translation, because the perfect beauty of the French style of Mrs. Craven, like the incommunicable fragrance of a flower, defies all rendering. The more exquisite is the mastery of a writer over his or her own language, the more utterly impossible it is to reproduce it in another. But it is also fair to say that I am conscious that an English *Life* of Lady Georgiana Fullerton must be, in some respects, different from a French biography. Lady Georgiana had lived long in France, and formed a great number of ties in that country. It is not unnatural that her intimate friend, a French lady, writing about her to her own countrymen, should dwell fondly and at length on those scenes in her life and parts of her character which would immediately interest those for whom she was writing. It was also inevitable that there should be some things in the life, both religious and literary, with which a French writer would find herself not quite at home, and also which would require greater expansion when put before the English public. The most absolute freedom has been allowed to me in dealing both with the materials collected for Mrs. Craven's work, and with the work itself, as it has come from her hands. As far as the time and strength at my disposal allowed of it, I have not spared any labour in making the English *Life* as perfect as might be, and for this it was necessary here and there to add or to omit.

There will be found, then, in the following pages, whatever the reader would have found in a literal translation of the French work, with a few exceptions. All the letters have been used, but I have taken the liberty of enlarging here and there Mrs. Craven's quotations, all the more as I had the advantage of being able to use the letters in their original language. Some few have been added, though those who know what has been still left out will be likely to wonder at the frugality with which the additions have been made. Nor has all Lady Georgiana's correspondence been at the disposal of the author of either work. There were two points on which it seemed to me that an Englishman could speak with more clearness than any foreigner. These two are the religious phase which passed over the country fifty years · ago, in connection with the Oxford Movement, and which landed Lady Georgiana and so many others in the fold of the Catholic Church. The other point relates to Lady Georgiana's position as an English writer. On these two points, therefore, I have ventured to rewrite some of the remarks of Mrs. Craven. But in one other matter also I have to some extent departed from my original, in this case by omission rather than by any substitution. Mrs. Craven had access to some of Lady Georgiana's private notes and memoranda concerning her own soul, and from these she has quoted largely. They have been transmitted to me, and I quite understand that, writing for a public to whom Lady Georgiana represents only an honoured name, she has not thought it necessary to shrink from the publication of what would be thought unadvisable in England. I do not act on my own opinion only, in being more reserved than she has been. Some few quotations from these private papers are made in the following chapters, and some account of them is given in an Appendix. In other respects, the chapters of this volume will be found to follow faithfully the contents of Mrs. Craven's book, and not to go beyond them.

I think I may venture to say both for her and myself, that we are perfectly aware that a much fuller and more detailed Life of Lady Georgiana might be looked for. The present is a sketch, which aims, above all things, in presenting her character to the world. It is possible that a character may be given without the greatest fulness of detail, and I at least shall be satisfied if that is the effect of the

present work. In particular, I feel the great imperfection of the account, given in the fifteenth chapter,
of the charitable works at which Lady Georgiana
laboured for a quarter of a century in London and
elsewhere. For even in Mentone, where she spent
several winters, and in other places abroad, she has
left traces of her work which abide to the present
day. If Lady Georgiana, had kept a diary of her
daily occupations of this kind, it would have filled
many volumes, and we might have written a book
as large as the lately published Life of the good
Lord Shaftesbury. Still, not to have done all is
not the same thing as to have done nothing, and I
hope that this incomplete sketch of a truly noble
and simple soul, may not altogether fail in making
her known to those who knew her not, and in
reviving her gracious, soothing, and consoling
memory to those who were so blessed as to know
her.

H. J. C.

31, Farm Street, Berkeley Square,
  Feast of St. Augustine of England, 1888.

DEAR MRS. CRAVEN,—Mr. Fullerton tells me that you have consented to write a Memoir of Lady Georgiana. I sincerely rejoice at the news.

Since I have been a Catholic I have looked upon her with reverence and admiration for her saintly life. A character and mental history such as hers make her a fit representative of those ladies of rank and position in society who, during the last half century, have thought it little to become Catholics by halves, and who have devoted their lives and all they were to their Lord's service.

May I, without taking a liberty, express my feeling that the treatment of a life so full of interest seems naturally to belong to you!

I bid you God's speed in your undertaking, and I add my prayers to the many which are sure to accompany you in the course of it in proportion as it becomes known. . . .

Nov. 17, 1885.

. . . I am glad that I have lived so long as to be able to send my blessing upon your work, that is to say, on a *Memoir of Lady Georgiana Fullerton, written by Mrs. Craven.* Thank you for so great a favour, and excuse the imperfection of these lines which I am unable to write with my own pen.

Most truly yours,
JOHN H. CARD. NEWMAN.

April 17, 1888.

CONTENTS.

b

CHAPTER I.

GEORGIANA CHARLOTTE LEVESON GOWER, better known to us as Lady Georgiana Fullerton, was the younger daughter of Lord Granville Leveson Gower and of Lady Harriet Cavendish. Her grandfather, on the father's side, was the Marquis of Stafford, on the mother's side, the Duke of Devonshire. She thus numbered among her near relations the Dukes of Norfolk, Beaufort, Sutherland, Westminster, Argyle, and Leinster, and the Earls of Carlisle, Harrowby, and Ellesmere. It was in the midst of rank and affluence that one of the simplest and humblest souls ever seen, perhaps, outside the walls of a cloister, was trained and formed.

We are so fortunate as to possess a short memoir of the early days of Lady Georgiana Fullerton, written by her own hand in the last year of her long life. This memoir is far from being as full as we could wish, and it ends abruptly at an early point. But it is too valuable a contribution to her history to be omitted. It must be premised, that it was written, in exchange for some similar confidences, for a friend with whom she had become intimate in her visits to Rome, long after she became a convert to the Catholic Church. Agnes Giberne,

B

the lady for whom it was written, had been intimate from early years with the future Cardinal Newman and his family. She had not long been a convert to Catholicism when she was called on to show her friendship and devotion to the then Father Newman, by a service which involved great anxiety and care. Father Newman had determined to expose the character of the well-known ex-Dominican, Giacinto Achilli, and, in one of his lectures on *The Position of Catholics in England,* had published, from authentic documents, 'a number of charges against his moral character. The famous case of Achilli *v.* Newman, 1852, was the result, and it became necessary for witnesses to be brought from Italy to support the charges. To take charge of these witnesses was a difficult task, and it was confided to Miss Giberne, who afterwards wrote an account of the journey in the autobiographical memoir which she exchanged with Lady Georgiana. Miss Giberne ultimately became a Visitandine nun at Autun, where she died suddenly not long after her friend.

The object of Lady Georgiana in writing the short sketch which we are about to print must be borne in mind in its perusal. She was endeavouring to trace out the incidents and scenery of her youth, chiefly with a view to recollections of a religious kind. It was natural to her to regard the whole past in that light, and to fasten on the few points which stood out in those early years which might mark her growth in the knowledge of God.

The autobiography begins as follows:

I was born on the 23rd of September, 1812, at Tixall Hall in Staffordshire. My father[1] rented it in 1808, at the time of his marriage with Lady Harriet Cavendish, and retained it for several years. It belonged to Sir Clifford Constable, the head . of a very old Catholic family. In the records of the days of persecution frequent mention is made of it. In a history of it by Mr. Arthur Clifford, which he dedicated to my mother, he speaks of her appreciation of the picturesque beauty of the ruins and surrounding scenery of the ancient abode. In the records of the days of persecution frequent mention is made of Tixall Hall and of its ancient possessors.

I cannot help connecting in some degree, in my mind, the fact of my birth and early years spent at Tixall Hall, with my eventual conversion to the Catholic Church. I must have been the first child born in that house[2] outside the visible pale of the Church. May not the Guardian Angels of the place, have asked for me the grace of conversion to the true Faith? My wet nurse was a woman of the village, the inhabitants of which were, almost all of them, Catholics. Who knows that she did not say "Hail Maries" for the infant at her breast? and perhaps she may have taken me into the chapel which was enshrined amidst the ivied ruins, close to the house. I remember her very well, for as long as we lived at Tixall she often came to see me. I was only six years old when my father gave up the place to move into Suffolk with his family. I cried much at leaving my nurse, and said over and over again I should never see her more, though my governess tried to comfort me by saying that when I came to visit my uncle, Lord Harrowby, who lived at Sandon, near Tixall, I should come to see her sometimes. But I never did see her again.

[1] Lord Granville Leveson Gower was the second son of the Marquis of Stafford and his third wife, Lady Susan Stewart. He was created Viscount Granville in 1815, and Earl Granville, and Baron Leveson, in 1833. He died in 1846. His son, the present Earl Granville, is called Lord Leveson in the earlier part of this work.

[2] Lord Granville Leveson Gower seems to have spent the autumn and winter at Tixall for the shooting. His eldest daughter, Susan (Lady Rivers), was born elsewhere. Tixall was given up in the spring of 1819.

It was perhaps a mere fancy, but the first time I heard Mass in the chapel at Slindon House in Sussex, there was something in the sight of a Catholic rural congregation which made a strange impression upon me. I had then that sensation, so often experienced and remarked by others, by which, when one is in a place for the first time, one seems to have known it before, and all that passes seems the repetition of something one has already witnessed. I had never been before, in England, in a Catholic church in the country, except in the magnificent chapel at Wardour Castle. I cannot recollect having ever been inside that one at Tixall, nor do I remember the outside except that it was amongst the ruins. I perfectly remember seeing the villagers walking on Sundays through the park on their way to it in long files, men, women, and children, and the first time I noticed it, and asked, "Where are those people going?" my being told, "They are the Roman Catholics going to their church." I did not go, I think, to the Protestant church at Tixall. It was in the spring of 1819 that I was taken, for the first time, to Albemarle Street Chapel in London.

One of my earliest recollections is my brother Granville's christening. I was then two years and a half old. I remember quite well sitting on a sofa in the drawing-room at Stanhope Street and people talking to me—also very distinctly learning to read at a very early age, about three years old I think, and the first time a notion of religion was conveyed to me. It was at Tixall. I was kneeling before a sofa with a large book open before me, in which I was finding out, and spelling all the words I could find, of three letters. I put my finger on one, and said in a loud voice, G. O. D.—God. My mother checked me, and said, "You must not say *that* word in that manner, it is a sacred word." She did not explain further, but the way she spoke and looked made me feel hushed and subdued. I may here remark that, imperfect and scanty as was the religious teaching I received in childhood, it had one marked characteristic. That was the inculcation of reverence and of the sacredness of matters and things connected with religion. We were never allowed to hold a Bible or a prayer-book in a careless manner, or to speak of a clergyman without respect.

The chapel was built among the ruins of another of earlier

date, and was very near the house. By a strange chance I have only last year (1882) made the acquaintance of a lady lately received into the Church, who had passed her childhood at Tixall, and she, like myself, had retained a deep indelible impression of the Catholic traditions of which the place is full.

At the early age of four years the little Georgiana was transferred from the nursery to the school-room, and was placed, with her sister Susan, under the care of a governess, Mademoiselle Eward. She seems to have been a person of much merit, and it is a proof of this that, after the relations between her and Georgiana ceased to be those of pupil and teacher, they corresponded for many years on the most affectionate terms. During the childhood, however, of the pupil, Mademoiselle Eward's severe and uncompromising character made her fail to appreciate her or to win her affections and confidence. Georgiana had probably been taken from the nursery too young, in order that she might share her sister's schooling, and there was an inclination to favour the elder of the two children which provoked the high spirit of the younger. She has herself related a trifling scene which she never forgot, an occasion when in a carriage drive she was told "not to pull her collar about," and took no notice of the injunction. She was punished by a threat, which was forthwith executed, that if she did not obey, her favourite toy rabbit should be thrown out of the carriage window. "Never," she says, "notwithstanding the long years that have passed since that time, have I forgotten what I felt, when I saw my poor rabbit falling on the hedge, and then from the hedge into the field, where it was lost for ever to me, and as I saw it gradually disappear from my sight."

She asks herself whether she had a rebellious nature, and declares that she never remembers a correction that did her any good, or an occasion on which she submitted without resistance. But the truth seems to be that her governess simply mismanaged her, and thus created in her young heart a sort of antipathy, which changed into warm attachment and the most sincere friendship as her pupil grew up. Her elder sister Susan, afterwards Lady Rivers, was the most attractive of the two girls. She had a soft, sweet disposition, and a charm of amiability which remained her characteristic through a life of much suffering. If her sister had been less generous than she was, she might have been jealous, but she was incapable of any rancour. The two were most tenderly devoted one to the other during the whole of their lives.

In the spring of 1817, when I was about four years and a half old, I went abroad for the first time. I recollect the horror of sea-sickness, then being handed by a sailor from the ship into an open boat, tossing on the waves, carefully wrapt up in a red shawl on the maid's knee just opposite to my father, and saying to him in a very reproachful manner, "I don't like it, not at all !"

My sister, two years older than myself, was very ill at Paris. We lodged at the Hôtel de Paris on the Boulevards, which had a large garden, in which I spent the greatest part of the day alone, much to my delight. I could read then and had an enthusiastic admiration for Mrs. Barbauld's hymns, several of which I knew by heart, and repeated aloud, when by myself,. with some sort of religious feeling. When my sister recovered,. we went to Switzerland, and remained some time at Neuchatel with our governess, whilst our parents travelled in Italy.

I perfectly recollect the first sight of the Alps, and, in crossing the Jura, our getting out of the carriage to look at the view, and Mademoiselle G. Eward exclaiming, "Voilà la Suisse!" But I was not much impressed at that time by beauty of scenery.

Two more autumns and winters we spent at Tixall Hall, which we finally left in 1819, taking leave for ever of my nurse whom I parted with sorrowfully and never saw again, of Cannock Chase, my favourite walk, where we used to run up and down the heathy hillocks, and of the Christmas "mummers" who had furnished one of our childish joys, for this old custom was not kept up in Suffolk, where my father then took a house. This was Wherstead Lodge, near Ipswich.

In London that spring, I first went to church. We had a pew in Albemarle Street Chapel, in the gallery. I now often pass by its doors and wonder whether it has been beautified since those days, when it was a perfect pattern of square ugliness. The services were dull. Church-going was most wearisome to me as a child, and I have hardly any religious impressions connected with it of a pleasurable kind, except of the holly and the hymn, *Hark the Herald Angels sing*, at Christmas. But I had fits of childish piety, and soon began to think a great deal about Heaven, and fancying what it would be like. I think I rather wished to die and go there, simply as a change. Hymns and religious poetry I delighted in. Reading was a passion with me from the age of seven or eight. We had few books in those days, but Miss Edgeworth's tales, *The Evenings at Home, Sandford and Merton*, and some French story-books, I read over and over again, and the rare happiness of a new book was ecstasy. I used to fancy myself the personages in my favourite stories, and set myself to imitate them, but not at all successfully as to their virtues, for I was a very naughty child, with very little conscientiousness. or sense of duty—kind-hearted and obliging enough, but ill-tempered, untruthful, disobedient, and idle, except when lessons.

amused me. History I liked, I detested arithmetic, and geography bored me.

When I was about ten years of age, the *Génie du Christianisme*, by Chateaubriand, was given to me to read, and this was quite an epoch in my life. It opened a new world to me, and for the first time, I learnt something about the Catholic religion. The poetry of the ideas and of the style fascinated me, especially in the chapters about Saints and Angels. I must have derived some sound ideas from the book, for one day I made my governess very angry by saying that, as the Apostles had founded the Catholic religion, [I thought it must be the true one.

About that time I suffered from a long fit of scrupulosity. Very angry with my governess, I had said to myself, "Méchante femme, je te maudis," and then I recollected that there was a text in the Bible which said, "He that curseth father or mother, let him die the death." It must be nearly as bad, I thought, to curse a person who had had so long the care of me, and I was horrified, supposing myself to be worthy of death! When I read in books of people who had lost their innocence, or that had committed crimes, I used to sigh and think, "This is my lot." A Catholic child would have been told by a confessor what had been the amount of sin, and would have received absolution. But I tormented myself some time about this, and then forgot to be sorry for it, till I made my general confession as a Catholic.

From the time I went to church I set a certain value on the Absolution in the Anglican Service, and if I had been more than usually naughty during the week I used to be vexed if we arrived too late for it. Once I remember grumbling inwardly that my governess was not making more haste, and saying to myself, "If she did but know all the bad things I have done, she would not make me lose the Absolution!"

This was but the natural effect on a religious-minded child of the Anglican formularies here referred to. Later on, in her first novel, *Ellen Middleton*, we find Lady Georgiana bringing out this feeling about "Absolution," and being severely taken to task by Lord Brougham in consequence. It is true, she then was speaking of the more precise and developed doctrine of the Prayer-Book, as seen in the Office for the *Visitation of the Sick*, and, at the time at which her novel was written, this doctrine had become a "burning question."

Living as I did almost entirely alone with the governess, and my sister being then in very delicate health, I spent a great deal of time by myself walking in the garden, thinking of all sorts of things, and living in an imaginary world. My punishment was always to be shut up in a room alone, and nothing I enjoyed more. I am sure that to confine a child in solitude without any employment is one of the worst plans possible. It leaves the mind at liberty to wander in every direction, and often in a mischievous manner. I began to write scraps of French verses, also, when I was nine or ten years old. Amongst my other attempts was a tragedy on the story of King John and Prince Arthur, *imitated* from Shakespeare.

These are my principal recollections up to the spring of 1824, when we went abroad. I remember my fears of an insane old sailor, called "Mad Jack," who used to wander about the lanes near Wherstead, singing psalms. I also call to mind visits to the shop of two good old Quaker ladies in Ipswich, who used to give me little dolls; in London, long drives taken for the sake of my sister's health, in the environs of London, when Paddington and Battersea were country villages; days in the summer spent in Kensington Gardens—a paradise to me, for *dogs*, of which I was dreadfully afraid, were not allowed entrance into them. There was the annual children's ball at Carlton House Palace, where on one occasion, when sitting on George the Fourth's knee, I told him I could not stay any longer with him, or I should lose a dance. Then we went yearly to the theatre : the first time to Astley's, where the piece was the *Siege of Londonderry*. I remember my brother Granville, then five years old, with the practical sense be has shown in after-life, crying out, when, on the arrival of loaves for the famished city, the chorus began to sing—"Why do they go on singing and don't eat the bread!" Another year there was a ballet—*Cherry and Fair Star*—which latter character I enacted every day for some time afterwards. In the last instance, we saw *Julius Cæsar*—my first acquaintance with Shakespeare. The scenes of this play remained deeply impressed upon me.

I should perhaps add, as relating to public events, that myself, my brother, and sister were, in 1815, taken out of our beds in the middle of the night, and carried off to Chiswick House, at the time of the Corn Law riots,—my father's house, in Stanhope Street, having been threatened by the mob. Also that from our nursery windows, in 1821, we saw the crowds assembled round Alderman Wood's house, in South Audley Square, where Queen Caroline was staying. Then in 1822, or 23, the Duke of Wellington was staying at Wherstead Lodge. Two incidents of his visit I remember, though I did not witness them. One was his accidentally shooting my father in the face, and the feeling he showed on the occasion, tears streaming down his face. Two or three of those shots were never extracted. The other incident was his acting in a charade, in which he personated an old nurse, dressed up in character, with the Russian Ambassadress, Princess Lieven, as the baby. He only requested that the performance should not begin till the officers from Ipswich had left after dinner.

Again I must recall the pleasantest hours of that period of my childhood, which were those I spent when I read poetry with my mother, Shakespeare's historical plays, Thompson's *Seasons*, some of Cowper's poems, and Walter Scott's. She used to hear us repeat the Catechism and the Collect of the day on Sundays. I did not dislike that, but very vividly do I remember my aversion to Blair's Sermons, one of which was read in the school-room every Sunday evening. It was a great relief when, now and then, our governess substituted one from a volume of sermons by a Swiss preacher, Cellérier. Two of those sermons I liked so much that I learned them by heart. There was a passage in one of them about Christian friendship, and it spoke of the Blessed Virgin and St. Elisabeth.

At the beginning of the year 1824 my father was named Ambassador to the Hague, and we went there in the month of March by Calais and through Belgium. The months we remained there are the pleasantest of my childish recollections.

The novelty of the scene, the dresses and manners of the people, were a constant amusement, and our mode of life was quite different from what it had been in England, where we were quite separated from our parents except for short periods of the day. At the Hague, we lived *en famille*, and were much more in the drawing-room. We walked and drove with my mother and my father, sometimes spending whole days in the beautiful wood which is the pleasure-garden of the place, or on the charming sands of Schevening, the fishing village at a short distance from the town.

I have never seen such sands as those, fine and shining, and strewed with the most lovely little shells of every variety of colour. The road that led to them was an avenue, lined on each side with dog-roses. The spring of that year was beautiful, it was like a long holyday. In May, I think, a fair was held under the trees of the public avenue in which our house stood. The booths, and shows, and shops of every sort, enchanted me. It seemed like something in a fairy tale, and this lasted eight days.

Again, in the early summer we went to Haarlem and Amsterdam. We heard a wonderful organ at the first of these towns, and looked with astonishment at the fields of tulips in its neighbourhood. Then at Amsterdam, for the first time I was taken to the opera, and that opera was *Der Frieschutz*. This enjoyment was intense. I cannot even now play or hear any of its music without a vivid remembrance of the excitement and delight I felt that night.

I remember hearing my mother say at that time, speaking of me to a gentleman attached to the Embassy, "That child has such a passion for books that one does not know how to supply them fast enough." He said, "You should give her a great deal of history to read, with voluminous details." I hoped his advice would be acted upon, for I was very fond of history, whereas books on Natural History always bored me.

We had at the Hague a master to teach us English grammar

and composition, in which we were extremely deficient, having been taught exclusively in French. He had a most interesting way of teaching, and I liked his lessons immensely, but unfortunately, during our little journey to Amsterdam, he ill-treated our little brothers, whom he was also teaching, and this was the first symptom of a brain fever. He went quite mad.

Much as I liked the Hague, it was not a subject of regret to me, when in the course of the autumn we heard that my father was named Ambassador at Paris. Change had attractions, and our governess told us wonders about our new destination.

We left Holland in October, remained a few days at Brussels, and arrived at Paris early in November, at that Embassy house where so many of the years of my youth were to be spent. The first sight of the house and its large garden was most satisfactory, and the streets, the Tuileries, and Boulevards and Champs Elysées were very amusing. But now again we were confined a great deal to the school-room. Business of course engrossed my father, and both he and my mother had such a number of social duties to perform, going into society and receiving at home, that we saw much less of them than in Holland.

CHAPTER II.

THOSE who are acquainted with the English Embassy at Paris will not be surprised to learn that the impression Georgiana received on first entering her new home, at about twelve years of age, was a most favourable one, and this impression was strengthened as time went on. It was there that the last years of her childhood and the first of her youth were to be spent. It was there that her heart and mind were fully developed, and that her soul began to seek those higher regions in which she was one day to sore so high. And it is also with her life at the Embassy that the sweetest and most important events of her life are associated.

After a few days, however, the vivid pleasure of the first moments was chastened by a great disappointment.

Lord and Lady Granville, occupied as they were with a multiplication of social and official duties belonging to their new position, were no longer free, as at the Hague, to spend the greater part of the day with their children. Both their daughters were too young to go into society or even to appear in their mother's *salon*, which soon became one of the most brilliant in Paris at a time which in this respect may be considered unique.

The brief interval between the final disasters of the Empire and the Revolution of 1830, which overthrew the newly established order, does indeed, now that it has become a part of history, present features belonging exclusively to itself, and differing from everything which preceded or which followed it. Several circumstances combined to give an interest and a charm to society which were wanting to it before and after this time. There were many women, who, perhaps full of frivolity and living on delusions in early life, had been matured and transformed by lessons of terrible reality. These ladies now made even the bravest of men wonder at the story of the sufferings they had borne and the difficulties they had conquered. The men, on their side, whether they had gone through the vicissitudes of exile, or borne a part in the famous battles the memory of which was still fresh and vivid, had something better than empty gossip to contribute to the conversation. Society at the same time, thanks to the cheerfulness that, in one and all, had outlived every trial, was neither dry nor wearisome. And then, all this was animated by the welcome breath of the peace now restored to Europe, which allowed foreigners to re-visit Paris and Frenchmen to travel beyond France, besides giving to public and social life an ease and security which had not yet lost the charm of novelty. Paris especially profited by the change. Numerous *salons* were re-opened, and it was once more easy to enjoy the pleasure of conversation in which the French delight so greatly, and shine so conspicuously. It must be admitted that their facility

often causes them to misuse it, and to talk when
they have not much to say. But this fault was not
so common then as it is now, partly on account of
the gravity of events still recent in the life of every
one, and even more because of the reviving hopes of
all. There was none of the bitterness and want of
hopefulness which have become so common now.
People were still a long way from supposing that
because there was nothing more to hope for, there
was no need for self-restraint and respect for the
feelings and opinions of others—a state of mind
which is the most fatal imaginable to the spirit of
conversation.

After 1830, however, social intercourse began to
be seriously affected by a spirit of bitterness and
animosity. Before that, if quarrels were not altogether at an end, they were discussed with a good
humour which blunted the edge of sarcasm. After
this fresh convulsion people began to draw off from
one another. *Salons* still existed, but they had
become hostile camps. Still their charm was not
destroyed during the life-time of those who had
created them. In several it was still to be found
at the close of Louis Philippe's reign. Under the
Second Empire their whole tone and character was
changed, and since the misfortunes which attended
its fall, no *salon* has been re-opened in which could
be found anything of the spirit, language, and
traditions of the earlier and better days.

Lord Granville was Ambassador at Paris during
the whole of the time occupied by the two phases
which, taken together, form the best and most

remarkable social period that France has known in the present century. This, then, was the atmosphere in which his daughters found themselves at their introduction into the world some years later. But as yet this time was not come for either of them. The beautiful gardens of the Embassy, and a walk now and then in those of the Tuileries or the Champs Elysées, furnished at first their only outdoor recreation. Indoors they saw but little beyond the walls of their school-room, in which Mademoiselle Eward reigned with absolute sway, as in the days before their residence in Holland. Soon after their arrival, however, a diversion, if not precisely an amusement, fell to their share, in the shape of a visit to the Duchesse d'Angoulême, who had expressed to Lady Granville a wish to make acquaintance with her daughters. This shall be recounted to us by Lady Georgiana herself.

Not long after our arrival my mother took us to see the Duchesse d'Angoulême, the daughter of Louis XVI. and Marie Antoinette. She was not prepossessing in look and manner ; her features marked, and her voice rough. She looked like one whose whole life had been a painful struggle. My English feelings were rather hurt, I remember, at what she no doubt meant very kindly. She said to my mother : " Vos filles sont si gentilles, on les prendrait pour des petites Françaises ! " The Duchesse de Berri and her children we were also taken to see ; Mademoiselle (afterwards the Duchess of Parma), then five or six years old, and the Duc de Bordeaux, about four. They were very nice little children, and we heard a great deal of them, as their governess, the Duchesse de Gontaut, had been a great friend of my mother's in the time of the Emigration. She was devoted to her charges, especially to the little Prince. I remember her saying that once a month he had to receive the visit of the Marshals of France, and was apt to get impatient, poor child! and to want to run away from his visitors. The Duchesse had to whisper to him: "Monseigneur, souvenez-vous du *pudding*!" He was particularly fond of pudding, and, if he was rude, was deprived of it.

One day, some time after our arrival in Paris, we went to the Palace of St. Cloud, when he was playing in the gardens. A miniature fortress called the Trocadero had been constructed for him, and this he and his little companions stormed and defended with their tiny cannons and swords. He led the attack, I remember, with great ardour.

It was one of my pleasures at that time to see the carriage of the "Enfants de France" pass through the Champs Elysées, then our usual walk. A detachment of the Cuirassiers rode alongside of it. They went almost every day to St. Cloud and back.

I will add here all my recollections of the Royal Family of France during our first residence at the Embassy, from 1824 to 1828, for I do not remember the exact date of each little incident. On Shrove Tuesday, 1825, we went to the rooms of one of the ladies of the Court, at the Tuileries, to see the procession of the "Bœuf Gras," an old custom which had existed from time immemorial. All the butchers of Paris escorted the prize ox, and the chief of them "complimented" the King and the Royal Family. One member of it, we were told, could never bring herself to look at that sight—the poor Duchesse d'Angoulême. It brought too vividly to her mind the scenes in that Court at the time of the First Revolution. The very name of the "Butchers of Paris" must have sounded painfully in the ears of the daughter of Louis XVI. and Marie Antoinette. I remember King Charles X., then Comte d'Artois, as one of the handsomest and most distinguished-looking men I have ever seen. His son, the Duc d'Angoulême, produced on me quite an opposite effect. As for the Duc d'Orleans, afterwards King Louis Philippe, he won my heart by his good nature. He was particularly kind to children. At the first children's ball I went to at the Palais Royal, however, he made a mistake which vexed me very much. He had taken me to the buffet and asked what I would eat. I said as loud as I could, "des pommes," looking

C

at a nice-looking *compote*, but he thought I said "des pommes de terre," and helped me accordingly, saying to my mother, who at that moment came up, "Je suis désolé, madame, vos filles ne veulent manger que des pommes de terre!" I was too shy to explain what I wanted, but was not the less much put out.

One great drawback to my pleasure at these balls was that they were presided over by our dancing-master, a certain M. Deschamps, who also taught the Orleans Princesses. He was most anxious that his pupils should do him honour, and cast severe glances at me when I did not perform my steps to his satisfaction. I think I have never in my life hated anybody, except perhaps this dancing-master. I am afraid I almost did hate him. He once missed coming to us on account of a sore throat, and ever afterwards I kept hoping he would have it again. If I had been a Catholic child how often I should have had to accuse myself of these bad feelings!

The Duchesse d'Orleans was then, as she ever was, dignified, kind, and worthy of admiration and love. One little incident I recollect at Neuilly. One day that we were there, the only one of her children at home was the Prince de Joinville—a very handsome little boy he was then. He was sent for to make friends with us, but this he was evidently determined not to do; whether because we were only girls, or because we were English, I don't know. At last his mother gave him a plate of sugar-plums and told him to offer them to us. He threw them all on the floor, and ran out of the room, the Duchesse calling after him, "Joinville, Joinville, je le dirai à ton precepteur!"

On one of the birthdays of the Duc de Bordeaux, we assisted at some plays acted by children. I can see him now seated in front of the stage, clapping his little hands and shouting with delight. It seems strange to think of at this moment, when he has just passed out of this world. The last child's ball I was at in Paris was the Duchesse de Berri's. I was then fourteen or fifteen years old. There I saw for the first time M. de Montalembert, who was about the same age. He asked me to dance a "Grand Père" with him, a dance I have never heard of since. It was a very active one, and having a bad cold I got exceedingly tired and said I wanted to leave off dancing. "No, no," he said, "I should not be able to get another partner !" My first impression of my dear holy friend of after years, was that he was a very selfish boy !

In 1837 the Duc de Bordeaux passed, as the expression was, "entre les mains des hommes." This was a sad trial for the poor Duchesse de Gontaut. The first night he slept in the room of his "gouverneur," the Duc de Rivières, she was sitting crying in hers. She described how the good Duke knocked at her door, and beckoned to her to come softly to his apartments, and gave her the consolation of looking at the little Prince asleep.

These are, I think, all my reminiscences of French Royalty under the Restoration.

From the fact of all the scattered recollections of many years being thus gathered up into one narrative, it might be supposed that Georgiana had a greater amount of gaiety than fell to her lot. But, in spite of these occasional visits and juvenile balls, the two young girls led a very monotonous life during this time.

I now return to the spring after our arrival in Paris, that of 1825. On account of repairs at the Embassy, Faubourg St. Honoré, we lived for six months at the Hôtel d'Eckmühl, Rue de Grenelle, Faubourg St. Germain, near the Invalides, which for many years afterwards was the Austrian Embassy. It was there that for the first time I was present at Mass, in the chapel of the Hôtel des Invalides. There was one at nine o'clock for the old soldiers, and very beautiful music. The English Protestant Service was at eleven, and, for the sake of the music, our governess took us very often into that chapel. We sat on a bench near the door, and I liked it very much. The presenting arms at the Elevation struck me as very impressive. Of course I did not in the least understand what was going on, and in spite of a certain pleasure in the names and sights connected with the Catholic church, I did not connect any religious ideas with it.

It was at that time that a poor woman on the Boulevard

begged of us. Our governess said she "never gave in the streets." The beggar answered, "Et où donnez-vous donc, madame?" Mdlle. Eward felt remorse at this question, for in truth, neither she nor her pupils, since their coming to Paris, had given anything to the poor. She proposed to us to give a trifle weekly, and said that she would too, out of our pocket-money, to two poor persons the French servants recommended. We agreed readily, but I soon became bored with this. Never seeing these objects of our charity, or hearing anything about them, I would much rather have brought presents for my friends. I suppose this would often be the case with children, and that to make them care for the poor, personal intercourse is necessary, or else some kind of excitement of the feelings and imagination.

When we returned to the house in the Faubourg St. Honoré, we began to take Italian lessons. A lady in reduced circumstances, the Comtesse Galvani, was our instructress. She was, I think, the daughter of the inventor of galvanism; a stout commanding looking person, who would have been handsome, but for a decided squint. She was clever, eloquent, agreeable, and I delighted in her lessons, which she continued to give us until we left Paris in 1828.

She was very poor, but full of energy, and very amusing in her descriptions of her *ménage*, and her makeshifts to meet emergencies. I read with her Metastasio's plays, and I kept in my possession those four volumes, which during subsequent years, I read over and over again, but with no benefit whatever to my mind. But they gave rise to all sorts of romantic ideas, such as good novels, like Miss Austen's for instance, would never have suggested. We read with her the *Gerusalemme Liberata* a little later on, and when I was fourteen or fifteen, I knew a great deal of it by heart. She never proposed Dante, that I know of. An English tragedy called the *House of Aspen*—I forget who wrote it[1]—she made me translate into Italian, and begged to keep the only copy I had made of it. From want of perseverance and practice I afterwards lost entirely the power I had then acquired of writing Italian. But I have never forgotten Madame Galvani, and the contrast

[1] It is a condensation from the German by Sir Walter Scott.

between her lessons, and those of music and dancing, which I hated. She went out of her mind, poor woman, and died in a lunatic asylum.

On my thirteenth or fourteenth birthday I received as a present Racine's works in three volumes. But the strictest guard was set over our reading any novels, and until I was seventeen I only read *Emma,* by Miss Edgeworth, and Walter Scott's *Tales of the Crusaders.* I knew *them* really almost by heart. Moreover every, even a child's book, placed in our hands was carefully looked over and pages cut out or sewn up. There was an extraordinary laxity about poetry. I have never been able to understand this. I read all Racine's tragedies, even *Phèdre;* Molière's plays, and Walter Scott's poems. My own attempts at composition, as I shall mention later, were modelled on French tragedies and Italian poems.

But now I must mention a book which I read when I was about fourteen, which had a strange effect upon me. That book was a controversial tale, entitled *Father Clement,* written by a Protestant of the Evangelical school, and intended to expose the errors and corruptions of the Catholic religion, Jesuit intrigues, and the like. It was well and pleasantly written, the characters well drawn, the conversations well sustained. Those of a controversial nature were tolerably fair, so far as to put into the mouths of Catholics *some* of the arguments they would naturally use. There was, to my mind, a wonderful charm in the description of the old Popish castle, and the chapel with its tall crucifix, pictures of saints, and dim religious light. Father Dormer, the Jesuit chaplain, was intended as a specimen of an excellent, pious, and in every way amiable and refined young priest, who, in the end, is made to waver in his faith, having been forced by his Superiors to act against his conscience. But, as represented at first, he excited all my admiration and sympathy, and I sided entirely with the girl in the family, who was a devout Catholic, and wished I could, like her, have gone to confession to Father Dormer, and thought how exactly I would have obeyed him. On the other hand, I took the greatest dislike to the other sister, who was being drawn away from the Church by her Protestant cousins, and I thought it very wrong of her not to submit to Father

Dormer. So strong a feeling had I about this imaginary Catholic priest, that being one day very angry with my governess who, as a punishment, had taken away from me for a fortnight a Bible which had been given me a few days before, I said to myself, "A strange way indeed of making one good!" But I suddenly remembered that Father Dormer had made Maria give up the Protestant Bible she had got hold of, and the beautiful things he had said to her about obedience, and I became quite humble and obedient *for once.*

In the course of the story there is a conversation between a Protestant and a Catholic about the invocation of the Blessed Virgin and the Saints, in which the Catholic says, "If we ask our friends on earth to pray for us, why not ask the Mother of Jesus Christ and the Saints to do so in Heaven?" This struck me as conclusive, and, acting upon it at once, I went into a little room adjoining the school-room, knelt down and said several times, "Blessed Virgin Mary, pray for me." I did not keep up to this, and I hardly think that I prayed to our Blessed Lady again till some time after my marriage, but I have a strong feeling that *that* prayer was not said in vain. For some little time I remained under these Catholic impressions,—so much so that I remember thinking that when I should be old enough to *come out,* I should tell my parents that I would prefer becoming a Catholic and going into a convent. This, however, was a very transient vocation. It is strange that it never occurred to me that my parents would disapprove of my plan.

A curious circumstance may be mentioned in connection with the book which made so opposite an impression on Lady Georgiana's mind from that intended by the author. The loan of *Father Clement* had exactly the same effect on Alexandrine d'Alopeus (afterwards Comtesse Albert de la Ferronays). It was lent to her, while still a Protestant, by a friend who was aware of her Catholic tendencies, and anxious to combat them. But, just as in Lady

Georgiana's case, the only thing which attracted her in *Father Clement* was the descriptions of character and of Catholic worship which it contains, so that the friend, who wished to turn her mind away from the Church, had the mortification of perceiving that she had brought about just the opposite result.

Another book fell in my way soon afterwards of quite a different sort—a volume of verses by a Mademoiselle Tastu, in imitation of the old French poetry. I was always scribbling something or other, and wrote some lines of the same kind, which I quite forget, except that the stanzas ended each by "Vierge Marie, priez pour nous."

When I was about fourteen and a half, my sister and I were sent to Dieppe with our governess, and remained there from the beginning of June to the end of September, I think. We had a pretty picturesque villa in a country suburb, with terraced gardens, ascending to the cliffs. The change was very agreeable. I had got—during the two or three years spent in Paris without leaving it—a kind of "Mal-du-pays" for the country. This reminds me of a day of cruel disappointment, such as children so often undergo, without any one intending or suspecting it. As a great treat, it was announced to us one day, that we were to go and have luncheon with our parents at the house of some friends, who had a villa in the forest of St. Germain. My delight was unbounded. I dreamt of running about under the trees, sitting on the grass, picking wild flowers, and I counted the days till all this was to happen. Well, we drove to the villa in question, and sat in the drawing-room till luncheon was announced. It lasted a long time, and we returned to the drawing-room, I, meanwhile, casting longing looks out of doors. Then carriages came to the door, and I sat "bodkin" between my mother and her friend. We took an interminable drive, along all the alleys of the forest and the terrace, and when we came back *our* carriages were ready, and we returned to Paris. I had hardly been able to keep from crying all the time, and I did feel injured when my mother said afterwards, "My dear child, you looked so glum and cross, that it does not incline me very much to give you, another time, a day of pleasure."

Once also, when driving with her mother in an open carriage, she heard her give an order in which she thought the word *jardin* was mentioned, and rejoiced to think that they were starting for some beautiful place out of town. She was quickly undeceived, and her feelings may be imagined when, in less than five minutes, the carriage stopped at the shop of the principal perfumer in Paris. What her mother had really said was, " Drive to Houbigant— *Chardin's !* "

At Dieppe we had the sea-shore, sea-bathing, walks on the downs, and country walks too, to pretty villages and farm-houses, and the garden was a great delight with its charmilles, bosquets, and flowers. There were roses by thousands with which we made rose-water which smelled very badly : and apples by thousands too, of which I secretly ate a great many, and unripe grapes also. Then we collected snails from the walls for the cook, who made broth with them for her consumptive mother. So unused had I become to any but town sounds, that I was once horribly frightened in the garden at what seemed to me the most terrible thing I had ever heard, so terrible that I ran alarmed into the house—this was the braying of a donkey !

It would have been a very happy time—that year at Dieppe—but that my sister was in an anxious state of health, and this so worked on the nerves of our governess, who was devotedly attached to her, that her temper became very trying, and she and I were continually falling out. When my brother Granville came from school for his holidays, we confided to each other how disagreeable she was, and we became great friends. He gave me *Goldsmith's Poems,* and wrote on the title-page :

> May this small gift, my dear Georgiana, prove
> A tender token of a brother's love,
> And our affection with our years increase,
> Until we both attain Eternal Peace.

I used to scold him at that time for his idleness and

indifference to *solid reading.* "Why, what do you want me to read?" he asked one day. "Suppose," I said, "you read every day a chapter of *Modern Europe.*" I little imagined I was speaking to a future Minister for Foreign Affairs!

Metastasio and Tasso continued to be my delight, and about that time I for the first time read some of Byron's poetry. My mother came to spend a few days with us in the course of the summer, and read to us some passages out of *Childe Harold* and the *Corsair.* The volume of all his works remained on the shelves in our sitting-room, I used to get hold of it and look out for those passages. I had a scruple about reading much else, though now and then I glanced at some of the other poems.

My mother had known him and his wife very well, and had the worst possible opinion of him. But somehow his poetry, his picture at the beginning of the volume, and the idea of his having been a wild, strange, and even bad man, took hold of my fancy, and I actually *fell in love* with him.

He had been dead some years, but it really was like being in love. I would have given up any pleasure for the sake of reading the least bit of his poetry, and kept constantly thinking of him. If his name was mentioned, I coloured, and my heart beat. For some time while in Paris, every time I went out in the carriage, my sole wish was that we might drive by the Avenue Biron! It made me very unhappy to think he was irreligious. I peeped at his Life in the beginning of the volume, to find out if he did not become good before his death, and thought I would have done or suffered anything, if I had been his wife, in order to convert him. Some months afterwards, when we were at Brighton, there was in a bookseller's window a small volume of *Beauties of Byron,* also with his picture. I had watched it as it lay open, with the most intense satisfaction. One day our governess took it home with some other books, to choose from. I passionately hoped it would be kept for our school-room library, but no, it went back again, and did not reappear at the window. This strange infatuation lasted nearly a year. I have often wondered whether, if I had read the Lives of Saints, I should have been so enthusiastic about them, and lived in thought with St. Francis Xavier or St. Teresa.

To return to Dieppe. I took the greatest delight in our walks to the neighbouring villages, where we used to drink milk at the farm-houses, and sit in the orchards. The Sunday dances I remember, and seeing a grey-haired curé sitting looking on with great complacency. The least details of those excursions are present to my recollection, but I must not go on dwelling upon them. They have no bearing on my religious life. One little book I read at that time with extreme interest, an Evangelical religious tale, *Harriet and her Friends*, I think, was the name. I was fond of everything religious of that kind, and though most inattentive at church and at my prayers, and not at all good in any way, I had moments and impulses of piety. The room where the English Service was held, was, I suppose, cold, or it was held at an inconvenient time for an invalid. For some reason or other, instead of our going there, the clergyman (Mr. Bauer was his name) came on Sunday afternoons and read the Service to us, and afterwards explained some part of the Bible. One day he expounded some verses in the Book of Revelations, and made rather a remarkable prediction. He deduced from the said verses that after awhile another Bonaparte would reign in France, and that he would do a great deal more harm to that country than the first. He concluded by saying, " I shall not live to see this, but you will, young ladies, and when it happens, you will remember the old clergyman at Dieppe."

Our governess, who would not have anything the least out of the common way, was quite shocked at this prophetic outburst, and we sat up a little later than usual (the Service having taken place in the evening), to listen to her remarks on the impropriety of mixing up such things with religion. Some means were taken to stop poor Mr. Bauer's ministrations, for he did not come again, nor did we go to the church at all that year at Dieppe.[3]

---

[3] Extract from a letter from Lady Granville to her sister, Lady Carlisle, in 1827. " The following is out of Georgy's letter to-day : ' The other day, as I was walking in the garden, I pushed in passing a little rose, just

opened, a remarkably pretty one, and it fell down. All that my poetical melancholy could supply on the doleful occasion was—

> Plucked from her stem, the morning of her days,
> Hid in the dust, the new-born beauty lays,
> 'Tis fled, the blushing hue that once did glow,
> With all the charms that music can bestow,
> No more thy doom to court the scented gale,
> Or rising sun with fragrant perfume hail,
> But pale and leafless, left to fade away
> The slow and dreary evening of thy day.' "

—The little bit of bad English in the second line is not unnatural in a girl of fifteen, brought up in France. Perhaps Lady Georgiana caught it from the object of her admiration at the time, Lord Byron, who, in his celebrated lines on the sea, makes the same blunder.

CHAPTER III.

In the month of September, 1827, the death of Mr. Canning having caused a change in the English Government, Lord Granville left the French Embassy. This does not seem to have been a subject of regret to Georgiana. What made her perhaps care less about it, was the unusual and pleasant way in which the journey was performed. People now-a-days would hardly consider it so delightful, as the object at present is to travel as quickly as possible. But the weather being fine, Lady Granville and Georgiana travelled in an open carriage, while Lord Granville, his eldest daughter, and his son, went on horseback. They slept twice on the road to Boulogne, from which place they crossed the Channel. They then went on to Brighton, travelling in the same manner. There Georgiana's pleasure came to an end. The rest of the stay at Brighton seems to have been, for her, a series of disappointments. Her secret wish, she says, had been that they might inhabit a pretty villa which they had seen, and where she hoped they were to live. Instead of this, by the advice of a doctor, they were settled in the very midst of the town, in its least pretty or shady part, and here the two daughters and their governess were left, while Lord and Lady Granville paid visits in the country, among their friends and relatives.

The same doctor who had chosen their abode, " no doubt," says Georgiana, " because it was most convenient to himself," had also decreed that Susan's health, for which they came to Brighton, required that the house should be kept very cool. This order Mademoiselle Eward obeyed most scrupulously. All this is mentioned in the autobiography.

Towards the end of October of that year, 1827, as sea air was still considered essential for my sister, the family doctor came over on purpose to take and settle us at Brighton for a few months. We crossed from Calais to Dover, and travelled along the coast, stopping at a pretty villa at Seaford, which a friend of my father's had offered to lend him for us. We had luncheon there, and ardently did I hope this lovely cottage, with a garden, might be accepted as our abode ; but the doctor opined that it was not as dry and bracing as Brighton. I rather suspected him of being influenced in this decision by the greater convenience to himself of looking after us at Brighton, than at Seaford, and felt very resentful.

Brighton, I intensely disliked. The first house we had there, was swarming with bugs. We tried another, and then finally settled in one in Cannon Place, the dreariest street and coldest house imaginable. It was altogether a dreary five months we stayed there. I never in my life suffered so much from cold for so long together. My bed-room looked north, and I never had a fire in it. I used to be kept awake by the iciness of my feet in bed, but as I was the strongest of girls, I was ashamed to complain of it. Our governess had been warned against hot rooms as unwholesome for us, and I cannot help smiling when I think of the description given by a dear aunt of ours, of the time she paid us a visit there that winter. She was delicate and chilly, but bore, heroically, the hardships of the day. In the evening the sitting-room was beginning, with the fire and lamp, to get a *little warm*, when to her dismay Mdlle. Eward suddenly threw the door wide open, exclaiming, "On s'étouffe ici !" Our food, too, was of a very austere description, and we had not very much of it. All our childhood and youth through, we were brought up on a system of extreme abstemiousness, which was supposed to be wholesome. At breakfast, milk and water and dry bread, the same for supper. At dinner, roast meat, vegetables, and a plain pudding, sometimes a little fruit. As to sugar-plums, I never tasted any, except, alas ! sometimes by stealth, or a small bit of sugarcandy my father gave us sometimes.

Once at Paris, I took, out of a box of bonbons in my mother's room (which had been sent her as a New Year's gift), a piece of chocolate. The taste struck me as so strange and nasty (why, I cannot imagine, I have been so fond of it in later life), that I thought I was poisoned, and underwent great apprehensions ! I did not dare speak of it, but I remember saying to myself, "But perhaps I shall die, and then I shall have committed suicide ! "

But there was a charming interruption to this dreary Brighton *séjour*,—undiversified hitherto by anything more exciting than lessons in Oriental tinting, a sort of mechanical painting. My uncle, the late Duke of Devonshire, came to Brighton and stayed some days at an hotel. He took us out walking two or three times, and into shops, and gave us presents. We dined with him one day at five o'clock, and the fare was a great contrast with our lodging dinners. And, moreover, as it was requisite for my sister to see a doctor in London, we spent, soon afterwards, a few days at Devonshire House. The luxury and comfort, the sight-seeing with my uncle, the variety and amusement of those days, were so different to Cannon Place, that the return there was like what boys feel when they go back to school. Our uncle Devonshire was one of those persons whose originality and funniness even children could appreciate. One was always on one's best behaviour with him, and much afraid of boring him, but still at one's ease. Even to spend a few moments with him was amongst the greatest pleasures of my life, up to the time we lost him, in 1858.

The Duke of Devonshire will often appear in these pages. In order to understand the charm with which he was endowed, and the influence he exercised, it is not necessary to add much to the picture which is drawn for us by his niece. On her return to Brighton, she was much amused at learning to play at whist, and she tells us of the fun which was excited at the way she translated from French into English the names of the different suits on the cards.

In the early spring of 1828 we returned to Paris. At Easter, I think, I was Confirmed, and received the Sacrament for the first time. I had previously read some religious works with my mother, amongst others, Jeremy Taylor's *Holy Living* and *Holy Dying*, which I liked very much. But my mother used to explain away or dissent from the Catholic part of its teaching. Especially I remember her saying we were not to attend to the Anglican prelate's injunction, to pay that honour to the Sacrament, to let it be the first food taken on the day on which we receive it.

I made a great many good resolutions, and on both occasions felt very pious, but no great change took place in my conduct. I have always reproached myself for the way in which I read some books, and parts of books, without leave. Our governess used to paste together chapters not to be read, but I found out a way of undoing her work and putting it together unobserved. This did give me great remorse, not because of my disobedience, but as a piece of ingratitude for the pains she had taken. It almost made me cry sometimes— but the temptation was too strong.

Again, having to take some medicine twice a day, I was sent to take it the second time alone in the bed-room, and generally threw it out of the window. That again I felt was ungrateful to my parents, who paid for it. I had no repentance for faults that did not wrong any one, and was not at all truthful. That year I had lessons from the famous pianist Liszt, then only just beginning his career. He played brilliantly, and with great "fougue." He would make me play his own music, which was very difficult, and my performance so unsatisfactory to him, that he sometimes started up and ran about the room, stopping his ears! I can still play some little bits of those pieces, which made me go through so much torment. At last I tried to persuade him that the best way to teach me would be to play himself the greater part of the hour the lesson lasted. I sent him a message by his friend Father Hermann some years ago. He said he remembered, if not my musical talents, my amiability!

In the summer of 1828 we went again to Dieppe, to our villa of Condi Côte, and I remember the Duchesse De Berri's coming there for sea-bathing.

It was about this time that she first tried to compose a poem. She wrote the first canto of a love story, in which figured knights and troubadours. This kind of thing was rather the fashion among young girls at that date, even among those who were not gifted with the literary talent which later on was developed in Lady Georgiana, and their minds were very much occupied with it. They were full of the fabulous exploits of bards and heroes, of whose deeds they sang, queens of beauty hopelessly adored, and for whose glory these doughty deeds were done, and upon whom to a certain extent was reflected some of the glory which these acts earned. Such were the themes which then inspired the writings of girls of the age of Georgiana. To their successors of the present day all this seems great nonsense, and it is likely that their minds are quite free from such romantic ideas. But if the fashion has changed now, is it for the better?

I forgot to say, that during the last summer I spent at Dieppe, I wrote the first canto of a poem, which was to be a love story of the days of knights and troubadours. The love in it was in the style of the French tragedies, and very extravagant in its language,—"Dying of love" and suchlike expressions. Having been asked by my governess what I was busy about, I produced my manuscript. I remember so well her look and manner, when she said, "Je n'aurai jamais cru qu'une de mes élèves écrirait un roman ! avant d'avoir quinze ans !" Poor dear Mdlle. Eward, she was more indulgent to novels, when in 1844, as she was travelling from Switzerland to England, to pay us a visit, she fell in with a party of English people who were talking of *Ellen Middleton*. One of them said, "Who is this Lady G. Fullerton?" Upon this my old friend, "se rengorgea," as she described it, and said, "She was my pupil."

To return to Brighton in October, 1828. I spent two dull months much like those of the preceding year, but before Christmas my parents returned and took a large house in Brunswick Terrace. My brothers were at home for the holidays, and we had some amusement. I had hardly ever made acquaintance with other girls. One I had seen, Lady Charlotte Thynne, now the Duchess of Buccleuch, and walked round the garden of the Embassy with her. Once or twice I had spoken with a beautiful girl of my own age, Mary Hardy, now Lady McGregor, and those had been events in my life. That winter at Brighton, I made acquaintance with Miss Wortley, who afterwards married John Talbot, Lady Lothian's brother. She was three years older than I was, and took a little notice of me, talking of drawing and scenery. I felt honoured beyond description. She became a dear friend of mine later on.

There was a great deal of discussion at that time about Catholic Emancipation. It seems so strange to think that the subject did not interest me more than arguments now-a-days about the Thames Tunnel or the Isthmus of Panama. Once, however, I was struck by my uncle Lord Harrowby saying one evening, "It is quite wrong to call Roman Catholics idolaters, because they worship the Host. They only worship

D

It because they believe that our Lord Jesus Christ is present in It."

The time was not yet come for her when this important subject would throw all others into the shade. Much that was very vague was then floating in her mind, her tastes and inclinations. Nothing appeared absolutely indifferent to her, though nothing interested her for very long. Her impressions of things were remarkably vivid, and in some ways her mind was much developed. But there was much of the child about her still, and this gives to some girls, when passing from adolescence to youth, a charm which others do not possess. For there are many who, from the natural quickness of their intellect, soon outgrow the dreaminess of youth. Better that dreaminess, than an unnatural maturity, full of premature schemes and plans, which surprise and sadden us, like the sight of a flower, faded before it is fully blown, or wrinkles on a young face before their time.

In February we went to London, and then followed for me six dreary months. My sister came out, as it is called (or rather was called in those days). She dined late, and went to balls and parties, whilst I was in a constant *tête-à-tête* with our governess, who was in a state of the greatest despondency at the idea of leaving us, which she was to do after the London season. No wonder, dear woman! after having lived with us nearly sixteen years. But her sorrow made her very cross, and I had a weary time of it. In August we all went to Tunbridge Wells for a fortnight, and lived all together, though she was still with us, and how enchanted I was!

It is no wonder that the absence of her favourite pupil, and the prospect of being soon separated

from the other, saddened Mademoiselle Eward's
mind. Next year, it would be Lady Georgiana's
turn. She too would "come out," and this would
put an end to the duties of her governess, and bring
about a final separation. One must suppose that
during these last months of her stay, having only
Georgiana to occupy her, and feeling less the weight
of a responsibility which was so soon to end, the
thought of which also, no doubt, touched her heart,
Mademoiselle Eward began all at once to view her
character and her faults in a new light. She began
to see, rather late it is true, how much she had often
mistaken the one and exaggerated the other. Being,
as she certainly was, a person both good and sincere,
she now conceived for her a sympathy and tenderness, which found expression when the time for
farewell came, and still more in the frequent
correspondence which followed between them.
More remarkable still, is the readiness with which
Georgiana responded to these tardy signs of affection, and appeared to forget all her former troubles
and wrongs, as well as the feelings of anger, to
which they had formerly given rise. Her feelings,
however, were deep and strong, but she was too
kind and generous to let anything like rancour
dwell in her heart. The least attempt at reparation
on the part of another, was enough to make her
not only pardon an offence, but forget it entirely.
Tunbridge Wells, of which she speaks as a charming place, became a spot of which she was very
fond all her life, and which always had for her
something of the attraction which she had felt at

her first visit there.   It was for her the dawn of
young life, and a dawn which her imagination
painted as that of a brilliant and cloudless day.

It was the end, too, of all the vicissitudes of
Mademoiselle Eward's reign, which though latterly
much softened, had not been such but that at
seventeen years of age it could be anything less
than a relief to be set free from it.   When the time
came, however, for the final parting, many tears
were shed on both sides.   The poor governess was
in despair at leaving those to whom sixteen years
of her life had been devoted, and her two pupils
gave signs of true sorrow.   They were, however,
quickly dissipated by the prospect of a journey
into Derbyshire, which gave them promise of much
pleasure.

From there we went for a few days to London, and parted
with our poor governess with tears, and great sorrow for her
great grief.   Our sorrows were quickly superseded by the
intense pleasure of the journey to Derbyshire, and our arrival
at Chatsworth, where I had never been before.   The second
night we slept at Derby.   The sight of Matlock next day
threw me into ecstasies, which were not diminished on seeing
Chatsworth.   I had never been before in any large country
house.   It seemed to me like a sort of paradise—what with the
beautiful scenery, the magnificent woods, the immense gardens,
the lovely winding rippling brook that flows along what is
called the two-mile walk, and then all the pictures and statues
in the house and gallery, and the beautiful drawings !

To these treasures of art, gathered in halls and
saloons worthy of them, it must be added, that in
this beautiful place were assembled a number of
people, full of intelligence and brilliancy, such as

the Duke of Devonshire had the gift of gathering round him, and we cannot wonder at the effect which all this produced on his young niece, who had always been a special favourite of his.

I was just seventeen, and had been kept closely in the school-room. It seemed a strange change of custom and existence. I suffered a little from shyness, but not very much. The night we arrived I sat at dinner by a grey-haired gentleman, whose name I did not know. He asked me if I admired the new wing which had just been added to the house. I answered that I thought the house must have had a better effect without it (which is still my opinion). But I was horrified to find afterwards that the gentleman was Sir Geoffrey Wyatville, the architect, who had designed the said wing. On this first coming out, I was surprised to find that some things I had up to that time looked upon as merits, were not approved of in a grown-up girl. One was being silent at meals, and another going to bed early. We were, however, kept much more under restraint than young ladies now are. My mother made us breakfast in our own rooms, in order not to begin the day at once in society. We were expected to study in the morning, and did not appear till luncheon, and our breakfast still consisted of tea and rolls without butter. But oh! the enjoyment of the walks with other young people ; the long drives in pony chaises and four that went as fast as the wind ; the expeditions to Matlock, Hardwick, Haddon, &c., &c. ; the dancing and acting of charades in the evening ! One of the party we met at Chatsworth at that time was Mrs. Robert Arkwright, who lived at a place called Stoke, four miles off. She must have been then between forty and fifty. She had a face beautiful still and full of expression. She was Stephen Kemble's daughter, and the dramatic talent of his family found vent in her singing. She had not much voice, but when singing the songs (which were mostly ballads by the best poets), the music of which she had composed herself, her intonation and the expression of her wonderful eyes had a strangely pathetic and exciting power. Her conversation was also singularly original and attractive. You can imagine what an impression such a person would make on an imaginative girl, and what was the enchantment of being noticed and liked by her. My enthusiasm was intense, both about her and her singing, and even now, if I play to myself some of these songs, I feel an emotion which carries me back to those days, fifty-five years back.

In these lines Lady Georgiana seems to give us a complete picture of what she was at this time of her life, when her tastes and faculties were showing themselves with a freedom which till then they had not enjoyed. She was passing just then through one of those phases of enchantment which occur at the opening of some lives, which are like some mornings of which we say "they are too beautiful to last," and which make us fear that clouds will soon appear and dim their beauty. When the morning is that of a human life, one may be sure that these clouds will not fail to come. That of Lady Georgiana was for the present destined to be transformed rather than to be overshadowed. From all the *éclat*, the luxury, and the magnificence of the high society which surrounded her at Chatsworth, she very soon and willingly separated herself. The sumptuous way of life with which her own was now associated was, nevertheless, that to which she was born, and her nearest relatives and their friends were of the highest rank in that distinguished circle. She was therefore truly in her rightful place, and could lead in it, as did many others dear to her, a perfectly good life. She might have been led into more frivolous ways, but she forsook the too pleasant and easy paths for others, into which we

shall by-and-bye follow her.   But it is well to
remark that the great change which then made
her life become one of greater austerity, never
modified the feelings with which she looked back
on this first phase of her youth.   After fifty-four
years she still thought of it with the same emotion,
though she had long reached that point of the path
of life at which the soul tends always higher and
higher, and regards the empty vanities on which
youth occupies itself in their true light.   We shall
find in her life always this characteristic of unity
and consequence.   She could sometimes blame her
younger years with some excitement, some errors
of judgment, some too vivid passions.   But her
thoughts and her soul itself were always noble,
pure, and clear.   So that, when old age was drawing
near, she could look back and view these far distant
pictures of the past, and could smile over them with
tender emotion.   For even while she walked in the
midst of the glorious light which then shone round
her, there was nothing in these recollections which
she could wish either to banish or forget.

Imagination, intelligence, sensibility,—these are
great gifts, and nothing can degrade them but the
use we may ourselves make of them.   No doubt
they are dangerous gifts, gifts which we cannot
possess here below without having often to struggle
and fight with them.   It is needful to have great
courage in using them, sometimes great courage in
keeping them under restraint.   But for those who
can master them, they are some of the noblest
instruments which God has given to the human

soul. By them we may raise it to Him, and by
them we may practise towards others that love and
charity which He has placed by the side of the love
which we owe to Himself.

My father and my uncle were going to the opening of the
first railway, from Manchester to Liverpool, which was to take
place that month. It was arranged that my mother, my sister,
and myself should spend the two or three days of their absence
at Stoke with Mrs. Arkwright. I think I liked that place better
even than Chatsworth. It was in the midst of wilder scenery.
Behind the house there were rocks and a torrent stream;
beyond these, the purple moors. We were all day with
Mrs. Arkwright, who was always ready to sing to us, and whose
conversations with my mother I listened to with intense interest.
They were both so clever, but so different in many respects.
Mr. Arkwright was a great contrast to his wife; no imagination,
or poetical element in his composition—a kind-hearted, hard-
headed man, devoted to everything practical. They had four
sons and a daughter, then eight years old, whom I made great
friends with during that visit. One of those happy days
Mrs. Arkwright took us in a carriage with post-horses, a sort
of journey, rather than a drive, through all the most beautiful
scenery of the Peak. The weather was beautiful, and my
happiness not to be described. We got out and walked in some
of the most lovely spots. She was telling us all the time
interesting things, past and present, relating to the places we
passed through.

On the day we returned to Chatsworth, terrible news came
there. Count Potocki arrived there with the news of Mr. Huskisson's accident and expected death. He was an intimate
friend of my father's, who remained with him till he had
breathed his last. He had been standing close to him at the
fatal moment, and my mother was very much overcome by all
the thoughts connected with this fearful accident, and my
father's narrow escape. A gloom was thrown over the party
assembled at Chatsworth. But young people soon get over
these impressions when their affections are not concerned. It
was during that month that I also made acquaintance with a

great friend of mine in after-life, Lady Newburgh. She lived
likewise near Chatsworth, at Hassop, the family place of the
Eyres. Her husband was a Catholic, and I remember a discussion taking place one day as to whether she was secretly
one or not.[1]

She here refers to the 15th of September, the
day of the inauguration of the first railroad in
England which was opened for public use, that
which runs between Liverpool and Manchester. It
was a great event, and enormous crowds of people,
not only from the neighbourhood, but from a great
distance, were assembled for the occasion, to which
the presence of the Duke of Wellington, then Prime
Minister, added great honour. It will, no doubt,
be remembered how this great day was saddened
by the death of Mr. Huskisson, at that time one of
the Members for Liverpool and one of England's
most eminent public men.

* Here, unfortunately, we come to the end of
these reminiscences of her youth by Lady Georgiana
herself. They cannot be properly called a journal,
for they were not written down till a very few years
before her death, but they preserve to us many
incidents which we should otherwise have missed,
and enable us to begin her biography, properly so
called, with a very great knowledge of her character
through life. At the very time that she was enjoying
her first sojourn at Chatsworth, her future friend

---

[1] This venerable Lady Newburgh still lives, and has rejoiced to see the
publication of the *Life* of the girl whom she then met at Chatsworth. She
was a Catholic, though her conversion was not then publicly known.

* An asterisk marks the passages in which there has been any important
deviation from the French author.

and biographer, Mrs. Craven, was suffering under the blow which destroyed the fortunes of her family in the French Revolution of 1830. That Revolution probably passed over Lady Georgiana at eighteen with, perhaps, more effect on her feelings than on those of most young English ladies of the time, because she had lived in France, but still without leaving on them any very deep impression. She lived to sympathize with France almost as if she had been born there, but that time was not yet come. Of course it would have been very diffierent if she had had the personal interest in the events which fell to the lot of her friend, who was the daughter of a distinguished and noble French diplomate and statesman, who had been Minister of Charles X., and who, after the exile of the elder branch of the Bourbons, felt unable to continue his career as one of his country's Ambassadors. Lady Georgiana at the time lived in a society which had political excitements of its own, not far inferior in importance to those which occupied minds on the Continent, and till then Paris had only been for her a place where her days were spent in the schoolroom, and her recreations passed with her sister and Mdlle. Eward. The time was coming when she was to return there under very different auspices, and to lay up a store of her best and happiest memories.

CHAPTER IV.

GEORGIANA and her sister passed the winter 1830—
31, and part of the next spring, in England, enjoying all the pleasures that country life affords at
that season of the year. They visited, with their
parents, many houses in Derbyshire, Staffordshire,
and Yorkshire, which were hardly less splendid than
Chatsworth. But Castle Howard, Lord Carlisle's,
was the house which Georgiana preferred to all the
others, and, during her whole life, the very name of
this beautiful place awoke in her the pleasantest
recollections. (Lord Carlisle's wife was Lady
Granville's sister, and thus Georgiana's aunt.[1])
These recollections included not only her parents,
her brothers and her sister, but also her uncle and
aunt, her cousin Lord Morpeth, who afterwards
won for himself an honourable place in public life,
and was remarkable for his many sterling and
amiable qualities, and his six sisters, endowed with

---

[1] Lord and Lady Carlisle had nine children, three sons and six
daughters. Of the sons, the names of Lord Morpeth (afterwards Lord
Carlisle), and Charles and Henry Howard, occur frequently in Lady
Georgiana's letters. The daughters were Lady Caroline Lascelles, Lady
Dover, the Duchess of Sutherland, Lady Burlington, Lady Elizabeth Grey,
and Lady Taunton.

peculiar goodness and charms of every kind, not excluding, in more than one case, the gift of great personal beauty.

The long absences from England, which Lord Granville's diplomatic services had occasioned, and the very retired way in which his daughters had been educated, had separated them a good deal from their relatives. This separation now came to an end. It was a new pleasure for Georgiana to become intimate with her cousins and others of her family, and with her natural quickness of understanding, enjoying, and loving, she entered into this fresh kind of life, though still preserving, as always, a certain slowness in becoming demonstrative, in spite of the strength of her impressions.

It is sometimes said, with questionable justice, that family ties are not so strong in England as they are in France. Many things give a colour to this. In England the boys go to school while quite young, and they return home only at intervals. After school comes the profession, which may be the army or the navy, and which may take them away from their country, and specially in the case of sailors, long voyages may detain them for years. English families are usually numerous. The daughters do not always marry, but they are allowed, even while still young, a great deal of independence. They can choose their occupations and friends, if they please, outside the family circle. To this may be added the custom which exists, almost without exception, of leaving their father's roof when they marry. Any other way of life would seem to them almost the contradiction of a law. Each man in his turn must, when he marries, found a "home" of which he is to be the head. It may be sometimes the case, that all this leads up to the fact that family life, as it is considered in France—where several young households often live together in the closest union with their parents—seldom exists in England. It is none the less true, however, that there is the tenderest affection between brothers and sisters and other near relatives. And among the English aristocracy might be certainly mentioned, as examples of this, the families of Leveson Gower and the Howards, which were exceptions to the ordinary rule of separation and dispersion which reigned in so many others.

In the month of May, 1831, after this winter of which we have spoken, when Georgiana finally left the school-room, she returned to Paris and again lived in the English Embassy there. No longer now as a pupil under the charge of a governess, but by her mother's side, entering a sort of new world, where she would be henceforth, more or less, in public society. Paris had, during the disturbances of the last few months, undergone many changes, and was not at all what it had been when Lady Granville first went there in 1824. In speaking, however, of the transformation which had taken place since then, it must also be noticed that the division was not very perceptible. It never was perceptible at the English Embassy, as long as Lady Granville presided there. Her talents, and the charm and grace of her manner, never failed to gather round her many, at least, of those who had before formed part of the circle in her *salon*. Balls, evening parties, and state dinners were for her the fulfilment of her duty, more than her pleasure. But she well knew how to choose from the crowd a certain number of people, who frequented her more private soirées, or dinners where her guests were few. At these were to be found the most distinguished men and women in Paris, as well as members of the diplomatic body. They each and all considered themselves honoured by being invited. To this excellent French society was added the best English, in which Lady Granville numbered many relatives and friends, all eager to bear part in a circle which, while very cosmopolitan, bore a " cachet " which marked it out from everything else of the kind in Paris.

Georgiana, however, cared less at first for all this agreeable society than might have been expected, and regretted the pleasant life which she had led for the previous six months in England. Her feelings on this matter were poured out in the many letters she wrote to Mdlle. Eward, who, from the moment she ceased to be her governess, had become her intimate friend. So intimate, indeed, that she always addressed her by her first name " Eda," and, what is perhaps more surprising, we find her " tutoyant " this lady, whose stern and cold demeanour had weighed so heavily on her childish years. Georgiana never lost the habit of confiding in Mdlle. Eward, and, at least for many years, she opened her heart to her on all subjects in the freest

way. A few days before she left England, she wrote
to her as follows :

To Mdlle. Eward.

To-night we are going to a ball, which they say will be
splendid. I am so glad. We breakfast at Lord Mansfield's
and go to the opera in the evening. It is certain that the more
I go into the world the more I like it. I can't precisely say that
I like never to be out of it, but conversation becomes such a
pleasure when one feels at one's ease and is accustomed to it !
Another advantage is that I find one thinks less about it the
more one goes into it. It seems strange—but I mean that the
evening's amusements occupy one's thoughts during the day less
when they are frequent. But I feel that this kind of life would
be bad if it was to go on long, and mamma would certainly not
let us go out so often if she did not know that it would all come
to an end in eight or ten days.

My uncle [the Duke of Devonshire, with whom they were
staying] is extremely gay, and delighted that we are going back
to Paris.

The country [England] is quieting down gradually. The
incendiary fires are less frequent. Last week the mob attacked
one of the Duke of Beaufort's places, and tried to seize him
himself. But Worcester saved his father, and captured the
ringleader. Since that, the country has been quiet. The
people generally submit when spoken to reasonably. The
other day in one of the towns of which my uncle names the
Members, the people made a great fuss and revolted violently.
But the moment the two Members, Sir James Mackintosh and
Lord Waterpark, came and addressed them, they were perfectly
calm. The Ministry seems very popular, and the Opposition
very quiet.

No doubt these remarks refer to the disturbances which occurred throughout England while the
Reform Bill of 1832 was under discussion.

A few days after writing this letter, Georgiana
left England with her parents, and as soon as she
reached Paris, she again took up her pen.

To Mdlle. Eward.

Paris, *May* 15, 1831.

MY VERY DEAR EDA,—Papa and mamma are gone for their visit to St. Cloud. Meantime, Susan, Granville, William, and I, are in the green drawing-room, the first playing the piano, the others reading, and all four as comfortable as can be. Paris is beginning to be excessively agreeable, the weather is superb, the gardens delicious. In short, I should be enchanted with our life here, if the remembrance of England and our uncertainty when we shall return there, did not often come to disturb my pleasure.

A few days later she writes :

We are expecting next week Charles Wortley and his wife Lady Emmeline. Three years ago she would have been my *beau ideal,* for she is a poet and very romantic. But happily those qualities, thanks to you above all, do not seduce me any more. How useful your advice has been ! I wish I had always followed it, especially to correct my vanity, which often makes me do what I regret. . . . I like being here more than at first, but it is always very different from the life we lead in England. But we are far too happy to complain. Balls are the only things we do not get to like, and this is very convenient to mamma, and I love to think that our tastes are like hers. I do not like either the manners or the conversation of the French. I can't bear their compliments and affectations. There are no nice English people here now. In short, except Madame de Flahaut, Mr. and Mrs. Fitzroy, Lord Harry Vane, Mr. Stuart, and Prince Paul Lieven, we have not yet made many pleasant acquaintances. Prince Paul is as clever as his mother. I hope between us Susan and I have put you *au courant* as to our society and kind of life. . . .

I don't know what is the matter, I feel rather sad to-day. I feel as if I could do nothing. But one must fight against it, it is so ridiculous to say one is out of sorts, without any reason to give. I like Sir J. Mackintosh's book. I have been reading Byron's *Giaour* and *Corsair.* They have enchanted me, for I like poetry excessively, though now I read little of it.

It is easy to see from these passages what were the new relations established between Georgiana and her old governess, now become her friend. We shall not quote much more from the letters which followed them, during the remainder of that year and the next. They are chiefly made up of descriptions of the various gaieties in which the two sisters took part, or in details about the new acquaintances they made in Paris, as well as of their old friends and members of their family, in all of whom Mdlle. Eward took great interest. There are no longer any of the comparisons between society in London and in Paris, or any mention of the "affectation" of the French. In short, she seems to have found it all most pleasant, and everything around them was "couleur de rose." They no longer regretted the past, or wished for anything but what surrounded them. Georgiana, however, soon perceived that this kind of life was distracting, and not altogether good for her. But she resisted its frivolity, and Mdlle. Eward's good counsels, which, when they used to be pressed upon her, had often been disregarded, were now remembered and obeyed, when obedience was no longer enforced. After all, this phase of dissipation did not last above two years. It was like one of those confused preludes to some piece of music, which appear incoherent till the theme of the composition disengages itself and becomes clear. The *theme* was there. It was "life," and the time was beginning to dawn for both of these two sisters when happiness itself takes a grave tone, and when amusements, gaieties, and interests of

E

earlier years came to be recognized as the things of children.

A great part of the year 1833 was passed in England. Before it was ended the lot of both of the sisters was decided. According to the English custom, in the case of both, their own inclination was the sole cause of their marriages. But while that of Susan with Lord Rivers met with no obstacle, that of Georgiana with Mr. Fullerton was much opposed, before the consent of the parents on both sides was obtained.

It is not necessary to explain to English readers that there was no objection on the ground of birth or rank, as might have been the case in France. Mr. Fullerton was the heir to considerable estates in Gloucestershire and Ireland.[1] He had been educated at Eton, where he was "next in school" to Mr. Gladstone, and had entered the Guards ("the Blues")—at that time, and probably still, one of the finest and most distinguished regiments in the army. The troubles which stood in the way of Lady Georgiana's marriage proceeded mainly from the difficulties raised about the securing her immediately a sufficiently independent position. It is easy to guess that her friend and *confidante*, Mdlle. Eward, was told from time to time the fluctuations of hope and fear which passed over the mind of her late pupil, and it may be allowable, at the distance of more than half a century of time, to quote some of the letters in which Lady Georgiana expressed her feelings with the utmost simplicity and freedom.

Ballintoy Castle, Antrim, and Tockington Manor, Gloucestershire.

The affection so warmly expressed in them was consecrated by long years of the tenderest and most exclusive devotion, which was never more conspicuously shown than in the hour of parting for this life. It seemed indeed rather transformed than extinguished. No one can tell us of its early phases better than herself in her confidences to her old friend.

The attachment seems to have sprung up and come to a head early in 1832. The difficulties seem, as has been said, to have been mainly caused by the fact that the father of Mr. Fullerton, who had other children to provide for, did not at first see his way to making such a provision for the young pair as was thought desirable by Lord Granville. In the course of the summer of 1832, the latter appears to have refused his consent, notwithstanding the influence brought to bear on him by the Duke of Devonshire, which was enforced, moreover, by substantial assistance to the provision to be made for his niece. This was the occasion of a beautiful letter to her uncle from Lady Georgiana, which is fortunately preserved.

To the Duke of Devonshire.

Paris, *July* 21, 1832.

MY DEAREST UNCLE,—I have long wished to write to you to tell you, although I never shall be able to express half what I feel, how grateful I am for your unbounded kindness. And at this moment, when I must give up what I had looked forward to as to happiness, I feel it, if possible, more strongly than before. It has been and is that sort of kindness which can never, never be forgotten. I will not speak of the disappointment, which has been severe, nor of the difficulty of making up my mind to papa's decision, which is most certainly meant, and may perhaps prove, for my happiness—nor can I, for I know I ought not to, ask you to say anything to Mr. Fullerton from me, although it would be a great comfort, could I be sure that he would know that it is no change in my wishes or in my dispositions towards him, that has contributed to the unfavourable answer, which I do not think he can regret more than I do.   The recollection of his affection and of your adorable kindness, in the midst of my sorrow, I look back to with a feeling of the deepest gratitude.   It is a consolation to me to tell you this, though my expressions are cold in comparison with my feelings.

I remain, my dearest uncle,
Your most affectionate niece,
G. C. LEVESON GOWER.

There can be no doubt that Lady Georgiana suffered keenly the temporary disappointment of her hopes and expectations.   There are a few interesting letters remaining to her friend Mrs. Talbot, which reveal her feelings during this interval, which, however, our readers will hardly expect us to publish. The difficulty was borne in the noble spirit which breathes in her letter to her uncle.   It was in due time overcome, as we shall see, having left behind it nothing but the ripening and strengthening of her character.   Her sister was married early in the ensuing year, and the following letter gives an account of the engagement.   It is written in English.

To Mdlle. Eward.

January, 1833.

MY DEAREST MDLLE. EWARD,—Here I am prepared to give you all sorts of details on the subject, every word of which will, I know, be interesting to you.   Our darling Sukey is as happy as your wishes even would have made her, and that is

not saying a little. There never were two people so desperately
in love with each other. Still they are singularly well suited.
His warm, eager nature and captivating manners have drawn
forth all her feelings of love and devotion to a degree which
perhaps no other person would ever have done, and her perfect
sense and unequalled sweetness of temper are wonderfully well
calculated to meet his little faults, which arise, not from anything unamiable, for I really believe there never was a sweeter
and more affectionate nature, but from being a bit of a spoilt
child. Those who know him most intimately agree that never
was such a passionate adoration ; it must be owned it is very
delightful to see what one loves so beloved, so appreciated.
He feels his happiness the more, that he has gone through a
great deal of grief and sorrow, young as he is. . . . It is certainly
a delightful feeling that this marriage has given them all the
greatest possible happiness. It does them credit in one way,
at the same time that it pays the greatest compliment to Sukey,
as it would have been, in an interested view, very advantageous
to them had he married a girl with money. But it shows what
an opinion they had of her that all along it has been Lady
Rivers' most ardent wish. She says the announcement of it
was the first moment of pleasure she had known since her
husband's death. Lord Rivers has two sisters, very nice girls
indeed, I believe, and a brother, Horace Pitt, two or three
years younger than himself. Lord Rivers went to London last
week, as his presence there was necessary to the final arrangement of law affairs. There was a most melancholy parting—
indeed any one would have thought it was for three years
instead of three weeks—but they correspond regularly, and
keep up their spirits that way. They are sometimes like two
darling babies together. I do wish you could see them, with
their sweet pretty faces close to each other, looking so senti-
mental, but at the same time so ungovernably joyous ! He
will be here probably by the end of this month, and, at the
beginning of the next, they will be married here quite privately,
and set off the same day for England. The first night at
Beauvais, the next at Abbeville, the third at Boulogne, the next
at some town between Dover and London, and then, without
stopping in London, straight to Chiswick, where they are to

spend the honeymoon, and some time longer, too, probably. We shall follow them to England in one, two, or at the very most, in three months. Where they will live afterwards is as yet uncertain. He is, and consequently she is, very anxious to live at his own country house, Mistley Hall, in Suffolk (it is on the banks of the Orwell, not very far from Wherstead). But, as for some time their affairs will require the strictest economy, it is considered rather an expensive place, as the house and the whole place are on a very large scale. However, all that will be settled afterwards. To you, my dearest Mdlle. Eward, I need not *say* what I feel at the idea of our approaching separation, though this time it will probably be for a comparatively short time. You can understand it without my dwelling upon it. I fear it for mamma, too, more than I can say ; the moment will be one of severe trial for her. Papa, too, though he may not feel it so acutely then, will miss her terribly, and in my present state of spirits I feel far more sanguine as to being able to be some comfort to her, than a cheerful companion for him. Granville and Freddy go back to England to-morrow. The former likes Oxford very much. They have had rather dull holidays, poor boys. We had a ball here on Friday though, and they liked it very much. I cannot say I did. It was the first I had been at since London, and Susan was not present, so that altogether my feelings were not inclined to gaiety. I should have written sooner, dearest Mdlle. Eward, but that Susan would not hear of not writing at the same time, and yet her time is so incessantly taken up, that she has scarcely a minute to herself. Mamma bids me thank you a thousand times for your letter. They all send you their very best love. Believe me always most affectionately yours,

G. C. Leveson Gower.

In your answer ask me all the questions you want to have answered on *the* subject, for I feel I have written to you an unsatisfactory letter.

There seems to be a fate against her (Susan) writing to you, she has been obliged to keep quite quiet during these two days, on account of a headache, and as I cannot put off any longer sending my letter, she bids me give you her *very very* best love, and tell you how deeply she felt the affection and kindness of your letter, that she knows what you feel for her at this moment, but that you cannot know how happy she is, or how grateful she feels to the Giver of all good. But it is impossible to send messages on such subjects as these, and she will write to you herself as soon as she can. The boys went this morning. I never saw them so sorry to leave home. They are both, in their different ways, nicer than ever. I trust G. will do very well at Oxford. The person he sees most of there is Charles Canning,[2] who is a very superior young man, and it gives papa much pleasure that it should be so. Freddy leaves Mr. Everard at Easter to go to Eton, which he does not like the thought of now, but will, I dare say, more so when the time comes. Baldwin goes with Susan which, though I am very sorry to lose her, I am very glad of, and I am sure you will be too. And now, dearest Mdlle. Eward, as I have some space left, I am going to indulge in a little frivolity, and describe to you the presents Sukey has got as *yet*, for *nous n'avons pas fini mes frères*, I hope. . . .[3] Once more adieu, dearest Mdlle. Eward. Yours most affectionately,

G. C. Leveson Gower.

January 15, 1833.

Lady Susan's marriage took place in Paris, February 2, 1833. The following is her sister's account to her friend.

Paris, *February* 3, 1833.

My dearest Mdlle. Eward,—First let me thank you a thousand times for your dear kind letter. It was just like yourself, and that is *tout dire*. When our darling Susan wrote to you, I was still so weak from my indisposition and its remedies, such as bleeding and starving, that I thought I should not have been able to be at the marriage, which vexed me exceedingly, but I got so much better towards evening that I was allowed to go down for it. It took place yesterday, Saturday morning, at twelve o'clock exactly, in the green drawing-room—nobody there but ourselves, G. Stewart, F.

---

[2] Afterwards Viscount Canning.
[3] Here follows a list of bridal presents.

Howard, Mrs. Arabin, and Madame de St. Clair (cousins of
Lord Rivers). Never did she look half as lovely as in her
bride's dress, a plain white silk gown, her long ringlets, and a
blonde veil. Dearest, darling sister! she was nervous, but
maintained perfect command over herself, and though very
much *émue* at parting with us all, one saw through it the *deep*
happiness of her heart. And no wonder she should be happy,
idolized as she is by him, whom since the first day of their
acquaintance she has thought the most captivating and en-
dearing of human beings. He won us all by the feeling he
showed at that moment, by the earnest sincerity with which he
uttered those beautiful but awful sentences which go to one's
heart even when they only are heard by the indifferent. Oh,
dearest Mdlle. Eward, what is it when one feels that those one
loves almost beyond anything in the world, are at that moment
sealing their fate for their whole life ! She then dressed, her
travelling gown and blue bonnet with a white veil ; oh, that
you could have seen that darling face of hers with her own
bright smile in the middle of all the crying !

They went to the Hotel de Toulouse at St. Germain, where
Ellen, the housemaid, had gone the day before to prepare their
rooms. Mamma had long letters from both of them this
morning. This is one of his phrases : "The treasure you have
given me is perfectly well, perfectly happy, and perfectly
adorable." It is the most perfect and beautiful expression of
deepest feeling and unbounded happiness. If it is fine to-morrow
they will leave St. Germain, if not, on the day after. They go
the first night to Rouen, then to Beauvais, and then Calais, they
will be at Chiswick on Friday. She charged me to write to you
directly, and to give you again and again her *very very* best
love. One knows not the value of such a treasure but when
one loses it, though, thank God, it is but for a time, and in all
probability a very short time, for we shall certainly go to
London in the course of one, two, or three months. It depends
entirely on Parliament. Dearest mamma is, and has been, far
better than I had ever ventured to hope. She was very much
overcome during the ceremony, but has borne up wonderfully
well since. The fact is, her nature is so invariably unselfish
that one ought not to be surprised at any new instance of it,

but I do suppose it never did exist in any one before to that degree. Papa is much better to-day, and will, I trust, soon get quite the better of this obstinate fit of the gout which has confined him to the house, and in fact to his sofa, for the last three months. I earnestly wish he may soon, for I do long for him to be able to have some distraction, for he misses her most dreadfully. Oh, dearest Mademoiselle Eward, what it was to go up to *our* room last night! No, I have been very unhappy before, indeed I do not call myself unhappy now, but still I had never before felt so strongly of anything, that it is gone never to return, the time of one sort of intimacy with her whom I love more than words can express. It is a great pleasure to me that Lord Rivers has been kinder and more affectionate to me than any being ever was, the contrary would have been so painful from *her* husband. She is so pleased at the thoughts of the box you are going to send her. I shall forward it immediately, and even without peeping, which, dearest Eda, you must own will be very meritorious. Thank you a thousand times for the pocket-handkerchiefs. Dear Mdlle. Eward, I am sure you tire yourself working so hard at that very fine and delicate embroidery. Do *ménagez* that dear head of yours. You ask me where —— is. He is quartered with his regiment at Windsor, but goes up now and then to London. The last I heard of him was from Granville, who heard from the Hardys, who know him intimately well, that he lives a great deal by himself, and when he goes out never alludes in conversation to anything relative to last year in London or to Paris. He has been to Brighton too for a few days, and has, I believe, in outward appearance recovered his spirits. That I was sure he would do, for not only has he the brightest and gayest nature I ever knew, but a delicacy of feeling that would shrink from any putting forward of his feelings. I feel a strong confidence in his fidelity, and shall be as surprised as disappointed if I am deceived in it. I feel very nervous at going to London *now*. It wholly depends, I think, on my uncle. Should he wish it as much as ever, papa would, I believe, entirely consent. I try and hope for the best, and am prepared for the worst.

Good-bye, my dearest Mdlle. Eward. God bless you. Pray write to me soon. I shall write very often and tell you all we hear of and from her. I only fear the postage must be very ruinous to you.

In a postscript she adds:

Ever and most dear Mdlle. Eward, you would not believe in me if you saw me. I am so happy and so calm. I have no *self* left, and for those two dear people and the two with me here, I exist, and am grateful.

Let me tell you her own words from St. Germain yesterday. "Very dearest mamma,—What shall I say to you to express my perfect happiness? Even you with all your devoted anxiety could not form a wish about me, beyond what are my feelings of joy and perfect bliss at my too happy fate. Nothing ever was so adorably kind to me as George is. It requires a very great deal, and I find it all in him, to make up to me for leaving such a home as mine was." God bless you, most dear Mdlle. Eward.

Lord and Lady Granville, with their youngest daughter, returned to London in May 1833, and it was during this visit, which was brought about by the necessity of her father's presence in Parliament, that Lady Georgiana's engagement was decided. The following letter gives details as to many interesting points:

MY DEAREST MDLLE. EWARD,—I have waited from day to day in hopes I might tell you something decisive about myself, but as I think you would be annoyed at not hearing from me I will not delay any longer, although nothing is as yet *decided*. But first, let me tell you that papa's gout is entirely gone, or rather his lameness, for he has been in reality well for some time. Both he and mamma have had the influenza—a sort of violent feverish cold which has been almost universal here during the last six weeks, and which sends one to bed entirely helpless—but we are both quite recovered now. Next I must tell you that we found darling Sukey in the best health and spirits, and looking as radiant and happy as possible but we have had *contretemps* about the time of being with her. Last Wednesday Lord Rivers went to a place in Essex a few miles from his home, in order to superintend some arrangements that are making there. He rode all the way, sixty miles, on a very bad rainy day, and the consequence was that the next day he was laid up with a violent cold and an attack of scarlatina. As soon as Sukey heard of it she immediately joined him, and though he is almost, indeed quite well again now, they cannot come back here till all chance of infection is gone, and so they are spending a few days at Harwich and will not be here till the 20th or 21st. It is a great disappointment to us, though we do not see a *very* great deal of her when she *is* here. The fact is, they are so desperately in love with one another that they can scarcely bear to be apart, he especially gets quite fidgetty if she is out of his sight for any length of time. His family all adore her, his mother (who is a very nice woman) looks quite another person, and says it is the first time she feels happy for years and years, and all the doing of that angel, as she always calls her. And now, dearest Mdlle. Eward, for my own story. I have seen Mr. F. several times since I am come, and I like him better than ever, and now the whole thing is coming to a crisis. I have met him at two Almackses, at a ball at Mrs. Baring's, three times at the opera, and last night at a ball at the Duchesse de Dino's. And there he spoke to me quite openly, for the first time in fact, for last year it was all arranged to me through Uncle D. He told me he was perfectly unchanged and more attached to me than ever; we talked on the subject for more than two hours. I find that he thinks his father *could* do much more for us.

I was just here, dearest Eda, last Friday morning, when my uncle came in and sent me packing off, as he wanted to bring Mr. Fullerton in to mamma. In my hurry and flurry I left my letter there, and as he stayed an hour and [a half I could not finish in time for the courrier, which annoyed me very much as I had already delayed it so much beyond what I intended. Mamma was *very* much pleased with him, in fact, she had never made real acquaintance with him before. She thought him immensely pleasing and attractive (a great *darling*, she says) and his conversation very sensible and intelligent. She told him she was very well disposed to consent, but that she could not speak to papa about it till he knew something more positive about his father's present intentions, and this is what they have settled together. We are going to Windsor to-morrow to stay till Thursday, and Mr. F. wrote to his father on Friday to entreat him to join him at his lodging at Salthill (which is close to Windsor, you know), on Wednesday, and mamma would arrange to get away from the Castle and meet him there somehow or other. . . .

(Friday morning.) It is all arranged, dear Mdlle. Eward. I met him at dinner yesterday at Chiswick, and he told me that his father had written the very kindest letter possible to him, and immediately consented to come and stay two days at Windsor, so that to-morrow morning after breakfast, mamma and I are to go to the inn, and there Mr. Fullerton and his father will meet us. I never felt so nervous at the thought of anything as of this first acquaintance with him whom I now hope and believe will be my father-in-law. Mr. F. tells me that he (his father) is quite annoyed at having been considered as so much against it, and that he is now disposed to do anything for us that can be reasonably required of him. I dare not be too sanguine, though it all seems to promise very well. He is quite assured it is going to be, and his spirits are quite ungovernable. I never spent so delightful a day as yesterday; it was perfectly fine at Chiswick, in greater beauty than I ever saw it, and we walked together till we were almost dead with fatigue. He is reckoned extremely like my grandmother, the Duchess of Devonshire, and that was the first thing that made Uncle D. take such a fancy to him. I wish I could give you a good idea of him. I doat upon him, and I must say I think he is very fond of me. Mamma is quite come round to it. She said yesterday that she felt sure he would be a great source of happiness to us all, and she told me that papa had often said lately that what he really must insist upon was that he and I should live a great deal with them, and that proves that, though he would have liked me to have made a greater match, he has no feeling of dislike to it or to him. Before I finish I must tell you what I had forgotten in the midst of more interesting subjects. Papa was made Earl

Granville the other day by the King, and in the kindest and most gratifying manner. Granville is Lord Leveson of Stone, and I, Lady G. Leveson. I know you will like it, dear Mdlle. Eward, for you never liked the appellation of Miss. Granville comes up from Oxford for a few days at the end of the week, I do long to see him again. Freddy is to meet us at the Salthill Inn to-morrow, and whilst we are in town he is also to come to us for a few days.

Good-bye, dearest Eda, I am afraid you will have been annoyed at my long silence, which has been caused by a number of little *contretemps*. Believe me, ever and always, most affectionately yours,

GEORGIANA LEVESON.

Since I began my letter we have heard two or three times from Sukey, both she and Lord Rivers are quite well. They had been to see their own place, Mistley, which quite enchanted her, and were going the next day to see dear old Wherstead, which she was delighted at.

The story of the engagement is carried on in the following, begun May 22, and ended May 27. The latter also gives an account of the unexpected death of her younger and invalid brother William.

To Mdlle. Eward.

May 22.

MY DEAREST MDLLE. EWARD,—I must write to tell you that at last I may say that my marriage is next to certain, indeed it is so, as far as one can be sure of anything in this world, although it is not yet declared. I have gone through a great deal of sorrow and anxiety since I last wrote to you. We went to Windsor, on the Wednesday morning, with some difficulty, got away from the Castle, and went to the inn at Salthill where Freddy immediately joined us, and soon after Mr. Fullerton came also, very much annoyed at his father's not having yet arrived. Afterwards he found it was owing to a delay occasioned by his having been ill with the general influenza. We all went back to London the next day, and

during the rest of the week the whole thing was in a most
critical state, twice on the point of being entirely broken off,
and I was miserable.   Then mamma's invariable kindness and
her influence with papa, who has also been kinder about it than
I ever can be sufficiently grateful for, and an interview of hers
with Mr. F.'s father, on Monday morning, brought it on again.
She was quite delighted with him, with his sense and feeling.
The thing which had made them most against it, and had been
most painful to me all along, was the idea that his father *could*
do much more for him, and did not, only because he disliked
the marriage.   This he proved to mamma was not at all the
case, he solemnly assured her that in justice to his other
children he *could* not do more for the eldest, but if on that they
would consent he would be gratified and delighted with the
connection.   Monday evening, at a ball here, mamma told him
they would consent.   She is gone to Brighton for two or three
days to see William, and at her return to-morrow all the minor
arrangements are to be made and the marriage declared.   I
need not tell you how happy, how grateful, I feel, how anxious
not to prove myself unworthy of the blessings that are showered
upon me—how at this moment I feel tremblingly aware of all
my faults and imperfections, now that his happiness will so
much depend on my character and conduct.   He remains in
the army, but leaves the Blues and retires on half-pay.

Chiswick, *May* 27.

My marriage is declared, dearest Mdlle. Eward, and on
that account I am happy beyond all power of expression.   But
now, dearest Mdlle. Eward, I must tell you something that
will give you great pain and sorrow, an event so shocking, so
sudden, that the blow came upon us when we were totally
unprepared for it.   Mamma was at Brighton last week, and the
day before she came away, the servant who was carrying our
poor William downstairs slipped and fell down.   At the moment
William did not appear the least hurt, excepting a blow on the
eye.   The doctor saw him, and assured mamma she might go
perfectly comfortably, that there was no mischief whatever
done.   We thought no more of it till yesterday.   When we
came home from evening church, we found poor mamma quite

miserable. Dear Mdlle. Eward, the worst had happened. On Saturday morning the blood had rushed to the poor boy's head, and by five o'clock all was over. But it was apparently without pain and without a struggle. For himself, dear boy, we ought not, we must not,.lament it. His life was not a happy one, never could have been a happy one, and we may hope that God Almighty has in mercy taken him to Himself. Papa and mamma were terribly shocked and bent down, but they are much better to-day. Freddy was miserable yesterday. His grief was violent, and the most affecting thing I ever knew. But of course with a child that can never last, and he is in very tolerable spirits to-day. We are all come to Chiswick to-day, and are to stay a week. Granville will come up from Oxford to-morrow and join us here. The quiet, the beauty, the charm of this place is beyond everything I ever felt. The Rivers are here with us, his kindness to all of us at this moment has been unbounded, as well as his anxiety to do anything that would please and comfort every one of us. Mr. Fullerton was with me some time this morning before I left London.

He had known poor William, and his feeling and sympathy on the subject went to my very heart. He is to come here to-morrow afternoon. I suppose we shall go back to Paris in about a fortnight, and that my marriage will take place towards the end of June or the beginning of July. Oh! sometimes I cannot, dare not believe, in the happiness of being his at last, of devoting my whole existence to him. . . . How can I speak so when I think of my poor brother? I feel it unfeeling to dwell so much on my own selfish happiness at this moment, though God knows we all feel that, for his own sake, this event has been one that has, in all probability, saved him from much future misery and disappointment, and this accident may have spared him a great deal of suffering, for the opinion of several doctors, consulted by Verity,[4] last year (we had never heard it till now) was that his life would not have been much prolonged in any case. Susan sends you her very best love and a thousand thanks for your last letter to her; in a few days she will write to you a long and detailed letter. She is a greater dear than ever. Good-bye, dearest Mdlle. Eward. Oh! that you could

---

[4] The family doctor.

see my own Alexander. It is the first time I have ever called him so, but I want you to know everything about him, even his Christian name. Good-bye again. God bless you, dearest Mdlle. Eward. Mamma sends you her very best love. Believe me ever and always, happy or unhappy,

Yours most affectionately,
GEORGIANA LEVESON.

Chiswick, *May* 27.

The next letter is written in Paris, the day of the marriage not being yet certainly fixed.

To Mdlle. Eward.

"MY VERY DEAR EDA,—A thousand thanks for the charming desk which I received on Saturday,—you are too good. I can never tell you how much I like it. The drawing inside is beautiful also. Again and again thank you, dearest Mdlle. Eward. Next, I must tell you that to my great regret I shall not see you so soon as I said. *We* do not go to Aix with papa and mamma. We shall pass some days at Fontainebleau, and then come back here to wait for them, and the only thing in the arrangement that does not please me is, that I shall not see you, which would have been an extreme pleasure. The day is not fixed, perhaps Saturday, perhaps next Monday, perhaps only after a visit which papa is obliged to make to London to give his vote. This puts mamma out exceedingly, for it will delay things for ten days, the beginning of August. The Rivers will leave at the same time, at least they intend it. I am glad that you will have the pleasure of seeing her, and seeing her so happy—of her happiness you will be able to judge for yourself. Mine is greater than I can express. I don't know how I can have deserved such happiness, but I thank God continually for it, and I hope every day to become a little more worthy of it. We have long walks together every morning. You see I am becoming active. I get up every morning at eight, and we are out of doors from morning to evening. Granville is here, Alexander came with him last Tuesday. We are expecting Freddy. I am a little nervous when I think of it, but happier than I can tell. Aleck is at my side now. It is he who makes me write in French, and says it is very lazy not to do so. He is quite right, and I know also that you like it.

The marriage of Lady Georgiana with Mr. Fullerton took place in Paris, on July 13, 1833. The same day they went to Fontainebleau, Lord and Lady Granville setting out for Aix. The newly-married couple spent the autumn and a part of the winter in England. They then returned to the Embassy at Paris, to which Mr. Fullerton was Attaché, having left his regiment. This continued till 1841. Lady Georgiana's first years of married life were thus passed under the roof of her parents, as they had wished. In the course of the few months which passed before her return to Paris she thus writes, after a visit to Mr. Fullerton's family, of which she speaks with the greatest affection :

I am in truth the happiest person in the world in every way. I suppose my husband is not perfect, for no one is in this world. But he is certainly very nearly so. His unutterable gentleness is joined to great firmness and the gaiety of a child. He loves application, and has a need of occupation which does not let him be a moment idle. If, with such a teacher as he is, I do not acquire a love for occupation, I shall certainly be incorrigible. I don't think there is happiness on earth equal to mine. I love him in a way which makes me tremble, for he is all I have in the world. As for my health, it is not very good just now, but they give me hopes that there is a good reason for this, and so I can but rejoice.

Lady Georgiana's prospect of happiness, which she thus hints at, was crowned by the birth of a son in Paris, July 15, 1834, who was christened by the name of William Granville.

F

CHAPTER V.

LADY GEORGIANA FULLERTON was twenty-one when
the birth of her son added the full crown to her
happiness. Up to that time we discern no marked
traces in her life of the two great features which
seemed at its end to have given it its dominant
character. Vivid and poetic imagination we have
already seen, but nothing has as yet revealed the
talent, approaching genius, which was to be developed in her and to ripen almost in a day. Again,
much that we have said of her shows earnestness
and thoughtfulness as to religion. If this was not
always evident, at least it was readily evoked.
Nothing, however, seems as yet to presage the
great conflict through which her soul was to pass,
and which was to end, after inexpressible sufferings,
in the deep peace of the certitude of faith. It might
be said of her that the very depth of her feelings
made them less quick to unfold themselves, and
they were longer in her than in others to reach the
surface of her character.

The English Embassy at Paris was the home of
the Fullertons for the first years of their married
life. They left it frequently to travel, and thus their

correspondence enables us to follow them. They always returned to it as their only home, till 1841. During these years we find Lady Georgiana frequently recording the pleasures of society in which she lived. She is, however, rather a spectator of, than an active sharer in, these pleasures. Her life and her heart were filled with her husband and the child whom she idolized. But she had many passing anxieties as to the health of both, and this gave a certain serious colour to her happiness, which belongs to all things in this world that are deep, and we may say, really happy. What is there that is worthy of the name of happiness, save that which comes from God alone, which does not cause us a secret fear from its very intensity? We say commonly, "It is too good to last." And the saying expresses only too exactly the thought that troubles us, even at the moment of our deepest joys, and indeed, then more than at any other moment.

We shall allow Lady Georgiana as much as may be to speak for herself in her correspondence. We find in her letters something of that style which was to give her writings so much charm, and it is interesting to follow the gradual and almost insensible transformation that she underwent. Her letters—certainly such fragments of them as alone we can make room for—do not show her, it is true, in that perfect openness which would have characterized her autobiography, if that had been continued. On certain subjects she probably never opened herself fully, even in letters to the dearest of her correspondents. But certain ideas were ultimately to come forward with a clearness of their own, and to take a dominant position of her mind. Her reserve, the excitement of her youth, and the noise of the world all around her, checked their influence for a time, and it is most interesting to watch them gradually disengaging themselves from all hindrances, and assuming the command of her soul.

Lady Georgiana travelled for the first time in Italy in the opening of the year which followed the birth of her son (1835). The journey was made less joyous by the necessity of a few months' separation from him. The object was to give Mr. Fullerton a change of air, which was necessitated by a malady he had caught during his sojourn in England that year. The child was not yet a year old, and remained at Paris under his grandmother's care, who came back from England in order to take charge of him, just as her daughter left. This journey was limited to a short tour in the north of Italy. Genoa was the first stage. They remained there some weeks. Lady Georgiana found there "her old friend Henry Fox, and his young, little, pretty, and charming wife."[1] They were afterwards to become Lord and Lady Holland. At that time Lord Holland, the father of Mr. Fox, was still living, and filling a great place in the world both political and social. It was under him, aided by his wife, a remarkable and original person, that his magnificent abode, Holland House, close to London, became the meeting-place of all celebrities. The inheritors of the title and of Holland House,

---

[1] Lady Mary Augusta Coventry, daughter of the Earl of Coventry.

as is well known, kept up the traditions of the
place. All its attractions were perpetuated and
are to be found in full life to the present time, as
its visitors can witness. During the early years of
their marriage, Mr. Fox and Lady Augusta were
almost always in Italy. They had taken up their
abode in the Palazzo Brignole at Genoa. There,
as was always the case, their house was most
brilliant, always full of life, and most hospitable.
Lady Georgiana and Mr. Fullerton were there constantly, and all their evenings were spent there.
Such were the easy and cordial manners of the
Continent, and especially in Italy, in those days.
There was a charm and pleasantness about them
equally difficult to describe and to forget.

In this charming and brilliant society it was not
likely, certainly, that religion should be often talked
of. It was no place for controversy. But the
atmosphere was Catholic, and not at all Protestant.
Mr. Fox and Lady Augusta had each a predilection
for Catholicism, as was proved later on by their
both embracing it. Besides, it was the religion of
all around them—the only one, it may be said, that
was known in Italy. Moreover, when Mr. Fullerton
and Lady Georgiana left the apartment which their
friends occupied, it was to pass down to the floor
on which the proprietors of the Palazzo lived, the
Marchese and Marchesa Brignole, whose name still
lives in the memory and veneration of many. There
they found themselves brought in contact with
fervent Catholics. Among them was the Marquis
of Durazzo (Gian Luce), whose Italian vivacity was

ready enough to enter on subjects of controversy, which his wife, the lovely Marchesa Durazzo, was equally ready to follow up. The Marquis Brignole himself would, perhaps, have preferred to hear grave subjects treated more seriously, but he did not hesitate to take part in the conversation when once started. This was something altogether new to Lady Georgiana. She was keenly interested, and although the religious traditions in which she had been brought up were unshaken, the attraction which she had always felt to Catholicism found a satisfaction in this society. Up to that time she had never had an intimate friend of that religion.

It was after this time that the powerful movement in Anglicanism itself, which took its name from the University of Oxford, gained great influence in England. English Catholics hardly took a direct part in it, though it was to draw to the faith a considerable number among the Anglicans, clergy and laity. One of the effects of this memorable crisis, which is still going on and which may have results as yet undeveloped, was that the rule of silence as to all religious matters, according to which it was a sort of impropriety to mention them in good society, came to an end. No sooner had the Anglicans brought before the world the belief and the ritual of Catholicism, than these became the topics of discussion and conversation everywhere, and were no longer the occasion of the same mysterious silence and dread as before. Meanwhile, Catholics in England had obtained their liberty and made use of it. By degrees they left

the poor and obscure chapels in which they had
hidden themselves to pray. As time went on they
acquired many churches worthy of their worship,
which was carried on with all befitting splendour
and reverence. Curiosity brought many to them,
who mingled with the faithful, it may be with indifference, but at least with respect.

In the present day all is changed in England as
regards the treatment and position of Catholics.
They are no longer in a strange country, certainly
not in a hostile land. It was very different fifty
years ago. Georgiana had never lived, even in
Paris, outside an exclusively Protestant circle.
Hence we find her showing quite new interests.
The least things had an importance to her. Genoa,
with its many beautiful churches, impressed her
much. All tended to foster the secret and inexpli-
cable drawing which she had felt from her childhood
towards the worship which was to become her own.

The importance of these vague religious impressions may not be very great. With a great number
they remain as barren *reveries*, and have nothing to
do with that manly act of the will which makes men
first seek and then embrace the truth. But to many
souls these things are the distant preparation. They
are the appeals of that good Spirit, Who can discern
beforehand who those are who will one day listen to
and answer Him.

All the impressions received by Georgiana at
Genoa were not of the same nature. There was
one, on the contrary, that for several weeks made
her acquainted with some of the agonies and

shadows of doubt. Our readers will no doubt remember her enthusiasm for Byron and his works, of which, perhaps, she had not at that time read the most mischievous, such as *Manfred*. Nor, perhaps, would the despairing and sceptical language of some of them have had much effect on her. It was not quite with as much freedom from danger that she, later on, fell in with some passages from Shelley, which seem to have caused her much disquiet, suggesting difficulties as to belief which she did not know how either to answer or to dissipate.

She was still in the same state of interior discomfort when she left Genoa for Turin. There she made a chance acquaintance, of which she shall speak herself. The Miss Ellices, whom she mentions in the letter, were very dear friends, and seem to have looked after Lady Georgiana's child in the temporary absence of Lady Granville.

To Lady Granville.

May 25, 1835.

DEAREST MAMMA,—If you have left London the day you intended, I suppose to-day you arrive at Paris. It feels very nice to have the space between us so much diminished, and our letters going and coming directly. This day week I hope to receive your first letter from there. How I do long for it. I wonder whether you will find my baby much altered. When you see the Ellices, will you tell them all I feel about their excessive kindness to him? I am on the whole very glad that he did not come here, for I hear so much of this climate being bad for children. Madame de Bombelles tells me she has a baby just teething who suffers very much from it. She is an Englishwoman (Miss Fraser she was), and I like her very much. They live close to us, we dine with them to-day. People think her dull and too much occupied with her nursery, which you may imagine I do not object to. Her children are the most beautiful little creatures I ever saw. Yesterday we dined with the Forsters, and met Mr. and Mrs. Legh, who are going on immediately to Paris. You see, even here, we are not without *company*, but the being in the country, and sitting out in the garden after dinner, makes all the difference. Our own little villa and establishment I am charmed with. We have made it look very nice and pretty, our garden is full of flowers, and from my berceau I see the plain of Turin and the Alps beyond. At the top of a steep grassy hill, just behind the house, there is an immense berceau of vines, with walnut-trees and stone benches, the view is still more extensive and really beautiful, the walks are enchanting, grassy lanes with quantities of wild flowers, little woods, brooks, and rivulets without end. In short, it is lovely. We get up at seven o'clock, walk till nine, breakfast, sit at home in the middle of the day, unless we drive into town to buy anything we want, dine at five, and walk afterwards. The only drawback as yet has been the variableness of the weather, tremendous thunderstorms, one, the day we got here, which quite shook the house. Alex is very well, with the exception of a headache he has had these two days, but they are very unusual with him now. He enjoys extremely this life, but chuckles at the thought of Paris in the autumn. I really hope that it will not do him any harm, as he is quite prepared to do everything prudent and good for his health, should we go there, instead of the reverse, which was the case last year. I cannot say how much I long to see you again, dearest mamma, it will be such happiness to talk with you again, and sit reading and stitching once more. Good-bye, dearest mamma, my best love to papa and Granville. I will not close my letter till the post comes in, as I may possibly hear from you.

Ever your most affectionate
GEORGIANA FULLERTON.

Would you send the enclosed letter to England? Alex sends you his best love.

She never forgot a little circumstance which followed on this acquaintance, and which gave it a real importance in her memory. Madame de Bombelles had been a Miss Fraser, of a Scotch family, which had remained always Catholic. In consequence of the state of things in her native country, such families were shut out from almost all careers, at least they had no hope of attaining any great position in any. The Frasers had in consequence emigrated to Austria, where they remained till the Act of Emancipation was passed in 1829, when many of these voluntary exiles returned home. The brothers of Madame de Bombelles did this, but the sisters stayed in Austria. The eldest of them married, some years later, Comte Henry de Bombelles, the son of a French *emigré*, who had formed connections in Austria and remained there after the restoration of the Bourbons. The father, however, returned to France, and having lost his wife, entered the ecclesiastical state. He became that excellent and venerated Archbishop of Amiens, the fame of whose virtues and zeal is not yet forgotten, although the generation that witnessed their exercise has almost entirely disappeared.

The son, Henry de Bombelles, was chosen at a later time to be the tutor of the now reigning Emperor of Austria. At the time when Mr. Fullerton and Lady Georgiana fell in with him at Turin, he had no thought of leaving the diplomatic career. His wife and himself were both fervent Christians, and probably their conversation often turned on religious subjects. In any case the little incident of which we speak left a profound impression on the mind of Lady Georgiana. We have already said that at this time the doubts that had been sown in her mind in Paris were still tormenting her. One day, while waiting for Madame de Bombelles in the drawing-room of the latter, she took up a book lying on the table. It was the *Introduction to a Devout Life,* by St. Francis of Sales. She lighted upon the chapter on "Doubts against Faith." She read it attentively, and as she went on, the troublesome thoughts in her mind were dissipated, and light seemed to come back to her soul. Madame de Bombelles, when she entered the room, found her so evidently moved, that she begged her to keep the book. Lady Georgiana did so, and never forgot the moment when she received the present. It was the first Catholic book she ever possessed. She was, however, still far off from the faith of St. Francis de Sales. We make a few extracts from some letters of this and the next years. They will help us to trace her movements, as well as the progress of her mind.

While she was in Turin and Genoa, her little boy was watched over by her mother in Paris, and in her absence, as has been mentioned, received many kindnesses from her friends, Miss Ellice and her sister. It is not likely that Lady Georgiana would be slow in showing her gratitude : the following is to her friend, announcing her decision that her little boy was not to join his parents in Italy. The letter is written some days before the last quoted letter to her mother.

To Miss Ellice.

Turin, *May* 11, 1835.

MY DEAR MARION,—We have come to a decision which I believe is wise, though it is the severest possible disappointment to me. This is, not to have our beloved child come to us till the hot summer months are past. An Italian summer is, we hear on all sides, extremely trying to a child, and well as he has hitherto been, I should always reproach myself, if, for the selfish though extreme gratification of seeing him three months sooner, I had exposed him to any risk. We are also to join papa and mamma at Aix in Savoy in August, which is by three days nearer to Paris. At the end of that month the intense heat will be past, and he will join us with more facility. I have written to Kulback to get him a cool airy apartment in the environs of Paris for those three months. I know it will be better, but I am anything but in spirits at this long delay of what I look forward to with the most intense impatience. Though you do not like me to thank you, I must tell you that I *never*, *never* can forget what your (and all your family's) kindness has been to my beloved darling.

She writes again a few weeks later :

To Miss Ellice.

Turin, *June* 1, 1835.

My DEAREST MARION,—I cannot tell you all the pleasure which your last long and most satisfactory letter gave me, and for the dear little sketch enclosed in it. You are too good and kind to think of everything that can be a comfort to me during this long separation from my dearest boy. Do not say you have been of little use, on the contrary, your constant kindness has been invaluable, and I never can express to you or to your mamma how deeply grateful I am for it. The comfort you have been to poor Hayes in all her troubles is immense. I hope by this time baby is established in his cool room at the Embassy. Dearest child, it is such happiness to hear of his being in such good health and looks. The little sketch is so pretty; you could not have sent me anything that would have pleased me more. We are very comfortably established in a small villa, and if he was with me I should have nothing to wish for. I have a nice garden full of flowers, and the environs are lovely ; such beautiful walks, the only drawback has been the weather which has been very rainy. We have had none of the heat you mention. We shall stay here till the month of August, when we shall join papa and mamma at Aix in Savoy. In the meantime we mean to go to the Vaudois valleys for one, and perhaps to Milan and the lakes.

We may as well quote a passage in a letter in the course of the next year, in which she speaks of her comparative want of enthusiasm for southern scenery.

This will appear to you strange—I do not like the quiet, blue tideless Mediterranean half as much as the briny stormy North Sea, and I get a little tired of the marked outlines and constant glare of a southern landscape. But it is very beautiful, one cannot deny it.

We may remark that Lady Georgiana's comparative indifference to a sea like the "blue tideless Mediterranean," at least her preference for a sea full of life, motion, and rage—dated from her early years. Later in life, she published the following lines, "Written in youth at the sea-side:"

Oui j'aime le murmure orageux de la mer,
J'aime de l'ouragan la sublime colère,
J'aime voir les vagues, menaçantes et lentes,
Rouler au loin leurs lames écumantes, bruyantes,
Et les flots irrités envahissant la plage
En longs mugissements y exhaler leur rage.
J'aime à voir l'oiseau blanc jouer dans la tourmente,
Sous un ciel qui s'abaisse sur la terre tremblante.
J'aime à voir un vaisseau lorsque l'orage gronde
Tracer un long sillon sur l'écume de l'onde
Braver des éléments l'impétueux effort,
Gonfler ses larges voiles et cinglant vers le port,
Défier de l'océan l'impuissante fureur.
D'où vient qu'en y rêvant-je sens battre mon cœur?
Quel est le lien secret dont les cordes sonores,
Dans mon âme troublée vibrent et frémissent alors?

Vous le savez, mon Dieu, car vous sondez l'abyme,
Vous lisez dans les cœurs, et votre main s'imprime
Sur les vants déchaînés, sur l'onde qui s'irrite,
Sur le vaisseau qui lutte et le cœur qui s'agite.[a]

There is a very fine passage on the same subject in her first novel, *Ellen Middleton.*

Our extracts from her letters during this period are made rather with a view to the light they shed on her mind and character, than with regard to chronological sequence. In the course of the next two years, a new reign began in England. Although there have been many descriptions of the circumstances of the accession of Queen Victoria, it may not be uninteresting to hear a few details from the pen of Lady Georgiana of the first days of a reign so prosperous and glorious, in which, whatever clouds may have passed over the country, the Crown has always nobly fulfilled its duty.

To Mdlle. Eward.

Paris, *June* 27, 1837.

We are in deep mourning for our King (William IV.). His death obliges my father to go to pay homage to the young Queen. No one can imagine how beautifully Princess Victoria has behaved since her accession to the throne. All who have seen her, of all parties, are delighted. At her first Council she made an excellent speech, full of grace and dignity, showing astonishing calmness. When she presented herself to the people on the balcony at St. James', the shouts and cries of joy so moved her that she burst into tears. Many charming little stories are told of her. She wished, at once, to write to her aunt, the Queen, to beg her to remain at Windsor as long as

[a] We print these verses—though they contain, we believe, some mistakes which would seem intolerable to French writers—because they show Lady Georgiana's predilection for stormy seas, and because she reprinted them herself in later life.

possible and to fix the day herself when she (the Queen) would
go to see her. When she was told that she ought to address
her letter to "the Queen *Dowager*," she refused, saying she
ought not to be the first to call her so.

She also refused to receive the Duchess of Northumberland,
her old governess seated. When it was insisted on as a
point of etiquette, she said, "Well, at least, it must be well
explained to her." But, when the moment came, she could not
bear it, she rose up, ran towards her and threw herself into her
arms. We are all enthusiastic about our little Queen. May
God keep her and preserve us from such a king as the Duke of
Cumberland, now King of Hanover.

The next is written after the Coronation, a year
later.

To Mdlle. Eward.

Paris, *June* 30, 1838.

I am trying to get a good engraving of our young Queen for
you. Everything went off splendidly. The enthusiasm was
extreme, never has a reign begun under more favourable
auspices. God grant that it may be long and happy. You ask
me if my brothers assisted in the Coronation? Leveson did
certainly, but I do not know if Freddy was able to get a ticket
for the Abbey. They both write so rarely now that we get
most of our news about them from others.

To the same.

August 25, 1837.

My uncle, the Duke of Devonshire, is at Chatsworth, and
mamma tells me in her last letter that Mr. Beamish, an Evangelical minister, a very eloquent preacher, came to dine *tête-à-
tête* with him, and that he found his conversation very interesting. He asked him to stay some time at Chatsworth, but
Mr. Beamish refused. I tell you this because I know it will
give you pleasure, as it did to me, that he had wished it.

To the same.

Chatsworth, *October* 18, 1838.

I love Chatsworth passionately. The woods and the
gardens give me intense pleasure. You ask me to tell you

something of my uncle. I love him more every day. There is such a charm about him, a sort of contagious gaiety, and now that all he does is under the influence of religious principle, I esteem him as much as I love him. Every morning we have family prayers, and on Sundays he always goes twice to church. On Wednesday evening he and I went together to an evening service at an old church near here, close to Buxton. The congregation was entirely composed of poor people and school children. The church was hardly lighted at all. We sat on the wooden benches. The singing was simple but pleasant, the sermon was touching. All this, and seeing my uncle so collected and attentive, made a great impression on me.

She was fond of recalling to mind a conversation that took place at Chatsworth during this visit. The subject of the conversation was the happiness of the next life, and the ideas which we have here below concerning that happiness. The persons present gave each their opinion about it. All seemed to dream of nothing more than a sort of transfiguration of what is happiness on earth. "As for me," said the Duke of Devonshire, "I ask and desire one thing alone—that is, to see God." Dr. Hodgson, the former tutor of the Duke, and at that time Provost of Eton, who was present, was much struck with the remark. He cried, "You are right: what you say is good, for it is the truth."

In a letter to her mother Lady Georgiana speaks of the guests whom she met at Chatsworth. She says of Lord Ashley, afterwards the well-known Earl of Shaftesbury, who spent his long life in working for the improvement of the condition of the labouring classes:

To Lady Granville.

October, 1839.

I like the Ashleys particularly. He is so very good and so very *earnest*, people call him visionary and enthusiastic, but *I* think it *refreshing* to find anybody ready to carry out in practice what so many only talk about. Another person I like, though quite in a different way, is the Speaker, who is here now. He is so agreeable, I think, and talked of Leveson with so much interest and kind feeling. He seems quite anxious about him, and considers this the turning-point of his life; that if he indulges himself in idleness much longer his *remarkable* abilities will be hopelessly thrown away and wasted; but that, if he makes an effort now, he may rise very high. . . . I had a long letter from Freddy yesterday. He is enthusiastic about Newman's preaching. How I do hope it may make a *real* impression upon him. He is so well disposed, that I feel great hopes it may.

Good-bye, my dearest dear mamma. Give my best love to papa and Leveson.

Your most affectionate
G. FULLERTON.

Lady Georgiana felt very deeply the loss of her cousin, Blanche, daughter of Lord Carlisle, and the wife of Lord Burlington, who died eleven years after her marriage, April 27, 1840.

We have a beautiful letter of hers to her uncle, the Duke of Devonshire, who felt her loss most intensely.

To the Duke of Devonshire.

May 9, 1840.

MY OWN DEAREST UNCLE,—I have wished and longed to write to you for the last few days, but felt as if I could not; you know better than I could tell you *all* that I have felt with you and for you, since the moment we learnt the overwhelming news, and knew that your lost angel was taken from you. To speak of my own grief or of my own regrets in presence of

G

sorrows so deep and so sacred as yours, would be wrong, but to have admired, loved, and appreciated her, to have looked upon her as the type and model of all that is good and excellent and lovely, and now to dwell often in thought on her blessed spirit as having gone before, where we may humbly pray and hope to follow her—*that* I have done and will do all my life. I feel gratefully to remember her angelic kindness to me when last we met, her indulgence, her sweetness, the effect that her example had in raising one's standard of what religion should be. It is a blessing to have known her, though only in time to feel and understand the whole extent of the misery you endure.

My mother is pretty well now, her love for you is very great, the first burst of her grief was for you, and it is with you I can see her thoughts continually to be.

My dearest uncle, may I tell you too how dearly I love you—how deeply I have felt your kindness?

Now and ever,

Your affectionate and devoted

G. FULLERTON.

It may be well to insert here some verses which Lady Georgiana wrote which will give an idea of her powers in French poetry as well as of her feelings—

ON THE DEATH OF BLANCHE, COUNTESS OF BURLINGTON.   1840.

Comme un lys moissonné, par la main du faucheur,
  Au printemps de l'année, au printemps de la vie,
Tu passas comme une ombre, O douce et blanche fleur !
  A la terre donnée, à la terre ravie.

Tu vivais belle et pure à l'abri des orages,
  L'amour et l'amitié répandaient dans ton cœur
Leurs fragiles trésors, et un ciel sans nuages
  Semblait lui garantir la vie et le bonheur.

Mais déja tu disais à la terre un adieu,
  Tu rêvais en silence un céleste séjour,
Ton âme s'élancait vers le sein de ton Dieu,
  Et tes bras s'entr' ouvraient à l'éternel amour

Et nous qui sur ton front summes lire le sceau,
  Que le divin Sauveur imprime à ses élus,
Pleurons, mais en pleurant levons les yeux la haut,
Et disons : "Prés de Lui vit un ange de plus."

Almost immediately after Lady Burlington's
death, she wrote about it to Mdlle. Eward.

To Mdlle. Eward.

April 29, 1840.

... You will be very sorry for a trouble which causes us
much grief. Lady Burlington has just died at the age of
twenty-eight years. A happy girl, wife, mother, and sister,
beloved by all around her. Oh, my God, it is sad, the news
has quite upset me. God has called this angelic woman to
Himself, we must not murmur, nor even be astonished. Nevertheless, the heart bleeds, and one thinks first of the husband,
then of the mother, then of my poor uncle who loved her more
than any one in the world. He said to me the other day, " If
I lose Blanche my life will be broken indeed. She alone takes
the inmost place of all." Morpeth[3] wrote a beautiful letter to
my mother, most touching and heartbreaking, but so pious and
resigned. An hour before she died she became quite calm,
with a sweet smile on her lips, and she died without any agony.
Susan will be deeply grieved, and I am so also. I have loved
her ever since my first visit to England. I saw so much of her
and knew her so intimately that I could appreciate her worth.
She was a good woman, whose deep piety covered all her faults
and turned them into virtues. She was an angel of peace in
her family. Her counsels and advice guided my uncle. I am
uneasy about my dear Fanny Howard,[4] who loved her like an
only and beloved sister. ... Dear Eda, is not it very sad ? Our
dear Susan will be deeply grieved, I wish I was with her. ...
Henry Howard is coming to give me news of the family. ...
My aunt has been most courageous and resigned. She was at
the funeral with her five daughters. It must have been a heart-
·breaking sight. After the service they all went down into the
vault, and knelt round the coffin of their dear sister. My aunt

Brother of Lady Burlington.　　　　 [4] Sister of Lord Burlington.

writes to my mother, " I have lost the joy of my life, my child
of predilection, the one who was the glory and the happiness of
my life.   It is an overwhelming blow ! but I trust that I shall
find strength in religion to help me to bear it."   My aunt was
always inclined to religion, but this trouble appears to have
awoken a piety and confidence in God which is truly to be
admired.   My uncle perhaps suffers more than all.   He is very
pale and changed, they say.   His inmost life is so upset that
I am quite uneasy about him, only happily, I know that he
seeks for consolation in religion.

The next letter is partly on the same subject.

To Lady Rivers.

Paris, *May* 15.

. . . I can entirely imagine your dreading the return to
London this time, but after the first moment I think it will be
a comfort to them all to see you and to talk with you of their
lost treasure, who you so truly loved and appreciated.   I saw
yesterday a beautiful letter from Mr. Blunt to Lord Burlington
which Lizzie had copied and sent to Harry.   It is so simple, so
touching, and describes exactly the singular beauty of her
religion, its being so real, so intense, and so free from show or
display.   Harry was very low when he arrived, but is much
improved in spirits since.   It is good for him to be with us, I
think.   He knows we feel with him and for him, and yet are able
to be cheerful and to draw his thoughts away occasionally from
this deep and heavy affliction. . . . I dined at Court a day or
two ago, and saw the Duchesse de Nemours, whom I think
quite lovely, and so gay and nice and young in manner.   She
is thought beautiful here.   Her dazzling complexion, large
hazel eyes, *et ces flots de cheveux dorés*, as Jules Janin describes
them, have a wonderful effect.   She has a strong German
accent, but it is not unpleasing.   She seems fond of Nemours.

What a sensation it makes in France this *Apothéose* of
Napoleon, as they call it ; the Carliste and Republican news-
papers join in predicting that it will electrify the whole of
France, and that L. Philippe will totter on his throne in con-
sequence !   All I hope is that they will not have returned from
St. Helena till late in the autumn, for I shall not like to hurry

back from England, and yet my husband is determined, and I shall be anxious, too, to see Bonaparte's interment. Fancy a military funeral, the most striking of all services, in the beautiful chapel of the Invalides, and to hear the cries of *Honneur à l'Empereur, Gloire à Napoléon* resounding all about one. The Prince de Joinville fetches the remains of Napoleon ; what a singular *rapprochement !*

The next letter introduces a new subject, the marriage of her brother, then Lord Leveson.

To Mdlle. Eward.

Paris, *July* 18, 1840.

Leveson's marriage is arranged, and will take place soon. If it is not too soon we shall go to assist at it. My mother is enchanted with Lady Acton,[5] and my father also, though he would rather Leveson had married an English girl. You will want to know what she is like, I will try to give you an idea of her. Imagine Susan (who is thought like her) smaller, with smaller eyes but of a pretty blue, a pink and white complexion, a quantity of light hair, beautiful arms, a pretty white neck. . . . She speaks English well, though with an accent, but a pleasant one. She is much loved by every one that knows her well. I think she has a quick temper, but never disagreeable, and her gaiety is pleasant to see. My mother writes from Chiswick, " Here come Leveson and Lady Acton in a little carriage as happy as two children, he teaching her to drive. They go boating every day, and she is learning to row. She tries to please all the family." They spend the honeymoon at Chiswick, then they go to Fulham where they have taken a little country house, later on they go to Aldenham. . . . What pleases me in my future sister-in-law, is her perfect frankness, extreme honesty, and her deep religious feelings—though these are not quite according to my ideas—a marked dislike, which she always shows, for all light or disrespectful words on serious subjects. She is perfectly strict in fulfilling her religious duties. The thing that grieves me in it all is, that their children will be

[5] Marie E. de Dalberg (married first to Sir Richard Acton), first wife of Lord Granville (then Lord Leveson).

of different religions, according to their sex. I know that Leveson ought not and that my father cannot consent that their sons or grandsons should be Roman Catholics, which is certainly unfortunate.

In the few words in which she has spoken of her sister-in-law, Lady Georgiana has naturally given but a very imperfect sketch of one whom at the time was hardly known to her. When she speaks of Lady Acton's frankness and honesty and religious feelings, she uses language which her more intimate acquaintance with her sister-in-law during the rest of her life, would certainly never have induced her to modify. The marriage took place shortly after the date of this letter. We shall have to record the death of Lady Leveson, in 1860, and the deep grief of Lady Georgiana, who was always most warmly attached to her.

We go back now for a time to Lady Georgiana's residence at Paris, a few months earlier than the letter we have last inserted. She then writes to her former governess.

To Mdlle. Eward.

Paris, *March* 19, 1840.

... It is a long time since I wrote to you, my dearest Eda. It is *not* from want of desire, I assure you, but my days are occupied from morning to night. I get up at eight o'clock. I occupy myself on my own account up to ten o'clock. I dress and breakfast up to one o'clock. I then give lessons to the children,[6] and read to my mother, or since the beginning of Lent I go to St. Roch to hear an excellent preacher, the Abbé Cœur. At three o'clock I ride with my father, and the rest of the day is passed with my husband and the children. In the evening we nearly always have company.

[6] She had a little niece staying with her for a few months.

My son is *a great darling*. He is always merry and good-
humoured, whatever happens, very obedient with me, and
devoted to his father, and he applies well to his little lessons.
He remembers wonderfully what I read to him in the History
of France or of England, and answers capitally as to all the
names and details when questioned. He is very fond of Susan
(the little girl) who is very young for her age, and loves to play
with him all day long. She is very fond of me, and I hope to
influence her character for good. Sunday is a happy day to
these dear children. They delight in hearing histories and
looking at pictures from the Bible. They always find the day
too short. Baba (her little boy) seriously reproaches me for not
reading family prayers in the evening as well as in the morning.
May God make my dear child a true Christian, that is the
dearest wish of my heart.

To the same.

Paris, *August* 7, 1840.

We all leave for Havre in two or three days. We are to
stay there some time, and then we—my husband and I—shall
go to England, or perhaps make a tour in France. Every one
speaks so much of the war, that we do not wish to be too much
away from Paris, though I hope much that it will end in nothing
save words, as has so often happened.

I have this morning received a most affectionate letter from
Leveson, pressing us to go to them in London [7] (they are going
to take a house in Berkeley Square), and after that to go to see
my sister-in-law at Aldenham, but I have told him the various
reasons that oblige me to remain here.

I went to see the consecration of the Archbishop of Paris.[8]
I never saw a more beautiful ceremony. This splendid Cathedral
of *Notre Dame* full of people, galleries, nave, and tribunes, the
centre of the church filled with all the clergy of Paris and the
neighbourhood, clothed in their sacerdotal vestments, the most
interesting ceremonies, the loveliest music you can imagine.
You may fancy how delighted I was, I who passionately love
the ritual of the Catholic faith.

---

[7] Lord Leveson had been married to Lady Acton, July 25th.
[8] That of Mgr. Affre.

To the same.

Paris, *October* 14, 1840.

As you are so interested in politics, you can understand how much we have been occupied lately. As for me, who for a thousand reasons would be miserable to have war, I cannot believe in it. Perhaps I have no good reason for being hopeful, for certainly no one round me dares give an opinion on the subject. It is quite certain that there is a war agitation throughout France which is frightening, but I remember there was the same thing at the time of the Polish Revolution, and now all is calm. May this terrible curse be spared if it is the will of God.

Thursday morning (same letter).

What a frightful attempt last night against the life of the King ![9] What thanksgivings we owe to God for saving his life and sparing this country, and perhaps Europe altogether, from dire misfortunes. War, revolution, and every imaginable evil might have followed. How I pity the poor Queen, so good, and in such continual fear and anxiety. It is said that the little Comte de Paris is very ill.

To the same.

Paris, *November* 5, 1840.

The Levesons have spent six days here. This has seemed a very short time, but it is very satisfactory to have seen them, and to see them so happy. We think her charming. She is so good and affectionate, frank and merry. She is very quick, and is easily put out, but it does not last a moment, and with one so calm as Leveson their harmony is never really broken. The Duchesse de Dalberg likes him very much, though her conscience obliged her to object to the marriage. It is easy to see that in her heart she is delighted to see her daughter so happy. Marie (Lady Leveson) seems to love my father and mother much.

The Hardys[10] are here. The more I see of them, the more I like them. We have been to the opening of the Chamber this morning. The King made a very sensible and practical speech.

---

[9] The attempt of Darmès.   [10] Daughters of Sir Thomas Hardy.

He was received with enthusiasm by the Centre, but with cold
silence by the Right and the Left. They expected disturbances
to-day, but all has gone tranquilly. I hope the Ministry will
keep in, but M. Thiers is a terrible adversary. *La Presse* is an
interesting newspaper. I am very glad that you have it. My
son is very well. He reads easily in French now, and writes
fairly.

To the same.

Paris, *January* 1, 1841.

I will write you a long letter another day about politics, and
the funeral of Napoleon. If you read *La Presse*, you will have
seen there the account of a melodrama which was played here
(the Embassy) with great success. I was not there, but I organized it, which amused me much. Our actresses were Miss
Raikes, one of my friends who is very clever, and the two
pretty Miss Ellices whom you know. Our actors were Freddy,
and all the gentlemen of the Embassy, Henry Greville, Henry
Howard, Lord Howden, and young Plunkett. I wish you could
have seen Freddy making love passionately. He played very
well. You would have trembled, as mamma did, when some
one shot at him from a pistol, and he fell to the ground !

To the same.

February 25, 1841.

I must tell you that I took my Granville, for the first time,
to a Court ball last week. Picture him in a dark blue velvet
blouse, with a collar of guipure, white trousers and gloves, his
hair cut *à la Vandyke,* as he always wears it now. He was
much admired, but it did not amuse him much, and we came
home early.

Here we have now the Ministry well established, but it may
fall at any time, and this keeps us in continual anxiety. I hope
at present that all is going well with France, and that we shall
not have war with America, but it is a good thing that the
Eastern question must be arranged before this could arise.

I am more amused by company this year than usual. We
have such pleasant society round us, but I shall be glad when
the Carnival is over. Lent is a happy time for me, because

of the excellent, eloquent preachers I can hear on week-days.
The Abbé Ollivier and the Abbé de Ravignan I prefer above all
others.

The next letter is written from La Jonchère, a
place of which Lady Georgiana seems to have been
fond. It is close to Paris, and was taken on account
of a sudden illness which disabled Lord Granville
during the last year of his holding his post of
Ambassador, which he would probably have resigned
sooner, but that a change of Ministry was impending
in England, and it was undesirable to create a
vacancy which would very soon have to be succeeded by another. The comparative quiet and the
country air of La Jonchère, did much for his health,
which, however, was seriously impaired, and never
completely recovered.

To the same.

La Jonchère, *July* 19.

We get fonder every day of *la Jonchère*. It is a delightful
place to stay at, combining all the charms of the country with
the enjoyment of a few intimate and pleasant friends. Oh, if
you could only see the delicious walks, and rides, and drives
through vineyards and charming villages ! Yesterday we had a
tremendous storm and hurricane, which lasted till four o'clock.
Then it held up, and we had a delightful walk that you can
imagine. My Granville (her son) is a good walker, and walks
several miles. He has a pretty little pony, and learns to ride, a
great delight to him. In the evening we have music or reading
aloud, and when the gentlemen of the Embassy are here (four
times a week) there are large billiard parties, and sometimes we
act plays. Last week we acted the principal scenes in the
Midsummer's Night Dream of Shakespeare, which amused
papa and mamma very much. The Tories are triumphing in
England. Sir Robert will have a large majority, but much
difficulty in governing, on account of the differences in his own.

party. It is certain that in six weeks, or two months, the present Ministers will be no more, and in consequence *we* shall no longer be Ambassadors. The Queen, it is said, is against the Tories, and wishes the Whigs to stay in.

We have hitherto taken many of the passages cited from Lady Georgiana's letters from her correspondence with Mdlle. Eward, rather than from those addressed to her sister. Writing to her former governess, she naturally enters into many details of her daily life with which her sister was already well acquainted. Her correspondence with Lady Rivers was all the time very active, and shows the close intimacy and affection which always existed between them.

This correspondence appears to have been at times almost daily, Lady Granville occasionally taking part in it by letters to her elder daughter. Only a portion of it survives, and the dates of the years are constantly missing. It is impossible to restore them accurately, and perhaps it is not quite necessary to attempt it. The letters tell us of an intimate sisterly intercourse, in which discussions about the education of children are mixed up with family incidents, and in which too we catch occasional glimpses of works of charity in which Lady Georgiana was constantly employed, even at this time. There is also a good deal of religious discussion interspersed. Thus we get a picture of all that occupied Lady Georgiana's mind, without being able to trace her life from day to day. We give a number of extracts, without binding ourselves to chronological accuracy of the arrangement.

To Lady Rivers.

Baby, or rather Baba, which is the name my little Granville
has given himself, is very flourishing, and gets every day a
greater darling ; he has added several words to his vocabulary,
amongst which the very French expression of *tenez*, when he
holds out something to one.   It will be quite enchanting to see
our two boys together.   I look a good deal to yours giving mine
a very good example ; he is in some ways remarkably good and
obedient, but I am always afraid of his growing jealous or selfish
from being the only one, and such a first object to us all.   As
to your ——, I will not talk about her, I feel so very envious of
you ; she seems by all accounts to be a perfect little beauty,
and *such* a darling.

I am afraid you will be quite afraid of my coming to Mistley,
as you deprecate so strongly the Calvinistic doctrines which,
with a single exception (which indeed I believe is generally
excepted by English Calvinists), they are my opinions, nor could
I join with you in rejoicing at any of my friends being free from
saintishness; for, on the contrary, my greatest wish would be to
see them what the *world calls* saints.   It always seems to me
so ridiculous to blame Evangelical people for the faults and the
humbug of *some few* among them, and those the unamiable or
narrow-minded which must be met with in any given number of
people, as it would be to consider the *unevangelical* responsible
for all the cold formality, the indifference to religion, and all
which *I* think results from that to me most singular dread of
people being *too* good.   I do not deny that there may be a good
deal of mannerism that might be dispensed with, *sometimes* of
cant that *ought* to be avoided ; but, on the other hand, how
much of offensive levity in speaking, how much of coldness in
feeling, which certainly is *more* blameable than their defects,
which even when they do exist are almost always mere manner ;
while they are thought uncharitable (that is the great word
against them) for reflecting upon others, more indeed by the tacit
reproof of a different sort of life and conversation than by actual
abuse.   My opinion, dearest sister, is so strong about their
being *perfectly right*, that I only regret, like on every other
subject, that a good cause should so often have ill-judging and
indiscreet professors and advocates.   I hope my having written

three pages on the subject will not have made you consider me as such.

To the same.

Baba has been unwell these last days with a violent cold, but he is better now, and will, I flatter myself, have recovered his looks a little by the end of the month, for when his poor little face is swelled he looks so very much to his disadvantage. Last Wednesday Monsieur Vallombrosa and Mdlle. de Castries spent the afternoon with him ; both of them exactly his own age, and they played to their hearts' content. I overheard him telling the latter that his cousins were coming, and she answered, " I have a little brother coming too," the mode of arrival being, however, somewhat different. The Duchess of Orleans is confidently stated to be with child, but perhaps it is only that people, whenever she is indisposed, choose to ascribe that reason for it. Like the wife of one of the National Guards, when at the *Nouvel au reception*, on the Duke of Orleans telling her in answer to her anxious inquiries for the Duchess, that she had a slight *erisipèle au pied*, exclaimed, " Ah, Monseigneur, *il faut espérer que ce sera un garçon.*"

To the same.

Your party at Mistley must have been very pleasant, and I like so much to hear of all your doings, dearest of Sissys, and can imagine how much you must have enjoyed your country ball and the drive home at night—all that sort of jolliness which makes me think, when I hear of it, of our girlish days, and which is *the* sort of enjoyment which in the middle of the hateful dissipation here is so very much wanting. I am not afraid of Baba's getting positively violent with his cousins ; I think when offended he will himself content himself with abuse in conversation, which he is rather prone to, and which they will probably bear with the most perfect equanimity. Baba had a visit the other day from Lady Abercorn's two eldest little girls, the prettiest little black-eyed things I ever saw. He was very civil, and only when he saw them in possession of his toys, kept saying to himself: " Well, it's my Noah's Ark," " Well, she's got my chair ; " and when they kissed him violently, only said, " That will do now ; now that's quite enough."

To the same.

Your account of the children delighted us, and I never tire of hearing of the darlings' sayings and doings. As to Granville, I have been taking great pains with him lately, for I found that he required to be kept in greater order, and nobody does it but me, and therefore I have him a great deal with me, and he is improving very much and in every way. His reading is getting on, though not very rapidly ; counting he is idiotic about, geography wonderfully proficient in, and very quick at learning little verses and answering the questions in the *Little Philosopher*, which I am pleased with, as you are. I cannot say how useful I think it will prove, in giving children a habit of reflection and comparison. I took him the other day to a *dejeuner danseuse* at Madame Apponys's, and his comments afterwards amused me extremely. First he complained that when he wanted to see the dancing, the ladies crowded round him, and bothered him. He exclaimed when he got into the carriage, " Now they can't get at me. What is the use of all this crowding and dancing ? It don't make me better, it makes me *wuss ;* gives me a pain in my head, and makes me very tired."

To the same.

How I shall like to show you Baba. You must not expect a pretty boy—his large fat face is too full-moonish for that ; but I think you will think him a love when he is at his ease with you. You must also make allowance if at first he is not perfectly amiable with his cousins ; an only child is so apt to get a little selfish, but he will, I am sure, be delighted with them, and it will do him a world of good to be with them. He gets on nicely with his spelling, though it is very difficult to fix his attention. What he delights in are the Bible stories, especially the history of the children of Israel in the Desert, which we are now going through. I copy out for you *à mésure* what I write for him, and will send it you whenever you tell me you want it. I intend to go through the whole of the Old Testament with him, before I tell him anything of the history of the New Testament. Now and then on Sundays, for instance, I show him a picture of our Lord Jesus Christ blessing little children, and tell him He is the Son of God Who came from Heaven to live some time on earth, and teach us to be good. This is all I have ever told him yet on the subject. I think the books for early religious instruction I have got, and which in many ways are very good (the *Peep of Day*, *Line upon Line*, *Mama's Bible Stories*), though they do not at all satisfy me—mix up too much the Old Testament and the New—if they do not explain themselves, advise one in notes to explain to the child the spiritual meaning of the Sacrifices, of the Passover, of the Brazen Serpent, which it seems to me impossible a very little child should understand. I write the facts themselves in some detail, and when once he is well acquainted with them, the application of them will be easy when he is older.

To the same.

Papa and mamma are dining at the William Bentinck's, and afterwards going to a *soirée* at the Duchesse d'Albufera, whilst we are sitting quietly at home, and I preparing this letter for the courier to-morrow. The weather has been raw and cold again, with heavy and frequent rain. I am quite stiff and aching to-day from the active evolutions at ball and hide-and-seek which I have been performing with Granville to supply the want of out-of-door exercise. As he grows older the more I can be his constant companion and playfellow the better, for a child requires one, and there are so few children with whom one can wish one's own to associate intimately. He is very well now, and the present system we follow with him seems to improve his health, his looks, and his character. What I am most anxious now to check in myself or others with regard to him, are attempts at drawing him out and showing him off in conversation. I have been reading *Emile* through lately, and though it is certainly too late (as in Miss Austen's novel, Emma discovers it to be too late at twenty-five to set about being artless and simple-minded) to turn Baba into *l'enfant de la nature*, and that if one *could* one *would* not follow Rousseau's system or admire his *Idéal*, at least not more than as an imperfect though attractive sketch of character ; still there is a good deal of sound reasoning and clever observation in it, and much which points out to me the errors in which one is continually

falling with regard to education. There is one letter on Education in the *Nouvelle Héloise,* which I like better than any of
Emile.

These extracts must suffice to show the occupation of Lady Georgiana during these years. There
are also, as we have said, many traces of good
works—a girl put to " pension," servants instructed
for Confirmation, and the like. She speaks of
Dr. Chalmers' preaching very enthusiastically.

I went yesterday afternoon to hear Dr. Chalmers preach at
the Teilbout Chapel, and had never yet heard such extraordinary
eloquence. In spite of an uncouth manner, a hoarse voice, a
Scotch accent which at first bewilders you with its peculiarity,
one feels fascinated and borne on by a flow of language, a
beauty of imagery, and strength of argument, beyond all description. His energy almost amounts to violence, but still has
nothing of ranting in it. His subject was an exposition of the
two great doctrines of Christianity, the Incarnation and the
Atonement, as peculiarly adapted to the cravings of human
nature, and he rose quite to the height of his subjects.

Lady Georgiana was at the same time going freely
to hear Catholic preachers, a thing she would not
have done some years before. At this time, and
during the following years, the French pulpit was
filled by some great orators, and she may have gone
to hear them out of curiosity. None of the names
which she mentions is second rate. If she went
at this time to talk with the Abbé Dupanloup about
her brother's marriage, there is nothing to show
that she allowed that great spiritual guide and
teacher of perfection to many souls to perceive the
thoughts which were maturing in her own. She
also went to hear the Abbé Cœur, the Abbé Ollivier,

and the Abbé de Ravignan preach, but she had no
acquaintance with any of them till after she became
a Catholic. But it was not a vain curiosity which
so often took her to the churches where she could
hear them. She listened to their teaching attentively, and took notes. There is an anecdote of her
doing this when the preacher was the Abbé Ollivier,
which shows him in not quite so amiable a light as
might have been expected.

He was at that time Curé of St. Roch, and was
preaching when Lady Georgiana had taken a seat
immediately under the pulpit, for the sake of hearing
better. She had taken a memorandum-book from
her pocket in which she wrote what she heard.
Many Catholic ladies, rightly or wrongly, do the
same, without having remonstrances addressed to
them, at least in public. But it appears that this
custom particularly displeased the Abbé Ollivier.
He first aimed one or two severe glances at the
delinquent, who did not perceive them. Then he
spoke directly, in a manner that drew the eyes of
all the audience to her, and it became evident that
the reflections he made upon the supposed offence
had a very personal aim. The effect upon so timid
and reserved a person as Lady Georgiana may easily
be imagined. Many years after this the good Abbé
Ollivier, who died Bishop of Evreux, came to learn
who it had been to whom he had addressed so
severe a rebuke, and he expressed his regret for his
part in the incident. In fact Lady Georgiana never
went into St. Roch for some time after. Happily
the thoughts which had been conveyed to her in

H

those sermons were not driven from her mind by this momentary explosion of impatience on the part of their author. The following passages are taken from letters to her sister at this period of her life, and may serve to complete what has already been extracted.

To Lady Rivers.

I thank you for your last dear letter, and I sincerely congratulate you on the news you give me.[11] Others might not consider it a cause of congratulation, but as for me, who desire the same, my love for children having in no way diminished since I had one of my own, therefore I congratulate you from my heart. Every child I see interests me. I have taken a great fancy to the little Vallombrosa, he is so handsome, graceful, and gay, with great black eyes, and very loving— which mine is not. In this respect he does not spoil me. He loves to be near me, he does not like leaving me, but he is not one of those children who care to kiss those they love.

You must have seen the account of the attempt on the King, in the papers. The man was a clerk who fired at the King just as he was getting into his carriage at the Tuileries. He was bowing at the moment, which saved him. The ball lodged in the cushions of the carriage behind him !

We went to Neuilly with papa and mamma the same evening. We found them calm and full of courage, though much moved.

To the same.

I envy you the active good you can practice on all around you, above all, to the poor whom I love, your presence is a real blessing. I know well that, in the position we are in the world, there is great danger of our wasting our lives in trifles. It does not do to think too much of what others do in this respect under their circumstances, but to do the best one can where one is. It is this I am afraid of not doing !

. . . Last Monday, the birthday of the Queen, M. Cousin, the Minister of Public Instruction, came to dine. You know

[11] The expected birth of a child.

he has written much on national education. We talked much, and though his ultra-Protestant and democratic opinions are not to my taste, the conversation interested me much.

Are you not much interested in this proposal about the changes in the Prayer Book? I am sure you are against it as I am. The Oxford Tracts make me wish to go back to the Book of Edward VI.

This is the first allusion we find in her letters to the Oxford movement, many phases of which had their influence on her, though she does not speak of them to her sister. We see, however, that she manifests much religious feeling, as well as the motherly care with which she strives to inspire her son with the same.

To Lady Rivers.

Paris, *October* 8.

MY DEAREST SISTER,—I received your dear letter yesterday and, at the same time, the very pretty frock you have kindly given to my dear boy. It fits him beautifully, and is just the sort I like and the colour that becomes him. Thank you so much for it, dearest Sissy. I suppose you arrive at Chatsworth to-day, and can imagine how lovely it must look in this fine autumnal weather, and the pleasure you will have in being there again, and in meeting so many of your greatest friends at once. Your arrival will give *such* pleasure to the whole party. . . . We have still here the same heavenly weather that you describe, and very enjoyable it is. I think we shall certainly spend at Versailles the time of papa's and mamma's absence, and if we have a tolerably mild November it will not be unpleasant. . . . I have begun about three months ago attempting to give my boy some idea of religion, and although at first one feels puzzled how to proceed, from the extreme childishness of his ideas and conceptions, still I am persuaded that it is no reason against going on. It seems to me a great mistake to expect children not to have childish ideas on that subject as well as on every other, and though they may appear to oneself ridiculous, yet probably they are scarcely more so in the eyes of God than many of ours. I was thinking so the other day when my boy asked me if in Heaven he should dig (gardening is his greatest pleasure). Probably his idea of heavenly happiness is not much more remote from the reality of it than ours are when we think of music, &c., such as we now know it, as ingredients in the felicity of a future life. All that one can require is that they themselves should not treat the subject with levity, not that their ideas should not often to us appear extremely ridiculous. I have not gone further yet than praying with my boy for a minute in the morning, and his nurse does the same for a minute at night. I have got a large Bible picture-book which I show him on Sundays, and now and then in the week, when he seems disposed to it. That is the Old Testament hitherto. All the books I have met with for giving the first instruction out of the Bible do not appear to me half simple enough. I enclose to you a sheet where I have written out the substance of the first chapters of Genesis. Should you approve of the style of it, and like me to send you what I write for my boy as I go on, I should be delighted to do so. You would do it yourself as well or better than I, but you have so many occupations that it might save your time, and I am sure that we agree on these subjects, at least on all those that touch the early education of our children, and you cannot think till you try how much time it takes to omit every word and expression one thinks a child would not quite understand and to find substitutes for them. I make my boy put aside his guns, drums, &c., on Sunday, and play with quiet toys, of which I keep some new one for that day, and soon I shall have puzzles and picture-books expressly for that purpose. This is a subject of such intense interest that I feel I could write for ever, but I must now leave off. Give my best love to Rivers, to Leveson, to Uncle D., to all my friends, particularly to Fanny, and believe me, dearest sister,

Your most affectionate

G. F.

To Lady Rivers.

Paris, *October* 16.

MY DEAREST SUKEY,—I received your long and most
interesting letter yesterday, and thank you a thousand times for
it. I am glad you like the sheet I sent you, and will despatch
another next courier. I perfectly agree with and deeply feel
all you say with regard to the unspeakable usefulness of the
subject. I have a great many books of the sort, but though
they give one useful hints, none of them are altogether satisfactory. *The* one great difficulty of all I think is to impress
them with the *seriousness* of religion, without associating any
gloom with it. You are often obliged to check their levity, and
in doing so you feel afraid to abate their cheerfulness with
regard to it, which nobody can have a stronger dread of than
I have, but, dearest, you *must* have misunderstood me about
Sunday. In withdrawing the military and noisy toys on that
day I substitute some quiet ones, which, from being new and
having them only on that day, he likes a thousand times better.
On Sunday I play with him more than usual. I paint little
things for him, I take the greatest pains to make the day
appear a very happy one to him (and he already does consider
it so), at the same time that I think it a great object that, as
far as is possible with a little child, he should think it different
from other days, and the pleasures of it of a different *sort* from
those which he usually enjoys, which can be my only object in
substituting a Noah's ark, or a box of lambs and shepherds,
for drums, guns, and trumpets. You say there ought to be no
cessation of innocent amusement, but you consider yourself
theatres, balls, &c., as very innocent amusements, and yet you
would not indulge in them on Sundays, and I do not see why
the difference should not be marked to them at an early age.
I so far agree with you that, did I see that the privation of his
usual toys was the *least* a grievance to Granville, I should not
enforce it, but I always so manage that his day is full of other
amusements which he likes better than those with drums. It
is not to convince you to do this that I have dwelt upon it, for it
is a mere little *accessoire* and of no consequence, but merely to
show you that my idea is as much as yours to render religion,
as far as lies in my power, a source of happiness and enjoyment

to my child. As I have begun before you, I will confess to you as I go on my mistakes, as well as everything else, because it may be of use to you. I think, that after giving Granville the first idea of God and making him say a few words of prayer, I too soon began telling him stories out of the Bible, which created a degree of confusion in his ideas, and that he mixes up too much the idea of God with that of the various persons in the histories I have told him. I believe it would have been much better to have accustomed him to the idea of God, and have done so in connection with the beauties of nature, the comforts of life, till it would gradually have become more clear and defined in his little head, before beginning my historic and religious instruction.

Your letter interested me to the greatest degree. I rejoiced to hear what you say about Leveson. Dearest boy, I am very fond of him.

It will interest some to read her account of Lady Powerscourt, then at the height of her beauty. She afterwards became Lady Londonderry, and, as is well known, the intimate friend of Lady Georgiana in her latter years, like her devoted to good works and labours for the poor. She died a little before her friend, leaving behind a multitude of regrets and a great void.

To Lady Rivers.

We have had here, *en passant*, the beautiful Lady Powerscourt. It is certainly a degree of perfection in features and in colouring that is imagined but hardly ever seen. Then there is little or no countenance, and she does not improve on speaking. She was on Saturday at Madame Paul de Ségur's, and quite mobbed, people were crowding round her and a buzz of admiration going through the room, which my beautiful and quite unjealous friend, Lady H——, enjoyed extremely. She is so unpretending, so childlike and uncoquettish, that it is impossible not to be fond of her.

The following passage is not dated, but it must have been written either before the incident which has been spoken of in the Church of St. Roch, or after she had made up her mind to go again to hear the Abbé Ollivier.

To Lady Rivers.

I read the debate last night with great interest ; the speech I like best is Mr. Charles Buller's. Whatever one feels about other questions, I cannot imagine not being a Whig on the subject of Ireland. If there is a general election, how awful the contest in that unhappy country will be. There seem to have been serious riots at my brother-in-law's election for King's County. I am so sorry for his wife, who is in delicate health, and whom it must have made very anxious.

I have been twice to St. Roch to hear the Abbé Ollivier and the Abbé de Ravignan. Nothing can be more different than these two preachers, or more perfect than each in his own style. The former is practical, persuasive, going into all sorts of details about one's daily conduct and practices, familiar in his manner, and almost conversational, though never too much so—he always seems to me the personification of my favourite saint and writer, St. Francis of Sales. I shall hear him throughout Lent twice a week, I am happy to think. M. de Ravignan's sermons are more like essays, and on general subjects—his eloquence is quite unparalleled. It is something that feels to carry one *hors de soi*, and makes one conceive how the crowd collected to hear him. At Notre Dame, one day last year, they rose *en masse* and began a thunder of applause. He said it was one of the most painful moments of his life. He actually, I was told, frowned that immense crowd into silence.

During a visit of a few days to the King and Queen at Fontainebleau, Lady Georgiana and Mr. Fullerton having accompanied Lord and Lady Granville, she writes to her sister as follows :

To Lady Rivers.

Fontainebleau, October 5.

MY DEAREST SISTER,—Mamma is gone out driving, and will scarcely have time to write a line to you, so that I will give you an account of our proceedings up to this moment. We arrived at this most beautiful place at five o'clock on Friday, were eighty people at dinner, and had a concert in the evening. The singers were Cinti, Ponchard, and Mdlle. Musi. Yesterday we had a private breakfast in our rooms, and at ten a public one, like a dinner ; then sat at the round table looking at prints for an hour; then during two hours walked all over the château, which is immense ; then went to the tennis-court and saw the two great players, Barre and Louis, play—a most extraordinary *partie.* This had brought it to two o'clock, and I was so completely knocked up that I was excused the expedition in the afternoon. Mamma was very much pleased with it, except the dashing down a sort of precipice (in the valley of the Lolle) in the britska and six. My husband rode. Another dinner of eighty people and a play—*La suite d'un bal Masque*—with which I was delighted, and the *Philtre* sung by Nourrit and Cinti. The theatre is pretty, and all the women being very smart, is in itself a very pretty *coup d'œil.* I was very unwell last night, and not being quite recovered yet have passed a very quiet day. They are all gone to the village of Thomery, which they say is beautiful and famous for its vintage. There is an Italian opera to-night, and to-morrow a great ball. Mamma is uncommonly well, and bears all the fatigue quite wonderfully. Nothing can be kinder than the Royal Family, and the look of the thing is very magnificent, but there is a sad want of comfort and good arrangement. Our party consists of the Ministers and their wives, the Maréchals and their wives and daughters, the Apponys, the Duc de Frias and his daughter, the Duc and Duchesse de la Trèmouille, the Labordes, the Lehons, and then the numberless people immediately about the Court. I am, fortunately, almost always next to mamma everywhere. When I am not, my companions generally are Mathilde Laborde, whom I like extremely, Madame de Rumigny, Mdlle. de Chabot, and Madame Montalivet, a great bore, but a good-natured sort of woman. I shall be very glad when Freddy comes, and I am impatient to see my little boy again (I had an excellent account of him this morning), and we shall all be happy to find ourselves home again. . . .

———

CHAPTER VI.

1840—1844.

LORD GRANVILLE's functions as Ambassador at Paris came to an end in the autumn of 1841, when Sir Robert Peel became Prime Minister. This brings us to the close of Lady Georgiana's sojourn in France. We must, however, retrace our steps somewhat, in order to speak of an incident which occurred in the last year of this sojourn, which had an important influence on her future. We must say first, what is sufficiently clear from her correspondence, that in the midst of the pleasant and brilliant life which she had continued to lead at the Embassy since her marriage, her interest in the poor was continually growing, along with the religious tendency which was at work in her. This interest was now very active, and had little in common with those "velléités" of charity of which we have heard while she was under the rule of Mdlle. Eward. Lady Granville, never indifferent to any work of beneficence, seconded her daughter in her occupations of this kind. Lady Georgiana took them up with a zeal and an intelligent perseverance which were to develope more and more as time went on, and fitted her not merely to share in great charitable works, but also to direct them, and in due course to become herself a foundress in this kind. It is to this time of her life that an anecdote related by an English lady who visited her belongs. She was calling on Lady Granville at the Embassy, when Lady Georgiana entered, looking weary and fagged. "My child," said Lady Granville, "you work yourself too hard." "Mamma," was the reply, "we can never work too hard for God!"

Lady Granville and her daughter, at this time, made the acquaintance of Mrs. Fry. This good lady's name has gained a well-merited renown in the annals of Protestant charity. She was a heroine, of whom Macaulay has said, that if a Catholic, she would have been a saint, and a foundress also, one of those for which the niches of the great founders of religious orders are destined in the great nave of St. Peter's. It was about the same time that Dr. Chalmers was also at Paris. Like Mrs. Fry and many others, he had a mind which broke through the cold tenets of Protestantism, and, although he belonged to one of the narrowest of sects, his language would not have been disavowed by the most fervent and eloquent orators of Catholicism. There is a great phalanx of such souls, and God alone can tell their number,—souls separated visibly from the perfect truth by obstacles which He alone knows and can measure. No eye but His can discern with certainty those whose will has been pure and right, and has remained unwarped by the involuntary error of their mind.

Lady Georgiana was certainly not inclined either

towards the Presbyterianism of Dr. Chalmers or the Quakerism of Mrs. Fry. It may be that it was a fresh argument, in addition to the others which she had heard in favour of the Catholic Church, to see these fragments of religion in others varying according to individual character. But these new influences helped to redouble in her the love of what was good, and she began to give herself actively to those charitable works which were in the end to absorb her whole soul.

Those who seek the poor, easily find them. Those poor, in fact, who interested her most were just those whom it was necessary to search for— those who hide their miseries, and to whom the dread of humiliation of being discovered is more formidable than all their privations. We cannot tell how many of these her charitable hand aided, how many tears she wiped away, how many hearts she relieved of some grievous weight, how many kind works she accomplished, hidden by her with the same care with which the sufferings she had discovered and relieved had been hid. No human eye can perceive this kind of charity. The Father's hand gathers these treasures, and makes them up into the "eternal weight of glory" which is to recompense them by-and-bye.

We know of one of these objects of compassion, a young girl, well born and brought up, who had lost her parents in Paris, and was left in the most complete destitution. Lady Georgiana found her out, and took charge of her with all her compassionate care. She placed her in security,

watched over her assiduously, and never ceased
her care of her till a happy marriage had made her
lot secure. She then lost sight of her, knowing
only that her husband had taken her to India,
where he held an important post. Thirty-five
years afterwards she was at one of those "charitable
sales" in London at which, almost to her last day,
she was always ready to help, when a lady came in,
still young, asking earnestly after Lady Georgiana.
She was pointed out to her, sitting at a counter, in
the humble dress which she had then for many
years worn. We may imagine the joyous expression
of her look of surprise, when the unknown lady,
whose dress and manner showed her to be well
educated and in good circumstances, came up to
her and told her that she was the daughter of her
protégée of Paris, who never, during all those years,
had forgotten her to whom she had owed the
happiness of her life, and whose name she had
taught her children from their youth up to bless.

Lady Georgiana found out, very early in that
career of charity which she was to follow out to the
degree of the highest heroism, a fact which is as
permanent and invariable as is the existence of the
poor among us. This fact is the surprising rapidity
with which the means of helping others pass from
our hands, and how truly we seem to have done
nothing when we have done all that we can. Our
resources are swallowed up, but the miseries remain
and grow afresh. This is the secret of the numberless expedients—not all of them excellent in themselves—to which charitable persons have recourse

in order to get money,—money, the sinews of charity just as much as the sinews of war. We do not mean to reproach truly charitable persons. It is not their fault that they have sometimes to take a very circuitous method of gaining what they want. They have often begun by giving all they have, reducing more and more their own resources for the sake of increasing those of the poor, and have themselves, in the process, come to taste a poverty which is not the less real because it is voluntary.

Who can be bold enough to reproach them? They are moved by a sort of despair, in finding themselves in contact with misery in all its various, its multitudinous, and its most cruel forms. Their desire to relieve them becomes a sort of passion, of the noblest kind, even if it has sometimes its phases of excess. With such persons we must use measured language, if we venture to blame them. Our severity should be reserved for the effeminate and frivolous crowd of worldlings, who shrink with horror from misery in all its ugliness and its nakedness, who would turn away their eyes instead of stretching out their hands, if they saw it in its true aspect. The alms of such persons can be won only by disguising what they are, and they must not be told that what they give is to fall into the hands of charity while they think they are giving to their pleasures.

Lady Georgiana gave largely and generously from her own resources, and soon came to perceive that they must be increased. And this, as must certainly be recorded in her story, was the great and the chief motive of her first effort in literature. It was charity that inspired her to become an author, and it was in the service of charity that she worked the mine which was soon opened by her talent. Probably, since those early years under Mdlle. Eward, when she began to write, she had never altogether laid aside her pen. It was natural, almost necessary to her, to write. But we find no trace of this among her papers, no mention of it in her letters. If, therefore, she now and then wrote something to please herself, she probably destroyed it as soon as written. We do not know whether the pressing need of increasing her alms prompted her first effort, or whether she had written it before and took it out of a drawer for the purpose. But it was at this time that she suddenly produced, not an original composition, but an English version from a poet of Languedoc, Jacques Jasmin. It was called the "Blind girl of Castel Cuillé." She read it over, corrected it, without telling any one, not even her husband and mother, and sent it to Mr. Richard Bentley, one of the most eminent of London publishers, who at that time had charge of a new Magazine, called *Bentley's Miscellany*.

A French poem by Jasmin, translated by Lady Georgiana Fullerton, daughter of the English Ambassador at Paris, was sure to excite the curiosity of readers. If it had been second-rate (which it was not) it would have been certain of a favourable reception. It was put in at once, and its two hundred and seventy lines brought the author twelve guineas on the day on which it appeared.

Georgiana was surprised and delighted. She had taken the chance of her venture without thinking that it would succeed. All her long years of success, different, indeed, in degree, never effaced the memory of this joy. It was the first revelation to her of a power of which she had hitherto been ignorant, and it was the tangible proof of what might be made of it.

In the course of a few weeks she set to work again, and sent Mr. Bentley another poem. It was received less favourably than the first. Mr. Bentley did not absolutely refuse it, but he remarked to her that poetry addressed itself to a much more limited public than prose. He advised her to seek another channel for the talent which she evidently possessed. It cannot be doubted that this answer caused her some momentary displeasure. Still the advice was not lost on her. Perhaps it corresponded to a secret thought of her own. Mr. Bentley's letter exists, and at the bottom of it are written in her own hand, these words, *That day I began "Ellen Middleton."*

Many years have passed since *Ellen Middleton* first appeared, but although it belongs to the most ephemeral class of literature, the book still survives, still wears it original charm, its keen interest, and that strange and inimitable stamp of beauty which ranks it among those few romances which pass from generation to generation, and take their places permanently among the intellectual treasures of their country and era. We shall speak presently of the effect which it produced. That effect was not entirely due to its literary merit, for it happened to appear at a time when the public mind was singularly well prepared to welcome such a work. But on this subject we do not at present dwell.

The pleasures of discovering a fertile vein of thought is certainly keen. But to give it form and shape and publicity, long labours and often weary sufferings are needed. "This," says Madame Swetchine, "is an universal law." Lady Georgiana found it so, and it cost her more than others. The book took its final shape under the influence of various causes, some of which changed her whole life, others caused her soul much sorrow. This gives a singular interest to the book as a revelation of her own mind, made at a moment when her imagination was at last set free to wield a pen, gifted with eloquence such as to enable her to express a thousand thoughts hitherto undeveloped, and to paint vividly and powerfully a thousand images whith had hitherto lurked in silence in her mind.

She had hardly begun her work, when the change of Ministry obliged Lord Granville to leave the Parisian Embassy, this time for ever. This put an end to Lady Georgiana's sojourn under the roof of her parents. She was no longer to lead the kind of life which had been hers more or less since her infancy. Personally the change was of more importance to her than is usual with those fluctuations for which the diplomatic career must prepare those who follow it, and their families. But it was to her the end of an epoch. She was to leave the place with which from her childhood she had been familiar, to know it no more, perhaps never revisit it. She always felt such events with keen vivacity. "When I was a child, she once said, " I could never leave an inn where we had passed the night, without a strange emotion in my heart that I should never again see the place. The word 'never' seemed to me terrible." It is easy, therefore, to imagine the melancholy she felt at having to leave, without hope of returning to it, the beautiful abode of her childhood, where she had grown up, where she had lived as a young woman, where she had been married, and where her child had been born. We may say more. The Embassy was the place where her intelligence was wakened up to new worlds, and where her thoughts, though as yet vaguely, had been turned in a direction which presaged an immense change. It was dear to her from every point of view.

Some verses which she wrote under the influence of these various impressions may be here inserted as partly expressing all this.

ON LEAVING THE BRITISH EMBASSY AT PARIS, IN 1841.

Farewell, old house! my ears will never more
Rejoice in the glad sound I loved so well,
When at a journey's end thy opening door
Roll'd back to greet me, and my heart would swell
And bound with speechless rapture in my breast ;
Exulting in the thought of hours to come,
Fraught with sweet converse and with welcome rest,
'Midst all the genial sympathies of home.
Of thee a final mournful leave I take,
Long as my life, and on this parting day

I

My eyes o'erflow, I weep for the dear sake
Of vanish'd joys and sorrows pass'd away.
A child, I came to thy wide spacious halls,
Play'd on thy greensward, wander'd in thy bowers;
My girlish dreams were dreamt within thy walls,
And years flew by like a few fleeting hours.
Since then all that mark'd life with earnest stress,
Each strong emotion, each momentous change—
More than I dare to dwell on or express,
Of thought expanding to a wider range—
Through joy, through suffering, through experience won
With thee are blended, link'd for evermore;
But chiefly, tenderly, will mem'ry run
On one dear spot, where I would fain live o'er
Days full of happiness, too great for earth.
Thy room, my mother! Shall we e'er again
Renew those communings in grief and mirth,
Those free outpourings of each joy or pain—
That reading, thinking, dreaming, side by side,
That ceaseless converse, whether sad or gay,
Which still was sweet, and, when the heart was tried,
Lighten'd its burthen, and chased gloom away?
God knows! the future may be dark or fair,
But never what the past has been to me;
Farewell, dear house! a parting leaf I tear
From mem'ry's book, and as I sadly see
Thy doors close on me, one blest thought renews
Grateful emotion and a filial pride,
That, through the bygone years my heart reviews,
Spent 'neath thy roof, and by my father's side,
I still beheld him labouring for one end,
Peace between two great nations to maintain,
England's true son, and yet to France a friend,—
For this he lived, and did not live in vain:
Erewhile, when the dense clouds of discord rose,
And war's dark vision showed its hateful form,
Threat'ning both kingdoms with impending woes,
To him was given to allay the storm.
Strong in his native rectitude of heart,
His fearless truthfulness by none denied,
And honesty, the statesman's highest art,
'Twas his to mediate, reconcile, and guide—
And on the surging waters balm to throw.

" Blest are the peacemakers ! "   God's children they !
Oh, who can measure, who can ever know,
The full deep blessedness those words convey !
The guerdon pledged to all who act the part,
Christ thus has sanctified ; who bear the name,
Which gladly, humbly, with a grateful heart,
For thee, my father, I can dare to claim.

In order to explain the last lines, it is sufficient
to recall the fact that Lord Granville's last year as
Ambassador at Paris included the very critical time
when, after the signature of the quadripartite treaty
between England, Russia, Prussia, and Austria, for
the settlement of the affairs of the East, by com-
pelling Mehemet Ali to relinquish Syria—a treaty
signed without the knowledge of France — the
friendly relations between that country and England
were on the verge of being broken by war.   The
resignation of M. Thiers put an end to the strain,
but Lord Granville exerted himself to the utmost,
both with the English Cabinet and in Paris, and
had a great influence in bringing about the pacifica-
tion.   Lady Georgiana used often to speak of the
excitement of that time, and of her father's most
useful and successful work.

These verses express with more than usual
clearness the intimate feelings of her heart—some,
perhaps, which she would have hesitated to express
more clearly.   She could hardly have spoken in
prose of those impressions which might transform
her life, and of the higher flights to which her mind
might soar.   We now know enough to see that
there was no exaggeration about these words, and
they help us to understand the influences under

which she wrote the first book which was to make her name famous, in which, under the form of fiction, she set forth some feelings which were really in agitation at the bottom of her soul.

It was in October, 1841, that Lady Georgiana and Mr. Fullerton left the Embassy, to return to it no more. Lord Cowley took Lord Granville's place. They went first to Cannes, which had few residents then, except Lord Brougham. He lent his villa to Lord and Lady Granville. It was then nearly the only house fit to dwell in in the place. Then they went to Nice, where they were to meet with a great trouble, of which we shall let Lady Georgiana speak herself, in the following letter.

To Mdlle. Eward.

Nice, *December* 24, 1841.

My son has been very ill since I last wrote to you, for some months he has lost his health, and seemed weak and suffering. For some days he has been worse, much fever, and his brain has been affected.

He is, thank God, much better now, but he will need great care for a long time. I do not know how I could bear the anxiety about a child, so fearfully precious, without the deep conviction I have in the goodness of God and of His boundless power, if He wills, to spare the life of my only child, as He often raises up children for whom we have never trembled. Dr. Verity treated him with much care and skill. He forbids his being taught anything, even to read. He thinks that his having lived with grown up people has made his brain too active, and that he must have absolute rest. He urges us to put him to school. He says that the society of other children, active games and exercise, are indispensable, and though our repugnance and trouble about this advice is extreme, we are thinking of acting upon it when we have found a completely satisfactory place where we could leave him without fear. On this account we shall return to England in February. The Italian climate would be bad for him, and travelling would try his little head too much, and he could not have the society of other children, which is so necessary. I cannot tell you how much it costs me to put this distance between my mother and myself! The thought of even a temporary separation gives me great trouble, but I must submit.

These sad anticipations were not realized. The child recovered from his illness completely, and his parents had to make no change in their plans. They intended not to return to England for some length of time, and to pass the interval of their absence with Lord and Lady Granville. Nice became their head-quarters. A numerous and brilliant company was assembled there that year. We find Georgiana naming the most often the Grand Duchess Stephanie of Baden and her daughter, Princess Mary (who, the year after this, married the Duke of Hamilton), the Duchesse de Talleyrand, the Marquis de Castellane and his young wife—above all, her uncle, the Duke of Devonshire, who was enough to give life to the circle in which he lived. We look in vain in her correspondence for a single word about the work on which she was engaged. Still less does she speak of the questions which then stirred her mind.

During the whole of this year, perhaps, her inner thoughts were, more than ever before, at variance with the exterior life she was leading. It cost her no effort to keep it to herself. Perhaps she was hardly conscious how much she did this. She was never quick to speak of herself, and besides, what she would have had to say was so vague that it cost her less to be silent.

In all appearance then, she gave herself at this time to her duties and the pleasures of society. Amongst these must be mentioned several amateur performances in which she took part. The actors in these were the Duchesse de Talleyrand and her daughter, the young Marquise and Marquis de Castellane, and even the child of the latter, a girl of barely three, who appeared one day in the costume of an old Marquise of the time of Louis XV., carried on a chair.

> I imagined [says Lady Georgiana] that the poor child would be much frightened, but she was not the least. She played her part with the greatest *aplomb*, and appeared much delighted with the applause lavished on her.

She speaks afterwards of the remarkable talent of the Duchesse de Talleyrand and also of that of her daughter.

> Every time that Madame de Castellane acted in a simple part, her delicacy and taste were perfect, but in the tragic parts of Marie de Rohan in *Le Duel sous Richelieu*, or of Margaret de Valois in *Les jours gras sous Charles IX.*, she did not seem to me to excel. Tragedy is not her *forte*.

When we think of a time ten years later than this, and of the lot which God had in store for the persons here spoken of, of the high perfection to which these two lives were to be raised, and of the profound sorrow which was to encompass both, it is difficult to picture them to ourselves as these recollections represent them. As to these pursuits of pleasure, the greatest certainly in Lady Georgiana's eyes, the only one indeed which she really felt as such, was that of the Drama. She was still young when she gave this up, with all others like it, but dramatic art had always an interest for her. She dreamt of its regeneration, the wholesome influence it might have, its interpretation of the greatest works of genius, the cultivation it brought to the mind, the strength it could impart to the character. To the end of her life she liked people to talk to her of this Utopia, which required but one impossible condition for its realization—that all the world should be such as she was herself.

As soon as the spring was far enough advanced for the warm weather to make itself felt, Lord and Lady Granville, with their daughter and son-in-law, left Nice. Lady Georgiana does not seem to have felt, this time, the least regret at leaving Italy. The southern nature had as yet little attraction for her. She was to see it with other eyes by-and-bye.

She writes to her sister, from Nice, March 21, 1843.

To Lady Rivers.

. . . The other day, when I saw the hawthorn in bloom, I felt myself carried bodily to Rushmore—it must be looking so charming now. The Italian landscapes do not entirely please me. I am never content till something in them reminds me of the North. The fruit-trees covered with fruit and white blossoms please me more than woods of orange-trees with their golden fruit.

From Nice they went to Wildbad, where Lady Georgiana met Mdlle. Eward, from which place Lady Georgiana seems to have paid Mdlle. Eward a visit, at which they met for the first time since they parted in England. It was a great pleasure to both. But notwithstanding the active correspondence which they kept up and the intimate confidence between them, we may doubt whether a single word was exchanged as to the work which was in the course of the next year to make Lady Georgiana famous, and for which her old governess was to claim some credit. Still less was there any talk of the religious doubts which were floating in her mind. Never was she so reserved as during this phase of her life, when her doubts had taken no decisive form. The time for the struggle was at hand, but had not yet come. The time just before it, looks like a time of slumber and forgetfulness. It was a kind of calm in the moral order, which is like that which goes before a storm in the physical world.

We must insert the account she gives to her sister of her old governess, Mdlle. Eward.

I must tell you now of my visit to Neuchatel. I arrived there at twelve o'clock on Wednesday before last, and immediately proceeded to Mdlle. Eward's lodgings, which surpassed my expectations of their extreme comfort and convenience. They are admirably distributed and perfectly well furnished. She gave us a *soi-disant* luncheon, in fact an excellent dinner, which did the highest credit to the culinary talents of Mdlle. Louise, her maid, whom I told her I was sure she had selected on account of her extraordinary shortness, which has the effect of making her mistress look a very tall woman by her side. We stayed the whole next day, too, with her, and she was as happy as possible. I was much interested by looking over all the little ornaments, the drawings and all relics of former times, and felt quite overpowered by the sight of scraps of drawings and writings we sent her during the first years we were out in the world, and which brought me back to those times with a vividness which was almost painful. The picture of you on a cup was thought to be extremely

like Baba, more so than like any of your children, which was
odd. It has been very satisfactory to see Mdlle. Eward so
happy and comfortable.

From Wildbad the travellers went to Herrnsheim, a fine dwelling on the Rhine, the property,
formerly of the Duke of Dalberg, and then of his
daughter, Lady Acton. While staying there Lady
Georgiana continued her work. Solitude was not
necessary to her. She was absorbed in it. She
wrote sometimes on the corner of a table in a room
full of people, sometimes in the garden, or on the
lawn, sometimes even in the carriage. Nothing
that went on around her distracted her. One is
astonished at this facility when we remember that
much that she was writing represented profound
thought, and that the pages which she wrote off
with so much apparent indifference were often
terrible. But one of her gifts, and a great one, was
to be able to absorb her mind almost in whatever
she chose. It was a gift which added great power
to her spiritual as well as to her intellectual life.
None of her letters mention either her work, or her
religious questionings. They read as if she had
nothing to do at Herrnsheim but to walk or drive
about, or frequently to boat on the Rhine—a
pleasure which Lord Leveson was fond of, though
it was there somewhat dangerous. In the evening
there was sometimes dancing, when there were
enough young people at the château or in the
neighbourhood, or there was music. *Ellen Middleton*
lost nothing on these occasions, although Lady
Georgiana fell into many reveries listening to the

singing of her sister-in-law, whose style was as
perfect as her voice was melodious.   She was the
niece of the Marquis de Brignole, and she inherited from her mother that pure and clear Italian
accent which it is nearly impossible to acquire, if it
be not natural.   Like all her mother's family, she
spoke Italian with rare perfection, and English also
very well, though French was the language of her
childhood and remained always the most familiar
to her of all.

We may here insert some verses addressed to
her by Lady Georgiana.   Lady Leveson apparently
had said that she did not love poetry.

TO MARIE.

You say you love not poetry :
    Can that be really true,
When poets find for verse and song
    No sweeter theme than you ?

And though you say you love it not,
    We hear it in your voice
When with its thrilling, bird-like note
    It bids our hearts rejoice.

You say you love it not, and yet
    Wherever you have been,
Your magic art in bower and hall
    Evoked a fairy scene.

You love it not, and yet your smile
    Its witchery betrays ;
And all you say and do, a charm
    Akin to it displays.

Your words float on the ear like notes
    Which in the mem'ry dwell ;
You laugh and sing, and speak and move
    As if you own'd its spell.

Well, hate it still, and all your scorn,
I ween, it will forgive—
If in your every word and look
You still will let it live.

After a short stay at Munich, our travellers
returned to Italy, arriving in November, 1842, at
Rome, with Lord and Lady Granville. They all
lived together in an apartment which belonged to
Lord Shrewsbury in the Corso. Before the end
of this, her first stay in Rome, an event was to take
place which had a decisive importance on her future,
though she was far from foreseeing it, and did not
know it till she had left. Meanwhile, her first
impressions were not what might have been
expected, after all she had experienced in her first
sojourn in Italy. She was to come to love Rome
very much and to understand it thoroughly. But
this time it was almost a sealed book to her.

In fact there is not one Rome—there are three.
There is the Rome of history, the Rome of art, and
the Rome of the Church. This third Rome on
which she was to look as on a mother, was as yet
a stranger to her. It is true that neither her mind
nor her soul could be altogether insensible to the
mysterious charm which all have felt, although not
all have been able to divine the cause.

She writes thus to her sister:

To Lady Rivers.

There is an indefinable charm in Rome—a charm that
masters one more and more. However short one's stay, one
could never forget the front of St. John Lateran, . . . the grass
covered with daisies up to the very steps of the church, and

beyond the line of aqueducts, recalling former times, the beautiful mountains in the horizon. One lives here in a state of feverish interest. There is so much to see, the climate is so soft and tranquillizing to the nerves, that one can enjoy everything without being more agitated than is pleasant.

After seeing St. Peter's for the first time, she writes:

> How grand it is—grand without conception! but I would not exchange the Abbey of St. Peter at Westminster, or the Cathedral of York, for it.

This opinion is no doubt allowable. A great number of Catholics would say the same. The two styles are two sublime languages, which the Church has spoken in different places and at different times. It is quite lawful to compare them. But it may be doubted whether Lady Georgiana would have thought of doing this later on. Perhaps, when she had felt for herself the Catholic sentiment, and measured it, not from without as a critic, but from within as a child of faith, having a share in that mighty life, she would then have seen how this was so admirably expressed in St. Peter's. St. Peter's is the song of triumph of the Catholic Church, it symbolizes her universality and her immensity. To wish for it less of space and light, would be like intoning the *Miserere* instead of the *Te Deum* in a service of thanksgiving. Somewhat later on, after having told her sister of the Carnival and its *fêtes*, she speaks of the Exposition of the Blessed Sacrament during the follies of the Corso—which, it may be said, at that time had a character of childish gaiety which was afterwards destroyed by the tone of disorder and moral danger which was imported into those public pleasures. The Church tolerates such scenes but she desires a reparation for them, not as days of sin, but as days of forgetfulness of God. For this end she prescribes solemn prayers, in which serious and fervent souls come to take part, while others spend the time in amusement and dissipation. There are two camps and two crowds. The one of them prays for the other. Lady Georgiana speaks as if they were but one, but she readily followed the persons who took her from the Corso to the Gesù.

Madame de Castellane, who has already been mentioned, was present at the same function, kneeling beside her, and was struck by her profound reverence in presence of the Blessed Sacrament. As she went out she said "she was surprised she was not a Catholic, and thought she soon would be one."

To Lady Rivers.

Rome, *March* 3, 1843.

. . . Mamma probably told you in her last letter how mad we all were during the Carnival. It is quite absurd how animated one gets in all the nonsense that is going on. One day that all the husbands (mine, Marie's, Lady Chesterfield's, Lady Powerscourt's, &c.), and other men, were going in a car on the Corso, masked, and dressed up as Normas, we all, and the Cadogans (George Stewart and Flavio Chigi to protect us) dressed up in dominos and masks, went to attack them. We could not meet their car, but pelted them violently at a window without their knowing us again. The *Mardi Gras* seemed to me more like a dream than anything I ever met with. From two to five there is the Corso, the fighting with the *confetti*, the military music in the streets, &c., at five the horse-races. Then one rushes to the Church of the Gesù—one of the most beautiful in Rome. The altar is magnificently illuminated, the body of the church only lit by lamps here and there, a crowd of people, all on their knees, having just come from the Corso, and, with that versatility so peculiar among the Italians, becoming absorbed in the deepest devotion. The most beautiful music, the deepest silence in the church, the Elevation of the Host, every head bowed down in adoration. Then in the streets again, where everything is in an uproar, the Moccoletti have begun, the Corso is one blaze of light, everybody in the windows, everybody in the carriages, carries a lighted candle—you hardly have turned into the street before yours are put out, snatched away, people scramble before and beside your carriage, and scream in your ears "*senza moccolo, senza moccolo.*" You get fresh moccolos, you defend them fiercely, you scream "*senza moccolo*" yourself till you are hoarse with excitement. The whole scene, the noise, the brilliancy, the confusion, is unimaginable when one has not seen it, and yet no rudeness, no violence, and at a given signal, all the lights are put out and everything subsides. We hurried home, dressed, supped at the Duchesse de Dalberg's, and came home, as you may fancy, nearly dead.

I went to see Mrs. M—— yesterday. She is pretty and seems clever. It is a hard trial for her, poor little thing, to be shut up in this manner for so long, and without result, but I believe she is going on well. Thank you a thousand times for the details about schools. My darling boy is very well. He was charmed with the Carnival, and altogether is very happy here. I hope we shall be able to place him quite to our satisfaction.

On Monday we all drove at an early hour to the hounds meet, at Cecilia Metella's tomb! It sounds very unsuitable, but it was a pretty sight, and the red coats scampering through the ruins and across the Campagna, looked very pretty, though certainly not in character. The weather cold, bracing—but we comfort ourselves with hearing of deep snow everywhere else, but I fear we shall enjoy but little spring here. Good-bye, dearest Sukey. Give my love to your husband and to your dear children.

Ever your most affectionate

G. F.

P.S.—You would not have known me again in a *vieille cour* dress, powdered, with my eyebrows blacked, rouge, &c., at a ball at the Russian Embassy. Nobody did ; which made it as amusing as being in a mask. Will you send my letter to Freddy. I have behaved very ill to him, and must tell him here that Madame de Castellane *lui envoye mille tendres amitiés*. . . I often wish he was here. I know he would enjoy it so much.

The reader may have remarked how much it seems that, during this stay at Rome, living with her parents in the midst of that cosmopolitan society which in those days assembled in Rome every winter, and surrounded with the noise and bustle of the world, Lady Georgiana shows no sign of having been more accessible than before to Catholic impressions, although these impressions must have presented themselves to her on every side. It is true that she was continuing her literary work, and was as silent about it as about religion. It is difficult to say whether her silence on religious subjects was a part of her habitual reserve on all matters that had a firm hold on her heart, or whether her thoughts were really less absorbed by religion. During this winter she shows a gaiety and interest in amusements which were not very natural to her. Festivities succeeded festivities, and she took part, and it seems pleasure, in them all.

It may be that, at this time, there was an effort to withdraw herself from thoughts which pressed on her with some importunity.. She may, perhaps, have seen then, for the first time, the logical issue of her fluctuations, and this she could not think of reaching without sacrifices and sufferings before which her courage quailed. We find among some verses which she wrote many years after, when the struggle was over, and her soul was reposing in the peace of certainty, the following :

TO MY MOTHER THE CHURCH.

Oh, that thy creed were sound !
For thou dost soothe the heart,
Thou Church of Rome, &c.

(Lyra Apostolica.)

O Mother Church! my spirit's home! long sought and found at
    last.
Safe in the shelter of thy arms, I muse upon the past ;
E'en in my childhood's days there rose a shadow of thy form,
And through the thoughtlessness of youth it show'd amidst the
    storm ;
Like angel visits came those gleams my startled soul before,
Wave upon wave advancing left a token on the shore.
Not e'en an adversary's art thy lineaments could hide,
And though disfigured by a foe, thy beauty I descried,
For thy deep love my spirit yearned, but trembled at thy creed,
And longing still to pluck the flower, refused to sow the seed.
"Oh, that thy creed were sound," I cried, until I felt its power,
And almost pray'd to find it false in the decisive hour.
Great was the struggle, fierce the strife, but wonderful the gain,
For not one trial or one pang was sent or felt in vain,
And every link of all that chain that led my soul to thee
Remains a monument of all thy mercy wrought for me.

It was this last feeling, as it seems, that influenced Lady Georgiana at the point of our history which we have now reached. In truth, the " decisive moment " for her was at hand. The question of creed was brought home to her in a manner probably most unexpected. While she was dividing her time between her husband, her child, and her

mother, Mr. Fullerton was spending the mornings
of his days in a very different manner. At Rome,
as every one knows, it is very easy for people to
lose sight of one another for a moment, and then to
meet again, employing the time some in one way,
others in another, but all agreeably and to the taste
of each. What the antiquities are to one, the
churches are to another, or the convents, the galleries,
or the studios, even the simple walks *fuori le mure.*
Nowhere in the world can people be more independent, nowhere do they meet again more easily.
Lady Georgiana did not dare do at Rome as she
had done in Paris, go into the churches at the time
of services and sermons. Her mother, and her
father also, who was now set free from his official
duties, accompanied her in her daily walks, and
they would have been astonished. If she was sometimes tempted to enter a church or a convent for
any reason but curiosity, she would not have dared
to confess it, much less to take any step in consequence.

For her husband it was different. He was quite
free, and he spent his time in studies and conversations which were the natural result of much reading
and long preliminary reflections. It is singular, but
yet it is easily explained. The same thoughts and
the same doubts were in the mind of both husband
and wife, without their knowledge, and from the
same motive they said nothing to one another about
them. In proportion as the growth of their convictions made the end of their researches more plain,
they could foresee the struggle that awaited them—

J

many sufferings, many conflicts, many sorrowful breaches. Each of the two shuddered at the thought of what the other might have to bear.

There was nothing exaggerated in these anticipations. There are some moments, and that which was now at hand was one of them, when the sword penetrates, even unto "the dividing asunder of the soul, the heart, and the spirit," and all that to which they are most closely united, when duty goes to the length of placing us under the necessity of afflicting those whom it also bids us love, cherish, and preserve, at the cost of all pain to ourselves,—of all pain that we can possibly spare to them. Such a moment comes, and then truth and duty require the sacrifice. Human weakness may well resist and strive to put the day off as long as possible. In the present case, husband and wife sought much less to spare themselves than to spare one another.

Mr. Fullerton kept silence, but he did not put off any longer the act which his conscience required of him. He had found at Rome an old friend, Vicomte Theodore de Bussiere, formerly Attaché to Prince Talleyrand when Ambassador at London. He had since that time become a fervent Catholic. He was also a man of large information, quite capable of directing the inquiries of his friend. His piety and faith had lately been vividly kindled by the conversion of Alphonse Ratisbonne. It had been accompanied by extraordinary and marvellous circumstances. He had himself been personally engaged in it. Rome was at this time full of the incident, which is still commemorated there by an annual service of thanksgiving.[1]

Spring was coming on, and April was the date fixed for the departure from Rome. Mr. Fullerton would not quit Rome without having taken the decided step, and united himself for ever to the Catholic Church. He was received, April 23rd, St. George's day, by the Père Villefort, and then rejoined, at Florence, his wife and her parents, who had preceded him by some days. He had not told her beforehand the decision to which he had come, what it was that modified his former belief and brought him gradually to the profound convictions which he had just obeyed. It is impossible to describe the effect on Lady Georgiana. It was an inexpressible mixture of joy and agony. On the most important of all subjects there was an echo to her own thoughts in the soul of her husband. He was able to give her authoritative answers to a thousand questions which had for a long time troubled her. All this was, no doubt, a great comfort and an unforeseen happiness. But, at the same time, it was a brusque and sudden shock. She had found pleasure in regions of vague unreality and surmise, and now they were at an end. A veil had been kept before her eyes, and now it was torn away. She must now look with resolution at the path before her, the end to which all the aspirations of her life, confused or explicit, were to lead. She was forced to see what it was that had been the reason why she had avoided the recognition of all

---

[1] See the *Récit d'un Sœur*, vol. ii. p. 307.

this, up till now. She saw, too, very clearly the sacrifices and sufferings which she was bound to inflict and to undergo. It was the most courageous act of her life, that she did not then of her own will close her eyes to the light. She had the courage not to do so. She was yet to be long on the way, but she no longer delayed to look forward to the end, and to move towards it firmly and faithfully.

This was her state of mind at this time. After another stay in Germany, they returned to England towards the end of 1843. Her book was now finished, and she had to submit it to the criticism of competent friends, before it appeared in public.

CHAPTER VII.

LADY GEORGIANA had chosen as her literary judges two men whose names are enough to justify her choice, Lord Brougham and Mr. Charles Greville. The latter was less celebrated than the former, but the publication of·his *Memoirs* has made him well known abroad as well as at home. They were very different one from the other. But both were friends of Lord Granville, both competent and sincere, and both with a warm interest in the publication. Mr. Charles Greville, grandson to the Duke of Portland, was Lady Granville's cousin, and an habitual member of their family circle. He had known Lady Georgiana from her youth, and remained closely attached to her to the end of his life.

The critics would probably feel some anxiety when the manuscript reached their hands. The literary *débuts* of ladies, especially of high rank, do not always inspire much confidence *a priori*, even in those who wish best to them. However, as soon as they began to read *Ellen Middleton*, they discerned the remarkable merit of the work, and they showed their esteem for the author by not sparing her either counsels or praise. The corres-

pondence which thus ensued has much more than
a purely literary interest, and requires some preliminary explanations.

The year 1844, in which *Ellen Middleton* appeared,
marks the end of the first stage of the great Oxford
movement. The famous Number 90 of the *Tracts
for the Times*, which was published between four and
five years before this date, had caused a crisis which
still lasted. Mr. Newman embraced Catholicism in
the course of the year following, and his conversion
was the *dénoûment* of the movement. Up to that
time its stages can be traced in the successive *Tracts*
which had preceded Number 90, and in the numerous publications of all sorts and from all kinds of
authors which succeeded it. The movement was to
lead to its legitimate conclusion, not only the great
man whose name was unanimously recognized as
that of the leader of religious thought of the time,
but a multitude of other souls, thoughtful, sincere,
and generous.

The object of the *Tract* had been to justify, in
the face of many passages in the Articles which
seemed to condemn them, the revival of many
doctrines and practices which the Anglican Church
had either forgotten or abandoned, but which had
not been formally renounced by her at the time of
the Reformation of the sixteenth century. Perhaps
even the Reformers had meant to leave some of
them untouched—though it is unreasonable to consider the Anglican formularies as the issue of any
one definite plan. The existence in the *Prayer-Book*
of these Catholic relics seemed incompatible with

some of the Thirty-nine Articles to which the Anglicans were bound to subscribe. It was this anomaly which the Oxford writers pointed out and availed themselves of, and it is certain that the great mass of Anglicans did not see in the fact any fatal inconsistency. In the sixteenth or seventeenth centuries the violence of feeling hindered reflection. People were Catholic or they were not. That was the whole question. In the eighteenth century religious questions did not occupy the thoughts of men, and the Anglican clergy were as relaxed as the rest of the world. But as soon as the retrospect was forced on them, pointing to so much that was Catholic, and, at the same time, permitted to them, the result was the awakening of a new spirit of zeal, devotion, piety, the dawn of a new day. Many think that the exiled clergy of France, who had been received in England with hospitality that can never be forgotten, contributed much to the birth of this new movement.

However this may have been, one of its first effects was to direct attention retrospectively to the origin of the Anglican Church, and to the number of observances there to be found which had been completely abandoned, notwithstanding their existence. They were not formally and authoritatively abrogated, except so far as such abrogation could be implied by universal custom, which, in a truly living system, has always the force of law. It was, indeed, to spectators outside, an additional argument against the supposition of any Catholic life in Anglicanism, that for so many generations it had been willingly and universally less Catholic than it was bound to be. The spirit of the body was shown in the fact that the Catholic elements had died out as heterogeneous. This was naturally not the view taken by the revivers themselves. For them it was important to revive these Catholic elements, if only because they presented something to offer to those whose piety was stirred and attracted to the Catholic Church. Here was some kind of satisfaction to their feelings, which would cost no difficulties and no struggles, no sacrifice of the advantages and benefits which their own position secured to them. And those who have studied this page of the history of our times know that this means has often been used with success. Men are always liable to the influence of a balance of motives. It is so still. What is equally known to such students, is that those who were the choicer spirits of the movement soon saw how to draw their own consequences from the principles set forth by their leaders. In many cases they accompanied them in seeking, in the Catholic Church, the conclusions of studies and labour begun in the University of Oxford.

Lady Georgiana had followed this movement with an attentive eye before she returned to England. She had sometimes envied those who were carried away from the shore to which she herself still clung. All her thoughts and all the tendencies of her mind felt the influence of the general current. The air was full of these opinions. It cannot, therefore, surprise us that we should trace them in many passages of her book, written while all around her were moved by them as well as herself, and especially after the conversion of her own husband. In the book they are the newly-found treasures of a mind—to imitate Tertullian's expression—"naturally Catholic," taking its own position for granted, without questioning the solidity of its foundation. To others, they did not seem quite so much in their native place in the Anglican system as they then seemed to her. We see, in the effect which these passages produced on her two critics, how very general was the interest in these matters. This effect was different on each, but equally sensible. We may read their judgments, and form our own conclusions respecting them. But we may fairly conjecture that, twenty years earlier, neither the one nor the other of her two friends would have cared anything about the matter. It may be added with equal truth that, twenty years earlier, no Anglican author would have thought of writing these passages.

In order to understand this, we must remember that the heroine of Lady Georgiana's book is made the victim of an undying remorse caused by the violent death of a child of which she had, unknown to its parents, been the involuntary agent. She is herself an orphan, the child's parents are her uncle and aunt, who are to her as father and mother, and she succeeds naturally as the one great object of their love. It is this trouble of conscience which is the misery of her life, rendered intolerable by the impossibility of confessing her secret, and the absence of any tribunal to which she might avow her fault and receive a sentence of mercy, and, at

the same time, of equity. She ultimately finds
peace of conscience in confession to an Anglican
clergyman. It is obvious that this situation would
of itself open the door to many ideas strange to the
Protestant world. At the same time, she is conscious from the first that the secret is known to one
or two persons, and as the story unfolds, the possession of this secret is turned to his own selfish
purposes by one of the characters in the most cruel
manner. The development of the story of such
miseries and trials involves dramatic effects of the
greatest possible interest. We have seen how, as
a child, Lady Georgiana set a very high value on
even "general" confession and on Anglican absolution. This was now one of the "burning questions" of the day, a part of the great controversy
which had spread far beyond the limits of the
University. It was talked about everywhere, and,
as was sure to be the case when such subjects are
so treated, much that was foolish was said in the
course of the dispute. The Catholics looked on,
but took hardly any part.

Neither Lord Brougham nor Mr. Charles Greville
can be classed among religious men. But they were
both essentially intelligent, and they could not but
see the importance of the movement. Each watched
it with equal interest, but different feelings. The
difference soon showed itself. The passage which
brought it out was naturally the passage alluded to,
in which the heroine, after many years of anguish,
which brought her to the edge of the grave, is
exhorted by the Anglican minister to confess to him

her sins, and receive the absolution which he had
the power to give. The passage startled Lord
Brougham beyond measure. He wrote at once to
the author to protest. He declared that these
words and the whole scene which contained them
seemed to him "rank Popery." Lady Georgiana
was in no hurry to enter into a discussion with so
ferocious a critic. She sent the letter which she
had received to Mr. Charles Greville, and speedily
received from him the following answer, which will
inform the reader as to the objection which it
refutes.

Letter from Mr. Charles Greville.

London, *Monday.*

I have been out of town since I saw you, and there was no
E. M. (*Ellen Middleton*) at Stoke, so I have not had time yet
to compare Brougham's criticisms with the text—indeed, I can't
read half of them till I do ; but meanwhile, I write a few lines
to say I think you may well do battle with him on what he says
about *absolution.*

"What authority has a priest to absolve from sin ?" (he
says), "absolutely none. It is rank Popery to say so. The
liturgy does not venture on it, except in the Visitation of the
Sick." You are much more competent than I am to argue this
question, and it is quite superfluous to suggest anything to you ;
but this criticism of his seems to me a mere tissue of errors and
impertinence. He may reject the doctrine of the Church of
England, and adopt any other creed he pleases, but most
assuredly the doctrine of absolution is the doctrine of our
Church, and, according to it, *a priest has authority to absolve
from sin.* If it is rank *anything,* it is rank *Church of Englandism*
to say so. Nor is it true that it is *only* to be found in the
Visitation Service. Not but what it would be quite sufficient
to establish it as the doctrine of the Church, if it were found in
any one of her authorized services, uncontradicted either by
her Articles or anything in any other part of the Rubrics. But

there can be no question on the subject, because *the Form of ordering Priests* contains, in terms the most clear and unmistakeable, this authority and power conferred upon priests.

"Receive the Holy Ghost for the office and work of a priest in the Church of God now committed unto thee by the imposition of our hands. *Whose sins thou dost forgive, they are forgiven, and whose sins thou dost retain, they are retained,*" &c. There is, in fact, no difference between the Church of England and the Church of Rome on this head, except that the latter requires confession previous to absolution, and the former does not.

"But what authority has our liturgy to teach paganism? and how can any rational being suppose," &c.

You may leave him to settle that with the liturgy. It is enough for you that whatever the liturgy does teach, must be taken to be the doctrine of the Church of England. I don't well know what he means by paganism. As to his sneers at the doctrine of priestly Absolution, and that of the Real Presence, the latter has always appeared to me to be a mere question of fact—whether the Catholic or the Protestant interpretation of certain passages in Scripture be the true one. Our Saviour might have made this quite clear if He had thought fit—why He did not, it is not for us to say. Perhaps it was left doubtful as a trial of faith. They who believe this mystery believe upon a Divine authority in contradiction and opposition to the evidence of their senses. That is a test of faith; if the accidents were changed sensibly, it would be no trial of faith at all. Supposing Jesus Christ had delivered this doctrine in terms so clear that it could never be doubted or cavilled at, that He had set it forth in the express terms in which the Church (Roman) does, why, then, all the Christian world would have received it and believed it as a matter of course, exactly as they believe all the past miracles, and all mysteries (Trinity, Immaculate Conception,[1] Incarnation, &c.) which both Churches acknowledge.

Then as to Absolution—who supposes that any "mere man has the power of saving other men's souls"? Nobody can

---

[1] Mr. Greville probably means to speak of the Virginal Conception of our Lord.

pardon or save souls, but the Almighty. But the priest is consecrated to His service, and receives with certain ceremonies a Divine commission, and God "hath given *him* power and commandment *to declare and pronounce to his people being penitent* the absolution and remission of their sins." This appears to me to be the office of the priest, his duty and his power. And this is the doctrine of the Church of England, of which I suppose Brougham would say that he was a member.

Having gone to the end of my sheet, I will spare you any more of my theology. Pray write to me.

Ever your affectionate

C. G.

This is a remarkable letter in every respect. It has been here cited entire without the omission of a word, that it may bear all the weight which the writer's pen can give it. It is almost superfluous to refute the one or two mistakes which are mingled with the truths which are so precisely and clearly stated. As to the opinion that the power of Absolution conferred on the priest can be exercised by him without previous knowledge of the sins to be remitted or retained, the new school of Anglicans themselves were soon to pass beyond it. Individual confession was soon introduced among them, and is practised by some of them as with Catholics. No doubt there are many defects in this system to Catholic eyes, to say nothing of the want of jurisdiction and the at least very doubtful character of the Anglican "priesthood." But it is a witness on the part of our adversaries to the doctrine itself, as well as to the ancient custom of the Universal Church.

Lady Georgiana was guided by a right instinct
in making her heroine confess her faults in detail
to an Anglican clergyman. The point had been,
in fact, left open at the time of the Reformation—
probably because every one was then as much
accustomed to that kind of confession, in practice,
as Anglicans are now accustomed to rest satisfied
with a general self-accusation. The Catholic offices
contain more than one instance of "general" confession and absolution, from which the Anglican
forms were taken. What had completely died out
in Anglicanism was the use and administration of
the Sacrament of Penance, as it had been universally practised before the Reformation. It had
died out, even without being forbidden.

We have not, unhappily, the materials which
would tell us how Lady Georgiana answered the
letter we have just inserted. She answered it, indeed, but the letter has been lost. We may judge
of the tone in which it was written, from a later
letter of Mr. Greville's, and we give this in another
page as well as the former letter. He does not
there enter into this question of sacramental absolution, but we may gather from what Mr. Greville
says that she made a kind of explanation of her
tenets to him, which was very likely not so explicit
and definite as would have been the case if she had
been already a Catholic. Persons in her position
are obliged to evade certain statements about the
Real Presence, in consequence of the very distinct
pronouncement of the Prayer-Book that the Body
of our Lord "is *not* here." Of this, however, by-

and-bye. The correspondence before the publication
of *Ellen Middleton* must first be concluded,—at least
those fragments of it which remain to us.

Mr. C. Greville to Lady G. F.

London, *March* 19, 1844.

I have just seen Harness, who has read four books, and has
only one and a half to read. He says he never read anything
more interesting in his life. Some of the writing (when you
are very much in earnest) really magnificent, as fine as possible,—but he still thinks a good deal of correction would
improve it, and there are faults of language and of style which
might be remedied, and which may certainly be in another and
final correction of the proof sheets. He has so nearly finished
that he is gone to Moxon, and I shall hear to-morrow what he
says. Harness thinks he will hold out for publishing on the
terms of a division of profits, and I am now so satisfied of the
great success of the book, that, as Moxon is really an honest
man, I should prefer that, and taking all chances, to accepting
a small sum.

I am the more confirmed about the success, from what I am
going to tell you. During the interval of Harness' clerical
avocations, I gave it to Adelaide Sartoris [2] to read. She is my
most intimate friend, and I have the greatest reliance on her
judgment and her taste, because she is both uncommonly clever
and also an immense reader of works of this description. I
was, in fact, very anxious to feel the public pulse through her,
besides having the benefit of her criticisms. This morning I
received the enclosed note from her, which I must send you.
I have since been with her, and talked it over. Her admiration
of your work is very great. She says for years she had read
nothing so clever, and the interest is not only very great, but
perfectly sustained to the end. She does not think the Introduction the least diminishes the interest of what follows, in
which I quite agree. I went to her, and went through with her
all the passages she had to object to or remark upon—some
verbal alterations, evidently necessary (how I could miss the

[2] Formerly Miss Adelaide Kemble.

places I know not, except that, as I told you, one always does overlook so much), I made at once, but there were others, involving the excision of passages of considerable length, which I cannot take upon myself to make, and on which you must decide.

I have taken notes of those, and I must say, if you will consent to the alterations, I think they will greatly improve the book, though I know not whether execution would ever be done on certain passages which you may be rather fond of. What she objected to was the language being occasionally inflated and the thoughts not natural, and that some very fine passages, beginning admirably, were spoilt by your not stopping in time, and the effect of their early strength weakened by long drawn out conclusions comparatively impotent. And I must tell you that she cried out lustily against, was perfectly horrified with, that passage to which I so strenuously objected—to which I feel still the greatest objections, and which are of course confirmed by the effect I see it produces. Harness is not yet come to it, but I have no doubt when he does he will concur. I must however tell you that A. objects to the whole of the passage in which this is contained, what precedes and what follows it; no doubt the omission she suggests would be an immense improvement.

It is, however, impossible to explain all this by letter, and you must wait till we meet to determine on the several points.

Here is a volume, but I think your work so excellent, and I am so anxious for its success, that I am as nervously alive to its defects as a mamma bringing out her daughter for the first time at Almacks!

During the printing of the book Mr. Greville was constantly making remarks or giving counsel to Lady Georgiana as each proof was corrected.

The following note marks the time when the book was very near its appearance, which took place in May or June, 1844. Unfortunately, very few of the letters are dated.

From the same.

G. P., *Tuesday.*

I forgot to say, yesterday, that you will probably want some copies to give away, as there must be some friends or relations, whom you would not like to buy it. So you had better let me know about how many you would like to have, that I may stipulate for them. Will a dozen copies do?. I should hope that it would be more than enough, for the great majority must buy, of course. I also quite forgot to tell you (as I have all along told you everything, in the shape of adverse criticism) that the critics all *rather* dislike the incident of the mad dog and the sucking the wound, and would have preferred the event it was to bring about, having been brought about by almost any other means, and that anything would have done, any sudden emotion, any commotion, to produce the confession on Ellen's part, which was the real matter of importance. I have not thought it of sufficient importance to urge an alteration, though I rather incline to think it is a little too melodramatic, and I should have preferred something more simple—but I do not know that it will not take very well, with many people.

I send you the *Fatal Marriage* that you may correct the motto.[3]

Ever your affectionate

C. G.

P.S.—You need not now keep the book a secret. It must be known—for you will speedily *see in every newspaper*, and Moxon has told Rogers and Moore already,

In the Press.

ELLEN MIDDLETON,

A NOVEL.

By the RT. HONBLE. LADY GEORGIANA FULLERTON.

Moxon, Dover Street.

We hardly think it would interest the reader to enter fully into all the minute particulars of the criticisms and remarks made to Lady Georgiana by Mr. Greville. But one more fragment exists of a

[3] The motto to one of the last chapters.

K

letter of his, on Macaulay, which we will insert. Lady Georgiana seems to have had some objection to him :

> Notwithstanding your refusal of Macaulay as a guide, you will find him, with some exceptions, a very safe and sound one —but, unhappily, the religious persuasion to which you are attached, is, of all shades of opinion, that which is the least congenial to Macaulay's mind. But what I like in his writings is the high feeling of honour and freedom, and truth, which universally pervades them. He detests oppression, and meanness; and deceit, in all the shapes they assume, and he inculcates the noblest principles of rational liberty, of Christian toleration, of political integrity, disinterestedness, and courage.
>
> Ever yours affectionately,
C. G.

It may cause some surprise to see that only one of her two critics has been quoted by us. Lady Georgiana had so much more confidence in Mr. Greville than in Lord Brougham, that she sent all his letters to Mr. Greville to reply to them for her. Most of Lord Brougham's letters have disappeared, but the following notes in his handwriting are too characteristic not to be inserted. They evidently accompanied some of the voluminous notes sent to Mr. Charles Greville, if indeed they were not copied after the publication of the volume.

Lord Brougham to Lady G. F.

Brougham, Sunday.

MY DEAR LADY G.—I arrived here, by Penrith, to-day, and have copied out my notes on *E. M.*

Now, dear Lady G., I almost fear you will think me impertinent to send them—as they are blunt and plain-spoken, being written for your good. But no—I have too high an opinion of your sense, and, therefore, *will* trust them to you.

They are *specks* in the sun, hardly anything like spots, and very few in the Second and fewer still in the Third Vol. So they may be unnecessary for a future work, which I hope to live to enjoy.

Indeed they are about *miseries* of diction.

I have a word on your plot, however. Why should a man like Henry, who is so full of honour, or of dread of disgrace, as to be unable to bear not paying a debt of honour, steal three thousand five hundred pounds, sure to make him both disgraced and hanged ?

Again, why is Edward Middleton let off so easily for his beastly and stupid pride, whereby he murders E. M., without, perhaps, meaning it, but certainly without caring whether he does it or not? He is to me the most hateful of men—and I say so, being the victim and the martyr of pride myself, to a degree that would furnish you with a subject of a horrid romance, if you knew all; but I try to conquer it and sometimes succeed.

Be assured that whatever is *most touching is most simple.* I never produced any effect on an audience except by the most simple ideas and the most simple diction.

But you shall, in the very most strictest confidence, see a novel (M.S.) of a friend of mine, which I am correcting with the same severe pen I have applied to *E. M.,* and because I take an equal interest in it. You must promise me solemnly not to say I lent it you. If you did it never would see the U. K. S., because it would be at once connected with my name, and the author will conceal his. So write if you wish to see it. You will say as I did, on reading it, nothing can be simpler.

Yours,

H. B.

Lord Brougham to Lady G. F.

Brougham, *Sunday.*

MY DEAR LADY GEORGIANA,—I have now finished copying these notes, and enclose them to you. But I want once more to say how much you must think me impertinent and rude in my remarks. Especially must they appear so, because I have only noted what I attacked. Had it been to note down all I praised and admired and was struck with the power of, I should have written a *book* as long as *E. M.*

You will, at least, deem the minuteness of my criticism a proof of the sincere interest I take in the book and in its excellent author. But in the book, certainly, because many friends I love much have written books, and no bad ones either, and I never wrote one line upon them.

Once more—excuse my free strictures and remarks on what seem trifles.

I never have even attended to one of them except in these pages.

I expect you to let me know both that you take my frankness in good part, not being offended with my *dogmatical* and *judicial* tone. I have, for seventeen years, been in the way of correcting the works of our *Useful Knowledge Society*, and I never give any reasons. I strike out firmly, and add or substitute, and this gives me the habit of deciding *judicially* on style.

Hoping to hear also on the offer of a perusal of a friend's manuscript. Write about seeing it and reading it yourself.

> I am affectionately yours,
> H. BROUGHAM.

I must once more remind you that I only put down what I had to say *against*. I could have written a book in three volumes to say all your three deserve of praise.

> Truly yours,
> H. B.

From Lord Brougham to Lady G. F.

MY DEAR LADY G.—I will send this to Aldenham, where I shall also send the manuscript about which I have written to you. Though it is only ten chapters, it is voluminous but not tiresome. Please read attentively Chapter Nine. It will make you understand, according to my ideas, that pathetic subjects are the most simple, and therefore ought to be described most simply. If anything can awaken emotion, it is this.

I beg you not to be revolted at finding one of the heroines of this romance committing a horrible crime. I think that the original of this portrait is none other than Lady Macbeth.

Ellen Middleton, as has been said, was published in May or June, 1844. Its reception was at once enthusiastic. It was reviewed in almost numberless papers, and, what is still more significant, several of the Quarterly *Reviews*—more influential then than now—criticized it at considerable length in their issues for the next July. We shall give below at least one specimen of these criticisms. But it should first be mentioned that a second edition was soon called for, during the printing of which some interesting letters passed between Lady Georgiana and Mr. Charles Greville.

Mr. Charles Greville to Lady Georgiana Fullerton.

London, *August* 24, 1844.

I cannot regret what I wrote, because it has brought me such a beautiful letter from you in reply. I honour and defer to your feelings upon certain high religious matters, and I will never again (if I can help it) bring them into discussion with you. There are, however, questions of theology and religion, which I will never promise not to talk to you, or write to you about, because I don't imagine that you could object or scruple to interchange thoughts and opinions on such as are of a more general and less profoundly sacred character.

The partitions, however, which divide the one class of subjects from the other, are sometimes thin and narrow, and I hope whenever (if ever) I write to you anything at variance with this engagement, that you will refrain from answering. I hope you won't think me inconsistent if I make one remark upon something you say about the Romish doctrine of the Sacrament, because I think it indicates some confusion of ideas or inaccuracy of expression. The R. C. doctrine is not "a theory," and it is not "an explanation or definition," nor are you called on "to define the precise mode in which this happens." The question is much simpler than this—it is a question *of fact*—not defining the mode in which or by which this *fact* takes place, but declaring whether you believe that it takes place at all. You may believe firmly and undoubtingly that Lazarus was raised from the dead, without being obliged to explain or understand by what process the vital spark was re-conveyed into his body. When you say that you "believe that, in the Holy Eucharist, Christ is *especially* present," &c.— you rather seem to evade the question, as if you were not quite sure what you do mean, and to what extent your belief really goes. Now it can never be necessary, even for the most sensitive devotion, to think obscurely, and not to be quite certain of its own meaning. Do you see what I mean by this? Merely that the doctrine in question is so simple—such a mere matter of fact (however sublime and incomprehensible the mystery involved in it)—that it must of necessity command a positive assent, or positive dissent. I will merely say this much, and leave you to ponder over it. To the other points I will make no reply or remark. Your religious opinions and feelings are entitled to every respect, and from me they have it with perfect sincerity. They make you good, and they make you happy, and if I thought that some error or exaggeration crept into them, or that they were not always logically consistent, I should still be sorry to see any alteration or disturbance in the source of so much goodness and happiness. For God's sake never talk to me again *of the superior acuteness* of my understanding, or of the extent of my reading on these subjects. Without a particle of affectation, I must acknowledge to you my perfect sense of the extreme superficiality of my knowledge, and the truth (with shame I own it) of how very little I have read and still less studied. If I can make my own very plain thoughts intelligible, it is just the amount of what I can do, and I can't bear that you should think me so vain and so foolish as to be unconscious of the extreme humility of my own powers and pretentions to reason on these subjects or any others. More shame for me, for I might have been better qualified than I am, if I had not neglected the means at my disposal.

I meant to have written to you to-day about *simplicity*, but will another day. I will write to Mrs. Arkwright, and try to find out about *E. M.*, and what she means. Good-bye.

Mr. Charles Greville to Lady G. Fullerton.

London, *Monday.*

I write a few lines, as I engaged to do, about the *simplicity*, though I don't quite know what to say on the subject. I do not understand that Brougham complained of your style, as not being sufficiently simple.

There is no doubt that, what is most simple is generally most touching. Simplicity, as opposed to amplification or exaggeration, is good. There may be very simple thoughts conveyed in very elevated language—simplicity and sublimity are closely allied. The Bible furnishes many examples of this. Many authors write well, whose style can never be called a simple style. Burke's is not simple, nor Bolingbroke's, still less Gibbon's, nor, indeed, is Addison's. Swift may be called simple, and Defoe still more. Redundant epithet, and over-wrought descriptions, destroy all simplicity, and may spoil many a passage. What can be more simple, and what more touching, than the speech of Jeanie Deans to Queen Caroline, in Scott's novel? On the other hand, glowing descriptions may be equally affecting, and the most elevated language may be employed without the slightest exaggeration. It would be endless to quote passages. But one just occurs to me, in which the language is grand, and yet I think there is no in-flation, nothing overdone. It is the opening passage of Burke's famous description of the irruption of Hyder Ali into the Carnatic. After giving an account of the disputes between Hyder and the Company, he proceeds as follows :

"When at length Hyder Ali found that he had to do with men who would either sign no convention, or whom no treaties and no stipulations could bind, and who were the determined enemies of human intercourse itself, he decreed to make the country possessed by these incorrigible and predestinated criminals a memorable example to mankind. He resolved, in the gloomy recesses of a mind capacious of such things, to leave the whole Carnatic an everlasting monument of ven-geance, and to put perpetual desolation as a barrier between him and those against whom that faith which holds the moral elements of the world was no protection." [4]

[4] Burke's *Speech on the Nabob of Arcot's debts.*

Nothing can be grander, and yet, on examination, it will be found quite simple, and there is not an epithet too much, or a word that could be spared. There is no doubt a charm in simplicity, but if by the opposite of simplicity ornament is meant, there is no harm in that either.

The same to the same.

London, *Sept.* 17, 1844.

I have not to guess where you are, for you said you were going to Morpeth Court, Monday, for a week, and to Chatsworth on the 23rd. I must write a line to tell you that I have had the corrected books from Moxon, have gone over the corrections and returned them to him. I did not go over the whole, only the corrections, but I hope you have put all the *whos* and *whoms* right. I have made one or two slight verbal alterations, and have quite changed one sentence, p. 147, vol. ii. I cannot bear the word *whif* (with one *f* or with two) and I have altered the passage thus : "The air from the garden dispersed the delicious perfume which it had stolen from a bed of mignonette."

It is a little more poetical in expression, because I thought of these lines, which are sufficient authority for the expressions :

> Here gentle gales
> Fanning their odoriferous wings disperse
> Native perfumes, and whisper whence they stole
> Those balmy spoils.

The lines are in *Paradise Lost.* I am ashamed to say I never read Miss Baillie's plays, but I will do so, and that very soon.

I have been junketing about and am just come from the Grange—such a charming place. Send me your whereabouts, though by the time I could have an answer you will be at Chatsworth.

Ever yours affectionately,

C. G.

* A perusal of some of the criticisms already mentioned would give a more complete idea of the opinions formed on the work than the letters from friends, which may be inserted in the next chapter.

It was an advantage to Lady Georgiana that she had not been tempted to write anything for the public before she was fully ripe for the authorship. She had not rushed into print while quite a girl. Although her book contains no traces of the influence of any particular model which she had set before her in her work, it reveals a perfectly cultivated and educated mind, familiar with a large range of literature both English and foreign. The author revealed herself at once as one of the foremost writers of her time in mental power and elevation, and in the gift of affecting and influencing others. There is nothing in the story, except perhaps some merely mechanical points, to show the hand of a tyro, and, besides the strength which it displays, it manifests also the greatest delicacy and refinement of mind and heart. This, however, would hardly have been enough to secure for it the reception which welcomed it, not only from the general reading public, but from some of the most thoughtful minds of the time. We shall presently illustrate this by an example, the authority of which cannot be questioned. The work was not designedly a religious work. It was, however, one of the most religious works of the time, and it was this because she had written it. If it had been otherwise, however brilliant, it would not have been hers. She could write in no other language. Without the slightest controversial purpose, which she would certainly have shrunk from at that time, she touched a point which was then becoming a subject of deep thought to many, a chord which vibrated in the recesses of many a soul, and she touched it with a master hand.

The intense and passionate interest of the story, with the beauty of the style, the high and pure feeling, the real eloquence of many passages, and the knowledge of character and of the human heart which *Ellen Middleton* evinced, would have sufficed to raise any such work to a very high level in the public admiration.   Every one felt that the author did not call forth emotions which she had not first felt herself.   The fact that she was writing the book, as has been described, during a year of travel and sight-seeing, without revealing to any one the depth of the emotions which must have passed over her own mind, before they could reach those of others with that power of absorbing interest which those who read the novel for the first time will fully acknowledge, speaks volumes as to the real history of her mind during that apparently gay and even thoughtless period. Her hours of recurring dissipation must often have relieved her wonderfully—perhaps they were necessary for her.   She was not a writer who could not feel for and live in the characters she created and drew, nor could she draw the history of *Ellen Middleton* without a most intense sympathy. And yet, without at all assuming the didactic tone, we see that the author stands above her heroine, and holds the scales of justice with a firm hand for her and for the other actors in the terrible drama.   She

has a high purpose throughout—a high purpose and
a merciful purpose too.

From among the number of contemporary criticisms which the appearance of the work evoked,
we shall select one which perhaps attracted less
attention than it deserved, on account of the comparative want of prominence of the Review in which
it appeared. At that time the *English Review* was
a new venture. It contained many very able articles
besides that which we are about to quote, but it
never took a great hold on the public mind, although
it lived, we believe, through nine or ten volumes.
When we say that the article in question was by
Mr. Gladstone, and that it appears to us quite
worthy of its author, we have said enough to justify
our statement with regard to the high class of minds
who recognized at once the ability and the lofty
tone of *Ellen Middleton*. After a few preliminary
sentences, the writer says:

Of the eminently able and eminently womanly work before
us we may state, that of all the religious novels we have ever
seen, it has, with the most pointed religious aim, the least of
direct religious teaching ; it has the least effort and the greatest
force ; it is the least didactic and the most instructive. It
carries, indeed, a tremendous moral ; and were this an age of
acute and tender consciences, practised in self-examination,
and intensely sedulous in making clean the inner chambers of
that heart of man which is ordained as to be the Redeemer's
abiding-place, we might fear for its producing, here and there,
wounds over deep and sharp. But our authoress has to deal
with a dull and hardened state of the public mind, and she can
do something towards quickening and arousing it. . . . She
has assailed that which constitutes, as we are persuaded, the
master delusion of our own time and country, and, in the way

of parable, and by awful example, has shown us how they that would avoid the deterioration of the moral life within them, must strangle their infant sins by the painful acts and accessories of repentance, and how, if we fall short of this by dallying with them, we nurse them into giants for our own misery and destruction.

It is not possible for us to follow Mr. Gladstone in his masterly analysis of the story itself. It is enough to cite him as a critic of unquestionable authority, whose verdict raises the work far above the ordinary rank of novels which have achieved even the highest contemporary success. As to the technical contrivance of the plot, he says:

We do not deny that there is some complexity in the accessory incidents of this story, nor do we hold the plot to be constructed with the highest technical skill as far as regards its details. But we are chiefly concerned with the far higher qualities of delineation of character in its finest and most fugitive shades, as well as in its broadest and deepest colours (that is according as modern life and habits admit these terms to be applied) for which the work is remarkable.

One of the few passages which he quotes is one which describes Ellen's first view of the sea—

As I would have chosen to see it for the first time, stormy, wild, restless, colourless, for the everlasting fluctuations of colour, brown, purple, white, yellow, green, by turns; billows over billows chased each other to the shore, each wave gathering itself in silence, swelling, heaving, then bursting with that roar of triumph, with that torrent of foam, that cloud of spray, that mixture of fury and joy, which nothing in nature but chafed waters combine.

We have here perhaps a reminiscence of Lady Georgiana's comparative indifference to the calm, motionless Mediterranean. Of the passage in which

Ellen describes her dream on the night before her marriage, Mr. Gladstone says that in his judgment it has so much dramatic grandeur as to be worthy of Scott in the *Bride of Lammermoor*, or of Æschylus in the *Agamemnon*. And he sums up his abstract of the book by saying :

It is, after all, a book that to be appreciated must be known in its details, in its eloquence and pathos, in the delicacy and fulness of its delineations of passion, in its always powerful and, we think, generally true, handling of human action and motive, grounded, not upon analysis, but upon that intuition which, as applied to character, seems to be especially and almost exclusively the possession of the mind of woman ; in the healthfulness of moral principle that sustains it, in the singleness of idea and purpose that pervades it from first to last. It is unnecessary, perhaps, to add the meaner praise of fidelity in the picture of social life, and its varied, we might rather say variegated, movements. And yet this too was obviously requisite in order to produce the general effect. But it is a rare pleasure to find the mastery of all human gifts of authorship so happily combined with a clear and full apprehension of that undying faith in its Catholic integrity by which the human race must ultimately stand or fall.

The article concludes as follows :

The writer of the work before us has given to the public, and likewise has given to the Church, an interest in her reputation, and a first achievement of scope and promise such as this, while it necessarily inspires a lively interest in those which may follow it, likewise suggests the hope that neither brilliancy of success, nor the ardour of a mind flushed with the glow of recent exertion, nor the benevolent and pious desire to strike another stroke for the sake of truth and human happiness, may tempt her to do injustice to herself by diminishing either the energy or the labour which may be requisite in order to sustain the character of any future effort. But we think that all those who desire to see even the lighter weapons of human influence, or those which are commonly esteemed to be such, wielded for the welfare of man or the glory of God, will invoke blessings on the career of one who dedicates no common gifts of mind to the advancement of these high purposes, and will long for the day when the principles of belief and conduct which she labours to enforce shall have free course, as among the community at large, so especially in those stations of especial power and peril to which she belongs by birth and rank, and which she thus adorns by genius and devotion.

The *Edinburgh Review* of the same date found several faults with the work, without denying its excellence. But the article concludes with the following passage :

These volumes teem with proofs that Lady Georgiana Fullerton could produce a work capable of standing the severest ordeal of criticism, and it is the high estimate that we have formed of her powers that induces us to dwell so much on the errors of the plan. It matters little what mode of thought or style of composition is adopted by any ephemeral novelist, though he or she may happen to stimulate the jaded appetite of the London world of fashion, or afford them a topic for a week. But we feel bound to take care that no wrong notions of art or false theories of conduct are sanctioned by a writer so well qualified as this lady to make sterling additions to our light literature, and influence opinion in more extended circles than her own.

In the same way, the critic in the *Christian Remembrancer* concludes :

With the hope that we shall often again meet the authoress of *Ellen Middleton,* and receive at each successive meeting renewed and additional pleasure from the growth of principles and development of powers which cannot fail to entitle her to a high religious, moral, and intellectual position among the writers of the present age.

These extracts are quite enough to make it evident that Lady Georgiana's first work placed her at once, in the judgment of the most competent critics, among those few writers who teach and improve society while they seem to be only delighting it and moving its emotions, and who do this unconsciously and unintentionally, simply from the elevation and purity of their own minds.*

CHAPTER VIII.

1845, 1846.

THE success of *Ellen Middleton* surpassed by far the expectations of the author and her friends. We have no time to accumulate the witnesses of this. It is Lady Georgiana's Life that we are immediately engaged on. Some letters and facts, however, shall be laid before the reader.

Lady Georgiana and her husband were then settled near the Park, 36, South Street. This was their first home in London. They often left for visits to their friends, or to rejoin Lord and Lady Granville in the country. But this was their first home after their return to England. The following letter to her sister was written after a dinner at the Palace :

To Lady Rivers.

Wednesday morning.

DEAREST SUKEY,—I meant to write to you yesterday, but could not find a moment's time. In the first place I must tell you that the dinner at Court went off perfectly well. It was neither hot, long, or fatiguing, and I think papa rather enjoyed it. The Queen was all kindness, and insisted upon his sitting down immediately. Both she and Prince Albert, your friend Charles Murray, and several others, were very flattering about *Ellen.* There has been a favourable review in the *Court Journal,* a very ill-natured one in the *Spectator,* but what has turned my head is a letter to Moxon from Miss Martineau, which if I have time I will copy out for you.

We are all so much annoyed, so very sorry for the Carlisles, about Naworth Castle [a fire]. It is certainly, short of the loss of any person one loved, the severest blow imaginable. I feel it from what I know would be my pride and love of such a place, and theirs was as strong as possible. One quite dreads the effect on Lord Carlisle. Nothing almost in England equalled the beauty, interest, and historic associations of Naworth.[1]

The passage of Miss Martineau's letter to her publisher to which Lady Georgiana here alluded, is as follows (Miss Martineau had at that time a great reputation, and her suffrage is all the more valuable because it was entirely uninfluenced by personal considerations) :

Extract from Miss Martineau's letter to Mr. Moxon :

Ellen Middleton is very fine surely ! I want to know something of the writer, though the book reveals much. If, as I augur from some touches towards the close, she is capable of giving us characters and events of moral freshness and cheerfulness, she is a genius of a high order, for of her power in passion there can never be a doubt after this book. It is *rich* too. One is not merely carried away by a torrent of passion, but practical people (writers themselves) are struck in the very

---

[1] This grand old Border Castle was the occasion of a very happy anagram made one day by Lady Georgiana. *Naworth Castle, War to the Clans.*

midst of the sweep of progress with the profusion of beauties scattered by the way. This is one reason why I rejoice to *have* the book. I can read parts again. It is almost too much for an invalid, however ; for two days I was ashamed to look anybody in the face. I felt such an infection of criminality. This is a stronger effect than the ordinary one in such cases, gladness that one is out of the scrape. I suppose everybody is asking you about Lady G. Fullerton. My correspondents are asking *me*, and I can only reply about the book, not having even heard of her. I don't say there are not gross improbabilities in the book, but if they come only as an after-thought, as now to me, they don't matter much *this* time.

This letter from so competent a judge in the matter of composition and styles was well calculated, we must confess, to turn the head of a young lady at the beginning of her literary career. Miss Martineau's judgment about the improbabilities may be thought too severe, but it must be acknowledged that, like other successful writers of fiction, Lady Georgiana brought about her " situations " now and then without caring much for probabilities. She divined rightly " they don't matter,"—at all events, as Miss Martineau says, the first time. Few people would care to be too particular about such points, when every one in England and elsewhere was asking who it was whose name had suddenly become famous. It was then that Mdlle. Eward, as has been said, hearing some travelling companions whom she did not know asking this question, took occasion to make the proud answer, " She was my pupil!" We have heard before from Lady Georgiana herself a reference to Mdlle. Eward's trouble on discovering her youthful compositions at the age of seventeen.

L

Let us quote another letter from a friend to
Lady Granville :

Not having been able to read *Ellen Middleton* at once, I
lent it to one of my friends, an American Catholic, and very
clever. He was delighted. "He did not know," he said, "to
which of its high qualities he gave the preference. He admired the power and simplicity of its style, its pure morality,
and that firm religious tone which gives it such a different
cachet from the flowery religion of our day." We have such a
high opinion of this critic, that I was delighted to hear his
enthusiastic expressions on Georgy's book, but what will she
say to the observation with which he closed his remarks : "*But
the author is as good a Catholic as I am.*" I denied this
strongly. "*Then,*" he said, "*she must be a Puseyite, which is the
same thing.*" How far these observations are true as to the
book and to Georgy herself, I cannot judge, but it seems
curious to me as an indication of the view that Catholics take
of Puseyism.

Lady Georgiana had a far greater satisfaction,
from a success of quite another kind, which her
book gained some months after its appearance,
which we cannot pass over in silence. It must be
explained that the anecdote refers to a distinguished
officer, eminent by the name he bore and the
brilliancy of his career. He had often talked with
Miss Louisa Hardy, one of the charming sisters
who have been already mentioned as friends of
Lady Georgiana, on the most serious subjects. This
lady, full of piety, intelligence, and zeal, was not
afraid of conversing on the subject of religion. She
even did not hesitate to enter on it with persons to
whom it was neither familiar nor pleasant, who
were drawn to her by the rare charm of her conversation as well as the extreme goodness of heart

which outshone all her other qualities. Admiral B. had confessed to her that he was an unbeliever, but, nevertheless, he was glad to listen to what she had to say on this subject, and to answer her. Sometimes he was very ill-disposed to read the books which she suggested to him. One day, however, he opened *Ellen Middleton*, which was lying on her table. He asked her to let him take it away with him. For many days nothing was heard either of him or of the book.

Lady Granville shall relate to us in her letter to her daughter the result of the incident :

Lady Granville to Lady G. Fullerton.

After sleepless nights and such emotion as he had never before experienced, A. B. came to Louisa.

" I have read this book, and will now read whatever you like to lend me." He has hitherto resisted all Louisa's attempts to be of use to him. She mentioned the Bible. " If you please, but I don't know where to look." She said, " The Epistle of St. James would suit you best." " But I've got no Bible." She is going to give him one.

He told her, he never was so deeply moved in his life, never shed such tears, never felt such emotion. When he was young on board a ship (I know not if captain, or only under him) a sailor boy offended him by disobeying orders. In a violent passion, he seized a rope and ran after him, but the boy escaped him towards the end of the ship. Cooled by the chase, he returned to his cabin, thinking the fright punishment enough. An immediate cry : "All hands, some one overboard !" He rushed to the end of the ship—some time elapsed—the boy was picked up dead. He felt it was in escaping from his rage, that he had met with his death.

For months he suffered all the agonies of a murderer, he dared not, and never did tell any one. Then came years of sin, a hardened conscience, and total forgetfulness. When he read *Ellen* it came to his memory as if it had just happened.

Then he talked to Louisa in detail of the book—detestation of Edward, adoration of Alice. " But Henry Lovell—who could have imagined anybody could have painted such truth ! ' I have done it all, worse than it, I have been worse than him —nothing ever was so real, so true to nature,' and so on." . . . I was delighted with your letter to-day, with all your intentions.

I *implore* you to read "The Clapham Sect," in an old *Edinburgh* of June or July. It is not controversial, only portraits of remarkable men—too beautiful—almost divine.

These few words sufficiently show us that Lady Granville was then seeking, without any bitter feeling, to combat the tendencies which Lady Georgiana no longer kept secret. We have seen Mr. Greville speaking of "the religious belief to which she was attached," as if the fact was no longer a mystery. Her book itself showed, far more clearly than she was conscious of, what were then the desires and needs of her soul, though she was striving to satisfy them in Anglicanism. We think we may give her own testimony in the Preface prefixed to a re-impression of her book, all the former editions being exhausted, so late as 1884.

Preface.

The tale which is now reprinted, after the lapse of more than thirty years, was published at a time when the writer was on her way to the Catholic Church, into which, two years after it appeared, she had the happiness of being received,—a happiness which, at the end of a long life, is more deeply valued and gratefully appreciated than even in the first days, when submission had brought peace and joy to her soul.

Some passages in this story contain language implying a belief in the intrinsic efficacy of Anglican ordinances, which, after her conversion to Catholicism, the authoress would not have used. They have, however, been allowed to remain, because they witness to needs of the soul which, especially

under circumstances at all analogous to those of the chief
character in the tale, are felt by thousands who never avail
themselves of the Divine provisions made in the true Church
for their relief.

Since *Ellen Middleton* was written many changes, and what
are called developments, have taken place in the English
Church. The tale exemplifies the feelings and longings of a
generation now passing away, but there are probably at this
moment many as dissatisfied with the partial and unauthorized
efforts made to produce a semblance of Catholicism in the
Anglican communion, as there were forty years ago longing
for the attempt to be made, and happily destined to find it a
failure. To such this story of the past—for so it may well be
called—may not be without some interest.

We have enough reason, therefore, even independently of the evidence external to the book, that
while her literary work was in progress, another
work was being accomplished in her own soul. At
all events, when the book appeared, much of the
irresolution of the author had ceased. The composition of the book itself had, no doubt, much to
do with this. Her husband's conversion, also, must
have had its due effect on her, and must have prepared those around her for her own step in that
same direction. Her uncle, the Duke of Devonshire,
had, we are told, thought it "*convenable*" that she
should follow her husband, and said that "religion
is a subject on which man and wife ought to agree."
Her mother and sister did not so easily make up
their minds to what they looked on as a cruel separation. As to her father, whose health was then
much shaken, no one could approach the subject
with him without causing pain and even danger.
This was, above all, the obstacle which she found

so formidable. She put off the moment when it must be met. It was a terrible struggle—one of those tearings of the heart which the Truth exacts if it is to be grasped, one of those sacrifices which seem so hard and difficult, until we come to know by experience that no lawful ties on earth are really shattered in the bosom of Truth, any more than in Heaven in the bosom of Love.

Lady Georgiana had to know all the bitterness of the chalice—bitterness which must be measured by the tenderness of the affections she was forced to wound. There were no reproaches, no harsh judgments in that chalice, and these would perhaps have given her a courage in answering them and resisting them, which was lacking when the hearts so closely united to her own were full of nothing but gentleness and tenderness. Lady Granville's letters at this time have often passages such as this:

God bless you, my dearest, dear child. I miss you all day, every day, miss your agreement, your tenderness, your sympathy, all that makes it so delightful to me to have you with me.

Every day I am away from you I feel more that we alone are ever together. There is a unity in our differences that is marvellous.

The first paragraph here quoted was written before Lady Georgiana's conversion, the last afterwards. They are enough to show Lady Granville's incomparable tenderness, and enable us to appreciate the power of a conviction which required her daughter to give her so much pain in order to obey it.

In February, 1845, Lady Georgiana was at Brighton with her father, whose health continued to cause her grave anxiety. She writes to Lady Rivers :

To Lady Rivers.

February 4, 1845.

DEAR SUKEY,—I hope that the absence of news of you to-day means *good news.* On my part this is the case. Papa is better, he looks better. I wish I could say that he is really convalescent. . . . I cannot say this yet, but the doctor is satisfied and mamma is less anxious.

Mr. Sneyd is here, and his conversation is a pleasure to papa. Lady Beverley and Lady Louisa Percy dined with us yesterday. To-day the Calthorpes and Mr. Hennaway, to-morrow the Palmerstons, Lord Polwarth, and Mr. Morier.

I have given up writing the *Life of St. Elisabeth.* I saw, by various signs, that my mother did not like it from the first. She told me since, that everything touching controversy causes my father such nervous irritation, that I dare not approach the subject for fear of his health.

As things are I should be very wrong to bring forward, without great necessity, my Catholic sympathies. It is true that they must appear in all I write (for one cannot conceal what one feels so deeply and strongly), but I have no doubt that it would be best not to publish anything at present bearing on it, even in the very name of the book.

I do not know if you have time to read the papers? As for me, with the exception of Mr. Gladstone, who appears to me to show himself a conscientious man, I am disgusted with all the world—with Sir Robert Peel for having changed his opinions and having stolen from the Whigs the very measures he condemned and fought against in them, also with Lord John Russell, who, for party reasons, rakes up extinct animosities and withdraws measures which he had himself thought opportune and essential.

I thought the letter of Sidney Osborne of last Saturday was very clever and very skilful.

Adieu, dear sister. I hope all the children are well. May God bless you a thousand times. G. F.

Lady Georgiana was in fact engaged upon a new novel, not a Life of St. Elisabeth. She began its composition in the course of the year after the appearance of her first work. The subject which she chose gave much greater opportunity to the pouring forth of the feelings with which her heart was now full, even than *Ellen Middleton*. It was called *Grantley Manor*, and we shall see how it was received by the public. As before, the time spent in the work was one of much suffering. One of the greatest sorrows of all those by which life can be marked was now to fall to her lot. At the beginning of 1846 her father sank under the malady which had for many years threatened his life. All the sufferings which precede and follow such a loss were coincident with the religious crisis in her soul. She had more need than ever of the succours of religion. And then, after the fear of afflicting her dying father, came the other fear of increasing her mother's pain.

It was a time of inexpressible anguish. During this period Lady Georgiana was an assiduous worshipper at the chapel in Margaret Street, which became so celebrated in the annals of "Puseyism." It was there that so many of those souls met who, soon afterwards, found in the Catholic Church the logical issue of their aspirations. Since her return to England, Lady Georgiana had striven to find satisfaction to what were almost now convictions, by joining closely the movement in which she had taken an interest at a distance. It was one of the strangest movements that have ever been seen.

For the Catholic Church then gained for herself a
number of glorious conquests, almost without a
combat. It was not by sending apostles and missionaries that she brought so many souls back to
her bosom. She was like a mother standing silent
and motionless, with her arms only stretched wide
to receive her children coming back to her from afar.

The year 1845 had seen what has been called the
"grandest victory which the Catholic Church had
gained since the Reformation." It is true that
Mr. Gladstone speaks of the conversion of John
Henry Newman. He might have named others
also of his most illustrious and dearest friends.
Mr. Newman was the first and the greatest of all.
He was to be followed, after some interval of time,
by such men as Archdeacon Manning, James Hope,
Robert Wilberforce, whom he called the pearls of
the Anglican clergy and of the Anglican laity.
Among them came the group of lesser stars of whom
the Oratory at its beginning were composed, under
Frederick W. Faber, himself already distinguished in
the Anglican ranks, and ladies, such as the Duchess of
Norfolk, the Duchess of Buccleuch, the Marchioness
of Lothian, the Marchioness of Londonderry. No
one of them surpassed in holiness the subject of this
history, the friend, the companion, the guide of all,
now reunited to her in the eternal Peace.

Up to 1846 Lady Georgiana frequented the chapel
in Margaret Street already mentioned. It was there
she often met the friends we have named. It was
there, in particular, that she was struck by the profound devotion of James Hope, as well as with his

whole appearance, which no one could fail to notice.
Few men have ever received gifts of different kinds
in greater profusion, and few men have been so able
to make them all supernatural. His intelligence
placed him above his contemporaries, and his soul
raised him still higher. He was handsome, his
figure fine, and these were only the outward reflection of qualities that made him the model of
Catholics and Christians.

Thirty years later Lady Georgiana thus described
Mr. James Hope, writing after his death, to his sister,
Lady Henry Kerr:

> I think it was in 1843 that I first saw your dear brother in
> Margaret Street Chapel, the favourite place of worship of the
> Puseyites in those days, and noticed him and his friend Mr.
> Badeley walking away together, and was more struck with his
> appearance than with that of any other person I have ever seen
> before or since. . . . It is only in pictures that I have ever seen
> anything equalling, and never anything surpassing, what was,
> at the time I am speaking of, the ideal beauty of his face and
> figure.
>
> During the next two years I used often to see him at
> Margaret Street Chapel, and I may say, that his recollection
> in prayer and unaffected devotion made a strong impression
> upon me. Having been very little in England since my child-
> hood, it was quite a new thing to me to see a layman in the
> Anglican Church so devout, but without a tinge of fanaticism
> or apparent excitement. In 1844 I made acquaintance with
> Mr. Hope, and met him occasionally in society. He was all
> that his appearance would lead one to expect ; the charm of his
> manner enhanced the effect of his conversational powers.

It would cost us a long digression to dwell on the
bright circle of virtue which is suggested to us by
the memory of this distinguished man. His sister

and brother-in-law, Lord and Lady Henry Kerr,
made the sacrifice of all that made their life happy
for the sake of the Faith. Henrietta, their eldest
daughter, became that holy religious of the Sacred
Heart, whose Life has lately been so admirably
written. Of their three sons, two are now serving
God in the Society of Jesus. Nearer to Mr. James
Hope stand the two wives who in succession bore
his name. The first was the sole grand-daughter of
Sir Walter Scott, a convert, like her husband, to
Catholicism. During the short years after her conversion she seconded him to the best of her power
in the blessed work which he undertook in Scotland,
where he succeeded in reviving the faith in a part
where it had been lost, and once again created a
centre of prayer and charity. When she had passed
away, her successor, Lady Victoria Howard, sister
of the present Duke of Norfolk, was well worthy to
fill the void in the desolate home, as James Hope
Scott was himself worthy to become a member of
a family whom exemplary virtues and good works
make more illustrious than their great name, and
give to them a nobility higher than that of blood.

. These few names will give an idea how serious
and fruitful was that Catholic reaction which was
caused by the Oxford movement. It will explain
also what we venture to affirm, that few of the
converts failed to take with them the esteem of the
Anglicans, notwithstanding the regret which their
defection occasioned. This respect never diminished.
We may add that the enthusiasm which drew to
Margaret Street Chapel so many, in the hope that

they might be Catholics without submitting to the Church, was to most of short duration. With Lady Georgiana it was merely a passing phase of thought. From the time that she arrived in London she asked and received a course of religious instruction which was to put an end to all her doubts. It was given her by a venerable Father of the Society of Jesus, Father James Brownbill. He was a man of great holiness and simplicity, and he had the rare fortune to receive the abjuration of many of the friends we have named above, and to see them become, by his means, devoted and faithful children of the Church. .

Father Brownbill was at that time a little short of fifty. He still wore the dress which is no longer used by the clergy, differing little from that of laymen. It had been necessary in the days of persecution. He might have been taken for a refined gentleman farmer, but as soon as his voice was heard the illusion was over. His fatherly goodness was touching. The calm and laconic wisdom which characterized all his answers was equally striking. No one could help respecting the authority in whose name he spoke. Now that we think of the importance at the time of men like Mr. James Hope and Archdeacon Manning among the Anglicans, the one in the Church, the other at the Bar, we are perhaps inclined to think that such men were not altogether free from the temptation to imagine that they were giving the simple priest some unusual satisfaction in kneeling before him, at least a satisfaction different from what he might feel in the case of less distinguished penitents. If any such thought did occur, it did not last a moment. Father Brownbill's manner was enough to teach them, better than a thousand sermons, that they could bring to the Church nothing, and were, on the contrary, to receive from her everything.

Mr. James Hope said afterwards that they knew well that it was so, but that for his part he could never forget the impression he received—it was better than any words, any reasoning, any preaching. Father Brownbill's manner and attitude made him understand that he was but a child, and that the Church was his mother. Certainly the lesson was a good one for so many converts of distinction to receive. But at the same time it would be quite wrong to deny that the Catholic Church in England was the gainer by the new blood which was now poured into her veins. It was a time of need, after long persecutions. She had lost much strength, and was now reinforced. She gained both in her priesthood and her laity, and the converts were in many cases men of distinguished culture and high education, as well as zeal and devotion, qualities which add greatly in England, as elsewhere, to power for good.

Father Brownbill—as we might be certain—received his new penitent as a father, without being dazzled by her high birth or the literary distinction she had gained. He was just the person needed by her, in the midst of all her sorrow, added to her last struggles and the disturbance of mind which so many various causes combined to produce. He dealt with her with a calm and gentle authority, listened to the sometimes incoherent and ill-arranged ideas which she expressed without surprise, let her move on almost in her own way, made her progress easy without hurrying her, and awaited tranquilly the end towards which her goodwill, her absolute sincerity of heart, and her love for God, were leading her on with infallible certainty.

One day, shortly before her submission, when she was under the influence of those fluctuations which will be strange to no one who has ever passed through a crisis of the same sort, she came to Father Brownbill in a state of mind altogether different from that in which she had parted from him the day before. "I am come to tell you, Father," she said, in a tone of resolution, "that I have changed my mind. I no longer think as I did yesterday, and decidedly it is not into the Catholic Church that I wish to enter." Father Brownbill was sitting near a table, in the little parlour in which he received his visitors. He listened to this declaration without moving a muscle. He sat silent, looking at the tips of his nails (as he often did). At last he said quietly, "And what is the Church, then, that you intend to enter?"

No answer was possible to this calm question. It chased away, as by enchantment, the passing fog which had fallen on her to darken her last steps on the road. The light returned, and was never afterwards veiled from her eyes. The troubles of life, certainly, were not over for her. Great and much trial awaited her still, but the trial of doubt never again touched her soul. Henceforth she was sheltered from this evil, an evil which makes all others harder to bear. She entered on the possession of the good which sweetens them all.

This blessing, it is true, did not make itself felt in all its fulness at once. It grew and unfolded itself every hour of her life. But it was that day that she received in her soul the indestructible seed, the peace and certainty of faith. Two days after this visit Father Brownbill received her abjuration. It was Passion Sunday, March 29, 1846.

CHAPTER IX.

1846, 1847.

AT the end of the last chapter an assertion was made, which some readers may perhaps think rash. But it is the exact truth. After so many troubles and fluctuations, Lady Georgiana found in the Catholic Church peace, just as a vessel finds rest when she has cast anchor in the harbour. It was not a peace which had no pain or sacrifices. But it was free from doubt. Doubt is a sore of the soul unlike others, and those who have known it and been healed of it, know that the healing involves liberty, calm, and the possession of joy and peace, which abide and live, not to the exclusion of trial and suffering, but in the midst of them and in spite of them. We may well suppose that the truth becomes even more sensibly clear and firm to those who have made the greatest sacrifices to obtain possession of it, than to others. We leave our direct path a little in quoting, as we cannot resist doing, two other memorable examples of this.

It was on April 5, the eve of Passion Sunday, 1851, that the future Cardinal Archbishop of Westminster, and Mr. James Hope, were both received into the Catholic Church by Father Brownbill. That they felt the same peace and joy of which we speak, will be touchingly proved by the following notes.

The Rev. H. E. Manning to J. R. Hope, Esq., Q.C.

14, Queen Street, *April* 7, 1851.

MY DEAR HOPE,—Will you accept this copy of the book you saw in my room yesterday, *The Paradisus Animæ*, in memory of Passion Sunday, and its gift of grace to us? It is the most perfect book of devotion I know. Let me ask one thing. I read it through, one page at least a day, between January 26 and August 22, 1846, marking where I left off with the dates. It seemed to give me a new science, with order and harmony and details as of devotion issuing from and returning into dogma. Could you burden yourself with the same resolution? If so, do it for my sake, and remember me when you do it. . . . I feel as if I had no desire unfulfilled, but to persevere in what God has given me for His Son's sake.

Believe me, my dear Hope,

Always affectionately yours,

H. E. M.

14, Queen Street, *October* 21, 1851.

. . . I am once more in my old quarters. They bring back strange remembrances. What resolutions have passed since we started from this room that Saturday morning! And how blessed an end! as the soul said to Dante, *E da martirio venni a questa pace!* . . . You do not need that I should say how sensibly I remember all your sympathy, which was the only human help in the time when we two went together through the trial, which to be known must be endured.

Rome, *March* 17, 1852.

. . . How this time reminds me of last year! On Passion Sunday I shall be in retreat. *Stantes erant pedes nostri*—and we made no mistake in our long reckoning, though we feared it up to the last opening of Fr. B.'s door.

H. E. M.

Let us now hear Mr. Hope, addressing another friend, not less dear than the companion of his sub-mission, but from whom, on the contrary, he had just parted.

J. R. Hope, Esq., Q.C., to the Rt. Hon. W. E. Gladstone, M.P.

14, Curzon Street, *June* 18, 1851.

MY DEAR GLADSTONE,—I am very much obliged for the book you have sent me, but still more for the few words and figures which you have placed upon the title-page. The day of the month in your own handwriting will be a record between us that the words of affection which you have written were used by you after the period at which the great change of my life took place. To grudge any sacrifice which that change entails would be to undervalue its paramount blessedness, but, as far as regrets are compatible with extreme thankfulness, I do and must regret any estrangement from you—you with whom I have trod so large a portion of the way which has led me to peace ; you, who are, *ex voto* at least, in that Catholic Church which to me has become a practical reality, admitting of no doubt ; you, who have so many better claims to the merciful guidance of Almighty God than myself.

It is most comforting thus to me to know by your own hand that on June 17, 1851, the personal feelings so long cherished have been, not only acknowledged by yourself, but expressed to me. I do not ask more just now—it would be painful to you : nay, it would be hardly possible for either of us to attempt (except under one condition, for which daily I pray) the

M

restoration of entire intimacy at present ; but neither do I despair under any circumstances that it will yet be restored.

Remember me most kindly to Mrs. Gladstone, and believe me,

Yours as ever, affectionately,

JAMES R. HOPE.

Let us remember that the two men who had attained this peace of which we speak, this supreme beatitude, as one of them calls it, were men who, humanly speaking, had renounced for the sake of it all that could tempt human ambition, as well as all that up to that time had been dearest and sweetest to their hearts.

These conversions had not taken place at the time of that of Lady Georgiana. That of Mr. Newman, as is well known, had preceded it. We cannot exactly measure how far she had been influenced by his example. But it is beyond all question that it must have profoundly impressed her, casting, as it did, into the scale to which her own convictions and wishes inclined, all the weight of the highest and most venerated authority. No one who has not lived in England at that time can understand the popularity and the reverence which then encircled that great name. No one who has not been there after the lapse of nearly half a century, can understand the extent to which that popularity and reverence still survive, to the honour of the nation itself and of the holy old man who is their object. He is separated from them by what seems an abyss. He is clothed with the highest dignity in a Church which is not theirs. But the place which he fills in the minds of his countrymen is the same as ever. His words are always welcomed with respect and sympathy. He is received with demonstrations of honour whenever he leaves his retreat, and his name remains a household word, dear and cherished in many an English home.

If it is so in our days, we can imagine what it must have been when Lady Georgiana was received into the Church. It does not appear that she had any relations with Dr. Newman before this time. But they must have known one another by name. In that great movement by which the lives of so many were influenced, those who reached the port first looked with anxiety on the struggles of those who were still battling with the waves, and these in turn counted on the aid of the counsels and prayers of the others. That it was so in this case may be judged from the following letter addressed to Lady Georgiana, in answer to one in which she announced her submission to the Catholic Church.

Dr. Newman to Lady G. Fullerton.

Mary Vale, *April* 15, 1846.

MY DEAR MADAM,—I feel the kindness of the information with which you have entrusted me, and which has given me very great pleasure. It has filled me with gratitude too, for, I assure you, I have ever remembered your ladyship's name in my prayers, and have listened for news of you with great interest. Nor will I fail to do so still, as you wish me, and while so doing, I shall not and cannot doubt that the peace and confidence which others have felt who have taken the same important step, will be granted to you as to them.

With all good wishes and kind thoughts,

I am, dear Madam,

Your ladyship's faithful servant,

JOHN H. NEWMAN.

A few months later Lady Georgiana wrote again to Dr. Newman, on a subject which occupied her attention more than any other from the date of her conversion. This was the education of her son. The heart and mind of the boy seemed already to answer to the tender cares of his mother. We do not possess her letter, but we may judge of it by the following answer.

Dr. Newman to Lady G. Fullerton.

Mary Vale, Perry Bar,
Birmingham, *June* 25, 1846.

MY DEAR MADAM,—First let me express my great satisfaction and thankfulness at receiving so happy an account of your state of mind, as your ladyship gives me. It has been, I fear, want of faith in me which has made me so anxious for you; but I know that persons who have been in the habit of exercising their minds have often much more trial than others in such a change as you have made, and I did not take sufficient thought of the grace lodged in the Catholic Church for the supply of all our needs, however diversified.

I am sorry for the retirement of Dr. Logan, having a great respect for him. His successor I have hardly more than seen. But it is the system of the school, and not the excellence of this or that official, which is its characteristic, and I conceive Dr. Logan's retirement can have no other effect than the introduction of a person of more or less popular manners and behaviour, as the case may be, instead of him.

All that I have seen of the school makes me think that it has those great advantages over an English public school, which a Catholic school ought to have and Protestant schools have not. The boys seem very happy, and Dr. Wiseman likes the oversight of them better, I do believe, than anything else. Perhaps it is rather a rough school, that is all I can think of to say against it, and, though there are many boys of good family, it is not in this respect like the best Protestant schools.

I am quite sure that Dr. Wiseman will take great care of

your son, and if, when he comes, I can be of any use in answering your questions of detail, or in any other way, it will be a pleasure to me to be made so.

I am, my dear Madam,
Your ladyship's faithful servant,
JOHN H. NEWMAN.

We have now reached the date of some verses which Lady Georgiana wrote, and which we have already quoted. They are those entitled *To my Mother the Church.*

The conversion of Lady Georgiana changed nothing in her habits of life. Neither then or at any other time was there the least alteration in her relations to her own family. Her relations with the world outside, which now took up a very small part of her time, remained much the same, till ten years later, when the blow which seemed to crush her life fell, a blow which was to open to her a path of more perfect renouncement, and breathe into her a more heroic love for all that suffer in this world. Providence was then to stamp her with the sign under which she was to bleed, and to make her find peace under an inconsolable sorrow in those lofty and calm regions which are reached by those alone who are so consecrated. But up to that time we find little change, and we can follow as before the external course of her life. It was very rarely, we know, that she spoke of what passed in the interior of her soul. Some of her letters, however, show that as soon as she was inside the Church, she began to mount. The spiritual life has many stages, and she soon passed through the earlier of these and aspired to higher things. No one, sooner or better than she, obeyed the command *Ascende superius*, which one of the great orators[1] of our time has taken as his text, when he has to trace the steps by which we are to mount from the common life of the commandments to that of the counsels, which enable us to get a glimpse in this world of a heavenly life.

Before we pass on to the exterior incidents of the next two years, which, without troubling the peace of her soul, made her more than ever forgetful of herself, we shall cite some passages from letters of advice which she received in answer to inquiries, and from which we can gather something of her own thoughts from what she must have laid before some person of experience.

The advice given to her in these notes is quite simple and practical. The writer begins—it may seem strange to some readers to hear it—with insisting on seven good hours of sleep, and more if the doctor, or her own experience, suggests more. But exactitude to the time of rising, say seven o'clock, is insisted on as a bit of useful mortification. Then as to austerities. They are things we soon become accustomed to, and it is well, therefore, to vary them. And we must be on our guard against a secret self-satisfaction regarding them. They are useful, but they are *bagatelles*, as a little reflection on our sins and on the examples of the Saints will show us. If we have not courage for voluntary mortifications, the sense of our weakness must help

---

[1] Père Monsabre.

to increase our humility. For reading she is recom-
mended Rodriguez and the Lives of the Saints,
St. Philip and his companions, and St. Ignatius.
They help us to understand what sanctity means.
Among "pious books" we are to stick to and read
over and over again those which touch us most.

Her ordinary prayers are enough. When she
cannot get to Mass, she is to adore in spirit our
Lord in the Blessed Sacrament. There should be
a portion of her day reserved for work, either intellectual or manual. This can be laid aside when a
press of occupations require it, but it is always to
be considered a part of the order of the day. Some
simple directions are also given as to the prayers
commonly used by Catholics, and as to the "intention" with which an ordinary prayer, like the *Pater*,
is to be said. In short, her daily routine is not to
be changed, only it is to be looked on as a fixed
rule of obedience to God. There are also some
instructions about habitually turning all praise for
self to God, and the consideration of the love of
the Sacred Heart which may be gained by patient
perseverance. These counsels seem to contain so
much wisdom that they serve to show how much
this calm and peaceful kind of direction must have
strengthened a soul which had been so long in a
state of change and fluctuation.

We have said above that the relations of Lady
Georgiana with her family continued as intimate
as ever after her conversion. The following letter
is a sufficient proof of this. She approaches without
reserve subjects which in such cases are forbidden,

even with those who have before been accustomed to say everything to one another. This loving confidence Lady Georgiana never left off with her mother, who was far too good, too reasonable, and too just, to make her ever wish to abandon it.

The letter of which we speak as showing how free was the interchange of thought between mother and daughter, is addressed to Lady Granville, in March, 1847. It appears that the latter had consulted her—not for herself, but for some one under her care—about the use of Avrillon's books, which were at that time somewhat in vogue on account of some translations published by Dr. Pusey, who was not always very skilful or fortunate in the books which he selected as manuals for Anglican readers. Lady Georgiana advises her mother by all means to pass over many passages in Avrillon. " I should do the same myself, if I had to read to the servants, or to such a person as ——, easily frightened and innocent." " It is much better to encourage than to disquiet souls. I have, for this reason, not sent the book to her, as I had promised, asking her to read what was marked day by day. Many things in those books would not suit her: there are very severe injunctions on fasting and mortification, which seem meant for religious persons or those accustomed to great austerities." " But of other people it is only required that they keep to the precepts of the Church if their health permits, and it may be, some little secret mortifications." She says there are many passages which she does not like in Avrillon. His is a kind of devotion which

she could never adopt. "You are to put yourself by
an effort of reflection and of will in various dispositions—terror, hope, peace, and so on." "His
meditations on the Passion are admirable." This
letter ends by a significant passage:

> Yesterday, Freddy, Osborne, and George Stewart dined
> with us. They made me play fifty times over—
>
> Mourir pour la patrie
> C'est le plus beau sort, le plus digne d'envie.

The last lines of this letter show us that it was
written in 1847, when so many grave events were
already casting their shadows before them, while
those who ought to have dreaded them the most
did not anticipate them or feel alarm at the future.
Germany was already a prey to agitation, but " the
news from France was still good," and Lady
Georgiana, like so many others, was playing fifty
times over the *Chant des Girondins*, without the least
foresight as to what was to follow, or the slightest
thought of what the revival of that revolutionary
air presaged. Lady Georgiana was not to be as
indifferent to the events of 1848, as she might seem
to have been to those of 1830. She was no longer
a girl of eighteen, and she had passed the years that
had elapsed since the Revolution of July almost
entirely in France. She knew personally the Royal
Family who were this time the victims, and we
shall see how greatly she was moved by their misfortunes. But at the beginning of 1847 she was
far from having any anticipation of what was to
come so soon, and her mind was fully occupied with
other things.

It must be remembered that, besides the important thoughts which now became always dominant in her mind, and besides the works of charity which from this time engaged a considerable portion of her time, she had just published another work which met with a success quite equal to that of the first. Letters of congratulation and felicitations poured in on her from all sides, and the papers were full of the praises of *Grantley Manor.*[2] She had thus an early opportunity of resisting that feeling of self-satisfaction which had been pointed out to her as a danger to her soul, and of keeping herself simple and humble in the midst of a burst of applause that might well have flattered her pride. It is not in our power to speak at any length on all her works. But this was the first which she published after her conversion, the first in which she had purposely chosen a plot which enabled her to show her faith openly, and it therefore seems interesting to observe some of the particulars of the reception which greeted it. We therefore select some of the letters written either to her, or about her to others, which seem most remarkable.

The Countess of Carlisle to Lady Granville.

Castle Howard, *July* 1.

I cannot tell you how beautiful I have thought that book, my dearest sister. I must now give you an account of the end of our reading it. Since Francis went, Liz and I have finished it together. The night before last (my maid's room has been new painted, which keeps her out of it, so that I cannot ring for her, and she appears of her own accord, at the right time) no words can tell how sorry we were when she appeared. Liz

---

[2] This novel was published in 1847.

magnanimously left the volume in my room, and I, as magnanimously, would not read on without her. But you may imagine our self-denial. Edmund just gone into Mrs. Fraser's box! Last night we came to the conclusion, but it made me quite ill, and to-day my eyelids, always inclined to be heavy, are looking like two great snakes. I am afraid the idea I present to your mind is not pretty or picturesque. Oh, my love, I like it far above *Ellen*. When Liz finished it, and stopped, I could not speak, I could only weep—yes, though it ends well, that was the effect—till Liz at last said that now we had better cheer up. She was very nearly obliged to give up reading, and thought it one of the most difficult feats she ever performed to go through with it. I think it rather unfeeling in Georgy to ask which sister we prefer, for though Margaret is also a beautiful fascinating *creation*, I do not think her quite to be put on the same *niveau* with Ginevra, and Liz quite agrees with me. Then, sister, I think it so beautiful on Religion—that it really does one good, that it is so free from everything to give offence—if there is anything at all dangerous, it is what I have always thought. The only thing that to me appears so fascinating in the Roman Catholic religion, is the picture of that more entire dependence it seems to give to its votaries—that more complete rest for their souls, which Protestants *might*, yet do not, always feel.

In short, I think it is a work with so much, not only merit, but *genius*, that I cannot but congratulate her in possessing it, you in having it in your daughter, my beloved sister, sure as I am that it will ever be turned to and lead to good, and not only to good in the common sense of the word, but to the highest objects, the most unfading results!

Ever your most affectionate

G.

Mr. Charles Greville to Lady G. Fullerton.

From all sides come praises and admiration for *G. M.* (*Grantley Manor*). Some say (as I expected), that it is less deeply touching than *Ellen Middleton*, but better written, and the subject more cleverly treated. Moxon is well satisfied with its sale, everything going well. I am told that you are coming to town. I shall soon see you. You must be over-whelmed with compliments and congratulations, which is very pleasant.

Affectionately yours,

C. G.

P.S.—As your book raises much discussion between Cath-olics and Protestants, I find myself often in an argument with one and another of my friends (Protestants), well-intentioned, but very ignorant. The other evening (as a specimen) it was affirmed that Catholics do not believe in the salvation of Protestants. Also, that their spiritual guides do not allow them to read the Bible, which means, I imagine, that as they do not read the Bible freely, the reading of the holy Books, if not forbidden, is not encouraged.

From the same to the same.

London, *Tuesday*.

MY DEAR GEORGY,—I must send you an extract from a letter I have received from the Duke of Bedford this morning.

I continue to hear one person after another speak in terms of high commendation of *G. M.*

I am just starting for Croxteth, near Liverpool.

Ever your affectionately,

C. G.

The Duke of Bedford to Mr. Charles Greville,
enclosed in the last.

I have had a pleasure here that I was not able to enjoy in London, viz., the pleasure of reading. The first book I have opened is *Grantley Manor*, and I cannot resist telling you of the gratification it has given me. I find, on reading it, that I have not lost my unbounded admiration for such writing and such sentiments as I find in that book, full of talent usefully employed, and giving interest to good principles. Next to the employment of a man honestly engaged in the public service of his country, I place this occupation of a clever woman.

The following letter is from Mr. Henry Greville, the younger brother of Charles Greville. Like his brother, he is the author of some memoirs which paint very exactly and interestingly the society of his time. They are less important for political facts than those of Charles. But like his, they have found many readers both in France and England. Henry Greville's agreeable manners, goodness of heart, and cultivated intelligence, gave him a position quite of his own in society.

Mr. Henry Greville to Lady G. Fullerton.

Sunday.

I have just finished *Grantley Manor*, and I can do nothing else until I have expressed to you how admirable I think it in all ways. First of all it is so *pure*, so thoroughly Christian in all its sentiments, that it will do its readers more good than many books which are put into their hands for the purpose of improvement and not of amusement. Then it is admirably written. The characters well developed. The story interesting, and the winding up to the last degree skilful. In short, it is almost faultless, and I think you will add immensely to your reputation, which I am sure you don't care for, except as a means of doing more good on a future occasion. Everybody I have seen, without one exception, is in the highest degree laudatory, and I think all prefer it to *Ellen M.* I do, very much. Nobody can rejoice more than I do in your success, or is more aware of how much you deserve it.

Your affectionate

H. G.

Letter from the same to the same.

London, *Monday.*

DEAREST DODY,[3]—I had intended to go to Fern to-day, but I have seen Leveson, who insists upon Stud House, but I shall be with you all on Wednesday. I am in the greatest hurry, so that all I can say is that your triumph is most

---

[3] "Dody" was the name by which Lady Georgiana was ordinarily addressed in her own family.

complete, and that your head must be a little turned. All like it immensely, much more than *Ellen,* and those who prefer the latter are, like me, its passionate admirers. You will have seen the *Examiner.* The *Athenæum* is very flattering, though less so. A good criticism to read. I shall expatiate on it all on Wednesday. How pleasant it will be with dearest Sukey.

Your most affectionate

H. G.

P.S.—I send you to-day a written criticism of a friend of mine.

Miss Fanny Kemble to Henry Greville (enclosure).

. . . I have finished the first volume of *Grantley Manor.* I am *charmed* with it, and prefer it hitherto *infinitely* to *Ellen Middleton.* I read it so attentively at my dinner yesterday that, with my eyes on the book, reaching for my glass of claret I carried the mustard-cruet to my lips. I prefer Grote, however, for last thing at night—for whereas, at the end of three of his pages, I generally can just feel for the extinguisher and go to sleep, *while* I put my candle out, I lay awake half the night last night, reading *Grantley Manor,* and the other half in consequence of what I had read.

She must be a very cheering person, not because she lets you correct her book, but to be able to write such books.

From the same.

I send you your book. I cannot hold up my head, I have cried so over it. It is incomparably superior to the other—it is a *beautiful* book.

The next letter on our list is from Miss Berry to Lady Granville. Miss Berry was then past her eightieth year. She is famous as the friend of Horace Walpole, and as highly esteemed by a number of the celebrated men of the end of the last century and of the beginning of this. She was able to gather them around her in her very modest rooms in Curzon Street, and these rooms became the *rendezvous* of the wits and politicians of the present century, richer at that time in this respect than it has been in later decades. Her name figures in many of the works which preserve the memory of that now extinct world. Her letter, therefore, will be valuable as giving her testimony to the value of *Grantley Manor*, and also because it paints the author of that work in a graphic manner.

Miss Berry to Lady Granville.

Petersham, *Monday, July* 5, 1847.

Although you would not see me when lately at the Stud House in our immediate neighbourhood, I am going again to intrude myself on your notice by expressing to you how much I admire the last work of your daughter.

The style is for the most part excellent, and I cannot enough admire her nice discrimination of character, while she probes the deepest feelings and most acute sufferings of the human heart with a power, an accuracy, and a delicacy of touch which few of our writers possess.

I feel the more anxious to express my note of praise independent of the general voice of public admiration, because I feel ashamed of not having long ago discovered the superiority of the author's talents. But, between the thick veil of modesty under which she was quietly perfecting her abilities, and the great difference in our age, I thought of her only as your daughter, and allowed her hardly to share in the inimitable charm of your society and conversation.

And now having made my confession both to mother and daughter (very necessary to my conscience at my advanced age), with equal truth let me subscribe myself to both—a very old, attached, and affectionate friend,

M. BERRY.

Here is another, which reports the high esteem of the French Royal Family.

Marchioness of Normandy to Lord Granville.

Paris, *June* 5.

MY DEAR LORD GRANVILLE,—Pray let me thank you a thousand times for thinking of me and sending me that delightful book of your sister's.

I never left it till I read it through, and I feel as if I could read it over again with pleasure, it is so full of truth and goodness, besides which, it is one of the most interesting stories I could read, and the interest never flags from the beginning to the end. But, instead of telling you my opinion, I may as well tell you what will be more gratifying, which is that I found them all enchanted with it at Neuilly last night. The Queen pulled the second volume out of her work-bag, to show me that she was so much interested in it that she carried it about with her. And she mentioned many parts as particularly delighting her, which she had marked in pencil. The description of Rome and Italy, for instance. She said, she thought it one of the most charming books she had ever read, and much as she admired the first she liked this better, and so do I also.

We have at last got the summer weather, and I can enjoy this home—it requires hot weather quite to appreciate all its merits. We devote ourselves to sight-seeing and the small theatres, and enjoy ourselves very much.

But we should never end if we adduced all the testimonies received by the author of *Grantley Manor* to the new and great success which she had obtained. Some of her correspondents, and we might ourselves do the same, ask whether there was not in all this a temptation to self-love almost irresistible? No doubt such a temptation may have made itself felt, and with the ardour after protection and sacrifice with which she entered the Church, it will hardly surprise us to learn that the idea of putting an end to the source from which it came, by the total relinquishment of any exercise of her literary talent,

had occurred to her mind as the best way of safe-
guarding her humility. We have reason for thinking
that the question did actually occur to her. At a
later period she herself formally considered it and
solved it, and, what she says at that time seems
to describe her whole literary career from this
moment. We shall give this solution at its proper
place.

Of one among the letters of this time we much
regret the disappearance. We have to gather its
contents from the answer made to it by Lady
Georgiana. This is the letter which she received
from Miss Edgeworth, the intelligent and beneficent
author of works which charmed the children of two
generations, and which are still read with delight
by those into whose hands they fall. In some ways
they have never been surpassed. We cannot be
astonished that Lady Georgiana should have been
so greatly satisfied with the praise she gained from
this remarkable woman, whose age now increased
the authority of her talent.

To Miss Edgeworth.

London, *November* 14, 1848.

How can I thank you sufficiently, my dear Miss Edgeworth,
for the letter I have received from you, or express as I should
wish my sense of your great kindness? To you I owed the
pleasantest hours of my childhood, many and many in after-
life also, and *last* certainly not *least*, that in which I received
and read this most kind and gratifying token of your approbation. To be praised by Miss Edgeworth is no common
honour and no ordinary pleasure. This letter I consider as
one of my most precious possessions, and shall ever value it as
such. My greatest wish would be to have the advantage of

N

your advice, my dear madam, as well as of your encouragement. To you I am indebted for the love of reading ; as a child I never took any pleasure in fairy tales, it was the stories of real life which your books contained which excited and rivetted all my interest, and laid the foundation of that taste for watching and describing characters which after awhile turns one into an author. It is said that everybody remembers *one* book, which took a peculiar hold on their fancy at the age when the strongest impressions are made. Your *Emma* was that one to me. It was the first work of the kind that was put into my hands, and I read it so often and thought upon it so much that I could almost have repeated it by heart. I was then fifteen years old ; if I could have been told that twenty years later I should have had such a letter from you as the one I have just received, it would have seemed to me an incredible happiness. Your book on education I read, when expecting the birth of the only child I have had ; so that your writings are associated with the most interesting recollections of my life.

Let me thank you again and again for having added another item to these stores of memory, and for allowing me to look upon you as a friend, now in a direct, as I have long done in an indirect, manner.

It was particularly gratifying to me to have your approval of the way in which religious subjects are introduced into *Grantley Manor.* Your opinion on controversial novels is so entirely mine, that I can never read one on either side of the question without thinking of the fable of the Lion and the Painter.

The only part of your letter which caused me regret was that in which you say that a similarity of incident and of character had made you suppress some part of a story which I rejoice to hear you are engaged in writing. This makes me feel guilty towards the public. At the same time it cannot but give me great pleasure to think that there should have been such a coincidence of thought between us. This was the most practical compliment that my book could have received.

I am not, my dear Miss Edgeworth, one of Lady Carlisle's daughters. It is her sister, Lady Granville, who is my mother.

I believe you were acquainted with her also. She, as well as my aunt, had the strongest appreciation of the immense benefits you conferred on our generation, as well as the greatest admiration for your writings.

With renewed thanks for your indulgent goodness to me, and for the encouragement you have so kindly given me,

I remain, my dear Miss Edgeworth,

Gratefully and sincerely yours,

GEORGIANA FULLERTON.

We have a letter remaining to us of the time when Lady Georgiana was writing *Grantley Manor*, which it may be well to quote. The letter is to her brother Frederic, who frequently assisted her in her literary efforts. It will show that the management of her story was sometimes a matter of great difficulty to her:

. . . It was so kind of you to write to me so fully about *Grantley Manor*—which, by the way, must I think change its name, as the plot is carried on during all the last volume far from the said *Manor*. I will do what you wish—consult on the point of the misunderstanding between Walter and Margaret. I will explain your view of it to Charles Greville, and see how it strikes him. In thinking over the change in Edmund Neville's letter, though I still think it ought to be sterner and manlier, I do not, on second thoughts, think there ought to be much reasoning on the subject of religion, as they must have *epuisée'd* that in previous discussions, but I will make him say, "I will not go over the often trodden ground again, but only remind you that what was desirable then is now become necessary," &c., or something of that kind. It is a horribly difficult story to manage. I feel twenty times over *Que diable suis-je allée faire dans cette galère?* But as I am in for it I must steer as well as I can. I shall feel very much about criticisms upon it, which I did not about Ellen's story, for that I never could myself admit was unnatural, and on this one I am ready to admit any degree of condemnation. I believe that Edmund Neville's character is developing itself well, and somewhat in the line you describe, but he never can be really interesting, not so much as Lovell even, because he has not the excuse of an ungovernable passion. His excuses, though very real, and, in fact, perhaps greater, are not interesting. I wish I had put in something about the poor, however, and shall see if I can still do so.

The readers of *Grantley Manor* may remember a fine passage almost at the opening of the tale, about the virtues of the poor, which does not seem to have very much to do with the development of the plot, but which may well be taken as a witness that Lady Georgiana felt herself, in her second tale, at liberty to put into print the thoughts that were uppermost in her heart. It is in the account given of the teaching of Margaret by her future husband, Walter Sydney.

He taught her that self-denial practised in secret, and pangs endured in silence for conscience' sake, no less deserve the palm of martyrdom than the courage that carries a man to the scaffold or the stake. He illustrated his meaning by various examples : he called her attention to those heroic actions which are sometimes performed by the poor with such sublime simplicity, such unconscious magnanimity. For instance, he made her read and compare the historical record of the noble answer of Louis XII. of France, when in the presence of an applauding court, he pronounced that sentence, which has been handed down to an admiring posterity, "It is not for the King of France to avenge the injuries of the Duke of Orleans," with the police reports of an obscure trial in the newspaper of the day, in which a poor collier, bruised and disfigured by a cruel assault, begged off his brutal enemy all punishment, and refused all pecuniary compensation, simply urging that the man had a wife and children, and could not well spare the money, and that he would himself take it as a great favour if the magistrate would *pass it over.* Then he asked her if the monarch's deed was not of those that have indeed their own reward on earth, and the collier's did not number among those which are laid up as treasure in Heaven—there, where the rust of human applause does not dim, and the moth of human vanity does not consume their merits, and forestall their recompense?

The virtues of the poor! Their countless trials! Their patient toil! Their sublime because unknown and unrequited sacrifices! History does not record them. Multitudes do not applaud them. The doers of such deeds travel on their weary journey through life, and go down to their graves, unknown, unnoticed, though perchance not unwept by some obscure sufferers like themselves; but a crown is laid up for them, there, where many first shall be last, and many last shall be first! Wearied creatures who, after working all day with aching heads, perhaps, or a low fever consuming them, creep out at night to attend on some neighbour more wretched than themselves, and carry to them a share of their own scanty meal. Mothers who toil all day, and nurse at night sickly and peevish children. Men, who with the racking cough of consumption, and the deadly languor of disease upon them, work on, and strive and struggle and toil, till life gives way. Parents whose children cry to them for food when they have none to give. Beings tempted on every side, starved into guilt, baited into crime; who still resist, who do *not* kill, who do *not* steal, who do *not* take the wages of iniquity, who do *not* curse and slander, and who, if they do *not* covet, are indeed of those of whom "the world is not worthy."

And *we, we* the self-indulgent, we the very slaves of luxury and ease, we who can hardly bear a toothache or a sleepless night, *we* go among the poor, and (if they are *that* to be which must require a higher stretch of virtue than we have ever contemplated) give them a nod of approval, or utter a cold expression of approbation! They have done their duty, and had they *not* done it, had they fallen into the thousand snares which poverty presents, had the pale mother snatched for the famishing child a morsel of food, had the sorely-tempted and starving girl pawned for one day the shirt in her keeping, stern justice would have overtaken them, and mercy closed her ears to their cries. And if they have *not* transgressed the law of the land, but for awhile given over the struggle in despair, and sat down in their miserable garrets with fixed eyes and folded arms, and resorted to the temporary madness of gin, or the deadly stupor of laudanum, then we (who into our very homes often admit men whose whole lives are a course of idleness and selfish excess) turn from them in all the severity of our self-righteousness; and on the wretched beings who perhaps after years of secret struggles yield at last—not to passion, not to vanity, but to *hunger*, with despair in their heart and madness in their brain, we direct a glance, which we *dare* not cast on guilt and depravity when it meets us in our crowded drawing-rooms, in all the pomp and circumstance of guilty prosperity ! (vol. i. p. 9).

We are tempted to subjoin another passage, a few pages later, on Italy partly, at least for the purpose of justifying the remark of Miss Martineau, that the works of Lady Georgiana are full of gems. Her eloquence is quite equal to her lofty purity. The reader will remember that Leslie, the character here spoken of, is travelling in Italy very soon after the death of his wife.

The acuteness of grief had subsided, and a vague desire for fresh interests and new excitements had taken its place. A latent taste for painting and for poetry ; for the artistic and imaginative side of life took strong possession of Leslie's fancy as he advanced into Italy. The influence of its brilliant skies, the magic of its natural beauties, the memories of the past, its departed glory and its living charm, operated more and more powerfully on his soul ; and for the time being the quiet English country gentleman was transformed into a passionate admirer of that strange land whose very name is a spell, whose very defects are attractions ; where desolation is bewitching, suffering poetical, and poverty picturesque, where life resembles a dream, where the past is almost more tangible than the present, where an eternal vitality springs from the bosom of perpetual decay, like pure flowers floating on the surface of

a dark and stagnant pool; life in its brightest and most
glowing colours, death in its most poetical and soothing form,
meet each other at every turn. With her cloudless skies and
her tideless seas, the unchanging grey of her olive groves, the
brilliant hues of her mountains and of her streams, the solemn
silence of her cypress groves, the noisy throngs of her joyous
people, her gorgeous churches with their myriads of living
worshippers, her gigantic tombs with their countless multitude
of unknown tenants, Italy is at once and emphatically the land
of the living and the land of the dead. This Leslie felt ; he
did not seek society, he did not enter into noisy amusements,
he left his hours and his days to take their natural course ; he
floated down the current of life, while nature and art unrolled
before him visions of beauty and scenes of enchantment which
appear to those whose souls they touch, not as novelties, but
as the realization of a presentiment or of a dream. Have we
not, some of us, in our hours of sleep, known a land, a spot,
a home, which in our dreams we recognize, which in our
waking hours we sometimes long to visit again ? Have we not
at times, in performing the commonest actions of life, in
opening a book, in shutting a window, in meeting (for the
hundredth time perhaps) with a person, experienced a sudden,
strange, unaccountable feeling, which suggests to us, in what
appears a supernatural manner, that we have done *that* action,
thought *that* thought, met *that* person in the same manner
before, and yet the whole impression is independent of the
memory, and is more a sensation than a thought? Such was
the effect that the first sight of the Campagna of Rome
produced upon Leslie. He had lingered at Genoa and at
Florence ; he had become thoroughly imbued with the order
of ideas and of taste which creates in men a sort of new sense
and new perceptions. I dwell much upon that change in the
whole intellectual being which is caused by a series of impressions and associations which, but a short while before,
were as strange to the mind they visit as colours to the born
blind, because it partly accounts for the sudden fancy which
soon after took possession of Leslie's feelings (p. 41).

These passages will suffice to give those readers
who do not care to make acquaintance for them-

selves with novels of a past generation, some idea
of the qualities which are to be found in this and
the other works of Lady Georgiana Fullerton. Very
few novels, indeed, can pass through a long course
of years with a perpetual and ever fresh popularity.
There are, on the other hand, some writers whose
name remains in honour, at least among literary
men, and maintains a certain amount of prestige
with the public at large. This is the most that can
be hoped for writers in so essentially an ephemeral
field of literature. The tastes of the day change,
new favourites inevitably shoulder out those who
have had their turn at earlier periods. It is something, that the charm of an author is not forgotten,
it is more that the effect and tendency of her
writings has been uniformly good, pure, and high.
This praise can certainly be claimed for Lady
Georgiana. Always successful, she never perhaps
surpassed, in later days, the achievements of *Ellen
Middleton* and *Grantley Manor*. We shall not have
time to speak in detail of the series of her other
works. Her next, *Ladybird*, published a few years
later, has much of the same charm, though it
may not have been quite so successful. The fourth,
Too Strange not to be True, has an historical or quasi-
historical basis, and the scene is laid partly in the
New World, and partly in the France of the time
of Louis XV. She wrote later the *Countess de
Bonneval*, both in French and English, and is considered by competent judges to have shown an
almost unequalled power in dealing with the difficulties of such a work. It is a most touching tale,

and describes, moreover, the France of that time, in a way that even few French writers have described it. Our admiration of the work is enhanced by the consideration of the scanty list of the existing letters out of which she has created the character of the heroine and the details of her story. *Constance Sherwood*, begun in 1864, marks her interest in the persecuted Catholics of the reign of Elizabeth, and the *Stormy Life* of Queen Margaret of Anjou, another professed autobiography, by one of that unfortunate Queen's ladies, is almost as full of beauties as *Grantley Manor*. And her two latest works of fiction, *Mrs. Gerald's Niece*, and *A Will and a Way*, though less known to the general public, have the same stamp of unmistakeable power, and ineffable purity and elevation. This must suffice here for an account of these graceful productions.

CHAPTER X.

THE public mind was soon filled by events far too important to leave it at leisure for literary engross-ments. Lady Georgiana herself was certainly one of the first persons to lay them aside. The thunder-bolt of the Revolution of 1848, breaking in upon a state of perfect serenity, fell upon those whom she knew, upon the country which she loved so much, the places around which her dearest memories clung. France has passed through many shocks of the same kind, and if any of us still retain the feeling produced by that, when first that country, and then all Europe, seemed struck with paralysis, they will remember what the effect was. We can easily guess what was her feeling under this as-tonishing and unexpected blow, and how anxiously she looked for the news from France. There was an unprecedented mixture of truth and falsehood in the first reports which reached the world outside of the catastrophe. The letters of Lady Georgiana reflect the rumours in circulation and the news, more or less exact, which the friends who had been suddenly scattered communicated one to another, and these have that historical importance, even after the events, which belongs to all accounts written at the time. It is also interesting to see how these terrible events were estimated by a stranger, a sincere friend of France, judging them from a distance, and with a full knowledge of the country where they took place. A comparison between the present and the past suggests very sad comments and reflections upon them.

A very slight summary of the incidents of the Revolution of 1848, as far as they affected Louis Philippe and his family, must suffice as an introduction to the following letters. Unfortunately, too many of them are dated only by the days of the week, and we are therefore not able to arrange them in any certain order.

The Revolution practically began on Tuesday the 22nd of February, when some barricades were erected, some shops plundered, and the like. It was on Wednesday the 23rd that the King determined to change his Ministers—that fatal step which involved all in confusion. It was on Thursday the 24th that the King abdicated and fled, first to Versailles, then to Dreux. After various adventures, during the intermediate days, the King, Queen, and Duchess of Nemours, left Honfleur in a small boat for a British steamer, on March 1st,[1] and landed at Newhaven the following day, hence they proceeded straight to Claremont. We may now let the letters speak for themselves.

---

[1] 1848 was a Leap Year, and March 1st fell on a Wednesday.

To Lady Rivers.

London, *Monday, February* 28.

DEAREST SUKEY,—George Stewart tells me he has written to you a long letter; as that and the *Times* which I trust you will get will have given you ample information. I will only add a few little particulars. I went to see Madame Delessert this morning. She arrived yesterday with her husband and her children. He was *mis en accusation* as Prefect of Police, and they got away without a change of clothes. Their equanimity under this awful *bouleversement* is wonderful, and the moderation of their language really admirable, but they deplore "*le fatal aveuglement du Roi et de ses Ministres.*"

The Duc de Nemours is almost out of his mind with anxiety. Nothing heard of the King and Queen, of his wife and four of his children. One child, who had been left at the Tuileries, fled with Princess Clementine of Cobourg, and recognized her father on the steamer by his voice. He was so disfigured by misery and change of dress, she had looked at him without knowing him again. The brother and sister (Nemours and Clementine) did not know they were on the same vessel. The meeting between them was heartrending. But the last news heard of the Duchesse de Nemours was that she was *lost* in the streets of Paris, having missed her way to the place where she was expected. Conceive the Duchess of Orleans losing her second boy in the press of the mob, on her way from the Chamber of Deputies to the Invalides, where they were taking refuge! It was some time before he was recovered. They are now hid, it is said, in the house of M. Anatole de Montesquiou. Neuilly and St. Cloud are reported to have been burnt to the ground. The Tuileries is transformed into an Ambulance.

Think of Lamartine! acting scenes out of his own book, as it were! . . .

There is a report of Louis Philippe's death, but it is not believed. The last place where they were heard of was Dreux. Gone perhaps to take a last leave of the tombs of their children. Some say that is the road to Brest, and that they will go to America, not to England. I am glad to hear our Queen has sent steamers with the kindest letters to all the parts where they are likely to be—they say she is very much overset by these events.

The Duchesse de Montpensier is arrived, and was expected every moment at Manchester House when we were there this morning with Madame de Jarnac.

There is a report that her husband has given his adhesion to the Republic, and asked for the command of the Artillery; that he has in view the Crown for himself. I should not think this was true. The most contradictory reports circulate. People are in a fever of excitement. We had quite a mob round the pony carriage in Manchester Square while Louis de Noailles was talking to us. He (being a Carlist at heart) blames violently all the Royal Family, and calls their flight "a disgraceful *sauve qui peut.*"

Some people are frightened about the *contre coup* in England. I am afraid of war—in short, one can foresee nothing, and feel sure of nothing.

God bless you, dearest ; I have not time for more.

Your most affectionate
G. FULLERTON.

To Lady Granville.

Wednesday, March 1.

. . . I have seen Madame de Lieven. M. Guizot was with her, very calm, but very pale and much changed.

She charged me with many affectionate messages for you. She is much touched by the interest shown towards her, and I find her much softened.

She is quite beside herself about Lamartine. "There," she says, "is a great heart and a gallant man." When he harangued the crowd, for the first time, on the abolition of the sentence of death for political crimes, he was struck on the cheek by many, and more than one sword was pointed towards him with a threatening air. But he never budged. He rendered numerous private services, and acted most generously. The Princess said that every one in Paris prays Heaven to spare his life and strength. But the situation is very precarious. "He governs the people by poetry," she said, "and his melancholy air—judge ·

if that can last." "I, I ! dear Lady Georgiana, at sixty-three years of age, to fly like a heroine of romance, with two chemises and some diamonds !" She showed much concern for the dangers run by M. Guizot. She depicted her own sufferings in a little house, where for hours she was alone without news of any one, trembling for him and fearing that each cry she heard in the streets announced his death. "For under all this there is ninety-three *tout pur,*" said she. M. Guizot expects that now at least there will be war to the knife between the Republicans and the Communists (or the Socialists, as we call them).

To Lady Granville.

London, *Thursday, March* 2.

DEAREST MAMMA,—There is no news to-day but what is in the papers. I will leave this open till I come home from driving, as one may hear something more. Prince Albert is rather anxious, they say, about the Queen. She is so very much overset and nervous, which is not pleasant just as her confinement is approaching. Her anxiety is intense about the Duchesse de Nemours, whom she is very fond of. Nothing has been heard hitherto of her and of her children, nor of the King and Queen. It is reported that the Duchess of Orleans and her sons have been arrested at Rouen, but that the authorities have offered to send her in safety wherever she chooses. If one can trust the newspaper accounts, the state of Paris is promising, and the Provisional Government acting very well ; but Lord Elphinstone told F. just now that he had seen an aide-de-camp of the Duc de Nemours who had made his escape, who says it is all in a dreadful state, and that they will not suffer any letters to pass that tell the truth. Lamartine seems to act a distinguished part, and, as yet, a courageous and humane one. Fancy a sitting of sixty hours at the Hôtel de Ville, and at the end of that time to be again summoned to harangue the mob !

I must tell you an answer of the Pope's which is much admired. The King of Sardinia was troubled at an oath which his predecessor had exacted from him, that he would never grant a Constitution, or act in a Liberal manner. He applied to the Pope, asking him to absolve him from this oath. He answered, "A Pope has no powers to absolve from an oath made in the Presence of God, but God does not accept oaths made against the welfare and happiness of men."

5 o'clock.

No news of the King and Queen, but they have heard at the Foreign Office that the Duchess of O. and her sons are still at Paris, and that it was the Duchesse de Nemours who was arrested at Rouen, and maltreated by the authorities, so that it is supposed she will soon be here. Private letters from Paris speak of order restored. It seems that the King showed great irresolution ; one cannot, in a man of such known courage, call it pusillanimity. The Queen, on the contrary, behaved heroically ; knelt to him, almost, not to leave the Palace, and had presence of mind, when it was determined they should fly, to return alone to fetch money, the King having left the Tuileries with only five francs in his pocket.

To the same.

London, *Thursday, March* 2.

. . . The contradictions we see in the present state of things in France are surprising. It is certain that it has produced an extraordinary religious change. The account given in the *Times* about the Queen's crucifix is quite true. It has been confirmed to me by a trustworthy person.

This crucifix was hung up behind her bed. It was respectfully taken down and carried in procession by a crowd of young men to St. Roch, where it was placed over the altar at which she had been accustomed to pray.

It is impossible not to admire the conduct of Lamartine now. His energy and courage are extraordinary. When the people clamoured at his proposition of abolishing the penalty of death for political crimes, he cried out : "Well, if this law is repealed, my head will be the first to fall, for in that case I shall betray the Republic." His power over the people, they say, is immense. His voice calms them, and it is always raised in favour of order and of humanity.

One cannot but hope that the most noble part of his character will tell now. The author of the *Méditations Reli-*

gieuses must have had some great capabilities for greatness; but the frantic wish for popularity, and the wish to play a great part, probably seduced and blinded him during these last years. He is supposed to be the vainest man alive, and to such, I suppose, it is comparatively easy to be generous and good, when, as with him at this moment, that passion is gratified to the utmost.

What I fear most is that the peaceable dispositions of the French will be overthrown by the horrible accounts from Lombardy, where Austria is laying her iron hand upon the people. Then, again, the Provisional Government is promising to the labouring classes a ruinous scheme of relief which must make the country bankrupt after awhile, or else, if withdrawn, draw down on itself the disappointed rage of the multitude.

There is an account in the *Univers* of Lacordaire's preaching at Notre Dame, on Sunday, to an immense crowd. When an allusion was made to the events of the week, a loud shout rose, but he seemed to rise too, and his voice was heard above the roar, bidding them remember they were in the house of God. They were silenced in a moment, and listened to the sermon in perfect stillness.

I fear these events will have a fearful echo in Ireland, and especially from the very reason that, happily for France, the clergy have there identified themselves with the popular cause.

To the same.

London, *March* 3.

DEAREST MAMMA,—I can only write a few lines to-day, though I hardly know when to stop in writing to you.

There have been some meetings here yesterday, but they were easily dispersed by the police. The news from Glasgow is not good, and Lady Morley tells me that Lord Clarendon is uneasy about Ireland. It is impossible not to feel troubled. I make great efforts to keep calm. It is strange how the words of the *Bible* which we have not understood or observed, suddenly spring to life.[1] I was quite surprised this morning to find that

---

[1] Lady Georgiana was in the habit, apparently, of reading a portion of the Bible every day, and perhaps her mother had taught it her, or practised it herself. On a slip of paper among Lady Georgiana's memoranda we

"clamour and indignation" were among the things forbidden to Christians. I see the proof of this now in many ways which I am sure you will understand. The violent language applied to King Louis Philippe and his sons, the insults and sarcasms heaped on them, seem to me so unjust, so exaggerated, and so ungenerous now in his great adversity, and when one's heart bleeds with compassion for the poor Queen; but I try to convince myself that to take fire at it does no good to others and only harm to one's self. Those words on "clamour and indignation" have been useful to me and have strengthened my resolutions.

It seems to me that the whole world is on the eve of great events, which will exercise the faith and the patience of all. We must take for our device the magnificent words that the Tractarians have taken for their motto: "In quietness and confidence shall be your strength."

Lamartine is certainly the hero of the day. He sent the King money, of which he had none. He has begged M. Guizot to go to his house, as to the safest and surest refuge, and in this he has given a proof of his courage, for it exposes him to great danger. They say that his colleagues grumble at him, and the story goes in Paris that he is still a Legitimist.

Adieu! dear mamma. My best love to dear Sukey and to the children.

Affectionately yours,
G. FULLERTON.

To Lady Granville.

London, *Saturday, March* 4.

DEAREST MAMMA,—Only one line to-day. The newspaper will tell you all about the arrival of the King and Queen. It is an immense load off one's heart and mind. Thank God they *are* arrived. The accounts seem to give the impression that he is well in health and not altogether cast down in spirits. I hear he has bought, at different times, portions of land in

find the following extract from the *Life of St. Vincent de Paul*, by M. Abelly, Bishop of Rodez.

1. *Adorer les vérités contenues dans le chapitre qu'on a lu.*
2. *Entrer dans le sentiment de ces mêmes vérités.*
3. *Se proposer la pratique des choses qu'elles enseignent.*

O

England. Perhaps, with that wonderful elasticity which belongs to the French character, and his in particular, he will turn into an active country gentleman, and the Queen may know peaceful days again. They were to sleep at East Sheen last night, and to proceed to Claremont to-day. Poor Madame de Dolomieu sank quite overcome in her last parting with the Queen at St. Cloud, where she followed her, and when the Queen charged her to return. Her health is quite broken. I have written to Madame de Montjoie, and if they receive any one at Claremont shall go there immediately. Madame de Lieven arrived yesterday. I called at the Clarendon in the evening. She was just gone to bed, but begged I would go to her this morning. I will tell you how she is when I come back.

The King's letter to our Queen was simple and touching. She burst into tears on receiving it. I do so love her for the feeling she has shown. He says it is of course *comme le Comte de Neuilly que je vous écris,* so that is the name he means to take.

The Government had a good majority in the House of Commons. Lord John is thought to be very ill, and that soon he must give up leading the House. Lord Palmerston or Lord Clarendon are talked of for that post.

It is said, there are great mob meetings in and about London, but that the newspapers do not choose to take notice of them.

F. says I wronged the Duc Ducazes yesterday, that he gave a very warm adherence to the Provisional Government, but nothing more than that.

G. F.

To the same.

London, *Monday, March* 6.

. . . Henry Greville has brought me the saddest news from Paris. The members of the Provisional Government are at open war. Ledru Rollin has perfectly cast aside the mask. No liberty exists for the elections. The candidates are frightened and menaced unless they are known as Republicans, and despotic powers are given to revolutionary agents. Except for the guillotine, it is the Reign of Terror. The army is discontented. They have taken away half their pay, and they are not allowed to be in Paris during the sitting of the Assembly. Forty thousand men of the new *Garde Mobile*, which is, in other words, the armed paupers of Paris, are to form a sort of pretorian guard for the Government. Every body seems to fear now that there must be some dreadful collision before a better state of things can arise.

Here there are many satisfactory symptoms that France has read a lesson rather thari given an example. They clamour at the theatres from the galleries for "God save the Queen," and order all hats off while it is sung, and one or two cries for the *Marseillaise* have been drowned by a general dissent.

Adieu, dearest mamma. Perhaps I may not write to-morrow, as we are going to Claremont.

To the same.

March 18.

. . . I came back from Claremont yesterday too late for the post. It is a most heart-breaking thing to see the Queen. She is an angel. I felt as if I could have knelt to her. Such intense piety—not a word of bitterness, of anger, of complaint. Nothing but heroic patience and courage, but much suffering, such deep suffering ! *Je tache de supporter, chère Lady Georgiana, je veux avoir de courage—mais mes enfants ! Mon Dieu, mes enfants ! . . . et puis mes pauvres, tant de souffrances pour nous, pour nous . . . ! Je succombe devant tout cela.*

All that with that angelic simplicity, I could do nothing but cry. It is the most affecting thing in the world. I was quite overcome too. There are rumours of every kind. Princess Clémentine goes back to Cobourg to-morrow. The young Prince of Wurtemburg, who had never left the Queen before, is in Germany with his worthless father. The Princes of Join-ville and Aumale, for some reason or other, are not coming to England, so that it is altogether a cruel separation. Then not one penny will they have from France. The Duchess of Orleans has written an adorable letter to the Queen, such tenderness and affection. She has refused all offers of asylums from German Princes, is going to live in strict seclusion at Ems, till the season begins, and then somewhere else, with her two boys and their tutor. She hopes to teach them to be good men, good Frenchmen, to bear adversity like their grandfather did in his youth, and *Et soyez assuré, chère maman, que je ferai tout au monde pour qu'ils soient toujours de bons et sincères Catholiques.*

This was real kindness, and shows such nobleness and delicacy of feeling.

The Queen said, *Hélène a été adorable dans ce tourbillon de malheur.*

The King came in, and sat some time with us. He was very different from the last time—silent and dejected. If there is not dignity about him, there is at least a touching absence of resentment or ill-will to any one.

The Queen kissed me over and over again, and really, I think, was melted by the ardent sympathy I felt for her.

The accounts from Paris are miserable. The Provisional Government are *literally* at daggers drawn with one another, Garnier Pagés threatening to kill Ledru Rollin if he moved from his seat to appeal to the mob out of doors. We dine with Lord H. Vane to-day, and go to Lady Palmerston's in the evening. Last night we spent an hour with Madame de Lieven and M. Guizot. Really I sometimes feel as if I was dreaming, and almost sick with excitement. Some days at Bourn would be very good for me.

Ever your most affectionate

G. FULLERTON.

P.S.—The nurses have *struck* at the Hospices, and went to declare to the Provisional Government that they would not nurse the babies at night ! Such tragic comedy. Young Guizot had a letter from a friend who heard a man get up at a Republican Club, and say, *Citoyens, j'ai le malheur de m'appeler Le Roy, mais désormais je demande qu'on me nomme Le Peuple et ma femme La Nation !*

After a time, as we all remember, came alarm for the stability of England, which henceforth mingled with the exitement as to foreign affairs. The kind of panic created by the Chartist movement and the state of affairs in Ireland, is reflected in the letters.

To the same.

March 14.

. . . The Kennington meeting went off as quietly as possible yesterday, the police say they have seen more people assembled and more tumult at many a Ranter's meeting. An immense number of gentlemen were sworn in as special constables, almost all the tradesmen, and even many workmen, two thousand coal-heavers (a formidable force) offered themselves. The fact is that the melancholy accounts of utter stagnation of trade in France, and the non-payment of the savings banks, are acting beneficially in England. The middle classes seem determined to keep the Chartists under. The saying at Paris now is, *Ce n'est pas la République, c'est la Ruine publique.*

Ireland seems to me a fearful subject. Leveson,[3] who never will allow danger in anything, says it is all nonsense, there may be some bloodshed, but no chance of a rising not being immediately put down. But Morpeth allows that one must count now on the independence of Ireland as a probable result of all this. I cannot but think that a desperate population who, as Sir A. A—— was telling me the other day, openly declare that they had rather be hung than starve, and who will certainly prefer being shot to either, may fight *à toute outrance.*

If a conflict should arise, it will be, I fear, the most dreadful that ever was seen, with the national and religious animosities which have so long smouldered, bursting into a flame. The Irish priests see the French on the side of the movement, and they do not consider that they, far from exciting the popular passions, are true ministers of peace, and only see in existing Governments what can best secure order. The Irish see the Sicilians throwing off the yoke of Naples, and proclaiming their independence, with the consent of their clergy, and in England there is evident sympathy with them. No wonder that they think the present is an opportune moment for throwing off the yoke of the religious supremacy of the minority, which is so galling. . . . I should be grieved at the

[3] Lady Georgiana calls her brother by his former name, after he had succeeded to the title of Earl Granville.

separation of these two countries, and, above all, I hate the thought of the horrible struggle preceding it, but I cannot be astonished at the Irish thinking that their time is come. I hope, at least, and I pray God, that if ever this conflict and triumph comes, that they will not forget the greatness of their mission, and that they will show themselves true ministers of peace and mercy.

I do not understand people talking of concessions to Ireland. I do not think that this is the question now.

Lord John Russell returns to-morrow. He is well again, but he seems to me to be far from equal to a great crisis such as this, only there really seems no one capable of replacing him.

Morpeth, Mary, Charles, and Henry Howard dined with us yesterday. It was very pleasant. So much is going on now of keen interest, that society is no longer the insipid thing it has often seemed to be.

Can you imagine a scene such as took place in the *Rue de l'Université*, after Madame la Duchesse d'Orleans left the Chamber by the court. She was pushed by the crowd as far as the door of the Duchesse d'Estissac. She took up the Comte de Paris in her arms, and, in doing this, had to leave go of the Duc de Chartres, who was lost for some minutes. She knocked at the door, and it did not open. She cried out in despair: *Oh! mon Dieu . . . ne s'ouvrira-t-il pas dans Paris une seule porte pour moi?*

My dearest mother, you may not perhaps need me, but I have the most longing desire to see you!

G. F.

To the same.

April 4.

. . . All the news received from the Continent is sad. Lord Clanricarde received letters yesterday from Paris, where they say that in ten days there will be a national bankruptcy, and this morning they say that civil war will break out in many places.

The Provisional Government are not agreed as to how they will receive the deputation from Ireland. They hope that Lamartine will carry his point, and that the reply will not be encouraging.

I wish much that this Government would make some concessions to Ireland, but at the same time place the country for
some time under martial law, for it would be frightful to see the
people arming themselves without check. But Ministers cannot
make up their minds to anything. Henry Drummond applies
to them the words of Holy Scripture : "They are like the
reeds shaken by the tempest." . . .

. . . The Duke of Wellington, they say, presses concessions
on Lord John, but he cannot make him decide. Lord Portman,
who told me this, says that if we do not make haste, there will
be a formidable rebellion. On the other side, I have just seen
my sister-in-law, who tells me that her husband, now in Ireland,
has no apprehension of this kind, and that we in England do
not know how to comprehend Irish violence, which often
evaporates in words.

The Salvos are just come. I am very glad.

The time is come of which the French general spoke :
"Now, at this moment, minutes are become centuries," and
with good truth. Our thoughts, like our bodies, go by express
trains.

To the same.

London, *April* 5, 1848.

. . . The accounts from Paris are as bad as bad can be.
Black despair reigns everywhere. It seems impossible that
Lamartine can stand till the meeting of the Assembly. M. de
Montalembert writes to Lord Arundel that nothing can exceed
the pecuniary distress in which every branch of society is
plunged, and that it is impossible to have the slightest insight
into the future. He says his own people about his château in
Burgundy have been cutting down his best trees and young
plantations, and threaten to kill him if he goes there.

The accounts from Ireland are very strange. There seems
to be a growing accession to the Repeal party from amongst
the more respectable part of society, and I begin to think that
the day is not far distant when it will begin to be treated as an
open question.

The Chartists are making proclamations about Monday,
and some people are afraid there will be a disturbance. They
are bringing troops into London. M. Delessert tells me that he

has recognized some of the worst characters of Paris in the streets. One does not feel afraid of any *result*. There may be riots.

We had a charming dinner-party at Holland House yesterday. Lord Walpole, whom I did not know before, was there, and was véry agreeable, also Mr. Thackeray, who does not please me much. I have met him before at Devonshire House, when he was asked what he thought of "Vanity Fair," now that he is admitted to it?

The walls are covered with placards bearing these words, *Liberty, Equality, Fraternity,* but the special constables are enrolled in large numbers, even among the workpeople.

To the same.

London, *April* 8, 1848.

It is impossible exactly to define what one feels about Monday. There are no *reasonable* causes of apprehension, every possible precaution has been taken, even large stores of provisions are laid up at the Horse Guards and Government Offices. Thousands of special constables from every class of society are daily sworn in, and it is very likely that the whole thing will end in smoke, like the last meeting at Kennington Common. Still there is a degree of vague anxiety on the subject, and the tradespeople are in a great fuss. It is just enough to make one feel that it will be a great satisfaction when the day is well over. Fergus O'Connor committed himself very much in the House last night, and Henry Greville said he heard he would be arrested at the first rising made by the mob,—but this is doubtful I should think.

The accounts from Ireland in the *Times* seem to me very bad, but Lord Clare said yesterday that he heard that the peasantry were disinclined to rise, and were more busy ploughing and sowing than they have been for years.

Paris still keeps to a certain degree quiet, but there are horrors which people do not talk of. The mob nearly murdered the Curé of Chaillot because he would not perform the funeral service over a man who had destroyed himself. They wanted to throw him into an oven and burn him alive, especially when it was rumoured that he had been Madame Adelaide's con-

fessor. The *religiosity* of the people goes against one, like all
the rest of their Frenchism. A large crowd went the other day
to St. Philippe du Roule, and announced that they would come
en masse to hear Mass the next day, which they did. They
then bellowed for the Curé, and insisted on his getting into the
pulpit and preaching to them. When it was over, they cheered
violently, and cried, *Vive la Religion!* Much as it goes against
one, there may be good in it, and may retrieve from crime
when the moment of general barbarism comes, though I hardly
can hope it has *root* enough for this.

A great many of the Communists are, it is said, really
religious men, and think that communism is a part of the
Gospel which has never yet been understood and practised.

I hear that the *gamins* of Paris no longer sing, *Mourir pour
la Patrie*, &c., but, *Nourris par la Patrie, c'est le sort le plus
beau, le plus digne d'envie.* . . . Adèle d'Hénin told me that the
Prince de Joinville had said to the King, when they parted at
the Tuileries, *Sire, nous ne nous reverrons jamais au Tuileries.*
It was from one of the tutors of the Prince she heard this, and
in a letter which was opened by the Provisional Government
from the Prince to the King, written from Algiers before the
catastrophe, there were these words, *Vous oubliez toujours,
Sire, que vous êtes l'Elu du peuple.* The distress of the Royal
Family is so great, that they live with the utmost self-denial, do
almost entirely without wine, and have nothing but the strict
nécessaire at dinner. He will not accept anything from our
Queen, or from Leopold. Lady Canning says our Queen is
very unhappy about them. She found her in tears the other
day about something regarding their difficulties. Lord H——
told me he heard that she (the Queen) is very low and frightened at the state of things here, but I do not much believe his
accounts. He is a great exaggerator. He says the artillery
soldiers at Woolwich are all Chartists, that so are the footmen
in London, and all sorts of stories of that kind. I believe that,
on the contrary, that set of people feel they have everything to
lose, and are much frightened at the example of Paris. Good-
bye, dearest mamma.

Ever your most affectionate
G. FULLERTON.

We now come to a letter written on the day of the 10th, which had been so anxiously looked forward to :

To the same.

London, *April* 10.

DEAREST MAMMA,—Everything has gone off quite well as yet. The numbers were insignificant compared to what had been announced, not more than twenty or thirty thousand at most, and of those not above ten thousand were real Chartists, it is said.

Mr. Mayne, the police inspector, sent for Fergus O'Connor, who came in a dreadful fright, and looking as pale as death. When he heard that the Government would not interfere with the meeting, but that not one step should they take beyond the bridges towards the House of Commons, he seized Mr. Mayne's hands, shook them, thanked him again and again, "Good Mr. Mayne, dear Mr. Mayne, then all is clear, then all is easy, I will speak to them. I am sure they will disperse now," and so on. He returned to the Common, and the petition, which was to have gone on a magnificent car placed on four gold lions, was forwarded to the house in a hack cab, and the last news we heard was that the meeting was broken up, and dispersing on all sides, no doubt egged on in this by a heavy shower of rain. Nothing can have been more satisfactory, and if it ends here, more gratifying—not a blow given by the police, or a red coat seen. But we must not forget that there are a number of these hungry, homeless people about, who may wish to make disturbances when it gets dark. The crowd is very thick round Blackfriars Bridge, and hoots violently at the police and the special constables.

A large number of Yorkshire Chartists, all armed, are arrived, but stand aloof, seeing the turn affairs have taken.

To the same.

London, *April* 12.

. . . How beautiful and striking that passage is from Ezechiel, which you send me. I have just been reading it. I know that you and I think alike on this subject.

Great mercies ought to make us humble. On Monday

evening when every one was crying out that "it was a day of which to be proud," I said to myself, and I said it out loud too, that it was not *pride* but *gratitude* we ought to feel.

The news from Ireland is enough to prevent our victorious songs. Lord Clarendon [then Viceroy] cannot go out of the Castle at night without a numerous escort, in the streets of Dublin. However, one of my friends, an Irish priest, assures me that the people have no desire to rise.

What absurdities Lord Brougham is saying against the Pope ! How a well educated man can be so ignorant ! He says : " How can the Pope have a Constitution and a responsible Ministry, being himself infallible, and not being able, I suppose, to communicate his infallibility to them." As if any one in the world had ever supposed or affirmed that the infallibility of the Pope applied to temporal questions, or to his own conduct as a Prince. It applies only to questions of discipline in the Church.

To the same.

London, *April* 13, 1848.

Last night we went to the Levesons. Lord and Lady John Russell, Lady Kerry and C. Gore, Lord Bessborough, and Morpeth were there. The little Premier seemed in better health and good spirits. Exceedingly amused at the premature accounts in the French newspapers of our revolution.

Dear Morpeth looked well and in good spirits. I warmly congratulated him on his speech about Repeal, which was after my own heart. He was a great dear about it, very much pleased I liked it, but a little frightened in consequence that he had been *too* Irish, as he was when the O'Connell shook hands with him and warmly thanked him on Tuesday night. I hope you read the speech. It was positive *against* Repeal, on the ground that it would do no good to Ireland, but it was kind and conciliating and courageous too at this moment. Uncle D. shakes his head at me, because Richard Cavendish tells him I am for the Repeal, which is not true. I think it a great misfortune, but it appears to me every day a more inevitable one, be the time of it far or near, and it seems to me a pity to make the very worst of it, by prejudging that the two countries must hate and ruin each other if it should come to pass. The article in the *Times* to-day seems to me written in the most mischievous spirit. Say that you banish all Irish workmen from England and renounce and cast her off altogether because she chooses to have a domestic legislature—Ireland may be made wretched, but England will not be made prosperous by such a line of conduct. . . .

I agree very much in what Lady Carlisle said in a letter to the Duke (of Devonshire) yesterday, of anxious desire that the Government should go on steadily now with liberal measures and reforms. I think the great danger for England is not revolution in the shape of a *coup de main* by the mob ; that is certainly not to be apprehended at present, but what alarms me are the symptoms of a Conservative re-action, and the anti-popular language held in society. I cannot but think the democratic principles are far too strong to be kept down by force, and that the only chance of ultimate safety is their gradual and constitutional development.

I send you the Pope's last allocution. I think it beautiful, and the French translation is so superior to the English that I cannot resist sending it you. Pray return it to me, as I should like to keep it.

Good-bye, my own dearest mamma. I go to Claremont to-morrow with Madame de Salvo, so it is possible that you will not have a letter from me on Saturday.

Your most affectionate
G. F.

In the same letter she says a few words on the preaching of Dr. Newman and Father Faber.

The sermon by Dr. Newman was very striking, all his thoughts are deep and original, and the very tone of his voice is moving. Part of his sermon yesterday was, however, a little too metaphysical for me, but the end was admirable. The paraphrase of the passage of St. Paul on those he calls "inconsequent Christians," that is to say, "as sorrowful, yet always rejoicing, as needy, yet enriching many ; "[4] all this part of the

---

[4] 2 Cor. vi. 10.

sermon was of extreme beauty, still, I am reproached with preferring Father Faber's sermons. This is perhaps true, but I admit also that it is a proof of bad taste.

To Lady Granville.

May 16, 1848.

. . . I have just seen Madame de Montjoie, who has been spending a few hours in town. She received, yesterday, a little book from Paris. For thirty years she had constantly written in it little religious extracts. It had been left on her table in the Tuileries, it had been found by the mob who had added blasphemous words signed by many names—this is painful enough to see, but years hence this book will be a curious *memento* of this time.

France seems to draw nearer and nearer to civil war. Ledru Rollin's ideas seem more tolerable. They call him *Coquin,* and the government *provisoire* they call the government *derisoire.*

In truth the world is in a frightful state.

Yesterday Father Faber spoke on this subject in the most eloquent sermon I have ever heard, many of the passages would have pleased you much. He preaches wonderfully, he moves me more deeply than Newman.

He painted the present state of things in strong colours, but not despairingly.

We had a lovely day for our drive to Claremont yesterday. We did not see the Queen, who was very tired after a long drive she had taken to Weybridge, but we saw the Duchesse de Nemours. She is very thin, but always beautiful. I cannot say how I pity them at this time, when the news from Paris adds poignant anxiety to their weight of care and sadness in their monotonous life!

I hope that you already know of dear Leveson having on Thursday made a protest, in the House, as to the words used by Lord Brougham to the Pope.

The word *charity,* which I suppose he did not understand, means *love,* and this is what the Pope meant, when he spoke of his love for all mankind and all Catholic nations, which did not allow him to say that Italy and the Italians are dearer to him than others. Though as God has placed him in their midst they have a right to special affection.

Every one remembers how the days of June succeeded to the days of February in Paris. We find an occasional allusion to them in the correspondence.

To the same.

June 29, 1848.

. . . I send you a little note from Madame de Montjoie. It has quite upset us, this news from Paris.

The King says "that he thanks God that all this bloodshed in France was not to keep him on the throne." Mr. Peel, who arrived yesterday, brought the news of the assassination of the Archbishop of Paris on the barricades as he was giving a message of peace to the insurgents ! . . .

All that one hears of Paris is frightful beyond description. But the Archbishop's death is glorious.

It is said that Cavaignac offers to retire, but they want to force the dictatorship on him. If he takes it he will know how to keep a firm hand. . . .

To the same.

St. Anne's Hill, *June* 30, 1848.

. . . Cavaignac is thought honest and a thorough Republican, but of his abilities, except as a military man, no one speaks. He is a friend of Thiers. Lamartine sided decidedly with the party of order, and, at the session of the National Assembly during the fighting, took his place between Thiers and Berryer. One has heard nothing yet of the promoters of the plot. On Wednesday, after I wrote, we saw young Delessert. He seemed *accablé:* one of his intimate friends, young de Rémusat, was dangerously wounded, and as there is no list published of the names of the numerous National Guards and officers who have been killed, they felt (all the French people in town) that any of their friends might have fallen. Madame Delessert arrived at Paris in the midst of all

the fighting. They had not heard from her, since a hurried note
on her arrival, and had had no private letters for two days.
On Saturday there had been a report that the Duc de Mouchy
had been killed.

I hope poor Sabine did not hear it. Her three brothers, it
is said, fought like lions. What a people of nerves they are!
But all that heroism without principle or sense only makes
their prospects worse.

What a scene the Archbishop's mission and his fall must
have been! The conduct of the insurgents does them honour,
I think, in that instance. In fact, in the midst of the atrocities
(and one cannot wonder at them when one thinks that
thousands of *forçats libérés*, the refuse of the Bagne, were com-
bating on that side), there does not seem to have been a
generally bad spirit among the insurgents, and it must be
confessed that the workmen had been cruelly deluded.

One almost wishes Louis Blanc had been killed in the
mêlée. I fear we shall soon hear of a similar conflict at Vienna,
where they are feeding thousands of workmen, a state of things
that cannot last much longer. We ought to live on our knees
at being thus spared.

I think sometimes of the prophecy, do you remember—after
the fall of the Orleans King : *Deux partis se feront une guerre*
à mort en France. Le sang coulera par torrents dans les
principales villes—après s'être entre-déchirés longtemps, le plus
faible (will that be the workmen) *aura le dessus pour un*
moment, et ce moment sera si horrible qu'on se croira à la fin
du monde, &c. . . . Certainly one has seen enough to be sure
that if the insurgent party gets the upper hand, the *République*
Rouge, as they call it, the horrors will be something appalling,
and it is curious too that a regular plan had been formed to
burn Paris to the ground, another of the facts foretold. I fear
it yet may happen. It is a fearful tragedy to witness, and the
interest deepens every day.

A letter written by the Duc de Broglie to M.
Guizot, has by some chance been mingled with this
correspondence. It seems worth insertion here, as
a conclusion to the subject.

Paris, *July*, 1848.

We are plunged in a dull stupor. Believe all we say and write—if you are told that Paris is perfectly quiet, that order is completely re-established, believe it. If, on the contrary, you are told that to-morrow all is fire and blood, believe that also.

Nothing appears more impossible than the return of the Monarchy, if it is not the establishment of the Republic, and nothing is less possible than the establishment of the Republic, if it is not the return of the Monarchy.

If there is not war, perhaps we shall have a Directory without going through '93. But with war will come massacres.

As there has been occasional mention of the Irish question in these letters, we may as well mention an incident which elicited from Lady Georgiana an expression of opinion on the subject which it may be well to record. Three years before the Revolution of 1848, Mr. Charles Greville published a volume on the *Past and Present Policy of England towards Ireland,* which attracted much attention and was very useful. It took a high place among the many works on the subject. Before it was published he sent the proofs to Lady Georgiana, with a letter showing all the simplicity and goodness of his character.

Mr. Charles Greville to Lady Georgiana Fullerton.

G. Place, *Sunday.*

I send you this thing, such as it is—you will see that its pretensions are exceedingly humble, being rather *extracts from the works of others* than my own composition. My object is to make out a case, and to call witnesses in support of it. It wants some correction, though I have erased most of the clerical errors (my scribe being no great scholar). The short introductory part is quite incomplete. I mean to do what

Clarendon suggests, but I am very doubtful if I shall even finish it so as to satisfy myself. Tell me pray (I am sure you will treat me as candidly as I did you) anything wrong or deficient that strikes you, and tell me truly if it really does answer your purpose at all, that I have in view.

Ever affectionately yours,
C. G.

Lady Georgiana replied as follows:

To Mr. Charles Greville.

I send you back with many thanks this admirable sketch. I have read it twice with intense interest, and the case seems to me made out unusually and most ably. How glad I am not to be Irish! I should hate England too much. How curious that opinion of Archbishop Usher's is of an original religious persecution carried on, on opposite grounds, for centuries before the Reformation. Have you seen Dr. Rock's pamphlet on the subject?

What an historian you would be! Your style so clever and forcible, and your judgment so acute and so dispassionate. Indeed, what I regret in this sketch is that it is only a sketch.

You hurry over the ground too fast, and though indications are enough for your purpose as *argument*, yet the *effect* would be greater, I think, if they were more developed.

I think you are unjust to Charles I. when you say that "he was only consistent in his *intention* to deceive all parties, and keep faith with none." Surely, if he did deceive them, it was out of weakness of character, and not from deliberate bad intentions.

In the passage about "fostering," it seemed to me that the quotation did not illustrate the peculiar Irish sentiment on the subject sufficiently. I know I turned over the page expecting something more.

I cannot tell you how it has interested me. It brings the whole course of that terrible history so rapidly and so vividly before one, and I cannot imagine how any one could withstand the propositions you wish to establish, in the face of that overwhelming evidence collected from such various sources.

P

Again I thank you for letting me see it. I shall long for the rest.

Believe me,

Ever affectionately yours,

G. FULLERTON.

Monday evening.

Mr. Greville's book did not, perhaps, attract at the time all the attention which it deserved, and the Irish question of that day was an entirely different one from that which is now before the public, as the book shows, which is largely occupied with the question of the establishment of the Catholic Church in that country. But its pages show us thus much, that their author was much in advance of other men of the day in the clearness and justness of his views.

CHAPTER XI.

THE letters with which the last chapter has been filled do not belong directly to Lady Georgiana's own history. But the vivid and interesting picture which is traced in them of a memorable page of the contemporary history of France will abundantly justify their insertion. More than that. No one can read them without understanding better her mind, her character, and her heart. No doubt, in course of time, some of the opinions which she then held may have been modified. She might have read over again at a later time, not without much surprise, some verses that she wrote on the Italian Revolution, but she never laid aside that generosity of impulse which led her so readily to take the side of those who seemed to her to be oppressed. She was always the same as to her readiness to waive all personal considerations and predilections of class in favour of those who seemed less kindly treated by fortune. Still less did she change that rare disposition which she here shows, which made her detest even the very shadow of boastfulness, and, in the moment of national triumph, made her desire to substitute the word "thankfulness," for that of "pride," and wish that, instead of pluming themselves on the success they had gained, her countrymen would "live upon their knees," thank‑ ing God for having spared them. We see herself in all this—herself, such as she was by nature, and such as she became more and more perfectly, in proportion as she advanced higher and higher in character and in soul.

We no not find any further letters on the affairs of France after the days of June. It is not that she ceased to take a deep interest in them, but the letters put before the reader in the last chapter are almost exclusively addressed to her mother, from whom she was at the time separated. When they again were together the correspondence naturally ceased.

As has been said, Lady Granville had with‑ drawn altogether from society since she had become a widow. She rented Fernhill, a house near Windsor, she stayed at Rushmore with her daughter and son‑ in‑law, Lord Rivers, or with her brother, the Duke of Devonshire, at Chiswick, or with her son, Lord Granville, at Stud House, a residence attached to the office he then held as Master of the Buck‑ hounds. There she spent her time, and there she was glad to find herself surrounded by her children and grandchildren. But no one was admitted to her family circle, not even her oldest and most intimate friends. Her retirement only drew more close the bond between her and her daughters, and especially Georgiana, with whom she had the most perfect sympathy, excepting only on the one greatest subject. Lady Georgiana's change of religion had produced no alteration in her perfect intimacy with her mother. It was perhaps hardly the same as to her relations with her sister. Their tender love one for the other did not in the least degree cease, but it was long before they got over the kind of *gêne* which ensues on the necessity of avoiding an important subject which was always present to the thoughts. Lady Rivers, surrounded by a number of children of all ages, was naturally desirous that there should be no conversation on religious subjects which might cast a doubt into their minds. Lady Georgiana conformed scrupulously to her sister's wish. Notwithstanding this reserve, all her nieces, the eldest of whom was then fourteen, and the youngest hardly three, loved their " Aunt Dody " most tenderly, and counted as happy days those which she was able to spend in the midst of them at Rushmore. The eldest of these nieces, who was always particularly dear to her,[1] has preserved some notes of this time from which we may make a few extracts.

I remember Aunt Dody ever since I was quite a little child. My earliest recollections are of her occasional visits to Rushmore, and the intimacy between her and my mother, the long *tête à tête* conversations they used to have. At that time, when we were quite small, her boy used to be more my eldest brother's companion than mine, as was natural. Their great point in common was a great love of playing with soldiers, and I came across only the other day, in looking over some old correspondence, some curious, badly written letters from Granville Fullerton to George, describing some new arrange-

[1] The Hon. Susan Pitt, now Mrs. Oldfield.

ments of "battalions" which he had decided upon ! One of
these letters is written from Midgham, one of the places which
the Fullertons hired for a time, but I cannot identify the date.

Granville Fullerton's other intimate boy companion was the
present Lord Acton, and I remember a visit to the Colosseum
with these two, which was a great enjoyment to us all. In
January, 1846, my grandfather (Lord Granville) died, and my
grandmother seems to have gone almost at once to Walton, for
I have found a letter from thence from my mother to my
brother George written during that month, in which she mentions Granville Fullerton as not at all well, and obliged to lie
down a great deal, and deprived of many amusements in consequence. She adds that he is very contented and finds plenty
of occupation, and that he is fond of reading. In the course of
the same year, my grandmother hired a house at Fernhill, near
Windsor, where my sister Fanny and I were with her with our
governess, and I remember the Fullertons being there a good
deal as well as at the Stud House, a house my uncle had as
Master of the Buckhounds, and which he lent to my grandmother in 1847.

I think it was at Fernhill that I remember my mother telling
us of my aunt's change of religion, and I also recollect that she
and my uncle went constantly to their chapel together at that
time, but generally slipped out without saying where they were
going, so that evidently, as was natural, a good deal of reserve
crept in between my aunt and her family at that time on the
subject of religion. I know that my mother tried very hard to
dissuade my aunt from being a Roman Catholic, and induced
her to correspond with an Archdeacon Lyall, who was a friend
of my mother's, with a hope that he might strengthen her in the
faith of the Church of England, but I fancy that, after the final
step was taken, the subject of the difference of religion was
scarcely ever mentioned between them.

My grandmother was very much interested in charitable
works, and besides visiting the poor, was also always working
for them in her own fashion, painting little pincushions, book-
markers, &c., some containing riddles or scraps of poetry, and
setting up old apple-women with things of this kind to sell, and
my aunt sympathized very much in all this. They also had the

great link of a love of reading and intellectual pursuits, and they were evidently a great deal together. In 1848 my grandmother writes to my brother from St. Anne's Hill, where she must have been staying with the Fullertons, and mentions an excursion to see some poor people at Midgham, with whom she and my aunt must evidently have made acquaintance during the time the Fullertons had that place. In April, 1850, my grandmother writes from Richmond, and makes some mention of my aunt, who, I suppose, was there also. You will see that my memories of my aunt, even helped by letters, are very vague during the time of my childhood, as children in the school-room do not see much of their elders.

Mr. Fullerton and Lady Georgiana passed the last months of the year 1848 at St. Anne's Hill, which they rented from Lord and Lady Holland, who were then in Italy. This beautiful place, the *beau idéal* of an English country house, is now the habitual residence of Lady Holland, and wears that inexpressible and inimitable charm which Lady Holland has always and everywhere been known to give to her place of residence, whether it has been at Genoa, or at Naples, at Florence, or at Paris, at Holland House, or at St. Anne's Hill. These places differ from each other in every respect, but not in the air and the charm which they have caught from their mistress. St. Anne's Hill was a pleasant retreat for Lady Georgiana after so much excitement from various causes. She spent there several weeks with her mother, who soon joined her, and in whose company she used to visit the poor of the neighbourhood. At that time, she did all the good that came to her hands, as it came. But the time was to come when her good works were to become so multiplied that she was obliged to make some regular system for her means and times of beneficence. It was a delight to her to help her mother, and be helped by her in turn, in all that they could do together. This time was perhaps the happiest of her life. Her soul was at peace, and she advanced with joy in the new paths which had opened themselves before her. This happiness she enjoyed without any alteration in her tender relations with her mother, and her son, meantime, was growing older and fulfilling more and more the happy promise of his childhood. We shall use the words of others to describe the tenderness which now filled his mother's heart, before the time came for it to be torn with anguish on his account.

> Your dear child becomes every day more dear to me [writes Lady Granville to her]. He is full of gaiety, without being boisterous, his manner to me and to all is charming, every one loves and speaks of his goodness and amiability.

The young Granville Fullerton was particularly happy with the numerous family of his cousins, children of Lady Rivers. Like all only children, he was timid and reserved, but he was also very affectionate, intelligent, gay, and communicative when at his ease. His first great friend was his cousin, the young George Pitt, but he soon was quite as much attached to his sisters. Lady Georgiana took great pleasure in gathering round her her sister's children, the two oldest of whom, Fanny and Susan Pitt, were special favourites. We again borrow from Mrs. Oldfield's recollections.

It was as we first grew up that we were constantly with my aunt and cousin. We saw a great deal of them in London, and my sister Fanny and I used to spend weeks with them in the country, for my aunt was so glad to have young companions for Granville, so that his home might be as happy as possible, for it was a great object to keep him at home, on account of his health, which was a constant source of anxiety to my aunt. It was at that time that she used to read aloud a good deal to us. The last book I recollect her reading in this way during his lifetime was Macaulay's *Lays*, which he and she were both fond of. He did not care much for general society, and professed to dislike young ladies. His mother used to ask him sometimes why, if this was the case, he was so fond of Fanny and me, but I think he never considered us in the light of "young ladies." He was a very pleasant companion, very amusing in conversation, and had nice intellectual tastes, and though his health debarred him from the ordinary occupations of young men, he was not in the least effeminate, and yet, on the other hand, he was also bright and cheerful.[1] He had set his heart upon going into the army, and his parents at last yielded to his wish on this matter. I recollect his reading for it one summer while he was with us at Rushmore, for it was in fine hot weather, and he used to come and sit with me while I sketched, bringing his books with him, and expecting me occasionally to examine him on what he had read. He passed his examination creditably, I believe, and when once in the army had to be a good deal in London. Then he went out a little in society, but I think that was a constant anxiety to my poor aunt. He made friends then with young men of his own age, many of whom he introduced to us, and they were a nice set, I think. Those among them whom we knew best were Count Wimpffen, who died so sadly a year or two ago, and Major Fitzroy, who is still a friend of mine.

[1] Granville Fullerton was for a year or two at Oscott before entering the army, and while at that College was a great friend of Edward Howard, afterwards the Cardinal. One who was at Oscott at the time remembers him as an attractive and pleasing lad, and remarkable for quickness and fluency in conversation.

Both Lady Georgiana and her sister knew well what it was to have a mother's heart, and it was through this that Providence destined each of them to the most intense suffering. Thus it is that God prepares the hearts whom He intends for the most cruel sacrifices as well as the highest rewards hereafter. The prophecy of the sword piercing the heart was to extend to many mothers as well as to the most holy of all.

In 1854 my youngest sister was born, and while my mother was shut up, my aunt took Fanny and me out a little. Balls were to her a long-forgotten experience, but I think she really enjoyed them with that childlike freshness which was such a characteristic of her nature, and that it amused her to see the dancing and to watch the people, and to be shown the special beauties of the day. She had very definite opinions as to which she admired most. We used to consider her on the whole rather silent and pre-occupied in society, except when any subject particularly interested her, when she would warm up and grow eager. On certain political subjects she would often talk with animation. But she was apparently a little inconsistent in her opinions, especially on foreign politics, which arose, I think, from a natural sympathy for the people in their struggles after freedom, which, if she had been a Protestant, would have made her even a little revolutionary, and yet a feeling of great loyalty to the Pope, so that there were, as it were, two influences pulling her different ways.

From 1858 till her death in 1862, my grandmother resided at Chiswick, which the Duke of Devonshire left her for her life. I, especially, spent much of my time there, and it was there, I think, that I began most thoroughly to enjoy talking over books with my aunt, who seemed to take great pains to develope my intellectual life, for which Chiswick with its beautiful pictures and delightful library gave full scope. My aunt used to encourage me in writing verses, and even persuaded me to attempt a novel, assuring me that it was quite easy, though, when I did try it to please her, she was not able to pronounce it a success ! I used to enjoy hearing her tell, as she did then, of her own authorship, how it began, &c., though she was very humble on the subject, and always said it only required perseverance. She astonished me by saying that writing was never a pleasure to her, and that she never thought about it till she actually sat down to write, and she did it as a task because she liked to get the money for her charities.

What is here said confirms the assertion already made about the motive which had first induced Lady Georgiana to enter on her career as writer. It is interesting to find it appearing again when she had already for many years enjoyed a success which might certainly have tempted her to listen to the suggestions of pride as well as to those of charity. It was to avoid this temptation that, after she became a Catholic, she had felt disposed to lay down her pen for ever. But she had not only discovered the real power which she possessed. The discovery revealed to her at the same time that she had a duty to perform by means of her talent, which might take its place by the side of charity towards the poor. She reflected on this, as she well knew how to reflect, without any sparing of herself. Her desire was to do good, and to do the most good possible. This was her only motive, and at the same time she humbly sought advice and knew how to follow it. The result was that she continued her work with perseverance. We may gather what was her motive in this, and what her thoughts concerning it from those which she has put into the mouth of an imaginary person, which seem to have been her own thoughts faithfully described.

The charities of this place, the hospital, the schools, the ladies' association for visiting hospitals and the poor, have been the recreations rather than the labours of my life. It is at that desk I have toiled. This may seem strange : but composition even in its lightest form is labour, and especially so when, under a light garb, it has an important object in view ; when imagination has to be exercised, and at the same time kept in check ; when the effort to persuade is accompanied by the fear of repelling, and an invisible hand seems to control the pen, which we feel to be God's instrument, not the mere servant of our own fancy.

Yes, I have worked here in sight of that crucifix. This little room has been my cell, my spiritual home. I have found here that happiness which the world cannot give. God has so far blessed my efforts that my books are read all over France, and have, I hope, done some good in their way. I have had the unspeakable joy of hearing that they have sometimes been the means of awaking or reviving faith, of kindling holy desires, and strengthening souls under trial.[3]

It would not be well to conclude from all this that Lady Georgiana took no pleasure in writing. A gift like hers is not possessed in vain. It involves a joy in its exercise, a joy impossible to control. But it is just this joy which she was ready to sacrifice if a higher motive had not made her continue her literary work without relaxation, as she continued also that other more difficult work, which was silently proceeding in her own soul.

Of this latter work, we shall, of course, find few traces in her letters. She never wrote to others for the sake of speaking of herself. We can guess of it only by its result, that is, by that increasing perfection which those who approached her the most nearly saw in her without her being able to conceal

[3] *Seven Stories.*

it. We have been allowed to read some pages which may be called the journal of her interior life, or rather of her daily examination of conscience. Some fragments of this have enabled us to see at what a cost it is that the summit of that holy mountain of perfection is reached—a mountain which we are all called to scale, though the height to which it is given to each of us to attain must be different. This journal begins by some rules which it would be useful for every one to meditate on, because it shows the secret of multiplying the amount of time at the disposal in the hands of those who know how to employ it, while in the hands of the idle it flies, being filled up, and leaves nothing behind it but weariness. But we must be sparing in our use of these private papers.

The following note belongs to this time. It was addressed to Lady Georgiana while staying at Aldenham with her brother and sister-in-law.

(Dowager) Lady Granville to Lady Georgiana.

Sunday.

A thousand thanks for your letter, my dearest child. It has more than satisfied me. It gives me happiness for the present and for the future. The life you lead at Aldenham ought to suit you perfectly. The readings with Marie, the rural dissipations which are just the ones you like, the quiet, with movement round you, and, I hope a new novel in progress, for the happiness and good of others, will soon be produced.

I hope that your stay will last as long as possible. Sukey will be with me. Do not trouble your thoughts about me—put aside the tender thoughts which would make you always think of me with too much anxiety. May God bless you ever.

A word must be said about the external circum-

stances of Lady Georgiana's life during the year
1849. While living temporarily at St. Anne's Hill,
Mr. Fullerton and Lady Georgiana were looking out
for a permanent home in the country, their intention
was to buy a property. This, however, was never
realized. They inhabited several houses as a trial.
The first of these was Midgham, in Berkshire. Here
they took up their abode in July, 1850.

Before leaving London for Midgham, Lady Georgiana had prepared herself for this new phase of
her life by a retreat, which was, it appears, the first
that she made. The director was Father Faber, her
confessor at that time, and the Superior of the
London Oratory. The notes which she made in
this retreat show an increase of severity with herself
as well as of piety.

It was about this time that Pauline Marie Jaricot,
the humble and illustrious foundress of the work
of the Propagation of the Faith, sent one of her
assistants into England, and to interest the Catholics
of this country in another work which was the fruit
of her zeal for the benefit, both material and moral,
of the working classes. Mr. Fullerton and Lady
Georgiana took a lively interest in the mission,
and also in the great work from which it was an
offshoot. Mr. Fullerton accepted then, and has
discharged ever since, the post of Treasurer of
the Propagation of the Faith, and Lady Georgiana
hastened to correspond to the appeal of Mdlle.
Jaricot's friend, by a letter inserted by the former
in a work published by her a short time afterwards.
She speaks of her meeting with Lady Georgiana at

the Convent of Mercy in London, and receiving from
her there a considerable alms, and then adds, that
a few days later, at a moment when she was in
extreme distress about sending to her holy friend in
France a sum of money of which she had great
need, she received, about ten o'clock at night, a very
heavy letter from Lady Georgiana containing the
following :

> *To a lady, sent by Mdlle. Jaricot.*
> [*Written in French.*]

MADEMOISELLE,—How much I admire the zeal which leads
to these results ! It is under these kind of circumstances that
one could wish to be rich. Unhappily, I am not. But it is with
much pleasure that I put these few gold pieces into the *Sac de
Marie.* I wish I could make a greater offering. It is such a
happiness to support such good works for the glory of God,
and also for the consolation of so dear and venerated a woman.

I admire the thought which inspired the holy foundress of
the Propagation of the Faith, and her plans for helping the
working classes. I wish I could help to keep up the work *not
as I am able, but as I could wish to do,* so that it may succeed.
I send you something from my husband, and if later I can help
you more, I shall do so with pleasure.

Pray accept the expression of my feelings, &c.

GEORGIANA FULLERTON.

CHAPTER XII.

LADY GEORGIANA soon found much to like at Midgham. She lost no time in considering whether it
was to be her permanent home. She set to work at
once. She had opened a poor school before many
days had passed, for the benefit of the poor Catholics
in the neighbourhood. This was the first of a
number of such schools to which she afterwards
gave so much of her time and affection. At the
same time she began her ordinary literary work, as
it had now become. She used to say that with a
book to write and a school to visit she had all the
pleasure she could wish for in this world. It was
the first time she had tried both at once. *Ladybird*
was the novel on which she was engaged. Her
promptitude was the secret of the great amount of
work which she accomplished. *Procrastination is the
thief of time*, is a favourite proverb in England, and
Lady Georgiana's example may well be quoted as an
illustration of the truth which it expresses for the
benefit of the indolent. She certainly never let
herself be robbed of a moment of time.

This year, 1850, was marked by a popular movement in the religious world hostile to the Catholics.

It was violent and it was short. Many persons would tell us that it was the last of English explosions in the "No Popery" sense—a fire which flamed up for an instant, never to be revived. In our own days, a Minister of the Crown has gone so far as to affirm that he did not think there is to be found an Englishman, who did not desire to efface the last remembrance of the measures formerly in vigour against the Catholics, and this Minister belonged to the party formerly most intolerant towards them. The agitation of 1850 arose, as is well known, from the establishment of the Catholic Hierarchy by Pius IX. The terms in which this step was announced to the English Catholics by Cardinal Wiseman, are thought by some to have had much part in the irritation of the public mind, while others find the cause of that irritation in the manœuvre of the Prime Minister, who adroitly used the events of the moment for party purposes in his letter to the Bishop of Durham. For a time the result was an agitation, baseless and unreasonable indeed, but not the less overwhelming. Articles in the papers, speeches in Parliament, cries in the streets, placards on the walls, petitions to the Queen for protection against "Papal Aggression,"—all were inflammatory in the highest degree, and the country seemed for some weeks to have gone back fifty years. In the midst of the storm, and the very day before the great petition was to be presented at Windsor, Charles Greville again showed his common sense and ability by writing to the *Times* a letter signed "Carolus," in which he pointed out the folly of the

Q

movement, and predicted that it would not last. He was particularly happy in characterizing the uselessness of this deputation, which was to go on the morrow to " complain of an imaginary grievance and to demand an impossible reparation."

These predictions were speedily verified, but the tumult did not calm down all at once. Lord John Russell had thrown oil on the fire in his letter to the Bishop mentioned above, in which he spoke of Catholicism as fettering the intelligence and enslaving the soul, and describing the act of the Pope as insolent and insidious. Parliament met, and a Bill was proposed making it penal for the Bishops to assume the titles granted by the Pope, and for others to give them those titles. Whilst the Bill was being discussed, the minds of men began to calm down. By the time it was passed, they had already become quite cool. The steps required before any application of the Bill, were never taken, and it was soon regarded as a dead letter. Thus, before it was used, it fell into disuse. The Catholic Bishops took the titles that were given them, and no one ever thought of denying their right to use them, much less of demanding the exaction of the penalties· which had been so violently insisted on at the time. As soon as this senseless panic had passed, the good sense of the English public resumed its sway. It was seen that no one was hurt, the effects of the Pope's action affected none but the Catholics, and that he had even considered the susceptibilities of the Anglicans, as well as the letter of the law, by not giving to the Catholic prelates the titles formerly borne by their predecessors, of sees now occupied by the Anglican Bishops, but titles entirely new, which no one had borne before them.

Towards the end of the crisis, Lady Georgiana wrote to her younger brother, who was then absent from England.

To the Hon. F. Leveson Gower.

London, *November* 18, 1850.

DEAREST FREDDY,—Your letters from Gibraltar and Malta have made us very happy, and we long for news from Egypt. Mamma's delight at your prosperous account of yourself and of your voyage was extreme, she takes an interest in your travels, and the first letters seem to bring one together, and associate one every step you take. We have scarcely had any winter yet, but soon it will be difficult not to think with envy of the sunny skies you will be basking under. I think mamma remarkably well, she has so entirely recovered her strength and not yet lost her prudence, so I trust she will keep so. We have had such a pleasant time here with her. On Wednesday we go to Danesfield for a few days, and return to remain here till the 3rd of December, when she goes to Bournemouth, and not to Midgham. We have had a private hint that Woodhampton House and estate will soon be sold. Though I should not like it near as much as Midgham House, still we might *coquet* about it, and frighten Mr. F—— into making up his mind at a fair price.

Granville has been very well indeed lately. Such a difference with last year at this time. He is as happy as ever with Mr. Simpson, but looking forward to coming home on the 20th of December. He is coming to town for the day to-morrow, and I am thinking of going with him the "Overland Journey,"[1] if he (which I am sure he will) likes to see it a second time.

I wish you, the great champion of civil and religious liberty, had been here this winter to fight our battles. I flatter myself that you will have been disgusted at Lord John Russell's letter, as I was delighted to hear that Lord Clarendon had been. He

[1] Mr. Albert Smith's popular Exhibition is perhaps not generally remembered in our time.

wrote to him in great indignation, and told him that he had made Ireland almost ungovernable, and I am sure Carlisle and many others are deeply annoyed at it. Cardinal Wiseman is about to publish an appeal to the good sense of the people of England. It is not come out yet, but its motto is an extract from a speech of Lord John's in 1845, in which he says, that he cannot conceive why the law should not be repealed which prevents the Catholic Bishops from bearing the same titles as the Protestant ones. If that was his opinion when in Opposition, how could the Pope suppose that he would consider it as "insolent and insidious" to do something of the same kind, but in strict accordance with the existing law?

. . . We have been all reading an exciting Chartist novel called *Alton Locke* by Mr. Kingsley, which makes one *very* democratic, and, a powerful, disagreeable, unnatural, interesting, American one called *The Scarlet Letter*. But your letters are what we look to as the greatest treats. G. Stewart is very much excited on the "No Popery" question, though in an amiable way, but longs, I believe, to blow up St. George's and transport the Cardinal. . . .

We may here cite the following letter addressed to Lady Georgiana, by Father Faber of the London Oratory, well known by his writings in France as well as England. She had been slightly ill when he thus wrote.

Father Faber to Lady G. Fullerton.

The Oratory, London,
February 16, 1851.

MY DEAR LADY GEORGIANA,—I grieved to hear from Mr. Fullerton how very unwell you had been, and I was half afraid you might have been naughty enough to have made matters worse by a little spiritual obstinacy—sticking to your observances when you clearly ought not to do so. I should be so glad to have a few lines to say how you are, and meanwhile I have put you especially into my Memento at Mass. You must not fidget during your convalescence because you cannot keep your rule, or are not strong enough to keep your mind on God as intensely as you would wish.

Devotion is to do what God wills, and if He chooses you should suffer instead of act, you must acquiesce in it ; and, if you find how much you leaned on rule and practices, you can learn humility out of that very discovery. Suffering and glory are the two most unmistakeable wills of God, and what suffering is on earth, glory is in Heaven, and so suffering, you see, is earth's kind of beatitude. See ! how I speak to you, I who cannot bear a headache with half the patience of a beaten ass.

Believe me, my dear Lady Georgiana,

Your very devoted,

F. FABER.

Another ·letter of nearly the same date is addressed to her brother on his travels in Egypt.

To the Hon. F. Leveson Gower.

99, Westbourne Terrace,

March 5, 1851.

DEAREST FREDDY,—Mamma received, the day before yesterday, at the same time, your letters from Ghiza and from Patnar (I dare say I spell them wrong), and it was great satisfaction to find from the second that you had got over the ailings you spoke of in the first. The frequency of medical opportunities gave us great pleasure too, and your accounts, though brief, of the country, scenery, people, made us long for the detailed ones you must give us when you come back. How did the Thug look? It must have been dreadfully curious to see such a man. Now for a home journal for you. Mamma is very well. She has had a cold, but has nearly got rid of it, and in all ways I think she is well, and able to bear things which formerly would have been great trials. We have very good accounts from Rushmore. Susan is well and pleased to see Rivers restored much to his usual state and able to occupy and interest himself about his farm as much as ever. Granville, for whom they had much feared the loss of the companionship and cheerful example of his dear brother,[1] has not apparently felt it

[1] George, the eldest son of Lord and Lady Rivers had lately died. Granville, the second, was born in 1858. William, the third, was born in

as much as they expected. I suppose the great interest shown him and the affections that are now centred upon him have been great consolations. He and Willy, if they are not better, which some think, are decidedly not losing ground, and Henry is most satisfactory. George Stewart has been staying there a month, and on Monday next escorts to London the two eldest Miss Pitts, who are coming to stay with mamma till the 14th of April, when she takes them back to Rushmore. For a wonder I have been very ill! Influenza, intermittent fever, and other little sufferings, but now I am nearly well, only *thin* (a good thing) and weak (a bad one). On Monday we are going to St. Leonards for, I suppppose, a fortnight. Then back to town for a week, and then to my dear Midgham, which I like better than ever. Granville is growing very fast, and strong at the same time. He is very well, thank God, and getting on as well as ever with Mr. Simpson. Everybody thinks him so improved in looks and manners, which gratifies me much. I was pleased at your remarks on Lord John, and amused at your thinking that by this time the Pope and his Bishops were out of men's minds, whereas people talk of nothing else, and the Papal Aggression has been the stumbling-block of all combinations during the crisis, and will yet, I fondly hope, turn the Whigs out. You can fancy that we must feel indignant with the conduct of such *soi disant* Liberals, and I cannot but think they must be ashamed of themselves when the Peelites on the one hand, and the Radicals on the other, take what *ought* to have been their line, and even the Protectionists accuse them of intemperate haste. We hear that the excitement in Ireland is as great, if not greater, than before Catholic Emancipation, and some people say this Bill *can't* pass. Sir James Graham says it will not, but Leveson thinks it will. On the other hand, if it does not, a dissolution will ensue at a most untoward moment, and against the wishes of all parties, except, I believe, the Protectionists. It vexes me to see Leveson and Carlisle supporting a Government which brings forward a measure so

1845, and Henry, the youngest, in 1849. He was the only one of the four who survived his parents, and that only by a year. The "Granville" mentioned presently in this letter as "growing fast" is Lady Georgiana's own son.

entirely opposed to their views and feelings. You say we Catholics are not *liberal* ourselves. We *cannot* be *latitudinarians* without renouncing our faith, and I can quite allow for men like Lord Winchelsea or Mr. Spooner, who on *their* side hold exclusive opinions; but it is to see men who *pretend* to be liberal, act as the Whigs are doing, that makes one indignant, and we might as well appeal to Parliament to protect us against the speeches at Exeter Hall, as for the Legislature to enact penal laws because Cardinal Wiseman and Father Newman hold what to them appears intolerant language. The utter prostration of the Protectionist party must have given you satisfaction, and I could not help being glad (though it might have been better for us if they had) that Lord Canning and Mr. Gladstone would not join Lord Stanley. There have been jokes about us in all times of crisis. It is said the Duke of Wellington gave the word of command to the Russell Ministry in the military phrase, "As you were!" but could not add the next, "Stand at ease!"

Good-bye, dearest Freddy. Mamma sends her best love, and does not write, as I do. Excuse this stupid letter in a *convalescente*. The Duchess of Sutherland is at Paris, where she and Constance are both much admired.

In the course of the same year, 1851, Mr. Fullerton and Lady Georgiana went to Paris for the first time since leaving it in 1841. Their first impressions were naturally sad, as everything around them awakened memories of the past. But Lady Georgiana soon found an abundance of reasons for liking what she saw, and it was then that she began to have that tender affection for France which she always preserved.

The travellers left Paris at the beginning of November for Pau, passing by Blois, whence she writes again.

To the Hon. F. Leveson Gower.

Blois, *November* 6, 1851.

MY DEAR FREDDY,—As I have a spare hour this morning, I will employ it in writing to you, and thanking you for your two kind letters, which I received at Paris. You see that we have not yet advanced much on our way. We left Paris at one, Monday, and arrived at Orleans at five. After dinner I went to the Convent of the *Sacré Cœur* to see Madame Henri de Castellane. She is looking very well, grown fat, and seems very happy. She has a small apartment that communicates with her daughter's room, who is at school in the convent, and her little boy is also at school near Orleans. Her brother the Duc de Dino's two girls and two boys are there too, and I saw him with her at the hotel. I suppose he is separated from his wife. I rather liked what I saw of him. As there was to be a magnificent service and procession on Tuesday afternoon at the Cathedral, we determined to stay for it. It was well worth seeing, but it lasted very long, and the weather was intensely cold. Fullerton, who had had a cold for some days, got very much chilled, and was very unwell in the evening.

. . . I am enchanted with this place. The Loire is so beautiful. The old château, and the view from its highest galleries, is striking. The streets and churches so picturesque. It was a bright moonlight last night, and the beauty of the river and bridge was very great. This morning, Granville, Charles Cavendish, and Mr. Wiles, went to Tours by an early train in order to have the whole day for sight-seeing, and Fullerton and I are to follow at two. Granville is wonderfully well, and enjoys himself immensely.

We are here under martial law, I believe, but there is nothing to make it apparent, and the people look animated and busy, and happy, as they seem to do everywhere in France, in spite of all present and threatening evils. The guide at the Château de Blois seemed to regret L. Philippe, and to execrate the Republic, but that was natural, considering all that the former had done, and the latter has left undone, in the restoration of its beautiful apartments.

Will you tell Marie that I paid a visit to the Bishop of

Orleans, who asked most kindly after her, and begged me to give her his best remembrances.

I evaded being given a letter to the possessors of the Château de Chaumont, where we should have found ourselves in the midst of a Legitimist literary society. . . . *Grantley Manor* is much read, I am told, in all the *cafés* and *Cabinets de Lecture.* I came across one number of it at Orleans, Margaret's proposing to old Walter, and I thought it very well translated. Much better, I thought, than *Ellen M.* was.

Mr. Fullerton and Lady Georgiana stayed at Pau some weeks, passing on from thence to Eaux Bonnes and Cauterets. They travelled slowly, enjoying the fine weather, and often stopping where there were celebrated shrines to visit, or fine scenery to enjoy. They spent some days at Marseilles, after having stopped at Toulouse and Montpellier, making their way towards Rome, where they were to pass the winter.

Lady Georgiana now found herself under the sky of the south after a lapse of six years, during which time much had changed around her and in herself. She could now measure these changes by the differences which she felt under the influence of the enchantment of the scenery and natural beauties of the climate, which she had before looked on with cold admiration, not far removed from indifference. Then she had said that she would rather see a single hawthorn bush in bloom than all the fruits and flowers of the south ; and that she preferred the tossing seas of the north to the calm and tideless Mediterranean. See held a different language now, for she saw all with new eyes. She had, as it were, gained a new sense, and she found charms where she had before perceived none. It was still a country which she loved, but the country and home of her soul. Those who have been born in the bosom of the Church are so accustomed to the singular blessings with which she surrounds every moment and step of our lives, that they do not understand what those persons feel who come to the possession of her treasures, not gradually, as those who inherit them from their childhood, but of a sudden, when mature age and personal experience, and above all, trials, have taught them to value them at their true price—often indeed have won for them the grace to appreciate them more than others and to enjoy them more worthily.

As she was leaving France to enter Italy, she writes thus:

To-day I have seen the Mediterranean again. I love its blue, which never seemed to me so deep, the sky so pure, and the sun so brilliant.

I cannot express my feelings at seeing again this southern vegetation. The beauty of sky and earth moves me irresistibly, and I feel full of gratitude as all these things pass before my eyes, and impress themselves on my memory.

It was in the Pyrenees that they heard the news of the *Coup d'Etat* of December 2, 1851. It made little noise in those peaceful regions, where indeed the shock of the Revolution of February was hardly felt. We may learn what Lady Georgiana thought of it from her letters in the course of the following year to her younger brother, with whom, then and always, she kept up an active correspondence. Both her brothers were equally dear to her, but the younger, although in Parliament, had more time to spare than Lord Granville, who, from that time, was deeply engaged in public life, and held an important place in the Ministry whenever his party was in power.

A few of her letters, scattered over this period, remain to show her interest in public affairs.

To the Hon. F. Leveson Gower.

Paris, Hôtel Bristol, *Oct.* 27, 1851.

DEAREST FREDDY,—I feel as if I ought to have written to you sooner, and it sounds ridiculous to say I have not had time, but I really believe it is true. I must confess that I think Paris *delightful*, and that I am afraid that if it was not for her [her mother] whom I can *never* live happily away from for more than a short time, I should have fears of thinking it too pleasant to be abroad. Everything has hitherto prospered with us. Fullerton is in excellent spirits. Granville wonderfully well, our doctor pleasing, satisfactory, and singularly unobtrusive. The first days I was here, I was haunted by associations that I could not shake off, that followed me wherever I went and were at first *only* painful and intensely so. Now I find something not altogether painful even in that, and the emotion which the sights and sounds that bring the past before me occasion, I would *not* feel if I could. I feel that I *love* Paris, as well as like it. There are a thousand new sources of interest here, and in many respects it is quite a new world to me. I see a great deal of the Arundels, and of Mrs. Craven, and have made acquaintance with several of their friends, and go with them to see all, or rather a very small part, of what is interesting in the religious and charitable way.

Amongst my new acquaintances those I have taken the greatest fancy to are Madame de Gontaut (the daughter-in-law of the old Duchesse), Madame de Thayer (*née* Bertrand), and the Marquis Val de Gamas, the Spanish Ambassador. I went on Sunday evening to Madame de Lieven's, accompanied by Granville. I may tell you that his manner is really charming, such tact, such courteousness, and no forwardness. I saw there several old acquaintances, and found Marion nicer than ever, and in very good looks. Granville goes to see her very often, and she instructs him in French politics. Yesterday we dined with Madame de Caraman and met only Mrs. Craven,.Albert de Broglie, the Nuncio, and my new friend, Val de Gamas. He and Albert de B. differed enough and not too much on political questions to make an animated discussion *possible* and very amusing. Afterwards I went to the Hôtel de Gontaut.

Now as to politics, I have no facts to tell you, but the aspect of things is most curious. Every third person has a different opinion, and everybody is more or less frightened—some to the degree that they go about with gold sewed in their clothes, ready to be surprised any morning by the red Republic. The new Ministry is insignificant and has no *colour* whatever, but they are respectable men and friends of *order*. They will carry the President's message to the Chambers, propose the repeal of the Electoral law, which will be rejected, and then retire, the President having gained (as he hopes) popularity in that way, and then he will make it up with the *parti de l'ordre*, and things will go on much as before. I think the *general* opinion is that *somehow* or other his powers will be prolonged. Some persons accuse him of having produced all this excitement in order to gamble with the funds, and make himself up a private fortune. The *Absolutists* are divided into two camps, the Legitimists and those who wish for a dictatorship, *Le dernier resort de la démocratie*—a military despotism that will rule with an iron hand. The Constitutionists seem to me in the minority. The general impression seems to be that that system has been tried and found wanting, and that the reign of the *Classes moyennes* through a representative Government has utterly failed. I do not know how far this is true, but I cannot see *good* in either of the other ideas. The Bourbons and Orleanists I should equally dread for France and for the Church, which is, I am convinced, the only means of saving her, temporally speaking. The last would oppress, the former protect her, and I do not know which would be worse. The present state of things, and liberty for the immense work which is doing amongst the people to extend itself, is what *appears* to me to be wished for, but lookers-on, perhaps, do not appreciate the sufferings of an unstable Government, and the impatience that people feel to have something more secure before them, but in grasping at that, I think they would lose their present footing, and not gain another.

I went on Sunday to a *reunion* of workmen and their families in the crypt of St. Sulpice. Nothing but blouses and uniforms, the Abbé Melleriot is an apostle among them. After they had heard Mass at a very homely altar, with no music but six hundred voices singing *cantiques:* I never heard anything so interesting, or so perfectly adapted to the audience addressed. The clergy is accused of Socialism, only because of their intense sympathy with an uninterrupted devotion to the labouring classes, and if anything is to save France from anarchy and a reign of terror, I believe it will be those symyathies and that devotion.

To the same.

Genoa, *Jan.* 26, 1852.

DEAREST FREDDY,—I received your interesting letter yesterday, and must begin by thanking you for having written a second time to me, though I have behaved so ill about answering the one you had so kindly written to me to Pau. I suppose you expect me to enter on the subject of politics. I feel a little afraid of doing so, for I am sure we differ so widely that you will only be provoked with me. But the fact is *opinions* depend on *facts*, and to ascertain the truth about facts seems more difficult than ever. We have spent some time in France, and travelled through it, and every chance individual we have spoken to has reiterated the cry that Napoleon has saved France. Everywhere confidence and commerce have revived, and abhorrence of parliamentary government seems to reign in every class except that of disappointed politicians. If L. N. is committing atrocities, and practising a system of lying and deceit, of *course* I must dislike his Government, and can hope no eventual good from it. But *we* hear that the system of his enemies and of the *Salons de Paris*, is to calumniate him in every respect, and in England you hear the accounts of the very people who are most likely to paint his acts in the blackest colours. As to the banishments, I cannot think them in themselves so bad. France has been *worn out* with struggles, and if he felt that he could not fulfil the mission which the *people* has intrusted to him, in presence of ceaseless intrigues and opposition, I think he is quite justified at a time of crisis in keeping the enemies of peace away from the scene of action. How far he is from putting the screw on too tight, or practising any *unnecessary* tyranny, I really have no means of judging, but I cannot take for granted that all you hear in England is true. We have seen, for instance, enough of soldiery in France, in every place and turn they were swarming, and not once have we seen a soldier drunk or disorderly. Then because the majority of the nation has risen as one man in defence of society, you seem to undervalue the frightful dangers which were impending, if the *rouges* had been allowed to mature their plans. How could the party of order have risen as one man to crush that powerful minority, under no other head but that miserable National Assembly, whose wretched fragments could not even agree amongst themselves on the 2nd of December, or with that little unprincipled Thiers, endeavouring to thrust a child upon the throne at such a moment? Many of the atrocities committed and planned by the insurgents have never been published. There are stories too horrible to relate, far *worse* than anything in the first French Revolution, and had they been successful they would have constituted a system generally pursued. I do not believe that Montalembert's indisposition was feigned. Whether right or wrong, it is so utterly unlike his character not to have the courage of his opinions, or to shrink before public opinion. I am no blind partisan or admirer of Napoleon— unfortunately, his character is not one that one can put any confidence in; I feel he may any moment turn out a tyrant (*perhaps* he is so already). He may, which I care about more than for anything else, turn against the Church which to-day he protects ; but that he has rendered a great service to society, that he is popular with the *real people* of France, and that they have spontaneously elected him, and prefer his Government to that of the National Assembly, I do not for a moment doubt. I am *very* democratic in one sense, but it is the interests of the *real people* I have at heart, not the tyranny of the middling classes, which I believe to be often more irksome to the poor than that of an absolute Sovereign.

An absolute Government founded on universal suffrage is such a novelty that one can hardly judge it till one has seen it work. If L. N. was a good man, I own I should be pleased to see the experiment tried ; as it is, I feel it is *anxious* and perilous, but not hopeless, and really before the *Coup d' Etat the situation was despairing*.

No one, perhaps, who has not let the lapse of time and the events which have since passed make him forget what were then the impressions even of those who became afterwards the most ardent adversaries of the Empire, will deny, boldly, that Lady Georgiana judged well of the state of minds in France at the time when this letter was written. What follows about Italy will, perhaps, be contested by some of our readers. In any case Lady Georgiana's opinions on this subject were never modified. The course of events only served to confirm them more and more, and this furnishes a double reason for recording them here.

I could not help smiling when I read your letter at your calling Piedmont a bright spot. It only shows how from different points of view things appear in various lights. It appears to me that this country is treading precisely the same path that has been so fatal in France, where with pain, shame, and sorrow, they are beginning to retrace their steps. The abominable publications, the blasphemous caricatures, the bad books of all kinds which are encouraged rather than repressed by the Government, the contempt they endeavour to throw on the clergy, the monopoly of education, that most detestable of tyrannies—the invention of the First Napoleon, and the strangest inconsistency in countries that call themselves liberal—will shortly end in demoralizing the people, and, unless they are crushed by their neighbours before, will probably bring on the same evils of socialism and anarchy in time—of a good deal of this I can judge by my own eyes. The accounts I hear are, I am quite ready to admit, *one-sided*, the Brignoles, Spinolas, Palaviccini, &c., being very anti-Government. We had an amusing *soirée* at the Palazzo Rossó yesterday. Every one was on that side except one poor senator, who is always there, and whom they all fly at fiercely. The Genoese are very anti-Austrian, however. Madame Meyendorf was cut dead here some time ago, because it was discovered that she had associated with the Austrian society at Milan, so she employed herself more usefully in copying pictures. M. de Brignole says she copied one of his Vandykes so that it could hardly be known from the original.

I have always liked this place, and Italian society amuses me. *Grantley Manor* in French has just got here, so that people talk about it, as if it was just come out, and make a great fuss with me, but partly, I think, as Leveson's sister. There is a universal cry of joy at his position. I was obliged to put in a good word for Palmerston, whom one lady seemed to think was a fiend in human form, and Leveson an angel come to repair all the mischief he had done. I did not contradict the last part, but said that P. was good-natured in private life, at which she looked quite incredulous, *cela n'est pas possible.* G. dined out for the first time yesterday, and behaved as if he had done nothing else all his life, and has great success. I must say he is getting very pleasing and agreeable, and speaks French quite fluently now.

The shops here are full of caricatures about French affairs. They call the President *Malaparte*, which I think funny, but I don't know if it is new.

To the same.

Rome, *Tuesday, April* 6, 1852.

DEAREST FREDDY,—As I shall not have a moment to write n during the next four days, I will prepare a letter to-night for the Saturday's post. For a wonder I am spending the evening alone at home, which has not happened to me since I have been here. Fullerton is dining out *en garçon*, and G. has walked with a friend to the Coliseum. I do not feel disposed to be argu-

mentative in this letter, though there were several things in
your last one which I was inclined at the time to dispute upon,
but the climate and the influence of Rome are essentially tranquillizing, and I feel more ready to thank you for it and for all the
pleasure it gave me, than to carp at some of your remarks.
The intense enjoyment of Rome in its religious, its poetical,
and its picturesque point of view, so fills my mind that it is
somewhat an effort to think of politics here, but I have spoken
to several persons of different ways of thinking, on the temporal
state of affairs, and this is what I gather by comparing these
accounts. In the first place, the Pope has little if anything to
do with it now. He did his best to correct abuses, to conciliate
all parties, and establish useful institutions previous to the
Revolution. Since the utter failure of these endeavours, he
devotes his attention wholly to the government of the Church,
and has ceased to struggle with the opposition which the spirit
of anarchy on one hand, and its result the fear of innovation
on the other, present to any schemes of improvement. The
characteristic of the Government here seems a systematic
passiveness. I cannot find out that it is harsh, arbitrary no
doubt it is, and minutely arbitrary in some respects, but this is,
I believe, from the wish to forestall plots which might lead to
greater mischief. People are often arrested apparently for
trifles, wearing colours, uttering cries, making bouquets of
particular sorts, &c., but these are all the signs of a party
which is incessantly at work. Mal-administration is the great
evil, and the difficulties of reform almost insuperable, but men
who betrayed every trust during the Revolution, and pointed
the cannon at the windows of the Quirinal, are only imprisoned,
and not executed as they would have been in most other
kingdoms, and if people are often arrested, they are also often
treated with more leniency than they deserve. There is a
good deal doing in the way of agricultural schools and education for the people. The Pope is particularly anxious on this
subject ; and, if it is persevered in, the character of the people
must in time become more efficient. The common people are
neither immoral nor stupid—very much the contrary, but they
are apathetic when their passions are not excited, and an easy
prey to the bad men who work them up in a wrong direction.

R

The generality of English people in Italy seem to me credulous to an excess. They see and hear the very persons most likely to abuse the Government, and make men into political martyrs who in England would probably be in Newgate. At Naples I believe that great improvements are taking place, and I must say that it speaks very well for the King that Mr. Gladstone's violent attacks, which were enough to irritate any sovereign, have made him investigate into the charges, in some instances relax the severity of the prison discipline, and diminish instead of increasing the rigour of his government, at the same time that he has a deep sense of having been most unfairly and unjustly attacked by a foreigner, who listened to every discontented person within his reach, and accepted and published every hearsay story that told against his government. I think this readiness to improve, even when the attacks were hard and uncourteous, is an excellent trait in a man, and a promising one in a sovereign. We are greatly relieved here at hearing that the French Government have *désavoué* d Canino's attempt to come back to Rome, and have ordered him to leave Civita Vecchia. . . .

I am amused at your finding *glimmerings* of liberality in my last letter. I wish you had heard me the other day disputing vehemently with M. Goudon, the *rédacteur* of the *Univers*, about the different nature of political and criminal offences. I think he considered me as dangerously Radical in my opinions. *Apropos* of Radicalism, I wish you every success in the Potteries, and am very glad you mean to pronounce yourself against the No Popery cry. As to Maynooth, I should rather like the grant to be withdrawn, as nothing would, as the *Times* truly observed, so assure the success of the Catholic University. I suppose we shall arrive in England when Parliament will be sitting and excitement at its height. I only want you to remain out long enough for your *Chef*, if your *Chef* he must be, to commit himself to a liberal policy, in religious as well as in other respects, and to eat back in spirit, if not in the letter, his last year's Bill.

Granville has been delightfully well here, and enjoying himself immensely. He is this moment returned from a second expedition—this time to Frascati and Castel Gandolpho.

The weather and the beauty of the spring are too charming. We mean to go to Albano in the Easter week. How much I should enjoy some time or other being in Italy with you. I shall think of you and long for you at Venice next month ; but, once away from Rome, my impatience to get back to England will become irresistible almost. I do so *long* to see dearest mamma and all of you again, and even here I think of Midgham with delight. Think of my winning the other day in a lottery a drawing of Overbeck's valued at £80! I could hardly believe in my luck. I have been very idle about the fine arts, but after Easter I shall go to some studios and galleries. Gibson's I have been to. The cast of his statue of Sir R. Peel is fine, but not very like. He has given him too commánding and intellectual an appearance.

To the same.

Florence, *Feb.* 17, 1853.

DEAREST FREDDY,—Many thanks for your long and very amusing letter. As you like the discussion, I will answer it in an argumentative, and I hope not in a disputatious, manner. And first I will at once admit that, as regards politics, I have not, in a certain sense, fixed principles—that is, no determined adherence to particular modes of government, independently of the thousand varying circumstances of time, place, and character. I believe that in one age or amongst certain people the very same laws which might be most beneficial under other social conditions might prove dangerous or mischievous. I think nothing immutable in this world except the truths of Religion and the Laws of God. Justice and kindness are, I consider, amongst these latter, and that makes me say that if L. Napoleon or the King of Naples transgress those laws, I am ready to condemn them as much as you do. But the question remains whether the severities they exercise are not necessary to maintain social order, and repress the attempts of the worse enemies of all justice and humanity. I do not say they *are*. I am now explaining what I meant by appealing to facts, not to principles. In this case arbitrary government is not in my opinion necessarily against those laws of justice and kindness, and therefore it is not its existence in all cases which I am prepared to condemn, but would rather judge it by the spirit *with* which and the mode *in* which it is exercised. All human institutions are fallible, and I see perfection in none. I readily admit that they should be changed and modified according to the divers wants and the changes in the history of mankind.

I think liberty a great blessing but not *the first* of blessings, free discussion and self-government, excellent things when the first elicits truth, and the last conduces to peace and order. But when they have directly contrary effects, and that they lead to disorder, impiety, mental and bodily suffering, they cease in my opinion to be good. I do not consider them in the light of absolute blessings in themselves, but only as the means to an end (and I quite admit in *general* the best means to that end), the virtue and happiness of mankind. And allow me to say that in this way I can justify what you complain of, the frequent changes in my political opinions, or rather wishes. With regard to the Divine Right of Kings, I am not aware that since my girlish days, I ever asserted it as something in which I believed, but what I have always said is this, that it is the only principle on which I could conceive that a sentiment of loyalty could be logically founded independently of any individual merits in the Sovereign, or of the respect due to the first magistrate of the country. . . .

Next with regard to the Radicals in England. I have a sympathy with them, first, because when democracy is not allied with the evil which it has been made the tool of abroad, my inclinations are all that way. I like the extension of the Franchise. I dislike monopolies and privileges of class, and their views of religious liberty and equality would tend greatly in my opinion to the advance of what I believe to be the true religion, which is the foremost thing I have at heart. There you see, my dear Freddy, is the rock we split upon—what makes it impossible that we can see these subjects in the same light. I consider the knowledge of religious truth, the religious education of children, the spiritual instruction of the labouring classes, as the first and most important of all objects and of all blessings, and civil liberty, comfort, temporal prosperity as very inferior points, highly desirable in themselves, but not to be put in comparison with what concerns the *souls* of men.

Abroad, the Radical party, with some few exceptions, has identified itself with the cause of infidelity and impiety. In England, though unintentionally, their political views would be favourable to the advancement of what I believe to be the truth, and hence the difference of my feelings with regard to them. I am afraid you will be annoyed at these frank admissions of the paramount importance I attach to that *one* point, but it is of no use to beat about the bush, and disguise one's real feelings, especially as the avowal of them is what explains apparent inconsistencies. My *sympathies* are all for the side of liberty. I should have been delighted to have seen the French Republic succeed, if it had carried out what seemed to be its good tendencies, if the National Assembly had been true to the people, and the statesmen honest in their allegiance to it. It would have given me far greater pleasure to see it succeed than to see L. N. in his present situation, even if he conducted himself as wisely and humanely as possible. But I believe it was utterly powerless for good, and was preparing the way for all the horrors of anarchy and socialism.

Again, in Italy my sympathies are all on the side of Italian Independence, and the sight of the Austrian troops is painful to me. But, having seen that in the present state of this country any attempt at Liberal institutions (and how could it be made with more spontaneous generosity, confidence, and earnestness than by Pius IX.?) is instantly swamped by Mazzini's party, that curse and bane of Italy, and that the amnesties, concessions, and paternal government of such a Sovereign are repaid by the most brutal and shameless ingratitude, not by the bulk of the people, but by that horde of wandering ruffians that mar all attempts at improvement, and labour incessantly to pervert the faith and morals of the Italians, I cannot but rejoice that they are kept at bay even by Austrian bayonets, and arbitrary arrests. When you talk of these at Rome and at Naples, I think you ought to remember that assassination is a regular system with the Mazzini party, and that it may be a matter of necessary precaution to arrest a man who may have been using violent language, or associating with bad companions, even though there may be no proof against him. It is a miserable state of things, but *à qui la faute?* When people are stabbed in the streets while standing talking to their friends, there cannot be such delicate *ménagement* about dilatory forms of justice as in countries where life is not so threatened. I suppose the rulers are timid, the administration of justice defective in many respects, and abuses great, but it is the perpetual intrigues of the demagogues that keep these suspicions alive. I see the King of Naples has released a number of prisoners now. If, in a short time, a plot is formed against him, and some of the persons thus released are implicated in it, as most likely would be the case, how can it be expected that he should not revert again to measures of rigour? I hear that the Pope is almost broken-hearted at the disappearance of his fondest hopes for the welfare of his people, and at his painful position between the continual intrigues of the demagogues, and the severe measures that are forced upon him by the necessity of the case, and the not unnatural fears of the Conservative party. Remember that he let out of prison, that he frankly forgave, that he blest, and helped out of his own purse, some of the very men who afterwards assassinated Rossi, killed his secretary by his side, and was obliged himself to fly for his life. And now, tell me if it is true, or false, that in the Ionian Islands people have been flogged and shot for political offences, that newspapers have been seized for advancing that they ought to belong to Greece and not to England, and that the decisions of the native Parliament have been arbitrarily overruled? Is it false that some of the Irish exiles have been treated with revolting severity? These things are *asserted*. I hope they are false. But it ought to make people a little cautious in admitting reports of that kind against other Governments. I do not suspect the Strutts or Mrs. Grey of Protestant prejudice—but perhaps of a little English credulity.

Lady Georgiana here recalls several acts of rigour imputed to the English, and says that if they are truly so imputed it ought to prevent them from blaming others for the like, while if they are falsely charged with them, they ought to suppose that the charges against others may be false also.

Mr. Scarlett, who is no particular friend of the Austrians, and is very properly alive to the hardship of Mr. Mather's case, said it was an exception to their general conduct, which was as mild and considerate as possible, and I should think his testimony was an unprejudiced one. But, to hear G.'s Italian master, one would think they were incarnate fiends, that they plunder the market carts, that they flay peasants without any provocation in the court of Prince Lichtenstein's palace, that they treat Florence, in short, as a place taken by assault. This is so glaringly untrue, that one sees at once that it is national antipathy, and Italian fervour of imagination, that conjures up these accounts, and I can imagine that at Rome and Naples, with some natural bitterness in their hearts, and doubtless some hard cases to recount, the sort of persons with whom English travellers generally associate may easily present to them a most exaggerated picture. About this I shall be able to give you a better opinion when I have been to Rome. I have still something to say in answer to your letter. You say, " I was lately an admirer of L. N.'s policy, and soon a severe condemner." I do not quite understand what you mean. I am still an admirer of the *Coup d'Etat*, and am not a severe condemner *yet*, though I dislike and disapprove of, his decree about the Orleans family ; but surely you do not think that consistency obliges me, because I admire his energetic conduct in the first instance, and the stop he put to the moral agony of France, by appealing to the universal suffrage of the people, that I am therefore bound to approve of him if he misuses the power they have entrusted to him, and should prove himself a tyrant and an oppressor. Such consistency would be the height of inconsistency. It is not his possessing absolute power that would make him guilty, whether for their interest or not the people have given it to him, but his responsibility in using it must be immense, and on that will turn my opinion of him.

It is very easy to talk of liberty, but most difficult to define it. In England, doubtless, we possess it, and cannot be too thankful for the blessing ; but how often it exists in name and

not in fact. The tyranny of a majority over a minority is, afte
all, as grievous, if not more so, than that of a despotic sovereign.
The Radical Cantons of Switzerland have oppressed and ill-used
the other party far more cruelly than many an absolute sovereign has treated his subjects, and, if the terrified populations
of France that were trembling under the threats of the Socialists,
are now breathing freely, won't they thank Louis Napoleon for
the *Liberty* he has restored to them ?

Your accounts of dearest mamma and Sukey delight me.
Give them my best love ; but this will be an old letter when it
reaches you, for it is to go by a courier.

I am much pleased at Lord John's including in the Reform
Bill the doing away of the Oaths.

What you say of the universal feeling about L. is delightful.
God bless you both.

Yours ever affectionately,

G. F.

I must just add that I have no doubt that the state of the
Italian prisons is as bad as possible, as to light, ventilation, &c.,
the fact of chaining people together, &c. ; but that I cannot
consider as any argument of the inhumanity of the Sovereign
or Government, though it is most desirable that this state of
things should be changed. They did not invent the system,
and, when people are used to anything, it is long before it
strikes them as shocking. I suppose that a hundred years
hence English officers and sailors will be horrified at the idea of
the floggings and the use of the cat in the army and navy, and
yet they will not perhaps be the least more humane individually
than those military persons who now advocate it. Observe the
way in which Madame de Sévigné talks of torturing criminals
without the least expression of horror at it, and yet I suppose
she was just as kind-hearted as any of us. If the punishment
of death is ever abolished, our descendants may shudder at the
cool way in which we speak of executions. All this must be
taken into consideration, I think, in judging of the characters
of men, and it is this sort of allowance that is so seldom made
by English travellers.

What were the English prisons fifty years ago, and when

Howard first visited them? In respect, especially to all that regards comfort, Italy is behindhand in civilization, and this would affect, in proportion, the prison system, without reflecting on the humanity of the rulers.

Some of the opinions here expressed may probably be contested by many among us. But that is not the question. The good sense, the lofty intelligence, the generosity of heart which the letter evinces, are incontestable. The writer seems to desire to sympathize with every one, to understand every one, and to take an interest in every one, though her own life was absorbed in the one thought which dominated and ruled it. We shall find Lady Georgiana reaching the highest grade of interior detachment from everything human. But to the very end of her life the ties of blood and friendship were never to be broken or impaired, and the fact that she was so detached only rendered and gave them a greater charm.

CHAPTER XIII.

IF the simple view of the Mediterranean had produced in Lady Georgiana an impression so different from that which she had received ten years before, and if the natural beauties which now surrounded her had seemed to her to speak a new language, the language of what was henceforth to be the country of her soul, what must have been the feelings with which she now saw Rome again? Rome was now a new city to her, and it would be no exaggeration to say that henceforth she never left it without feeling a sinking of heart like that which those who are fondest of their homes quit them. It is an impression which cannot be described or understood by those who do not feel it, *Intender non la puo, chi non la prova.*

Rome, the Rome which she loved, no longer exists—or if it exists, it is only on account of that indefectible majesty of the Papacy, which none of the blows that have been struck at it can destroy. Rome has lost, not only her ancient crown, but also the crown which belonged to her as queen of the Christian world. To be the capital city of Italy is a paltry thing indeed, for the Rome of history and

of the Christian Church. We have nothing to
describe in modern Rome. We know nothing of it.
But our recollections of the past are untouched,
and untroubled, and it is these alone that we have
now to recall, for those alone did Lady Georgiana
keep in her memory and heart to the last day of her
life. In her first visit to Rome, she had been like
other strangers. She had taken a number of interesting walks or drives. Intelligent guides had enabled
her to pass back over the great spaces of history.
She could thus add to the pleasures before her eyes,
those that are to be found in the great memories
which rise up at every step in that famous and
charming country. Her imagination had been fed
by visits to all the galleries. But neither history
nor art in itself was ever able to call forth in her
any vivid interest. She could quickly make herself
at home in a period of history, and give it its local
colouring. But to interest her thoroughly it required
the further spur of the attraction furnished by
persons or subjects which she cared for. It was
the same with works of art. She entered into them
when they gave shape to her favourite ideas or
sympathies. Art by itself, ancient or modern, found
and left her comparatively indifferent. Thus it was
that in her first stay at Rome she had seen everything and been interested in everything, but she had
been deeply touched by nothing.

Now she could begin her study of the monu-
ments of the Christian religion. She went down
into the catacombs, not out of simple curiosity, but
to venerate the tombs of the martyrs. She visited,

one after another, the numberless sanctuaries consecrated to the memories of heroic saints, or the
honour of the several great mysteries of her
religion, or to that of the Mother of God under
the various titles with which the piety of centuries
has adorned her name. She now came to know the
multitudinous works of charity, in which so many
ladies, noble or untitled, took their part without
noise or ostentation, and often at the cost of much
personal service, and which were carried on also by
men of all ranks. The spirit of the whole came on
her as a new thing, and she understood at last what
was the true Rome. By the side of the treasures
which are devoured by the eyes of *savants*, the
students of antiquities, and of art, she found there
was in Rome another world. Antiquities, science,
and art, were certainly not banished from this, but
there was one ruling idea, from which all went forth
and to which all returned. This was the true Rome,
and this she came to know, and at the same time,
as she said to herself, to love like a person. She
was very soon to love it like a mother.

It cannot be expected of all readers that they
will understand this. Those who have known what
this Christian Rome is, and who have lived in it,
will not question what is said. It is a luminous
and blessed atmosphere, and those who have once
breathed it, find it difficult to live outside it. When
they leave it, it is with the hope of returning, and
of carrying with them from it some of its warmth
and brightness. A thousand details therein may
have displeased the taste. There are imperfections

to which it is hard to be blind. There are even abuses which cannot be denied. But in no place in the world but Rome is the presence of an atmosphere of supernatural truth more evident. Nature reigns in full magnificence on the summit of the Alps. It is true there are many rough paths to be seen there, brambles and thorns which are banished from the sheltered and well kept garden. But who would prefer the best kept garden in the world to the view from the summit of the Alps, or of the hills which look forth on the Bay of Naples? or indeed, to any view whatever which places him face to face with the works of God?

That such was the impression on Lady Georgiana is proved to the author of these pages by her own recollections of the time.[1] She came from Naples, then her home, to spend, for the sixth time, the last days of Lent and the Holy Week at Rome. They were memorable days indeed. Those magnificent solemnities are now numbered among the things of the past, or are at least suspended. They must be revived some day, for they belong to the very soul of Rome, whatever may the fortunes of the visible city. The present generation is deprived of them, but the next will know how deep and holy have been their effects on that which is passing away.

English travellers and others, who take advantage of the freedom with which all are admitted to these splendid ceremonies, regard them as wonderful spectacles, and may be surprised to be told, that to us they are something very different. It is well

---

[1] The author here meant is, of course, Mrs. Craven.

to call to mind what Cardinal Bona said in the sixteenth century, speaking of the revelations to be found in mystical authors—that we should always be content to believe what the best people in the world affirm when they are speaking of things within their own personal experience. Catholics should be believed when they say that what touched them in the ceremonies of those holy days at Rome was not the mere artistic or æsthetic satisfaction, however complete, of their curiosity or their taste, but the deep significance of all that met their eyes or entered their ears. No doubt the chanting of the *Miserere* in the darkened chapel of the Sistine, or in St. Peter's, as the day was declining, made an impression which even the most indifferent could not escape. But for fervent Catholics, this simply expressed the mysteries of their faith. On the Wednesday in Holy Week those sorrowful and pathetic notes were the language of penitence, the Sacrament of which they had received the same day. On Holy Thursday they spoke accents of gratitude for the Holy Communion they had made that morning, and at the same time a preparation for the greatest and most terrible day that the world has ever seen, the eve of which had begun when the chant was entoned the second time. On Good Friday they sounded for the conclusion of a day which no other in the whole year could equal, every minute of which had been consecrated to the faithful by the remembrance of that to which it is consecrated. It was filled by that memory everywhere, not only in the churches in which the faithful assembled, but in all places and for every one. It was a single day of human life entirely withdrawn from the noises and movement of the world.

And then, at the end of the Holy Week, Easter Day! All are agreed that there is no sight so fine as that of the Pope giving the benediction from the Loggia of St. Peter's, and the greatest scoffer in the world is not tempted to break that solemn silence which enables all, to the very utmost limits of that vast area, to hear the sacred words. What is passing in the hearts of Catholics? Assuredly, something more than the admiration and emotion that all persons can feel—something divine, something of infinite tenderness and power, strengthening at once their faith and their love, drawing closer the ties which unite them to the Church and to our Lord, Whose representative on earth has just blessed them. And in dwelling thus long on these recollections, the writer is justified by knowing that her own feelings were shared by Lady Georgiana, who shared her religion, and she can but faintly describe what she must have felt, though with far more ardent faith, and far more fervent piety.

During this winter Lady Georgiana formed a close intimacy with the family of Prince Borghese, and especially his mother, who became her special friend as long as she lived. Princess Borghese (*née* De la Rochefoucauld) was a person who gained a great influence with all who came near her. She was a faithful and devoted friend, of great nobility and generosity of character. She filled the highest place among the Roman society while she lived, and left in it an irreparable void when she died. There was a peculiar charm about the fine *salon* of the Palazzo Borghese. The conversation was interesting and serious. The young people were many, and gave it brightness and animation. It was the rendezvous of the most distinguished foreigners who frequented at that time the Holy City. It was a place of delight to Mr. Fullerton and Lady Georgiana, and they were well pleased to take their son with them. He enjoyed this residence in Rome as much as they did. And this was a fresh delight to them, that they could share with him their new impressions of the religious and even of the social life of Rome.

Lady Georgiana had kept up her relations and correspondence with Father Faber, as her confessor. The following letter is addressed by him to her, and has much to interest us, as well as many character- istic touches. It was written from a place in the country whither he had to retire for the purpose of restoring his health, already gravely shaken.

The Rev. F. Faber to Lady Georgiana.

Hether Green, Lewisham, Kent,
March 12, 1852.

MY DEAR LADY GEORGIANA,—I have been writing and writing to you I don't know how often, and have never accomp- lished it yet. Even in this my exile, one thing comes after another, and then I get lazy, and then your long letter has never reached me, and so I am somewhat at sea about you. As for myself, I suppose I am better, but Mr. Tegart has now prolonged my exile to the 3rd or 5th of May, and it is very, very tiresome, as you may well suppose,—however, *La Volonta!*

It feels very odd to be called upon in the midst of work to

stand aside, and be a looker on. I can hardly tell you how it
affects me. The world looks so much more wicked, good people
so shabbily good, men so unconvertible, truth so entangled and
hard to put, error so mixed with truth, everybody, in short, so
wicked, and at the same time so candid, that I can't see what is.
to be done with anybody.

I find nobody to agree with but Lady Arundel, who the
other day when I said, "Well, we can't live long," exclaimed,
"Yes, it is just the thought that supports me all through."

This you see is not a very apostolic frame of mind; yet I
am not indulging unmixed misanthropy, for I have tamed a
wild cat, which, I take it, is a work only surpassed in difficulty
by the conversion of a sinner, and the keeping of an Irishman.
to his duties, or getting a pious lady to be quiet and common-
place.   Indeed, I cannot help hoping that my increased hard-
ness and hopelessness about the state of things may make me
a better workman than I was, for I trust it will enable me to
work more quietly, because I shall expect less, and shall have
to do it more entirely on supernatural motives.   I wish we
English people would work quietly with less eager-heartedness
and more simple trust in prayer.

I believe a sweet peaceful resignation when God has let one
of our plans fail, would go further to get a blessing on our next
plans than all the talent in the world, or all the most abundant
gift of miracles.

But it is so hard to possess oneself in peace, for nobody
cares for souls, or understands what you are at, when you plead
their cause.   Catholic associations, Catholic clubs, and a better
understanding between the English and Irish Catholics, a new
Cathedral, a Cardinalitial residence, putting one's foot on Lord
John—all this may be very well.   But—but—but! There are
the Irish courts—there are the famishing souls—there are your
little ragged thousands! Everything in England is crying out,
Blood! Blood! Blood!   The Precious Blood!   And to see
good men wild about consolidating the Catholic party, eager,
loud, anxious, bright-eyed, eloquent, with every perception and
zeal sharpened; and speak of *souls*, obscure, dirty, redeemed,
snobbish, vulgar, unshowy souls, and you have in a moment,
the dull eye, the gentlemanly languor, the listless assent, the

S

courteous but unsuccessful effort to hide what a bore it is, and stupid admission that all you have said is very important, and the offer of a guinea subscription !!!

The remedy, my dear Lady Georgiana, for keeping one's temper under all this ! Why, there is no remedy except keeping alive the remembrance of what a selfish beast one is oneself, and to stick to that. Oh, what a world ! By the grace of God, we are what we are,—and by whose grace is Johnny Manners a member of an Orange Cabinet ? See now, I am setting sail into the inviting land of censoriousness, and so good-bye. Please remember me in all holy places.

Ever, my dear Lady Georgiana,
Most faithfully yours in Jesus and Mary,
F. W. FABER, Cong. Orat.

Like most persons who have made a long stay at Rome, Mr. Fullerton and Lady Georgiana left it with a well-formed intention of returning the next year. It is said that Pius IX. said once to two strangers who were taking leave of him, How long they had been in Rome? The one answered, Three weeks. " Only three weeks ! " said the Pope, " then I must bid you good-bye." The other answered, that he had been in Rome six months. " Then," said the Pope, " *au revoir*, you will certainly come back." In fact, the Fullertons went away only for the summer. They returned to England through Switzerland, where Mdlle. Eward had the pleasure of once more seeing her old pupil.

Although her stay in London was short, Lady Georgiana occupied herself actively in the works of charity carried on by the Oratorian Fathers, of whom Father Faber was the Superior. With her almsgiving was the last part of charity at least, incomplete unless she took some part herself, some care, some time was spent in the works which she aided. She loved to go and teach the catechism to the children of the rising schools, in class time, and when the time for play came, she entered into their games, and mingled good advice which they could understand, informing herself the while of the wants of each family. Children always know the persons who love them, and they loved her in return, and her presence among them was always a feast-day. Her example in this respect is worth mentioning here. During the summer of which we speak, Lady Georgiana knew well that her stay in London was to be short, and that her return was uncertain.

The idea of their purchasing Midgham was now given up. Another home in the country was thought of, whither they were to go on their return after another winter in Rome. In any case, she was soon to leave for Italy. Many other persons would have used these circumstances as a reason for sitting with their arms folded and doing nothing. But with Lady Georgiana, when there was a personal effort to be made, she only thought of accomplishing what was to be done without loss of time as far as was in her power. She did not look far either forwards or backwards, and left all this kind of precaution for the time when she might have to call in the aid of others, organize resources, or take counsel as to work in hand. It was then her way to reflect with full deliberation. She became, if not slow, at all events circumspect, and applied all the vigour and perspicacity of her mind to the con-

sideration of the line to be followed and the means
to be employed. Her humility never failed. She
was, as we shall see, the life and soul of the works
on which she occupied herself, but she always
avoided appearing so. In attaining this object she
often strove to leave to others all the merit and
honour. Her works of charity in no way made her
relax the other kind of labour by which they were
fed. They only served to make her more active
with her pen.

It would be a pleasure to enlarge our remarks on
all her works as we have been able to do on the
two first. But this would delay too much the story
we have to tell. Her new novel, *Ladybird*, which
was published in 1852, had the same success with
the others. But the public was now more severe
with her than at her *début*. Her talent was now
well known, and she had to take pains to keep up
the high reputation she had acquired. Yet she
succeeded in this, and her literary reputation was at
least confirmed.

The end of the year had found Mr. Fullerton
and Lady Georgiana on the way to Italy. They had
settled themselves in Rome in the first days of 1853.
Granville Fullerton had regained his health, had
entered the army, and was to join the Grenadier
Guards at the end of the year. Meanwhile he
accompanied his parents to Rome, and was as glad
as they were to find himself there again. His
character had now attained its full development,
and the promise of his childhood was fully realized.
One of those who knew him best, describes him as

of attractive appearance, ready wit, animated and amusing in conversation ; easily led to interest himself, and with an ardour and courage by no means in keeping with the delicacy of his constitution, which only served to deceive himself and others. No words can describe what he was to his parents, and all description would be superfluous.

The following letters were addressed by Lady Georgiana to her brother, Mr. Frederic Leveson Gower, during this sojourn at Rome and the few months which followed, and will enable us to follow the incidents of this period, which bring us to the eve of the time when all earthly enjoyments were extinguished for her. She thus describes the society ·which they found at Rome :

To the Hon. F. Leveson Gower.

Rome, 3, Maison Serny,
February 10, 1853.

DEAREST FREDDY,—We arrived here on Friday after a very prosperous journey, and the weather, since our arrival, has made us feel how fortunate we were in that respect on the road. It has rained a good deal, and there have been frequent thunder-storms, which is very strange at this time of the year. We are all delighted to be here, and it is as charming as usual. The air as soothing, the mode of life as pleasant, the charm of everything one looks upon as peculiar.

Indeed, I believe I feel it more than ever. We have the same apartment as last year, only with additions which make it still more comfortable. The Carnival was rather a failure, owing to the rain partly, and to the prohibition of masks. On Monday, however, there was some animation on the Corso. The *Moccoletti* on Tuesday evening were very different from what I remembered them formerly, but still a pretty *coup d'œil.* There are very few English people we know here, though great numbers of others, and crowds of Americans—the Sartoris's, the widow Lady Grey, Lady Hermione Graham, and her husband, are all here—except those I made acquaintance with last year, English Catholics and converts. Maurice Esterhazy tells me that the Sartoris's have very pleasant society. They are at home always on Sundays and Wednesdays, and have beautiful music. We are to dine there on Sunday. Madame Arthur de l'Aigle is looking handsomer than ever, and I think her quite charming. Mrs. Norton and Mrs. Kemble are expected here, so we shall be a good many authoresses assembled. I have a long list of people to whom my book is to be lent. At this moment Madame Usedom has got it, who was the first person who called on me, and carried it off. Granville is delighted at finding himself with some of his friends again. He had, on Sunday morning, something of an attack again, but still slighter than what he had at Genoa. He had too soon after that one, we think, tired himself, and it seemed only to affect him just for the moment. However, he gave up in consequence, the Monday's ball, and Tuesday's also. He seems now better than he has done for a good while. Mr. Wiles thinks that though his previous state of health enabled him to bear it at that time, still the life he led in London knocked him up. He has given up smoking, and taken to music again, which is a happy exchange. I was so glad to receive your letter at Genoa, and I hope you will write to me soon again. It is such a great pleasure to get letters here. We just missed the Grenfells, they went to Naples the day before we arrived. Poor Lady Shrewsbury is here, quite broken-hearted. I hear the young man very well spoken of, but I fear he is very delicate. . . . I hear Mrs. —— has been acting at Naples with great success. We just missed here a spectacle of that kind at the French Embassy. Madame de Rayneval acted in perfection, I am told, and Madame de S—— well, only as the piece turned on the ravishing beauty of the heroine, it did not quite match her face. People here seem to have an extraordinary idea that England wants to go to war. Foreigners are much perplexed about the Cabinet, and cannot at all understand how they all pull together. It will be very interesting to watch the course of things when Parliament meets.

I am so glad you spoke at the School of Design meeting,

and should like to see your speech. That pretty little singer, Piccolomini, whom I have told you of, has been singing here during the Carnival. Her relation, the Cardinal, begged the Pope to try and persuade her to leave the stage, which he did, but vainly. She told him, as she did the Grand Duchess of Tuscany last year, that she should go out of her mind if she did not act.

Good-bye, dear Freddy.

I must go out, and have not another moment.

Ever your most affectionate

G. F.

Is it true that Madame Odier and my friend, Madame Thayer are Ladies of the Empress ? If, as I am told here, she smokes all day, I should like to see their faces the first time she offers them a cigar. They say the marriage is not popular in the army here. Why not a French girl ? they ask ; but really to that the answer is, that he was in love.

A few months later she writes to her brother on the announcement of his marriage with Lady Margaret Compton, daughter of the Marquis of Northampton.

To the Hon. F. Leveson Gower.

Rome, *April* 14, 1853.

MY DEAREST FREDDY,—Your letter coming so soon after the last, and written, as I saw at one glance, in a great hurry, made my heart beat. The first words reassured me, and I need not tell you what I felt as I went on. With all my heart I thank God that such a great blessing has been granted to you. Deeply I rejoice with you and for you, and I know well that few things now could have given mamma such happiness as this. Yes, I forgive you for having disobeyed my injunction, but mind you write as soon as the time of your marriage is fixed, for I am not without hopes that we might modify our plans, so as to enable me to be present at it. I wish it very much. You may imagine how I long to know Lady Margaret, how already I feel the strongest interest about her—what I feel she will be to us all.

Dear Freddy, what overset me quite was the thought of that first interview between her and mamma. To her who has no mother it will be giving one, and such a one—and I feel such a strong presentiment that she will be an immense comfort to my mother.

I have never seen her that I know of. Lady Marian I used often to see, and liked her countenance so much, though I never made acquaintance with her. I am writing in a great hurry, and hardly know what I say, for this is luckily the *Via del Mare* day, and you will get my letter very soon. I think it is such a charming family to be connected with, and everything one could wish for seems united in your bride. I expect mamma's letter with intense impatience. She will make me *see* her, and almost *know* her. Fullerton and Granville send you their most affectionate congratulations. The latter is very much excited—and impatient to make acquaintance with his future *aunt.*

We are foolish enough to be glad that she has such a pretty name. I am so very happy, dearest Freddy, that I hardly write reasonably. I have wished you so much to marry, and to be really, truly happy, and I see your happiness in every word of your letter. God bless you, dearest brother, and her whom you have chosen, whom you so much love. May you ever make each other as happy as you are now, and may *every* blessing be granted you. We have not been, after all, to Subiaco. The snow on Sunday stopped us. Tell mamma I am well, and will write to her as soon as I shall have received her letter.

Your most affectionate
G. F.

She was not able to be present at her brother's marriage, and writes about it thus:

To the Hon. F. Leveson Gower.

Rome, *May* 6, 1853.

DEAREST FREDDY,—I received your letter yesterday only, and perhaps you will understand I felt almost relieved that it made it *impossible* for me to return in time for your marriage. If it had been delayed, as I almost expected it would be, till the middle of June, it would have been *possible*, but I should have had to overcome many little difficulties, and for *my own sake* to get plans altered which *they* are very much bent upon. As it is, I feel that it cannot be, and though it is a *great privation* to me, I also feel that there is quite enough joy in the case, to make it wrong to have a selfish regret that I cannot see it with my own eyes.

I hope I shall know for certain the actual day, that my thoughts may be with you, and my heart follow you with blessings and prayers. My mother's feelings about Lady Margaret are everything you could wish, and what you tell me of her health and good spirits, which Susan also confirms, makes me feel almost wicked in being in the last degree low at being at such a distance from all at this moment. But I must confess that I have a little touch of *mal de famille* when I hear of the assemblages in Brook Street.

I have met the Courtleys here every week almost, at Mrs. Sartoris', but never happened to make their acquaintance. By an odd coincidence, he inquired of Mr. Sartoris yesterday what sort of person you were, being very anxious to hear about Lady M.'s prospects of happiness, and hoping you were worthy of such a treasure. The next time we meet I shall get introduced to him. I wonder if there would be any chance of your coming abroad after your marriage, and of our meeting somewhere. It would be delightful. Louisa Hardy wrote to me such a nice letter about you, and everything I hear of Lady Margaret makes me happier, and more inclined to love her.

We lead a very agreeable life. The weather has become warm, though very unsettled. It rains almost every other day, but the intervals are delicious.

On Wednesday we spent the day in the beautiful little green valley near Veii, by the side of a torrent, and amidst bushes of hawthorn and clusters of broom and honeysuckle. To-morrow we are going to do the same thing at Adrian's Villa, and on Monday are going to Frascati again for two or three days.

I am glad that the Government is stable, very glad that Gladstone distinguished himself so much, and hope it is not true, which was repeated last night, but which I do not see in *Galignani* to-day, that the Lords have thrown out the Law Bill.

Mrs. —— arrives in two or three days. I am rather curious to see more of her, but at the same time we have quite odd people enough without any addition.

Granville is sitting for his picture. I hear it is wonderfully like. . . .

On their return to England this year, Mr. Fullerton and Lady Georgiana took up their abode in their new dwelling at Wilbury Park. She does not seem to have liked it as much as Midgham. There was a strange instability about all the projects which they formed, which seemed to haunt them, and to be a presage of the blow which was to annihilate their plans for the future, which was to turn out so different from their anticipations. She writes from Wilbury to her brother, then travelling with his wife in Italy, the year after his marriage.[2]

To the Hon. F. Leveson Gower.

Wilbury Park, *Sept.* 2, 1854.

MY DEAR FREDDY,—I do not know if you ever received the letter I directed to Berne. It was a very dull one, so make no effort to get it, if it has not reached you.

How I envy you your journey across the St. Gothard, and by that lovely Italian Switzerland. I hope you stopped at the hotel at Lugano, which we regretted so much not doing, having put up the night before at Bellinzona, which is beautiful, all but its inn, and now I suppose you are lingering about the lakes or making your way to Venice. In the doubt, I suppose I had better now send this to Milan.

If you have had heat in proportion to what it has been here, you must have found it trying, I fear. It is unusual for England at this time of year. Some days too hot to go out in the middle

---

[2] Wilbury is near Amesbury, and therefore on the confines of Salisbury Plain.

of the day. But glorious weather for the Harvest, and a glorious and blessed sight it is to see cartload upon cartload of the most magnificent looking corn from every field that one looks upon.

You will be curious to know how we like this place. This is what I think : That it is a cheerful, sunny, comfortable house —a most healthy spot, with smart fresh air and smells. It has nice shade, and is very rural—a very pretty village at the gate of the small park. It sadly wants flower gardens and putting to rights. It has the somewhat neglected look of Rushmore, without its picturesque beauty. *That* would all be remedied when it belonged to one, the neglect, I mean. What could not be changed is the surrounding country, which consists chiefly of cultivated downs, an ugly sort of landscape—bare without wildness. It has, however, pretty towns and villages in the neighbourhood, and excellent riding on grass, green alleys for six miles round the place.

It is a much more *eligible* place than Midgham, a reasonable purchase, excellent sport for G. The railway is just making, which is to bring a station, at most, a mile from the house door. It is, above all things, much more healthy, but you, who I think admired Midgham as I do, will understand how much I miss at first its, to me, singular beauty and charm, and the extreme variety and loveliness of its lanes and commons.

Mamma came to us on Wednesday. She is very well, and going, I trust, to spend a whole quiet month with us. Then she intends going into Yorkshire. Rivers and the two eldest girls came over from Rushmore on Tuesday for the day, twenty-six miles and back. The accounts of the little boys are cheering again.

How melancholy the accounts of the ravages of the cholera and the climate are in the allied armies ! But G. tells me that, from letters received from some of the officers, it appears that the accounts of the correspondent of the *Times* are very much exaggerated and highly coloured. But, allowing for that, there remains enough to fill one with horror and with a sinking apprehension of the continuance of this dreadful war. One sees no end to it now. There seems no chance of any brilliant exploit that might bring it to a conclusion.

Thank God that the plentiful harvest in England and France has saved us from the additional sufferings of famine at home.

I saw Uncle Devonshire a fortnight ago at Chiswick, and thought him very well. He *then* appeared delighted with Mr. Wiles. . . .

G. has been very well lately. It is now three months since he joined, and during that time he has only had one attack—a month ago—which certainly proves that his present mode of life suits him better, on the whole, than that he previously led abroad. His zest and pleasure in his military duties is unabated, though, from the few officers at home, they are really pretty laborious. He has been here for two days' shooting, and brought with him a young Ponsonby and young Malet. It is pleasant to see the enjoyment of the whole party, who have been shut up in London so long.

You will have been shocked to hear of poor Lord Jocelyn's death. She is in great grief, I hear, though behaving very courageously and going to the funeral. The cholera is intense nowhere, but hovers over the whole country. One of Mr. Gladstone's children nearly died of it the other day at Broadstairs.

It hope you will not go to Venice while it is too hot and the mosquitos in force. I should be so sorry that anything interfered with your enjoyment in showing it off to Margaret. We have all been so delighted at the happiness which your visits gave to Mdlle. Eward. She was quite captivated with Margaret. She calls her now nothing but *la charmante Lady Margaret.*

When mamma leaves us, early in October, we shall go to Rushmore, and one or two other places perhaps. Later that month I hope we shall have your visit. I hope you have never seen Stonehenge, our *Lion.* It is six miles from this place.

Good-bye, my dear Freddy. I think you ought to have secured, before you went, more amusing correspondents than your own family.

Give my best love to your wife.

Ever your very affectionate sister,
GEORGIANA FULLERTON.

Granville heard from Leveson this morning, who says he spends his time at Carlsbad in "longing for news which does not arrive, seeing plays which he cannot understand, and shooting with toy guns at birds which will not allow themselves to be hit. Drinking the waters and a little literature fills up the day."

Lady Georgiana speaks in this letter with terror about the Crimean War. It caused her great suffering, so great that even when the great blow of her life had fallen upon her, she said she had never felt much more. Her son's regiment formed a part of the army that was then serving in the war. For some time she had felt revived apprehensions as to his health. But she had to resign herself to silence and let him depart. Naturally she was not one of those timid mothers who would turn their children away from the dangers which are involved in their duty and their honour. But a too truthful instinct told her of the gravity of a relapse which he had lately had at Rome. It was, indeed, but passing, but it showed the existence of an evil that was always threatening. She knew that her son's energy gave him a fictitious strength. On this point, however, she did not dare to speak. She had to await in silence and an inexpressible anguish the decision of the doctors who had to examine the question. It came, and was adverse to the wishes of her son. The mother was thus spared all the increase of alarm which comes from distance and the dangers of war. But in itself it confirmed the anxieties of her heart, which gave her no rest, and together with the bitter disappointment of her son, troubled the last days of relative security which she was to know here below. Certainly, if that beloved son had been struck on the field of battle, or if the cruel malady, more cruel than the enemy's fire, had carried him off in a distant ambulance, then his parents would have been in despair, increased by the distance which forbade the possibility of their reaching him and by the sense of responsibility incurred. But it was at a great sorrow that he was spared. This increase of sorrow was spared to them, but, nevertheless, they were deprived of the consolation of being present at his last moments. It was on a short stay with his uncle, Lord Rivers, at Rushmore, the day before he was leaving, and before he had reached his twenty-first year, that death took away quite suddenly this adored and only son, leaving in the hearts of his parents a wound which nothing on earth was to be able to heal. He died May 29, 1855.

These words belong to another place, but they are transcribed here because they express so faith-fully what is and what is not to be said at this point of Lady Georgiana's life. It was thus that she suffered, thus that she kept silence, imposing it also on those who would have liked to speak to her of

No amount of years can efface the remembrance of such an hour, and time, which softens all grief, never gave her the power to speak of it. Mothers, who have been pierced by this sword, cannot, they will bear me witness of this. Women who have no children, in the presence of her who has lost one, can but bow their heads, as before a sovereign majesty of grief.[3]

[3] *Mot de l'Enigme,* v. ii. p. 221.

her sorrow. From this day a great change was wrought in her. It was a change which was at first almost imperceptible externally. But it was none the less a transplantation of her soul to the very highest regions of the Christian life, towards which she had so long been on her way.

Her niece, Mrs. Oldfield, in the recollections which have already been used in this work, gives us all the details of his sudden illness. "Then came the Crimean War," she says, "and of course Granville wished to go to it, but this was positively forbidden by the doctor, much to my aunt's relief. He died at Rushmore, in the summer of the following year, 1855. He had not been less well than usual, and well I remember what good spirits he was in, and how one evening, when we were walking on the lawn in front of the house, he spoke of some arrangements which his father intended to make on his coming of age, if he lived so long, and saying something to the effect that there was then every likelihood of this, as he would be twenty-one in a very short time. Only a day or two after this conversation his end came suddenly and painlessly. Father Faber—I think, but I am not sure—broke the sad news to his parents, and they bore it with great resignation.[4] But they could not speak of the sorrow nor of him, and she never mentioned him to us in conversation from that time. On the 29th

[4] Mrs. Oldfield names Father Faber, but says she is not sure. It was Dr. Manning (now Cardinal Archbishop). Lady Rivers telegraphed the sad news to him, and on his way to the house he met Mr. Fullerton in the Park, and took him home. Lady Georgiana was carried to her bed, and Dr. Manning sat beside her for some time.

of May of the subsequent year, she wrote me a beautiful little letter from Richmond, saying that, though she had seen me the day before, my twenty-first birthday, she could not trust herself to say anything upon it to me, remembering how Granville and I had been together on that day of the preceding year, and she even asked me not to answer her letter."

The letter is as follows:

DEAREST SUSAN,—I could not say anything to you yesterday about your twenty-first birthday, as I was afraid of being overcome. I could not help thinking how much of that day you spent last year with my beloved child. But I cannot let you suppose that I do not form very earnest wishes for your happiness, or that I have not a very peculiar affection for you. Coming of age seems a new starting-point in life. May you make a fresh start towards everything holy and good, act up in every respect to what Almighty God requires of you, as far as you can discern His will, and may He grant you the best blessings for time and for eternity! Kneeling this morning at the grave of my child, I felt an ardent desire to call down blessings on all whom he had loved and who had loved him, and you and Fanny were as sisters to him. May you both be happy, if it be God's will, with every blessing that this world can give, but above all with such as it cannot give.

I do not expect you to answer this note, dear child. Indeed, I had rather you would not.

Your ever affectionate
GEORGIANA FULLERTON.

CHAPTER XIV.

THOSE who remember the character of Lady Georgiana, as it has been sketched in these pages hitherto, will not be surprised at the silence which followed the immense blow of which we last spoke. When she gave the reins to her imagination, she could command at will the most ardent, the most expressive, and the most eloquent language. But she had no language in which to express her personal feelings, in all their intense and deep reality. It is often said that "there are sufferings which no language can describe." With some persons this is a mere figure of speech. With her it was the absolute truth. She had already passed through two severe trials of a somewhat different kind, the trial of her soul during her conversion, and the trial of her mind before the production of her first work. Of neither of these is there any trace either in her correspondence nor in the recollections of her most intimate friends. The shattering blow which had now fallen on her was one unlike all others. It reached the most profound depths of her soul. It was to break irrevocably all her ties with earth. It is no wonder if she could not speak of it.

T

Father Gallwey, who became at this time and continued to the end the spiritual guide of her conscience, thus expresses himself of this period of her life :

> The wound of the death of her only child was so deep in her maternal heart, so bitter, so incurable, and above all so dumb, that one might ask, if during the thirty years that succeeded it, one single of her most intimate friends or neighbours, ever dared to mention his name before her. [1]

He goes on to say :

> It was only during the last days of her life, when the disease that was to kill her had nearly run its course, that, from time to time, she spoke of this inconsolable and silent grief. One day she said, turning her eyes towards a curtain that hid the picture of her son, "I wish I had the courage to draw the curtain and look at him !"
>
> About the same time, when reading to her out loud the passage from the Holy Scriptures, "And they shall mourn for him as one mourneth for an only son," [2] her burst of tears warned me that I had touched an open wound, and made me understand the significance and the power of the Sacred Text.
>
> But this great grief was for her the source of new graces, and elevated her to a higher sanctity. From that day her soul was absolutely detached from this fleeting world, and all her thoughts were turned towards that country where our God and our Father awaits His children. . . . She never revolted against the good God Who had given him to her and then withdrawn her son. On the contrary, she turned her heart more and more towards God and received in return wonderful gifts, a hundred-fold, for the happiness she had lost.

This testimony would suffice, if we had no other. Some of the effects of the blow were to be seen

---

[1] We believe, however, that with one friend at least she sometimes spoke of him—the Duchess of Norfolk.

[2] Zach. xii.

afterwards in her works, of which we may speak later on. It was as fruitful as it was terrible. But it had other effects deeper and more sublime, of which we should know nothing, for she never uttered a word to make them known, but that in her journals of retreats, and other scraps of paper which she wrote for the sole purpose of examining her thoughts and actions, we find traces of a new kind of work which became so clearly defined in her mind as to fill up all her life, and which we must call the search after perfection. It is a work which the world can neither know nor understand. Even when it makes itself perceptible by some outward sign, the world holds it a mystery, or perhaps even takes scandal at it. But holy souls go on along their path without troubling themselves about the surprise of the world, and those who write the lives of persons who have been stamped with the mark of sanctity, something far above the highest human virtue, must be as indifferent as they. Lady Georgiana rose up after she had been crushed by the weight of the heaviest of crosses. She rose up to embrace it, and to give to God without restriction the remainder of her life. The life thus given to God had henceforth but two great thoughts to rule it. The first of these was to devote herself even more than ever to him who, smitten like her and inconsolable like her, must perhaps have sunk under the grief, but for that firm and tender support which never failed at any moment to the last hour of her life, and which made him a sharer in the alleviation which she found in forgetting her own sufferings. The second thought was, after him, her poor. She consecrated to them with the most generous surrender all she possessed, her time, after that which was reserved for her first duty, her money, her strength, her health, and her mind. All were directly or indirectly given to their service. In short, her whole life was now made over, in its entirety and in its details, to that which surpasses all compassion, all pity, all merely human goodness, that charity which is but one thing with the love of God, and which will remain when hope is merged in possession, and when faith is perfected by knowledge.

This was brought about by degrees in her, although her life was already transformed. Before speaking of the active works by which it was filled, it will be well to study reverently the source from which all came, which brought on her activity its blessedness and its fertility. There is no harm now in glorifying her of whom we are writing. Her humility can no longer be wounded, and pride cannot approach her. The few extracts we make from her private notes will serve to show that a great trial alone, even when accepted without a murmur, is not enough to kindle in the heart the fire of love, human and divine. There must also be a deep and persevering work in the soul, of which these notes enable us to form some idea. We do not know exactly when these notes were written, certainly, however, between 1855 and 1860. The first portion of them is in French. It seems as if the great French writers had been her first teachers in spirituality, and when she came to apply their teachings in practice she naturally used their language. She occasionally mingles some Spanish passages. Spanish is the home language of Christian piety, and she had taken the pains to learn and study it on this account. (We make, with regard to these notes which illustrate her life after its great blow, an exception to our general rule, and insert some of them in the text.)

Lord abide with us! This is what I ask of Thee. Thy Name is *Emmanuel*, God with us. The air that we breathe, the ground which we tread on, the sky, the trees, the flowers, the waters, the clouds, all are full of Thee, all speak to us of Thee. By these visible objects Thou drawest nigh to our souls, Thou commendest Thyself to our spirit. Enlighten my understanding with the brightness of Thy Presence. Thou remainest with us in the lights which Thou givest us in prayer, in holy reading, above all in Holy Communion. Abide with me, my God, this day! Thou wilt enter my soul when I have the happiness to receive Thee. The Bread of Life is the one only object of my worship, of all my desires. Vouchsafe to take possession of my whole being at that ineffable moment. O holy Virgin, who didst conceive the Almighty in thy maiden womb, make Him to dwell in me in the Blessed Sacrament of His Love, make me keep Him with me by fervent prayer, boundless devotion, continual watchfulness against the lightest faults. Abide with me, Lord, by Thy grace until the time when Thou shalt enter really into my body and soul. Cause my rebellious thoughts to remain ever in obedience and recollection, may I never cease to think of the blessing which Thou dost promise me till the happy time comes when it shall be given me to receive Thee under the sacramental species.

These prayers were, no doubt, written out to be read when she was in church, and on the same paper we often find other prayers added. Thus between the lines of the passage just transcribed, we find the following:

[*In pencil between the lines.*]

Abide with me, O Lord, all the hours that are about to follow. Leave me not a single instant. Jesus Who reignest in Heaven, Jesus Who dwellest on earth, abide with me. I beseech Thee, O Lord, inspire me with all that Thou wilt have me think and say to-day, that I never offend Thee willingly, one single time, may I neglect no opportunity of doing good.

I ought to love God with all my heart, with all the fervour, warmth, and tenderness possible. I desire it, my Lord, I will it. Thou knowest well, Thou seest well, O Lord, that I desire it, but that, nevertheless, my heart is cold, hard, and dry. O that Thou wouldst take my heart, as Thou didst to some of the saints— take away from me this cold, hard heart, and wouldst give me a heart on fire with the most sweet love. O my God, teach me to cut and break and put fire and sword to my evil inclinations, so as to have a simple eye and a right heart. May I endeavour to understand God as much as my feeble mind allows, to strengthen my spirit by good and solid reading, some continued study, some wholesome reflection which may put an end to the license of useless thoughts of this or that, distracting me so powerfully and raising a cloud between me and my God.

And then, when I once get to love God in this way, I must also love my neighbour as myself. I must bear pain for him as for myself. I must fear still more sin for him, as for myself. I must never permit in myself aversions, antipathies, coldness. I must labour without ceasing or relaxing, employ for him all my care, all my time, for the sake of God and to please Him. No more contempt, no more weariness! May I see on the brow of all creatures the image of God, in every Christian the mark of the Blood of Jesus Christ! May it be ever so, my God!

.   .   .   .

Thou hast given me my heart, therefore I owe it entire to Thee! I have from Thee the power of loving, let me not then ever love outside Thee or without Thee. Let me love Thee, O Lord, somewhat like the Angels and Saints, somewhat as the Blessed Virgin loved Thee ! Kindle my heart with the divine fire of Thy love, let that holy flame purify it and consume it, enlighten it, and devour it ! I put my poor wretched heart at Thy feet, as St. Francis has taught me.

Lady Georgiana and her husband went to Rome for the winter of 1856—57. We find, from the following extracts, that she was admitted into the Third Order of St. Francis. The date of what follows is fixed thereby for the April of the last named year.

April 24, 1857.

Have I hitherto followed Thee, Lord ? I have known Him perhaps as the sons of Zebedee knew Him before the memorable day when He said, "Follow Me." Does He not address the same words to me now ? Does He not call me to follow Him in a most perfect manner, an obligation I incur in entering the Third Order of St. Francis, meant to mark a fresh starting-point for me ? My faults rise up before me, they seem to increase rather than diminish. Now is the time to begin in earnest to conquer myself, and do penance according to the strength and the means for this which God gives me.

Vouchsafe, O Lord, to suggest to me good thoughts, let them arise in my mind by reflection, ripen in my soul by prayer, become fruitful in holy affections. To hunger and thirst after justice ! Let me know what this spiritual hunger and thirst are. These are the thoughts I had put into my mind this morning as I woke. "To watch in God's Presence and do God's will." If I can only be penetrated with their meaning and live in this spirit. "God seeth me." This is the first lesson I teach my children, and the last which the perfect saint comes to learn. Vouchsafe, Lord, to make this lesson penetrate me more and more deeply, that it may take root in my soul and bear fruits of life !

Further on she writes, in English, the resolutions she had made, and observed with a faithfulness to which all who knew her can testify, though very few persons, perhaps no one, knew of her engagement to the Apostle of poverty.

To be poor in spirit—poor as regards one's tastes, as much as in me lies, practising poverty in the midst of wealth, being glad instead of sorry when for myself I have the opportunity of suffering some privation akin to poverty. To give away more than I have done things that I really care about. To try to detach myself more and more from all I possess.

I am about to become a daughter of St. Francis of Assisi, the Apostle of poverty. May his favourite virtue grow every day dearer to my heart. O Blessed Lord, help me to practise it in every little way that I can. Above all, by fighting against any wish to be esteemed, considered, thought highly of. Give me that love of self-abasement, that delight in self-abasement which is the characteristic of saints. Let me accustom myself to like blame in little things and never to defend or praise myself, so that by degrees that spirit may grow in me. I beseech Thee, O my God, to inspire me with all the graces necessary to be a perfect Tertiary, that I may not consider it as a light thing, but that I may endeavour to be really a religious in the tone of my thoughts, in the conduct of my life, in every respect that I can.

The next paragraph begins with two lines of Cardinal Newman's, well known in England.[3] She inserts them in her prayer, not by way of quotation, but as the expression of her own thoughts. Lady Georgiana writes:

Lead Thou me on. I do not ask to see the distant scene. One step enough for me. My dearest Mother Mary, let me

---

[3] The original is as follows:

Lead, kindly Light, amid the encircling gloom,
    Lead Thou me on!
The night is dark, and I am far from home,
    Lead Thou me on!
Keep Thou my feet, I do not ask to see
The distant scene,—one step enough for me!

pay to thee thine own sweet month of May, a month of tears,
of prayers, of grief, and of hope. Beautiful earthly flowers,
more beautiful than the flowers of Paradise.

I have many flowers to ask of thee, my Blessed Mother.
Now, I will lay them all before thee. Forgive what is pre-
sumptuous, pardon what is foolish, grant what is pleasing in
God's eyes, and above all things, obtain for me a deeper and
more fervent love of God and a greater devotion to thee.

I. *First Point.* . The purity of heart which I must seek to
maintain, in order not to lose in the least degree the graces
which God intends for me. How much time have I lost !
How many occasions of thanksgiving have I neglected ! O
my God, I have reached more than the middle of what would
be a very long life, but I have done very little, advanced very
little, laid up very little treasure in Heaven. Even, if I reach
a great age, I have only twenty years more to live, certainly
no more than that to work in. O my God, there have been
saints who have become such in a less time still. Give me the
grace to-day to make a firm resolution to work with all my
might to fill the time well.

Second Point. To ask continually the protection of the
Blessed Virgin, my Mother, my Mistress, my Lady. I wish to
have recourse to thee at every instant. Clothe me thyself on
Tuesday with the habit and cord of St. Francis. Make me to
be a true religious, to enter deeply into the spirit of the holy
Third Order which I am about to embrace. Let me prepare
myself these last days with much zeal and fervour, above all
by meditating on thy life, thy example, listening to thy voice,
keeping, for this end, deep silence in my heart. I will try to
avoid the very slightest faults, practise profound recollection,
humble myself before God, and, in all possible occasions, before
men also. Mary, my Mother, pray for me !

Rome, *May* 4, 1857.—Behold now is the accepted time,
behold now is the day of salvation. To-morrow morning, the
anniversary of my beloved child's last Communion, I am to be
admitted into the Third Order of St. Francis, and I firmly
purpose and intend, by God's grace, that it be the beginning
of a new life, strictly dedicated to God and to His service. In

the first place, I renew the vow I made with Father Faber's consent nineteen months ago. Secondly, I make a firm resolution to practise poverty in every way in my power in everything, using such things as are poorest, and oldest, and cheapest, within the limits of discretion and what is due to others. To consider my money as not belonging to myself but to God and the poor, only to take for myself what is strictly necessary for dress and those things I have to pay for. Not to spend anything that is not either directly or indirectly for the glory of God, little presents of affection and kindness being, as I consider, included in the latter class. If I feel any doubt on any question of that kind, to refer it to my confessor. To try not to allow in myself anything that I am not obliged to, that would be unbecoming in a religious. Over-excitement in conversation, complaints at want of comforts, negligent and self-indulgent postures. To try, as much as is possible in my position and without neglecting any duty, to lead a religious life. To do nothing from fancy or impulse, but as much as I can to practise obedience, submitting myself to circumstances in a spirit of religious obedience, remembering that "patience is to seculars what the rule is to religious." I will try, as the rule directs, to keep to two meals a day. If I take anything else, to let it be only a bit of dry bread. This I may be obliged to change at times, but at present I will at all events keep to it.

To make a careful and attentive study of my rule, observing every point of it. Keeping to the spirit, if I cannot to the letter, examining myself upon it, and noting down my transgressions.

I will make my meditation to-morrow on the Five Wounds of our Lord, with ardent prayers to St. Francis to obtain for me the five virtues of humility, obedience, mortification, love of poverty, and patience.

May 5, 1857.—Blessed anniversary of the one great consolation of my remaining life,[4] the most precious remembrance treasured in my heart ! Without it all would have been gloom and darkness which is now full of hope and consolation. Come,

---

[4] Her son's last Communion.

my soul, rouse thyself, and show thy gratitude to Almighty
God by less ungenerous dealings with Him, by a more complete
surrender of thyself to His service.

These lines were written a little after the end
of her sojourn at Rome. She continued, however,
to note down from time to time her inmost thoughts,
so precious and full of information for us. These
notes help us even in following her exterior life after
her return to England. Now again she was to dwell
in a new home. They had given up Wilbury, which
had no longer any attraction after the loss of him
for whom alone, and with whom, it had been
chosen. Death, which tears the heart, often does
more, it demolishes the plan of life, and it was so
with the parents of Granville Fullerton. The misfortune which had fallen on them left nothing fixed
in their life. For several years their existence was
homeless and unstable. This was but a small trial
when compared to the great cross which weighed
them down. But it had its part also in her sanctification. It destroyed in her the last traces of the
satisfaction of her own tastes, her personal prefer-
ences and desires, to make her practise what she
had sincerely asked and prayed for, detachment
from places and things, very much resembling that
which makes a part of the religious vocation.

The passages which follow show us that at this
time her doubts as to the usefulness of her literary
labours again revived. She was now making a
supreme effort to scale the heights of perfection,
and we cannot be surprised at the recurrence of
this question, while at the same time it makes us

admire the honest and generous spirit in which she deals with it.

Speak, Lord, for Thy servant heareth! Especially after Communion, when there is great silence in the soul, words often come from Thy mouth, my God, which are the life of the soul. May it be so to-day, my Lord. Let me hear Thy voice, and gather up Thy words. And since, Lord, all nature speaks of Thee, trees, flowers, mountains, men, books, animals, all speak to us of Thee, it only needs that we should know how to give ear, and hear all these voices in silence and recollection, amid the voices of our imagination, and gather ourselves up at Thy feet, and feed ourselves on this Sacred Manna, which Thou givest to us. Let our Communions be the fruit of our whole life, and our whole life the fruit of our Communion.

June 28.—To-morrow we leave Paris. I have suffered much this week. I feel ill at ease here, my recollections are sad. I have offended God much here, I have lost whole years, wasted the precious time of my youth, and now I have sadly experienced my own weakness and misery. I am discouraged, and more than ever uncertain as to the line I am to follow in my life. On the one hand standing literature, a little good to be done in writing, on the other the little time I have for prayer and works of charity. I do not know how to settle between these two kinds of life, and family cares are likely to distract and occupy me more than ever.

My God, I pray Thee to show me what Thou will have me do. Vouchsafe to give me Thy orders to regulate my life, to possess my heart, to enlighten the guide of my conscience. I seem to see that what God wants of me is a life always occupied, and always recollected, but in which all my occupations shall depend on circumstances, always ready to change, according as I have signs of that adorable Will which I wish to do and love with all my strength—writing patiently for a quarter of an hour a day, if I have no more time to dispose of, cutting off all idleness and dissipation of mind, doing all the good works I can, and submitting with resignation to all the hindrances which present themselves—always reading things useful for my sanctification, either in order to learn, or to serve the poor better, or in a literary point of view, submitting myself to lead a wandering life, to great change of plans, and of places, which are a great part of my lot. I wish to bring myself to think of nothing but of the present, and of my God, and of my dear child for whom I work, and who awaits me. Alas, I ask to suffer for him, and when God in His goodness sends me light inconveniences, I am not able to bear them with patience and without complaining !

Behold me, my God, prostrate at Thy feet, look at me, O Lord, with compassion, and send me the help I need in order to overcome my defects, to advance in virtue and in piety, and bear with patience my sufferings in soul and body !

The last quotation we shall at present make was written at Slindon, their new residence in Sussex. This was, perhaps, among all the homes which Lady Georgiana inhabited at this period of her life, the one which she preferred, the last in which she found the complete satisfaction of her tastes. Slindon Cottage was a small house, but situated in a charming country. It stood in a large garden full of beautiful flowers, among which the roses were remarkably fine. It was near Arundel Castle, the home of her dearest friend, the Duchess of Norfolk, and at the end of the village stood Slindon House, the residence of Lady Newburgh, belonging to a family that had never lost the ancient faith. The chapel in their house served as a parish church for the Catholics in the neighbourhood. It was on first entering this chapel that Lady Georgiana felt that strange sensation of which she speaks in the account of her infancy, when we feel as if all that was passing before our eyes belonged to some forgotten memory, and that we have seen exactly the same scene before, without being able to tell when or where. She explains this by supposing that she may have been taken, while a young child, into a Catholic chapel by her nurse. She was then so young, that the accuracy of her memory would seem almost as wonderful as the fact which she supposes it to explain.

This "cottage," where she passed many years when not in town, was always a place of peculiar predilection for Lady Georgiana. She quitted it with great regret, and it was her last sacrifice of the kind. She became, after this, indifferent as to the place of her abode, as she was already indifferent to most things she had formerly cared about. She went to place after place henceforth, as circumstances required, without any repugnance to or preference for any. Her soul gained in freedom, and she became more and more completely detached from the things of earth. We have a passage written by her soon after her arrival at Slindon, a presentiment that she would not reside there very long.

                                              Slindon.

Help my weakness. Let me become a stone in Thy Church, a very little stone, very poor, hidden, but, nevertheless, a stone of some use in its place. The hand of my Divine Master changes my place very often, puts me in a place, and then takes me away. His will be done. Only let it be given me to work with zeal and ardour where He leaves me, if it be only for a few days. Yes, my God, my heart and soul is sad to-day. It frets against my will, which is firmly fixed to serve Thee faithfully, to live in recollection and fervour—my poor soul opposes my will, and my body is feeble. Give me grace to conquer both, and walk on with firm steps in the path of obedience and patience.

We must now leave these scanty notes in order to study to some extent the external results of the many energetic resolutions which she made, as we gather from her prayers. For this, the difficulty is rather how to deal with the multitude of facts in a few pages. In truth, an entire volume would be insufficient to speak of her good works in detail. Details, however, are scarcely necessary for the sufficient understanding of what her life now became,—a life of Christian generosity and devotion, which it is not only useful to be acquainted with, but also to imitate.

About the end of November, 1857, Lady Georgiana received on the same day two pieces of intelligence very different in character, both of which called forth her ever ready and tender sympathy. The first was the engagement of her niece, Miss Fanny Pitt, to the Marquis of Carmarthen, now Duke of Leeds. The other was the death of her dear friend, the Duke of Norfolk (father of the present Duke). She wrote one of her characteristic letters to her niece's sister, Susan Pitt, expressing her deep joy on the marriage in prospect, which she looked forward to telling her mother the same afternoon, and mentioning also the long-expected but not less painful sorrow at the loss of the Duke. He, as well as his wife, who survived him nearly thirty years, had been among her most intimate friends, and the intimacy, in the case of the Duchess, was a continual source of the deepest consolation.to Lady Georgiana and herself as the span of their lives was lengthened. She speaks in

the letter of her confidence that the sorrow of the
Duchess will be as calm as it is intense and inconsolable, and that she will find the greatest support
in her children's affection.

Besides Slindon, Mr. Fullerton and Lady Georgiana had a house in London, in Chapel Street, in
which they spent some time every year. This was
the time which Lady Georgiana devoted to her
active works, heart, body, and soul. Activity of
this kind has its bustle as well as that of the world,
a perpetual movement which must be resisted and
kept under in a measure, and which will otherwise
drag down in its confusion the whole existence.
The whirl of all this engrossing activity was never
enough to make Lady Georgiana, however excusable
it might have seemed, steal a single moment from
the time which she ordinarily spent with her
husband or on her family cares, and she always
managed to find a portion of time, long or short,
for the literary labours which, notwithstanding all
her hesitations and scruples, she nevertheless
pursued perseveringly to the end of her life. Her
order and regularity enabled her to accomplish the
miracle of multiplying the hours of the day. Madame
Swetchine has said that money and time have a
strange lot in the hands of Providence. They are
as unlike as possible to one another at first sight, and
yet what can be said of the one is almost always true
of the other. Those who waste the one or the other
soon come to the end of either. The inexact and
heedless never pay their debts as to either, and
those who keep their time all for themselves, and

know not how to give it to others, are almost as detested and detestable as the misers of money. Lady Georgiana was both generous of her time and did not know how to waste it. She managed her money well, and she was at the same time generous of it. She never lost what was at her command, and she never cut short what she gave to others. Every one who came to see her and talk to her might suppose that his business was the only matter she had to attend to that day, especially when the subject of his visit was one which could interest her charity or the goodness of her heart. Considering the multiplicity of good works on which she was engaged, it was marvellous how much free time she had to spare for her friends and relations, who availed themselves of this without suspecting the great exactitude and order which had to be observed in order that time might be kept for them. It was like a perfectly supplied dinner-table, which costs immense cleverness and economy to secure its plentifulness and good arrangement.

In the next chapter we must, very superficially, watch Lady Georgiana in the numberless paths of charity which she followed, and enter into that world of the poor which she made her own, and which enabled her to recover the lost happiness of her life.

U

CHAPTER XV.

WE have now reached the period in the life of Lady Georgiana when she began to devote herself more than ever to the service of the poor. They had, indeed, always had her sympathy and her exertions. Even her literary occupations, as we have seen, were undertaken for their sake, and the good she did by her works tended in more ways than one to benefit them. She had indeed toiled and laboured for them incessantly. But now the care of the poor became, we may say, her principal devotion. It was a most thorough work that she undertook for them. The thought of all who suffered, whether in body or soul, was constantly present to her. It gradually became overwhelming and engrossing, as it must with all those who give themselves to it seriously. It was something which we have to admire in her, that she was so firm with herself in reserving the remainder of her time, while giving up so generously whatever she could of it to this work of devotion.

On settling in London, she put herself in immediate communication with the clergy of her district, that of the Bavarian Chapel in Warwick

Street. From them she learnt the wants of the
poor Catholics of the neighbourhood, and she began
regularly to visit them. This, when she could, she
always did herself; but as there were some days
when she was not so free, she got a friend to take
her place, or she paid a respectable woman, whom
she charged with her charitable works at certain
times, thus taking care to hide her almsdeeds
occasionally, by entrusting them to another hand
than her own.

It was in one of these visits to a poor bedridden
woman, many years later, that some of Lady
Georgiana's charitable habits came to be known to
one of her substitutes. This lady had placed on
the bed of the poor woman the money and the
contents of the basket of provisions with which she
had been charged, and was taking her leave after a
few kind words, when the patient said, with an air
of sadness: " You are going away, ma'am ! "

" Yes, are you surprised ? "

" But the other lady did not go so soon. She
made my fire."

" Oh, that's nothing," and the good substitute
set herself to rekindle the fire which had gone out.
After this was done she again thought of departing.

" That's nice, is it not ? "

" Yes, but it is not all."

The lady urged her to let her know all that Lady
Georgiana used to do, for she was there to do as
she did. She found out that this included the
sweeping of the room and putting it in perfect
order. Lady Georgiana used then to dress her

entirely, without seeming the least tired or troubled. She did not go away till she was sure that her poor patient would want nothing till her next visit, and often stayed a long time before leaving her, either reading to her or talking to her. Her substitute did the same, and from that day her duties to the poor whom she visited were discharged with greater perfection.

Lady Georgiana soon found out that her individual labours were insufficient. She must labour in other ways and more permanently to cope with the miseries all around her. The idea quickly ripened in her mind of calling to her aid the Sisters of St. Vincent de Paul. This was not easily accomplished. No house of their Order existed in England, and to bring them over was beyond her means. While she was thinking and praying on the matter, she suddenly came across another lady, as generous and courageous as herself, and to her was added a new convert who, even before her conversion, had given singular and even heroic proofs of her charity. The first of these was Lady Fitzgerald, who from that moment devoted herself to good works, till she finally entered a religious institute. The other was Miss Mary Stanley, sister of the well-known Dean of Westminster, a man who played a great part in the intellectual and religious world in his time.

The high intelligence and generous views of the Dean were shared by his sister, but she had, besides, a manly courage and a firm and logical mind, not content to remain for ever in the vague uncertainties which satisfied him. His brilliant eloquence too often served to disperse light, rather than to bring it to a focus on any subject whatever, even on the adorable and divine image of the Redeemer of mankind. Mary Stanley loved her brother with an affection which was the dominant passion of her life. But neither her admiration nor her affection for him kept her in bondage. She acted and reflected for herself. We purposely put action before reflection in this sentence, because it was in the midst of an active work of charity of an unusual kind that she was struck by the logical beauty of the truth. She had not confined herself to ordinary services of beneficence. At the beginning of the Crimean War she was one of those ladies who set out, under the direction of Miss Nightingale, to give to the wounded such succours as English soldiers had never before received on the field of battle or after the battle was over. The Catholic revival in England had drawn attention to the Sisters of St. Vincent de Paul, an attention which they had hitherto not received, on account of the wall of prejudice which had hidden from Englishmen so many Catholic institutions. That wall is now happily, in great part, demolished, and those who wish to see what passes on the other side of it, are no longer shut out from the sight. Mary Stanley, then, was of this courageous company of ladies, who found in the ambulances of the French army the Sisters devoted to the care of the sick, and learnt to catch their spirit and follow their example. When she returned to England she embraced Catholicism. Her affection for her brother remained what it had ever been, and she made no change in her life, which was, as before, devoted to the poor. But she understood better than any one what might be expected from the Order with which she had come in contact, and we cannot be surprised to find her join her two friends in the efforts to call to their aid such powerful helpers.

At the beginning of 1859 [writes the Superior of the Sisters of St. Vincent of Paul, now for a long time established in England] Lady Georgiana Fullerton, Lady Fitzgerald, and Miss Stanley, wrote to our Superiors in Paris to ask for three Sisters of Charity to begin in London the visitation of the poor and the foundation of a Créche. The work proposed was only a provisional effort, but the three ladies engaged to find all the expenses necessary for the maintenance of the house for two years. The proposal was accepted, and on the 22nd of June, 1859, three Sisters took possession of the small house which had been got ready for them by their patronesses, in York Street, Westminster.

Lady Georgiana was delighted. She could now begin the work, for which, as for everything else, an apprenticeship is required, which she was glad enough to make under such guidance, devoting herself to the infant community, as she knew well how to devote herself. As soon as the community was established, she came every day to the Sisters, to go with them, not, as before, among the poor in her own neighbourhood, where she found them in a certain relatively easy condition, but into the dismal purlieus of the most miserable parts of London, where, for the most part, the poor Irish were huddled together. The mission of the Sisters naturally found in them its principal object, on account of their religion. Lady Georgiana was well prepared to interest herself in them. Charity has no predilections, when it is perfect. But the poor Irish were in her eyes the personification of her faith. She had never lived in or visited Ireland, but she knew its traditions and its poetry, she could make excuse for the prejudices and even the passions of its children. She was much touched to find herself at work among them in their extreme misery. She could detect and admire the remarkable purity of manners which so many of them retain, even under such trying circumstances, in the miserable dens in which their lot is cast. It was a delight to be of service to them, to wipe away their tears and pour some little drops of comfort and even joy into their cup of suffering. The children were, of course, the objects of her tenderest care, and she was never more happy than when she could gather them round her and give them such amusements and enjoyments as were within her reach. She used to insist on taking some of the children in her carriage, that they might breathe the fresher air of the country, but it was soon found that this could not be continued.

The work of the little community in Westminster increased as time went on. For, in a city like London, there was misery enough to occupy the time of hundreds of workers. A small orphanage was added to the Créche, before the time came when the responsibility of the ladies who had brought over the Sisters came to an end. After a time Lady Fitzgerald retired into a convent, Miss Stanley found other work to which she devoted herself to the end of her life, and Lady Georgiana found other helpers as well as other fields of labour to satisfy her insatiable zeal for works of charity. But she always preserved her lively interest in the sisterhood at Westminster, with which she was in constant communication. As late as the year 1877, when an attack was made on the Sisters in the public Press, on account or occasion of an accidental mortality among the children, she came forward, as she was so well able, to vindicate them in the columns of the *Times*, and her letters had a great effect in turning the opinion of the public in their favour.

Apart from her own constant devotion to works of charity, which she carried through with all the completeness of personal labour and self-sacrifice which was a part of her character, Lady Georgiana was always forward in the introduction of religious communities into London, especially those connected with the service of the poor or the afflicted and the sick. It would be hopeless to attempt to give an account of her labours in this respect. It would probably be true to say that very few of the good works of this kind which either came into existence or required assistance, from the time when she began her work in London till the days when her strength began to fail, would not have some story to tell of her encouragement and support when it was most needed. Whatever her hand found to do, she did with all her might. The Sisters of

Charity may have been the first, but they were by
no means the last, of the communities whom she
befriended. Her pensioners were countless, the
orphans for whom she helped to provide, the bedridden and destitute old people whom she cared
for; scarcely, indeed, did she pass the day without
either receiving fresh applicants or visiting and pro-
viding for those who were already known to her.
She never denied her full attention to individual
cases, however much she might be pressed, and no
one was like her for her power of sympathy and
consolation. One of her dearest friends[1] applied
to her the words of Isaias: " When thou shalt pour
out thy soul to the hungry, and shalt satisfy the
afflicted soul, then shall thy light rise up in the
darkness, and this darkness shall be as the noonday.
And the Lord will give thee rest continually, and
will fill thy soul with brightness." And she adds:
" Among all her great gifts one of the greatest was
her power of consoling the afflicted, and did she not
indeed pour out her soul to those in want ? Surely
we may feel that the Lord has filled her soul with
brightness. When did she ever fail to help in good
works ? . . . It was this wonderful power of sympathy
in her, and universal charity, which makes it difficult
for me to remember the many good works in which
she was always engaged."[2] If we were to begin a
catalogue, it would be with a sense of necessary
imperfection, which might seem almost to imply
injustice to those the names of which might be

---

[1] Minna, Duchess of Norfolk.
[2] Letter to Mother Magdalene Taylor.

omitted. We must be content to say that from Tower Hill to Hammersmith and Hanwell, and from Finchley to Roehampton—and far beyond those limits too—she made herself beloved and revered by the workers for the destitute and afflicted.

There was in the days of which we are speaking a powerful movement throughout the country in general for works of charity, and especially works concerned with the most miserable classes. It is natural enough that Catholics should have been the first to catch the infection, and those among them especially who, like Lady Georgiana, had had the happiness of finding their way, after many struggles and sufferings, mental and moral, into the Catholic Church. Those who had originally been Catholics rivalled them in zeal and devotion, and the services of both were gladly accepted and employed by the large-hearted prelate who then occupied the chief position among Catholics, both in hierarchial position and in the minds of his countrymen.

The history of the episcopate of Cardinal Wiseman has yet to be written, and if it ever sees the light, it will naturally tell us much concerning the charitable movement of which we speak. It is not possible in the biography of one worker who had so many associates and companions, to chronicle the details of the many good works to which those years gave birth—works for the poor, or the orphans, or for the fallen, for the visiting of prisons and hospitals, the care of discharged prisoners, and the like, or for education. The work has been carried

on, especially in the last-named department, with
great success, under the present Eminent ruler of
the diocese to which the larger portion of the
metropolis belongs. But we are speaking at present
of the work which can be discharged by Christian
ladies in particular. The impulse in this direction
dates back, at least, to the days of which we are at
present speaking, and we need hardly say that in
all works of this kind that fell under her hand,
Lady Georgiana was a chief partner to the utmost
that her time, strength, and resources permitted.
But it would be invidious to name only one out of
a large body of active workers at the time. She
was soon joined by Lady Lothian, who gave, like
her, almost all her time to works of this kind.
Lady Londonderry, the Duchess of Buccleuch,
Lady Newburgh, the Duchess of Norfolk, Lady
Denbigh, Lady Herbert of Lea, Miss Bowles, were
among the workers, and quite a swarm of ladies
bearing the well known names of the Catholic
families of England, Stourtons, Langdales, Max-
wells, Cliffords, Petres, and others. The more
conspicuous figures in the lists of such workers are
now passed away, like Lady Georgiana herself and
her constant ally, Lady Lothian. But it is to be
hoped that the work begun by them remains and
will remain spread through a larger number of
hands, but animated still by the same spirit of
generosity and self-sacrifice.

It would be impossible, as has been said, to give
even a catalogue of the various works of zeal to
which Lady Georgiana now gave what time re-

mained to her amid her multitudinous cares, and
for which she managed to find room in her very
active life. What was remarkable about her, was
the thoroughness with which she entered into every
individual case which invited her charity, and also
the calm with which she passed from one to another,
and the punctuality with which all fell into order,
without the least neglect of her home duties, as the
time when she walked with Mr. Fullerton, any more
than the long spaces which she was accustomed
to spend in devotion in the church. She had
gained the art of doing a multitude of things
without letting them interfere one with another.
One of the works to which she was most devoted
in its infancy, was that called after the Immaculate
Conception, for the rescue and protection of the
children of the Catholic poor. It was in connection
with this charity that she now wrote one of the
smallest of her many works—the life of a young
girl of the poorest class who managed in her own
poverty to begin a work for the reclamation of a
few poor orphans, which afterwards came to be
established on a permanent footing under the care
of a religious congregation. No one will regret
the few minutes which are required to read through
her biography, the first of a short series called
Our Lady's little books, by Lady Georgiana. Elisabeth Twiddy, the subject of the memoir, died at
the age [of thirty-one in what would be called in
Catholic countries the odour of sanctity—one of
the many holy souls whose path in life **Lady
Georgiana** came across.

Elisabeth was a cap maker, the child of a Protestant workman, who deserted her Catholic mother, the last few years of whose sorrowful life were supported and cheered by her devoted child. For the eight years during which she survived her mother, Elisabeth lived 'one of those apparently ordinary lives which are made precious in the sight of Heaven by the perfection with which their common actions are performed. The greater part of the day, after her morning Mass, was spent at her work, the spare time allowed for food was often given to visiting the poor or the sick, or for counselling some poor companion of her own class. When her work was over for the day, she was found in the church at her devotions, and her modesty and recollection edified all who saw her. Gradually other girls gathered round her, and she became a centre of holy influence, without the least assumption of extraordinary goodness or authority. In time she collected a few orphans and destitute children into a little home, which was supported no one knew how.

One day [says Lady Georgiana] she entered the low set of rooms where the infant community was lodged, and said to her friend, "Why are you not getting ready the children's dinner?" The answer was, "I have nothing to give them." "You have no food, have you got a penny?" Yes, there was one penny left, the last penny in the house. "But what was that among so many!" might have been said then, as it was said by the disciples before the miraculous multiplication of the loaves and fishes. "Well," Elisabeth said, "I will tell you what to do. Give that penny to the youngest of these children, let her go . into the street and give it to the first poor person she meets." No sooner said than done. It was not long before the little messenger fell in with one of our Lord's representatives ; but before she had time to retrace her steps, that gracious Lord had sent one of *His* messengers to repay what had been lent to Him. A person called at the orphans' home and left five shillings, which quickly served to procure food for the children, and fill the two friends' hearts with gratitude and joy.

Elisabeth Twiddy died in the last weeks of 1859, and, as has been said, her work for children was taken up after her, especially by the promoters of the Immaculate Conception Charity already named. It was a work of a kind that can never be exhausted; and even within the last few months the needs of the destitute Catholic children in London have been again forcibly urged by the Cardinal Archbishop on the notice of his flock. Writing in 1860, Lady Georgiana says of it :

The Charity of the Immaculate Conception was established in London in the month of July, 1859. It was at the foot of our Lady's altar that the first idea of it arose. Many prayers prepared its way, much thought was expended on its detail before it assumed its present form. The need was urgent, the condition of thousands of our poor Catholic children deplorable, individual resources well-nigh exhausted. A great effort was wanted, and combined action indispensable. The rich must give, but they must also work. The poor must be called on to assist in the rescue of their own children. All classes must join in one great scheme, for the promotion of one great end. Our Lady's aid had to be secured, and her interest in it established, and so, as a thank-offering for her great privilege, twelve hundred children were promised to her, and many prayers in honour of her Immaculate Conception. . . . Several persons have dedicated themselves to the work and look upon it as their special vocation. In less than ten months an instal-ment of one hundred children has been paid, and the original debt to our Lady is daily decreasing. As the devotion to her matchless prerogative was the origin, so will it ever be the mainstay of this charity, the hope and the condition of its success, the pledge of its continuance.

These words are quoted here as showing the spirit in which such works were undertaken at that time, but we cannot find time or space for an enumeration of the charitable works of zeal which came into being during that spring-time, as it may be called, of Catholic devotion in London, and in none of which, multifarious as they have been, did Lady Georgiana fail to take her part as long as she lived, while she was the mainstay of many and the actual originator of some. Those who were workers then, had no time to preserve records of what they did. Those who were not living with them find it hard, indeed, to collect the memories of what survives only, we may hope, in the records of Heaven, and in the holy traditions of those who have inherited the labour of charity. One work will be specially mentioned, because Lady Georgiana made it in a peculiar way her own—the foundation of a religious congregation in which poor girls, who could not enter other convents, could follow a religious vocation, must be spoken of by itself in a later page.

It is needless to say that Mr. Fullerton helped on in every way in his power the charitable works of Lady Georgiana. There are necessarily so few records of this that we are tempted to quote a few lines from some of the very few letters that ever passed between them, from the simple fact that they were so seldom separated. But in 1862 Mr. Fullerton went for a few weeks to Italy, and Lady Georgiana, who was anxious about her mother's health, remained in London. Some letters of this time are preserved, and they show how anxiety for her mother divided her thoughts and cares with objects and works of charity. The first letter, written at the beginning of May, mentions a correspondence between Father Rowe of the London Oratory and the Privy Council Committee about a grant to a boy's industrial school. Then there is a trouble about an orphanage for girls with which Mr. Turner, the Government Inspector, is dissatisfied. Then the Rev. Mother of St. Elisabeth's Hospital returns thanks for a donation, "she says it is the largest donation she had as yet had." Then there is a great deal about the affairs of the Immaculate Conception Charity, then in a critical state. Then comes an urgent appeal from the Sisters of Mercy at Belfast, who have been turned out of their convent by the sudden claiming of a debt upon it. " Shall I send something ? " The next letter says, after a number of other matters, " I paid £25, the remaining half of your subscription, to the Sisters. Perhaps, before the end of the month, you will send it me, and the £20 you promised for May and June, and £10 10s. for Nazareth House in May, and £1 1s. for Dr. Todd's Orphanage, and £1 for the nuns in Belfast, £1 12s. 6d. for three months for Mrs. M——, and 6s. 6d. for Peter's Pence. Lady E. Howard, who wrote to claim it, £1. Total, £60." A little later we find :

The appeals from Ireland are heartrending. There is a letter about the expenses of the Workhouse Committee for you from Canon Morris. They are in debt, I think about £170.[3] I should hope there will not be much difficulty in raising that. Three persons had given £150 each, and that balance still remains. And, I think, we shall have to help the Sisters of Charity a good deal this year, and after that much less. I say this, not to check your generosity in other quarters, but that you may bear it in mind.

We read in another letter: "Mr. N—— was with me yesterday about the question of borrowing the £3,000 for the Sisters. It turns out that they won't borrow it. He thinks it will be necessary that the land be made over to you, and one other trustee, and the money borrowed in your names. . . ." These letters are but three or four in all, as Mr. Fullerton's absence was short, but if we had more such they would probably reveal to us the same story of active benevolence, for which Lady Georgiana's natural recourse was to her husband.

During these years, as has been said, Lady Georgiana's occupation in good works was not allowed to interfere with the time which she set apart for writing. In her later years she naturally

---

[3] This Workhouse Committee deserves to be held in remembrance among Catholics, as it was the beginning of the better state of things, with regard to Catholic children in workhouses, under which we now live, and which it required so much exertion from Cardinal Wiseman, and his successor Cardinal Manning, to win for them. A Committee of the House of Commons was obtained, of which Mr. Charles Villiers was chairman, to investigate the condition of those children. The evidence was voluminous, and it had to be gathered mainly at the expense of the Catholics. The result was embodied in a Blue Book, and it may be said that it was then that the foundations of the work of rescue were laid. After all exertions and much help from charitable Catholics, a considerable sum remained which Cardinal Wiseman had to defray.

V

wrote more or less with a distinctly religious purpose before her, and we may perhaps attribute the gradual lessening of her popularity with the public in general, at least in part, to this cause. In the year 1864, a fresh Catholic periodical was started, and Lady Georgiana was ready to contribute to its success by two successive novels, which had a very large share indeed in that success. *Constance Sherwood*, the first of these, is a beautiful sketch of the condition of Catholic society in England under the hard rule of Elizabeth, and might be considered by some readers as controversial in its tendency. The same charge could hardly be brought against *A Stormy Life*, which deals with a period before the Reformation. Still the characters of Henry VI. and Margaret of Anjou might be considered as attracting the reader in the direction of the religion which was the source of the sanctity of the one, and which soothed and elevated the sorrows of the other. Both these tales were rich in the gems of which Miss Martineau spoke in her letter concerning *Ellen Middleton*, and will be read again and again by those who know them. A full list of her works would be a long one indeed. A saint's life had seldom been made more attractive to ordinary readers than that of *St. Frances of Rome*. *Laurentia* sets forth in vivid colours the early Christianity of Japan. We see in these two works another characteristic of her literary efforts—the comparatively great amount of reading which she set herself to get through for the composition of what seemed to be a work of fiction. The same remark may be made as to the *Life of Luisa de Carvajal,* a Spanish lady who lived in England under Elizabeth, and who was the means of keeping alive in many an English heart the courage that was needed for the maintenance of the faith under severe trials.

In her later years, when she was induced to work at translations of the lives of more than one holy woman connected with the religious institutes which she befriended, perhaps few were aware of the extent of severe toil imposed upon her by what it was thought was a task which cost her "nothing," but at all events took up much time. Of the three lives of English women which she was anxious to write [4]—those of *Lady Falkland,* the mother of the famous Lord of the time of Charles I., *Lady Buckingham* in the last century, and *Lady Lothian,* her own most intimate friend—she only finished the first. The second she had no time to attempt, and the third, which she took up too shortly before her own death, as a duty which must be accomplished before anything else was begun, she left half written, to be completed, at her request, by the same hand which has had to set this her own biography before English readers.

It was, indeed, wonderful how Lady Georgiana accomplished all that she did, whether in works of charity or in the field of literature. She had the characteristic of the saints in this respect, that she

[4] She says in a letter to Father Coleridge : "I have always been wishing to publish Lady Falkland, the Marchioness of Buckingham's, and dear Lady Lothian's biographies successively. Though each is very different from the others, there is a likeness in their positions in those three epochs, which would add interest to their lives."

never seemed to be in a hurry, never let the coming business disturb her attention from the business which was before her at the moment. Thus she seemed to move easily through everything, while at the same time she gave full attention and very often indeed the labours of hours, to that which, when it was done, appeared to have cost her the thought of a moment only.

As we have mentioned the Life of Elisabeth Twiddy in connection with what was certainly a most favourite good work of Lady Georgiana, the care of destitute Catholic children, the need for which led to the organization of the Charity of the Immaculate Conception, it may be well not to pass over a second little book of hers, called *A Child of the Sacred Heart*. This was the Life of Mary Fitzgerald, a young convert lady, who came to the Church from the ranks of the bitterest Calvinism, and, after a short experience of work in London, entered the Congregation of the Sacred Heart in France, with the seeds of consumption already sown in her constitution. She died after seven years of Catholic life, in 1865. We have not time to sketch her character, very different indeed from that of Elisabeth Twiddy, inasmuch as, with her, sanctity had to be conquered by some of that holy violence of which our Lord speaks. But the short biography which Lady Georgiana wrote of this young person, whom she had come across in the course of her work for the poor in London, shows us how the idea of the particular Congregation which was to be specially associated with her own name, was in her mind a long time before it was carried out in practice. She thus writes at the end of this little book:

Those who have watched the good which persons in the position of Elisabeth Twiddy, Mary Fitzgerald, and many others even now quietly labouring amongst the poor in various parts of London, effect, must often be struck with the usefulness of this sort of ministrations, and, at the same time, with the inevitable uncertainty which attends their continuance in any particular locality. All secular work of this kind is necessarily subject to constant interruptions and changes. Often, at the very moment when it is beginning to establish satisfactory results, and to tell beneficially on a poor neighbourhood, family reasons, other duties, sometimes a mere change of abode, put an end to what seems so promising, and at once remove from the scene of her labours the person on whom everything depended. Another high and holy reason often will account for these sudden endings of hopeful beginnings. Those who love the poor out of love for our Blessed Lord, and divide all their leisure time between works of mercy and prayer, are often led to desire a more entire consecration to God, and surrender of worldly ties. Religious vocations will often spring up by the bedside of the sick, or amidst efforts to win back souls to God, or during ardent prayers for conversions; and, according to the various inspirations of grace, the resolution to become à Sister of Charity, or of Mercy, a nun of the Good Shepherd, a Little Sister of the Poor, or a Poor Clare, withdraws from the world the devoted girl whom God thus rewards for her good works. And God forbid that we should regret this tendency or deprecate what is the strength and glory of the Church. . . . But does not the thought occur that the present condition of our poor, and the special difficulties with which Catholicism has to contend in London, call for something we do not possess, that there exists a want which no Religious Order amongst us quite meets as yet? Are not religious workers needed in every parish, and yet, how is it possible with our scanty resources and the numerous calls upon them, to erect a convent or establish a house of Charity in each poor locality? And furthermore, inestimable as are the blessings conferred by the ministrations of Sisters of Charity and Mercy, is there not a work to be done which the very nature of their Orders cannot admit of? the peculiar work which can only be effected by those who associate with the poor, labour with them, in a certain sense live with them, and exercise the daily influence of their example in a mode of existence similar to their own?

Lady Georgiana goes on to describe the work that had begun and prospered in Poland, out of which arose the Institute of the Little Servants of the Most Holy Mother of God, and which was to give birth later on to the English Institute of the same name.

Those who have read the short biography of Elisabeth Twiddy, will at once perceive how exactly her life and that of her friends indicated the sort of Institute we have endeavoured to describe. One of the associates took care of a home of a few orphans, and worked with her needle to support them. Another, Elisabeth herself, the little cap maker, carried on an apostolate among poor girls. A third worked and collected pence for the maintenance of the little family. Why should not this mode of life be sanctified and organized, and perpetuated under the name and with the rule, and perhaps in connection with, the Institute of the Little Servants of the Mother of God?

It may be well to quote here a letter written by Lady Georgiana in these years to Father Faber, who appears to have written her a letter of condolence and sympathy on the anniversary of her son's death, or perhaps of his last Communion, either in the year 1858 or 1859. Father Faber, it may be remembered, had lately published his beautiful book, *The Foot of the Cross*, which he had dedicated to Lady Georgiana " in affectionate remembrance of a season of darkness which God consecrated for Himself by a more than common sorrow." The letter will show the new life which had been breathed into Lady Georgiana after the blow which had fallen upon her, of which she speaks calmly and resignedly.

DEAR FATHER FABER,—My husband is deeply touched by your most kind and affectionate letter, and, from my heart, I thank you for it. The eve of St. Philip's day ! the eve of the day when I saw my boy for the last time ! It seems as if I had no leisure for grief now, and those with whom I labour are strangers for the most part to that former existence, in which joy and anguish are so strangely blent. I never hear his name, never speak of him now. I sometimes scarcely feel as if I were the same person I used to be, so absorbed has my life been by a wholly new direction, so dedicated to a special line of work and thought. But it is lying there in my heart, only buried deeper, the love, the grief, the *purpose*, formed in those first days of sorrow, when I leant upon you, my dear, dear Father Faber. I never can forget what you did for me then. How wonderfully I see now God's fatherly hand in the removal of my child ! What fearful dangers stood in his way, had he been left on earth ! What fearful suffering it would have been to see him falter, if not fall, like others, in these days of trial ! God has been very good to me. Pray for me that I may not always be the "whited sepulchre" which I feel myself to be, that I may not be unworthy of the teachings and example I am constantly receiving. Ask St. Philip to obtain for me the grace of purity of intention. Give me your blessing, and believe me ever gratefully and affectionately yours,

GEORGIANA FULLERTON.

May 25.

We may subjoin to this letter two extracts of an earlier date, taken from the private papers to which reference has already been made. The first is a prayer *for the Month of May,* 1856, written therefore a year after her great loss.

Blessed Virgin Mary, most holy and dear Mother, accept my homage, see me prostrate at thy feet. O Mother of Sorrows ! hear the prayer of my bruised and aching heart. First, for him, my loved one, that as in this thy own month thou didst snatch him suddenly away from earth and its dangers, so thou wouldst snatch him out of Purgatory if his soul is still detained there, and obtain from thy Almighty Son his immediate admission into a region of light and peace.

Next, that thou wouldst grant me during this month a great accession of grace to love thee more, and serve thy Son better. Thirdly, I beg most earnestly that thou wouldst obtain for me the conversion of one most dear to me to the Catholic faith. Fourthly, and if it be for the real good of those for whom I ask it, a temporal blessing earnestly desired by one I dearly love.

The following verses may also be quoted, as expressing Lady Georgiana's feelings under her loss. She wrote them evidently for no eye but her own, and without a thought of finishing their versification and adjusting the rhymes.

> Dear child ! thou hast become
>   A guardian angel to me,
> And distant Heaven, like home,
>   Through thee begins to woo me.
> Those whom I loved on earth
>   Attract'st me now to Heaven,
> And thy soft touch has cut
>   Full many a chain that bound me.
> I feel thee, dearest, near me,
>   Thy noiseless step beside me.
> O dearest child, to Heaven
>   With grudging sighs I gave thee
> To Him,—be doubts forgiven !
>   Who took thee home to save thee.
> Oh, get me grace, my dearest,
>   To love thee yet more truly,
> Pine for my home above,
>   And trust my God here blindly.

These extracts show us two things : the abiding depth and intensity of the grief which coloured her whole life, after the loss of her son, and also the calm strength and serenity with which she dwelt upon her sorrows, in the light of her religion, and drew from them the power which bore her up, for the rest of her years, in the service of God to which she devoted herself.

CHAPTER XVI.

In the last chapter we have had somewhat to anticipate the course of our history. It was necessary
to enable the reader to master at once the general
tone of the remainder of the life of Lady Georgiana,
and to describe the sort of occupations to which she
devoted herself to the very end. There was sure to
be no trace of these occupations in her correspondence, which may now be resumed. We may find
her speaking less than ever of herself, but, at the
same time, each page will bear fresh witness to the
warmth of her affections, and the ardent interest
which she always preserved for all in this world
that deserve to be cared for. We also find repeated
proofs that her religious piety, which always was on
the increase, never in the slightest degree narrowed
her mind or lessened the warmth of her heart.
During the years which now ensued, her family
met with frequent and great sorrows, in which she
herself naturally shared. The following passage from
the papers of her favourite niece, Miss Susan Pitt,
found in these trials frequent and sad applications.

It was in sorrow that my aunt shone pre-eminently. I think
she comforted one not only by sympathy alone, but by strengthening one to bear the grief, whatever it was, by rising above it,
so to speak, in just the best way. I once went with her to a
hospital, and was struck by hearing her say, almost in a cheerful

tone, to a poor man who was complaining of his sufferings, "Make it a sacrifice." Even in little daily trials, such as small difficulties in housekeeping, she would advise one to learn to make whatever duty of that kind fell to one's lot an interest and almost a vocation, by throwing one's heart into doing it as well as possible, and that thus it would become less distasteful. No one, I think, seemed to feel more herself, or to inculcate more, religion in common life, and, though I cannot recollect her ever saying to me in so many words that one's whole life, even the part of it which seems most secular, should be devoted to God, I think one could not help seeing that this was her aim in life, and wishing in this to follow her example. I believe she never began her writing without a short prayer, and I know that she used short ejaculatory prayers applicable to the different parts of her dressing, and advised others to do so. This she told me herself, and I think she gave my dear mother a paper containing these little prayers.[1]

The writer of these lines had herself often to seek the support here spoken of, and her mother, Lady Rivers, the tenderly loved sister of Lady Georgiana, found by her side the strength so much needed under the strange sorrows which were reserved for her by Providence. Lady Rivers and her daughters also were indeed extraordinarily tried.

[1] Lady Georgiana certainly sent to Lady Rivers some prayers she was herself in the habit of using on her journeys. She says, in a note dated October 11, 1854:

I cannot resist giving you, dearest, this little set of prayers which I used *every day* during our long and frequent journeys, and in which I found inexpressible comfort. When used in that way, it was wonderful how each word came home to me ; we were mercifully preserved from all accidents, and greatly blessed even in the midst of trial. The collects that begin, "O God, Who didst preserve," I always felt particularly comforting. I shall constantly say these prayers for you during your absence. "May God bring you back to your still happy home, in peace, in safety, and in joy." God bless you and yours.   G. F.

What were these prayers? They were probably a simple translation of the *Itinerarium* which is in every Catholic Breviary, and in many Catholic prayer-books. The collect which Lady Georgiana mentions is a part of the *Itinerarium*, and the wish with which she ends is a quotation from it. She seems to have been fond of distributing these prayers to her friends.

God did not take away from her, as from her sister,
all she had in one day. She had a fine and numerous
family which grew up around her, only to give her
the opportunity of cruel and repeated sacrifices.
She had four sons, three of whom she saw sink into
the grave. A few years later she herself died, with
the knowledge that the last was struck in the same
way and could not long survive her. She had eight
daughters, all of them beautiful and healthy, but
one of these was taken away in the full bloom of
life and happiness, by an accident as rare as it was
fatal. It seemed as if she always had to suffer in
some unusual manner which made the blow seem
more heavy. When her sister's second son sank
under the same malady which had already carried
off his elder brother, Lady Georgiana saw plainly
that Lady Rivers was to have no peace here below.
Sorrow had taken its place by her in her home,
once the happiest in the world. Her own sufferings
may be imagined by those who have learnt to understand her character. The disease which thus mowed
down the four sons of Lady Rivers, one after another,
was nothing sudden or even rapid—a gradual diminution of all muscular strength, beginning as early
as at four or five years of age. All could thus look
forward to the termination. All these sons died
before attaining the age of eighteen. Their sisters
entirely escaped.[2]

These remarks are almost required by way of
commentary to the passage last quoted. The writer

[2] The four sons of Lord and Lady Rivers died, George Horace in 1850,
Granville Beckford in 1855, William Frederic in 1859, and Henry Peter in
1867, having succeeded to the title by his father's death the year before.

may well speak of the exceptional character of the sorrows to which Lady Georgiana had to use her power of consolation, of communicating to the will of the sufferer the gift of bearing the burthen of a grief of whatever kind. Lady Rivers bore her heavy cross with Christian heroism. She acknowledged and blest the mercy which guided the hand which laid it on her. The life of anguish found her calm and resigned, and her friends often heard her console herself in the most touching manner with the thought that the physical infirmities of her sons, which left their minds clear and untouched, added to their moral stature, preserved them from the dangers of the world, and ensured them a blessed recompense for their short lives of suffering.[3]

[3] Some lines, written in 1849, give Lady Georgiana's own portrait of her sister.

> *" Her children shall rise and call her blessed."*
>
> Oh, how fond mem'ry wakes again
> Thoughts of the time, when with a pen
> Unskill'd in verse, I sought to pay
> A girlish tribute to this day !
> Since then long years have onward roll'd
> Their chequer'd course—we now are old !
> The pen I held thy daughters take,
> And turn young poets for thy sake ;
> Thy children rise and call thee blest ;
> Their hearts fulfil that sweet behest ;
> And I would raise my voice with theirs,
> And blend thy name with fervent prayers.
> Oh, strong of heart ! go on and bless
> Thy dear ones in calm loveliness !
> With thy serene, tenacious will,
> To noblest aims devoted still ;
> Ever alive to duty's call,
> Cherish and guide and cheer them all.
> Oh ! blest with temper firm and mild,
> Joyous and guileless as a child,
> Scatter thy smiles on a sad earth,
> Yield us the sunshine of thy mirth !
> And if the days of trial come,
> If sorrows gather round thy home,
> Then like a guardian spirit stand—
> The angel of that youthful band.

During the time while their common grief united them more than ever, Lady Georgiana wrote thus to Lady Rivers:

To Lady Rivers.

Eastbourne, *June* 25.

My DEAREST SUKEY,—Depend upon it that the depression and anxiety you speak of is the result of what you have gone through lately. You suffered intensely, my beloved sister, and at the same time you were too much occupied with others to think of what your own share of nervous anxiety had been; and then instead of repose, which the body as well as the mind requires after a severe shock, you have had to think, to arrange, to decide, to look forward—no wonder that you have felt more oppressed than usual with the weight of daily solicitudes, hopes, fears, and cares. I rejoice that you are now in London; I believe it will be the best thing for you just now; your mind will be forcibly directed into other channels which, though not congenial at first, will *rest* your mind. I pray constantly for you and yours, more earnestly than ever. Yours is a very chequered path, my beloved sister, and hope and fear are often more difficult to bear up against than hopelessness; that is, hopelessness as far as this world's happiness is concerned. I feel ashamed of your praise, though grateful for your kind thought of me. God knows that courage you speak of has been, with the source it springs from, a gratuitous and most undeserved gift.

Dearest mamma is gone to Brighton to-day. She has been very well for the last two days—quite free from pain. Indeed, she has had very little since she came here. She was bent on seeing the Duke.

Fullerton is well, and takes a ride every day. He finds more and more comfort in talking with me of our beloved angel, and can often do so calmly.

God bless you, dearest sister. It is *you* I admire, my own, with your manifold cares and your unmurmuring performance of every duty.

Your most affectionate

G. F.

On the same subject she wrote to her brother.

To the Hon. F. Leveson Gower.

. . . We have received admirable letters from dearest Susan. She bears her trial with a courage and resignation that astonishes all around her. But, however sharp her *actual* grief is, it must be aggravated by the anxiety for the future for her sons. . . The constant alternations of hope and fear must be harder to bear than a broken heart. The deep tranquillity that comes with a hopeless grief (I mean of this world) is not given to her. May God strengthen and help her to bear the weight. . . .

Shortly after the time when this letter was written, we find many letters written from Paris. In the succeeding years Lady Georgiana often spent some time there, in going or returning from the south, where, at Mentone or at San Remo, she passed many winters with her husband. As she advanced in life, Lady Georgiana became more severe on the time of enjoyment which she had passed at Paris when she was young, and reproached herself with the time wasted, or spent in the pleasures of the world. This retrospective scruple came upon her when she became accustomed to look at everything in the white light of the lives of the saints, and she judged herself with excessive severity. It did not prevent her from enjoying her visits to Paris whenever they came about, and she took special pleasure in finding herself in the place where her childhood and a part of her youth had been passed. One day she spent one or two hours quite alone in the garden of the English Embassy. She said at a later time:

There I gave myself unreservedly to my recollections, and began to live my life over again, joys, pains, regrets, remorse, sorrows. I recalled my feelings in this spot and since I had left it. This vision of the past caused me almost an intoxication of distress, and at the same time the greatest possible, the most inexpressible, gratitude to God.

During these passing visits to Paris she always found time for some visits to friends, but she never re-entered society. Her days were passed in visiting the hospitals, schools, asylums, in order to gain information as to the progress and management of the numberless works of charity that were at that time multiplying themselves in Paris. She studied them with the view of using her acquaintance with them on her return home, with that perfect knowledge which can only be gained by long and serious attention, and with that kind of passion which a much loved pursuit engenders. Her companion in all these researches was the friend of her youth, Madame de Salvo. This lady, who became a widow in 1860, led after that time a life of the strictest retirement from the world. Those who were allowed to penetrate her retreat, in which her occupation in art, study, and religion were blended in a cheerful and sympathetic harmony, will understand the attraction that Lady Georgiana always felt for her friend and her quiet home.

There were many traits of resemblance between the two. Both had consecrated their lives to the poor. Madame de Salvo had a great talent for painting, and she used it, as Lady Georgiana used her writing, for the service of her works of charity. Thus they had the same interests and occupations. When they were separated they communicated frequently with one another, and they helped one another's works. Lady Georgiana used every year to organize some charitable sales, of which Madame de Salvo's marvellous paintings often formed the chief attraction. Thus the Marquise could reckon on the support of her friend in the interests of her poor, whom both loved equally. Their intimacy grew with years, and we find the proof of the faithful affection in the last words and last lines written by the hand of Lady Georgiana.

Other persons with whom Lady Georgiana was in intimate relations during her last visits to Paris are mentioned in the following letters to her brother:

To the Hon. F. Leveson Gower.

Hôtel Bristol, Paris, *June* 24.

. . . I have seen hardly any one. Harry called here twice, and Fullerton twice on him, without meeting. I saw Princesse Wittgenstein, a great friend of mine. To-night we pay the Montalemberts a visit. To-morrow I am to see Sabine, perhaps, and have an appointment with Madame de Gontaut. That is all the company I expect to see here. I am quite afraid of the violence of the M——'s. He has lost his election, and is frantic about it, I heard. Cavaignac will probably be returned, and another man, I am told, who is quite a Red Republican. But in general the elections have been most favourable to the Government.

Paris is certainly quite beautiful, and there are many out-of-the-way parts I like to go to. But what I care for now is the country. I hope to be at Slindon by the middle of July. I trust, dear Freddy, that you are going on as well as when you wrote last, and still like your quiet valley.

My best love to Margaret.

Your ever affectionate

G. F.

W

To the same.

Paris, *June* 28, 1857.

DEAREST FREDDY,—Although I have nothing interesting to say, I will write a few lines again before leaving Paris, which, to my great satisfaction, we do to-morrow. The heat has become intense, and disagrees with me. I cannot sleep, and quite pine for quiet and purer air. We go to Boulogne to-morrow, and I hope to swim over very soon, as in this weather, I suppose, the sea must be calm. I hear good accounts of you from England, so I trust that the baths continue to agree with you. Mamma continues to write excellent accounts of her health, and I rejoice that she is at Castle Howard during the heat. She thinks of coming to London on the 7th. I saw Harry yesterday. He has been suffering from what he supposes must be gout, lameness without any apparent cause. He is going to London on Tuesday, intending to consult Weber, the German doctor, about waters. He says the Government are not quite satisfied about the elections, that, although very few have succeeded against their candidates, they have been obliged themselves to support men not altogether so devoted to them as the last time. I made a great mistake the other day in supposing Cavaignac was going to be elected. I misunderstood something I saw in a newspaper. Harry says the Emperor is very imprudent about going about everywhere and anywhere without the least precaution, and yet that plots are now more than ever formed against his life. There has been one very lately found out. We paid a visit to the Montalemberts on Wednesday evening. They said they would be *en famille*, but that term includes, I suppose, the editors of the *Correspondant*. I was glad to make acquaintance with M. de Falloux and the Vicomte de Melun. The latter devotes his life to works of charity. There is no institution, and scarcely a poor family in Paris, that he is not acquainted with. I found M. de Montalembert very unwell, and out of spirits about his health. He was very gentle, and did not show any irritation about politics. He talked chiefly on literary subjects. I have seen the Duchesse de Galliera twice. She is going to England next month. Her little boy is much improved in looks and manners. Sabine is out of town, at Versailles. *Madame de*

Bonneval sells very well, I hear. M. Sainte Beuve is going to
review it in the *Moniteur.* I am extremely indignant with
Hachette, a bookseller here, who has published, without my
permission, and consequently illegally, a new translation of
Ladybird, and left out passages in it, in particular one that
contains a cut at Voltaire, which makes me very angry. It was
pointed out to me by M. Nicolas, the author of *Les Essais
philosophiques sur le Christianisme*, a work of great reputation
and merit. He said that passage was his favourite one in my
book, and that it disappointed him very much to see it left out
in what was meant to be the popular edition in France. . . .

G. F.

Not long after her return to England, Lady
Georgiana lost her uncle, the Duke of Devonshire,[4]
whom she had loved most tenderly from her childhood, and her sister-in-law, Lady Margaret. Soon
after this blow, her family was saddened by the
death of her other sister-in-law, Lady Granville,[5]
with whom she had been united for years by the
most affectionate love, and who, during the last two
years of her life particularly, had become dearer
than ever under her great sufferings, in which she
showed her ever increasing piety and courage. Lord
Granville's loss was shared by London society in
general, as well as by many friends of Lady Granville's youth, who loved her as she loved them,
faithfully, warmly, and with an affection as unalter-
able as their grief was inconsolable. Outside the
great world in which she lived, she had many
friends among the poor, and she was fond of
forming intimacies with a number of fervent and

---

[4] The Duke of Devonshire and Lady Margaret Leveson Gower died in
1858.

[5] Lady Granville (Marie) died in 1860.

pious souls. No doubt their prayers were joined with her last prayer on earth, and her first, it may be thought, in the next world, for those whom she loved so well. Her death caused a great desolation.

These three great misfortunes were soon succeeded by another, which she had feared even when a child, and which had haunted her all her life. Her mother might die. She repelled the vision with terror, when as yet her heart had not experienced its greatest wound. When the long-expected blow fell, she was prepared, to quote her niece's expression, to receive from the hand of God any trial, however great. She had stood at the foot of the Cross, and she used these sorrows to cultivate in her soul the fortitude which must be watered by bitterness. Lady Granville's health had become gradually weaker and weaker, but there was nothing to make her children apprehend a sudden coming of the end, when, in 1862, she had a stroke of paralysis in London, from which she never recovered. Madame Swetchine says that suffering is good for everything. It teaches us to suffer, it teaches us to die, and it teaches us to live. This lesson Lady Georgiana learnt most completely. Whether the path was rugged or smoothed under her feet by the goodness of God, suffering always taught her to mount higher and higher, and her life was one continual effort to rise. We shall easily see this from the following notes, made in a Retreat in the year 1859.

My God, my will is fixed. I was created to praise Thee, to show Thee reverence, to serve Thee, and I *will* do it. I will stop at *nothing*. Only show me the way. I lie at Thy feet like Saul in his blindness at the feet of Ananias. "What wilt Thou have me to do? Speak, Lord, for Thy servant heareth." Open Thou a way before me, especially to a fuller and more perfect practice of obedience. Give me some one to obey. Show me what Thou requirest of me in the way of humiliation. I will refuse nothing, for I deserve the worst in that way that can happen to me. Even though it be through poverty, disgrace, and sorrow, bring me to Thee. I will not stop short of that point which Thou dost wish me to reach.

April 14.—Every insult, every disgrace, every humiliation I could possibly meet with, reviling, open shame, blows on the face, would be far less than I deserve, and anything of the sort that I could meet with should be received with joy. God has forgiven my neglect of Him for so many years, but I am not less for that a sinner forgiven by His free grace.

Of Thy great goodness, O my God, grant me a deep shame and confusion, and an abiding repentance for forgiven sin.[6]

The rule of life which she had set herself became at this time more and more severe. She rose earlier in the morning, and lengthened the time of her meditation. She confessed twice a week, and communicated every day. Her acts of renouncement and mortification were multiplied. She no longer shrank back from any kind of penance, even those kinds which frighten not only the children of the world, but some of those persons who are familiar with Christian ideas on the subject. Those who firmly study the sufferings endured for us by our Master and Model will understand this. This consideration will enable them to understand the feelings of those who perceive the necessity of giving back to Him suffering for suffering, love for love. At least, the less we feel ourselves capable of imitating such examples, the more shall we be full

[6] See the Appendix.

of respect for those who have the courage to set them. With some it is probably more difficult to deny their self-love or their egotism, than to inflict on themselves some bodily penances, which, nevertheless, have so much power in self-conquest, the secret of every good here below.

We shall not be surprised to find the scruple relating to her literary efforts reviving at this time. We quote from some notes of the same date as the last.

> My difficulty about employment is this. If I propose to divide my time between writing and works of charity, the latter invariably usurps all of it, because writing can always be put off, and the others cannot. People coming to me for advice and consolation, letters to write about finding people situations, all these things do not brook delay.

> On the side of writing. Money gained, perhaps from £200 to £300 a year, if I gave myself assiduously to it, and wrote works of fiction. How many orphans could be provided for, and good works promoted with such a sum! A *little* good done also, perhaps, by such tales, especially if in French.

> Then writing religious tales, or lives of the saints, much less money gained, much fewer children provided for. I suppose the *Life of St. Frances of Rome*, such as it is, has done more good than my novels. Questionable if they have done any, though I hope a little in some cases.

> But then, if I take up literature as a vocation, I give up, in a great measure, personal work amongst the poor, which seems much more directly to benefit my own soul. Also, personal influence over others from associating in the same pursuits, and having common objects. I must withdraw from much I have engaged in, and give a check, perhaps, to the zeal of others by so doing.

There were many considerations on the other side, especially connected with her charities and labours among the poor. The result of these reflections was that she continued her writing. But there is no appearance of any diminution in activity in any of her charitable works. On July 1st of this year, 1859, the feast of the Sacred Heart, we find entered in her Journal a particular offering of herself to the service of poor children. She proposes to honour and serve our Saviour in the persons of those little ones, whose angels always see the face of His Father in Heaven. She desires that this offering may not be a passing emotion, but a firm and lasting determination of her soul. If she went on with her writing, we shall see how severely she kept up her guard against any self-love that might result from it. It seems to us that the self-denial which she imposed on herself in this respect was among the hardest for nature to yield to.

Some notes made in a retreat at Roehampton, in one of these years, show a good deal of the state of her soul at the time. Some extracts from these will be found in a separate place.[7] On one subject mentioned in her notes of this period we may give an account of what she says. This was the advice given her to relax her retirement some little, in consideration of the good which she might do, and the influence she might have in society. She discusses the question in a few lines. She says she is ready to obey, but she finds a difficulty in seeing how the following this advice would fit in with the kind of life she has been for some years leading. In order to exercise influence and be agreeable in the world, she must cultivate the talent of conversation, and give up the self-restraint she has imposed

[7] See Appendix.

on herself in checking her desire to talk, in aiming at silence, except when charity or the good of others do not oblige her to speak. She may not always have succeeded, but it has been her aim to do this. Again, it would be necessary to read the papers, and keep up with the current literature of the day, if she is to aim at being agreeable in society. But for the last four years she has read none but religious books, and if this is given up, she fears she may lose the little greater facility in prayer that she has acquired. She is just beginning to feel drawn to longer and longer prayer. The thought of God takes her away from all others. Is this an attraction that should be resisted ? The idea of an apostolate in the world is quite intelligible to her, but she has adopted a direction of thought quite the reverse of it. Two years ago, she says, at the end of her retreat, she had resolved to make her life more and more, as far as possible, like that of a religious person who was, by some accident, obliged to live in the world.

The end was that she continued to live as before, for the great good she might do, and for the happiness of her friends, but without throwing herself any more entirely into society. In this case, certainly, God was no loser. The severe watchfulness over herself by which her exterior life was guarded proves this, as well as the long list of the daily prayers by which her soul was continually raised to God, so that she seemed to accomplish the precept which the Apostle is not afraid to give us, of "praying always." We need mention further one point only, as to which, even the most virtuous among men may learn something, for there will be few who may not read with some confusion her inventions of humility, so to call them, in mortifying the pride of intellect. Lady Georgiana had never had great personal beauty in the ordinary sense. The charm in her was the charm of countenance and expression. She had never had the least feminine vanity or love for dress. Her dress was always plain, and, at the end of her life, even poor. This was not any reaction against her former tastes, but simply a consequence of the charity with which she denied herself in everything, and her humility which gave her a certain pleasure in appearing and being treated as a person of no importance, and, in some cases, as we shall see, as actually poor. But she could not conceal from herself that she had great intellectual gifts, and it was here that she found in herself some temptations to pride which she might fight against. How she dealt with it we have already seen. She thought it right to lay the matter before her spiritual guide, and it was decided that she should continue to write.[4]

[4] A little before this she had proposed to her guide in all such matters the question whether it would not be well to give up reading all reviews and notices of her works, which she found gave her ordinarily an intense pleasure, to which was added a certain usefulness which she found in the criticisms and remarks of the writers. This resolution she was advised to make at least for a year. Now, again, she raised the question we have been speaking of, whether it was best to continue her works of fiction at all? She says very humbly, on the one hand, that she has reason to think that her works do good to some souls. Another consideration is that, without this resource, she may have to give up a number of good works she has undertaken, orphans for whom she has made herself responsible, and the like. On the other hand, she says that her works are read by many to whom they can do little good, her name being so much connected with pious undertakings and religion generally. They are read even in convents. She does not herself think this is good, perhaps because, as she says, it is impossible to make novels interesting unless some *love* is introduced. The answer to this query was, as we have said, that she should continue to write, with carefulness in the selection of stories and materials.

CHAPTER XVII.

IN the course of the years which now ensued, Lady Georgiana was struck by new and sudden sorrows. The first of these blows, and the most appalling, was the death of one of the daughters of Lady Rivers, the young and charming Mrs. Arbuthnot, Alice Pitt. She was struck by lightning two months after her marriage, while travelling in Switzerland with her husband.[1] "Death in any form seems cruel, when it thus shatters happiness in its first bloom. What must we call it, when it is not only premature, but so strangely sudden and terrible? It is said that lightning strikes down, according to well founded calculations, about one in a million of those whom it might strike. And now it had chosen out one so charming and so dear!" Lady Georgiana thus wrote to her sister in the first moment of her anguish. This sorrow filled up the chalice of griefs which Lady Rivers was to drink. It was her last great suffering. Before a year passed, April 30, 1866, she was to rejoin the child she had so cruelly lost.

It was by a favour of Providence to Lady Rivers,

---

[1] In June, 1865.

almost as extraordinary as her sorrows, that she was not parted by death from the husband whom she loved so tenderly. Both were taken ill at the same time, and in the case of both, no danger was feared. Lord Rivers died, without his wife's knowing it, just two days before her. They met in the next world without having had the pain of parting in this. Lady Georgiana and her husband were absent from London at the time. The news of the death of her brother-in-law came to her suddenly, and she was reckoned on as the person who could break it to her sister. With her heart already full of anguish she arrived at the station, and was met by a messenger asking her to call on her way home at Hill Street to see Father Gallwey. Some kind friends of hers had thought of prevailing on her venerated guide and father to tell her that her sister had not survived her husband. It was thought that he, if any one on earth, could give her the courage to bear this new access of grief. She seemed at first to be thoroughly crushed. For many years she had been faithful in keeping under with great firmness her strong natural affections, but now, for a moment, they seemed to overwhelm her in their vehemence. She broke out into sobs and cries of grief, and it required all the authority and all the persuasiveness of her director to bring her back to the peaceful acquiescence in God's will which was her habitual state.

After the date of these sad losses, we find that the ties which united Lady Georgiana to her nieces were drawn still closer. This was especially the case with the two eldest, always loved by her with a peculiar love. Fanny, the second daughter, had married the Marquis of Carmarthen in 1861. The eldest, Susan, had more need than ever of her aunt's tender support. Her heart was full of peaceful strength, and we have spoken of that power of warm sympathy which enabled her to lead others to know the source whence her own serenity was derived.

The following letters written in the course of the year to Miss Susan Pitt, are dated from Mentone, where Mr. Fullerton and Lady Georgiana passed the winter of 1866—67.

To the Hon. Susan Pitt.

Mentone, *Jan.* 15, 1867.

DEAREST SUSAN,—Thank you very much for your long letter written on Christmas Day, and for your affectionate words.

They are precious to me ; though I love you all, you and Fanny are those most dear to my heart, and I can never expect that the others will feel the sort of intimacy with me that exists between you two and me, and I shall be indeed glad to find myself in England again.

I never say now, that I *long* for a future moment to arrive, for the sense at my age of the shortness of life gets so strong that I dare not wish to hurry over what remains of it.

The value of each moment seems so great. It is such happiness to do anything for God, and when one has begun late in life to love Him, there seems so much to make up for. To be cut off from active work is the greatest trial sometimes, but I am sure a useful one, like everything that God ordains.

I was thinking this morning, when reading the Gospel for the day, that just after our Lord had said that He must be about His Father's business, that He went to Nazareth and for *eighteen* years lived in seclusion there, apparently doing nothing.

His Public Life only lasted three years. I believe *the work* any one is intended to do, the object for which God has sent them into the world, occupies sometimes a very short space in their existence, and that the various positions they are placed in gradually train them for cotresponding with His grace at some appointed time, which proves the most important of their life, though this is not always evident.

It is such a comfort . . . that Henry is well in health.

Dear, dear boy, what you tell me would depress me did I not feel, as I know you do also, that we cannot about him form any deliberate *wish* of any sort. Happy in life and fit, I firmly believe, for death, let God do with him what He wills.

I am sorry Mrs. Craven's book has not been sent, I will write and inquire what has become of it.

She has lately lost her remaining brother, Fernand. He died suddenly while taking a drive with the Comte de Chambord.

I think you would like the three Lives Lady Herbert has published. The first, *St. Monica*, would not quite do for your younger sisters.

Ever your most affectionate

G. FULLERTON, *E. de M.*

To the same.

Mentone, *Feb.* 11, 1867.

DEAREST SUSAN,—I meant to have written to you long ago and thanked you for your last dear letter, but, for the last ten days, I have been troubled by gouty swellings and irritation about my ears, at first painful, now much better and only troublesome, but it made me feel lazy.

I do not feel sure if you are at Torquay or at Rushmore, but I think by the time you receive this letter you will have moved to Rushmore, and so I direct there. We are going at last on Friday to San Remo, on our way to Rome, where we have written to take apartments for the first days in March.

If you write this month, direct to Hôtel de Londres, San Remo, as Pièrre will forward our letters on the road ; but after the 1st of March to Serny's Hotel, Piazza di Spagna, Rome.

I am most glad to go back—not to leave Mentone. It is a charming spot. So full of beauty and within the reach of the lowest capacities in the way of walking. It has done my husband great good, but I think a change will be good also now, as the mistral will soon begin to blow on this coast.

How you would enjoy the spring flowers here, they are so beautiful! Our doctor brings me back lovely nosegays. He explores the country in every direction. We went on the 2nd of February to a Carmelite monastery, with a church which is a famous place of pilgrimage in this part of the country, at about eight miles from here. It is in a wild valley closed in on three sides, with one opening which has a distant view of ridge after ridge of hills and mountains.

On certain festivals, as many as ten thousand persons sometimes assemble here, encamping in covered carts all round the monastery.

There was a poor peasant woman in the church, who was aware she was out of her mind and was praying to be cured. She kept constantly coming up to me and saying, "I am the mother of four children and I am out of my mind, ask the Madonna to have pity on me."

And then she began again praying and sobbing with such wild imploring eyes. She disturbed my prayers, but I could not help feeling that she put me in mind of the Syro-Phœnician woman, "Send her away for she crieth after us." If I had any poetry left in me that would be a subject.

There are two or three anecdotes in Lady Herbert's book on Spain which would make pretty subjects for verses, particularly the story of the idiot boy who could never learn anything but the words, *Creo a Dios, Espero a Dios, Amo a Dios,* repeating them before the altar.

Mrs. Craven's book, which you must have read, I hope, has gone on to a tenth edition. I believe I am going to translate it.[2]

The journey to Rome, which is spoken of so hopefully in this letter, was prevented, as Lady

[2] She speaks of the *Récit d'une Sœur.* It was not Lady Georgiana who translated it into English, but Miss Emily Bowles, with help from her counsel, and under her direction. M. de Montalembert said it was the best translation he had ever read.

Georgiana came to see, providentially. She thus writes about it to Lady Herbert of Lea, who had been converted to Catholicism two years before this time, and soon became one of Lady Georgiana's intimate friends.

> . . . This is our history. On the 16th of February we left Mentone to go to Rome. But as I was very unwell with an inflammation in the ears and neuralgic pains in the head, we were to begin by staying a few days at San Remo. Though I was dying to get on, my husband and the doctor would not make a start till the 28th. We went to Alegrio. I was in extasies at being, after four months putting off, at last fairly on the way to Rome. But in the night my husband was taken ill with a stomach attack and great nervous exhaustion, and by the doctor's advice, the next morning our *voiturier* horses' heads were turned the other way and we returned to San Remo, where we stayed till yesterday. This was certainly a severe disappointment, for some reasons almost a sorrow, but I felt I had set my heart too much on the thoughts of it, and I have no doubt it is all for the best—a blessing in disguise, as all trials are. England is, after all, where I would soonest be, and the change will probably bring us home a month sooner. I hope to be in London early in May.

This letter is dated March 15, from Mentone, to which place they had by that time returned on their way to Cannes and Hyères. It turned out that they were to hear news which made them not regret their change of plans. Of this we shall speak presently. The same letter contains a passage which may interest us, concerning the good that may be done in the most apparently unpromising society.

> I can perfectly understand your dread of the London season. The only comfort is that that sort of mortification, when it is

really keenly felt, is perhaps the most meritorious of any. It furnishes no food for self-complacency, and satisfies no natural feeling. Then, again, there may be opportunities of doing good in a ball-room as well as in a House of Charity, especially in these days when amongst the higher classes are so many anxious, unsettled minds. It is good perhaps that some of God's workers should be compelled to go into scenes which they would not voluntarily frequent, but where seed may be sown which may some day bear fruit. I remember how, twenty-two years ago, one night at a large party, when I felt very miserable about Mr. Oakeley's dismissal from Margaret Chapel, I found comfort in talking to Sir R. T——, not a brilliant specimen of a Catholic, but simply because he was a Catholic; and again at a party at Windsor Castle, three years afterwards, how the Duchess of Buccleuch came and sat by me all the evening, seeking evidently the same sort of consolation. Are you in the habit of invoking the Guardian Angels of those you are about to converse with? I have been told that this often obtains graces for them.

The letters which follow next, relate to the last of the sons of Lady Rivers, who, as has been said, survived her. Henry, mentioned with such anxious rejoicing over his health, was now the head of the family, and the tenderness with which his sisters regarded him was mixed with the fear that was to be truly justified by the event, that he would follow his brothers to the grave. He was now approaching his eighteenth year, which, like them, he was not to attain.

It would hardly be possible to think calmly of the pathetic and mysterious lot of these brothers, but that there was a purity and a nobility about these young lives, thus gathered in their first bloom, which shed a light upon them more beautiful than the realization of any human prospects could have given. Life has no significance or importance but that which is given to it by the end to which it leads. These sons of Lady Rivers may have reached that end with more safety and more happiness than others who had many and long conflicts to wage, and their mother, through all her trials, had good reason to give unceasing thanks to God for having granted her the blessing of giving them birth.

To the Hon. Susan Pitt.

Mentone, *March* 11, 1867.

MY OWN DEAREST SUSAN,—I have received this morning a letter from Freddy which gives me the deepest anxiety about our beloved Henry. The account in itself would have left me little hope, only as six days have elapsed since he wrote, and, in the meantime, no telegram has come, I cannot but hope a little.

We have all so long looked this fear in the face, that I can feel and write calmly about it. If the worst should happen then, dearest, we can bless God those beloved ones are spared the terrible trial, and He will bless you all and help you to bear it.

I am so thankful now we did not go on to Rome. What was a severe disappointment, as so often happens, turns out such a mercy.

It is a comfort to me to get nearer to you if the worst does happen.

I shall hope soon to return to England, as now the bad time of the year is over and my husband is well. I am a great deal better.

God bless you all with all my heart.

Your ever affectionate aunt,

G. FULLERTON, *E. de M.*

On Tuesday we go to Nice, Wednesday to Cannes till Saturday, then to Hyères.

X

It was at Cannes, on the following 21st of March, that Lady Georgiana received the news of the long-feared and long-expected death of her nephew.

To the same.

March 21.

After writing to you, a fresh letter gave me a little hope, when your message came. . . . In spite of all I was not prepared for it. For our dear Henry, we must only adore the will of God and think that for *him* it is more than well, and for your beloved parents, how can one thank Heaven enough that they were spared the trial.

It is for you, my poor darlings, who have to bear the full weight of the blow that I feel. The loss of your last brother, so carefully tended and deeply loved, and the loss also of your home, both at once. How I feel for you ! If my old heart, hardened by grief, feels so much at the loss of the home, rendered dear as the place where I have witnessed so much joy and so much sorrow, what must it be to you all to whom it was *Home*, where you have lived with all your lost ones. But God calls you in your early days to bear the cross, and I have no fear of your shrinking.

Send me the photograph of our Henry, and also the one he intended for me of his favourite dog.

To the same.

Cannes, *March* 27.

DEAREST SUSAN,—This letter will probably reach you at the moment of your great trial, though indeed I am not sure if a little time hence you will not feel even more acutely than in the act itself the separation from your loved home.[3]

I was so touched by your finding time to write to me from Rushmore. I received your letter yesterday. The sharpness of this suffering in one sense is its consolation. The work done in the place appointed to you, and the mutual love between your poor neighbours and yourselves, is the painful, the most painful cause of your suffering.

[3] On the death of young Lord Rivers, Rushmore went to his uncle, and after him, to a distant cousin.

Well, there is sweetness also in that pain. You may say of your share in this work of this portion of your life, *Consummatum est*—"It is finished," and in a very humble sense, "My God, I have finished the work Thou hadst given me to do." Now you leave behind one stage of life's journey. He only knows where and how He will next employ you. Your motto now should be St. Paul's words, "Forgetting the things of the past (only in one sense, of course), stretch forward to those beyond."

Perhaps you have sown seed which you will not see the harvest of, but every effort to do good is counted, stored up, and the sufferings of to-day are earning, perhaps, special blessings on future years and future works. Have you meditated often on these words, "Unless a seed falls into the ground and *dies*, it does not produce fruit"?

The kind of uprooting you are now going through is a real dying to self, if generously accepted, and will bear fruit.

God bless you, dearest ones—all of you. Give every one of them my tenderest love.

Ever your most affectionate
G. FULLERTON, *E. de M.*

Direct to Hyères. It does not lose time. I do not know which day we shall get there.

The next letter is written apparently from Paris.

To the same.

April 28.

DEAREST SUSAN,—The days seem to pass slowly when I think of England, which I do so long to reach, although quickly, as regards the number of things I have to do here.

We have put off our departure from the 29th to the 30th. I wished to be sure of being able to go to church that morning.

As our time of crossing always depends on the weather, I shall telegraph when I leave Calais, and you could send me a line to Dover to the Lord Warden Hotel, in case you could not receive me at the time I should name.

The weather has been rather wet and stormy this week. I perfectly understand all your feelings, dearest Susan, and if you have found any comfort in my letters, I hope that when we are together it may be still more so. There are characters for whom *action* is the greatest rest, but work, when the body is weak from all the soul has gone through, though it might relieve, would quickly wear out.

Make it your work *to rest*, and then, after awhile, work will be the best rest.

This Paris is a wonderful place, full of interest, and I should like some time or other to spend some time in seeing *leisurely* the charitable institutions.

I often think how wasted were the sixteen years I spent here in my youth. The regrets I feel on this point make me so anxious to persuade those who have life before them to think of the value of time as I now do.

But some of the best spent hours of our life may be those of *apparent* inaction. How little others and even ourselves know the moments in which we are doing most for eternity ! There will be, I imagine, great *surprises* on the Day of Judgment.

God bless you, dearest Susan. With kindest love to all your sisters.

Ever affectionately yours,
G. FULLERTON, *E. de M.*

Mrs. Craven's book is going through the tenth edition, and is about to be crowned by the French Academy. I believe I am going to translate it, an arduous and ungrateful work in some respects, but I hope a useful one.

During these days of sorrow, Lady Georgiana wrote as follows to Lady Herbert of Lea. Rushmore was not far from Wilton, and Lady Herbert took a lively interest in the young sisters, struck down by so many afflictions.

To Lady Herbert of Lea.

Cannes, *March* 25, 1867.

MY DEAR LADY HERBERT,—Many grateful thanks for your kind note and affectionate sympathy, and goodness to my poor dearly-loved nieces. The trial is a heavy one, and made

heavier to me by absence. However, I am now glad of the
great disappointment I had about Rome, as it will bring me
back to England, at all events, sooner than if we had gone
there. I long now inexpressibly to get home, and hope to do
so by the beginning of May. How *very* kind of you to have
offered Wilton,—but they had, I know, accepted at once to go
to Walmer Castle, as soon as they depart from Rushmore. I
was in spirit with them yesterday when, within a year, they saw
this only brother, the object of so much tender care and
affection, buried by the side of their parents. Yes, the trials
of my family are strange and mysterious, but I doubt not that
those numerous prayers, so many of which I owe to you, have
obtained strange blessings also for them all. Indeed, I can
never doubt it. They are a pledge, as it were, that those *three*
specially pleaded for in that appeal have been taken in mercy.[4]
Dearest Henry's end was as beautiful and hopeful as any death
not visibly in the Church can be, and the heavy load of sorrow
laid on his sisters in their youth will, I doubt not, prove an
earnest of future spiritual blessings. The trial of leaving
Rushmore, which they are now preparing to do, is severe.
They almost idolized the place, and had lived and worked there
ever since they could remember.

I am so sorry you have anxiety about your second daughter.
That, added to the coming season, is another suffering to offer
up. If you are obliged to go to a warm climate with her next
winter, how I wish you would return to Mentone. Whether we
do so ourselves, which is very probable, or not, I should be so
glad you did so. There is so much good to be done there just
at this time. I will tell you all about it when we meet, and I
have one plan in particular in which I want you to help me.

We have not been able to have good apartments at Hyères

---

[4] Lady Georgiana here alludes to an appeal for prayers which she and
Mr. Fullerton had made as widely as possible, during the last year, for her
nephew and also for his parents. An account of her industry in this appeal,
which was spread through almost every European country, prayers being
offered at many famous shrines, and by hundreds of religious communities,
is given in the Appendix. She considered the strange mercy of the almost
simultaneous deaths of her sister and her brother-in-law, neither of whom
knew that the other was in danger, as an earnest that the prayers were
answered, though in God's way, not ours.

yet, at the hotel near the church, but by the end of the week I believe they will be vacant, and we shall then proceed there.
Yours, dear Lady Herbert,
Always affectionately yours,
G. FULLERTON, *E. de M.*[5]

These letters will serve to show us how, in the midst of her increasing austerity, Lady Georgiana kept up all her natural affections with tenderness and faithfulness. Her return to England this year was, it can be easily imagined, a great joy to her nieces, who had now losses of so many different kinds to draw them to her sympathy.

[5] We subjoin to this letter that which Lady Georgiana had written to Lady Herbert on her conversion.

To Lady Herbert of Lea.

May, 1865.

MY DEAR LADY HERBERT,—As you sent me a kind message by Lady Londonderry, I venture to write and tell you with what sincere joy and gratitude to God I heard of your being actually received into His Church, to which you have long been in heart devoted. I have now been just nineteen years a Catholic, and never ceased to wonder with an adoring heart at the infinite mercy of God in bestowing on one so unworthy as myself, that blessed gift of Faith not vouchsafed to so many who would make a better use of it. *You* have a great part of life before you, and He Who has called you into His Church will, I trust, give you many many years to work for Him and to bring many others to the Faith. It gave me great pleasure to hear that you were affiliated to the Sisters of St. Vincent of Paul. So have I been for the last three years, and I am happy to think we shall have a common object of interest. I suppose you have to look to many trials and many heartaches in consequence of your conversion, but I doubt not that strength and courage will be given you to bear whatever cross it may please our Blessed Lord to lay upon you. May such crosses be lightened and sweetened by heavenly consolations. Believe me—I may venture to say so now when, although we have not very often met, we are linked by the same faith,—
Yours affectionately,
GEORGIANA FULLERTON, *E. de M.*

Easter Sunday.

She writes after arriving in England to the same niece :

To the Hon. Susan Pitt.

27, Chapel Street, Park Lane, *May* 28.

DEAREST SUSAN,—Many thanks for sending me that photograph. It is a deeply affecting one.

I can scarcely look at it without tears. How strange it is that it should have upset me more than dearest Henry's own likeness. God bless you.

Ever affectionately yours,

G. FULLERTON, *E. de M*.

She writes again on hearing of the death of Mrs. Talbot—wife of a brother of Lady Lothian—who had been her own intimate friend many years before, and with whom she had lately renewed her intimacy. Miss Pitt felt her loss, not only as that of a very dear friend, but as that of the mainstay of some charitable works in which she was herself engaged. One of the chief helpers in this work had been Miss Laura Oldfield, who had died a few months before Mrs. Talbot.

To the same.

June 13.

MY DEAREST SUSAN,—Cross upon cross ! In the midst of my grief for my oldest and dearest friend,[6] with whom my intimacy had revived within this last year, and for whom I had anticipated such an advanced and active old age, my first thought was for you.

So soon after your irreparable loss you are deprived of one of the props on whom you would have leant in carrying on your work of charity.[7]

How strange it seems, dearest Susan, when we think of Holmbury last year, that those two souls so full of energy—

[6] Mrs. Talbot.   [7] Miss Laura Oldfield.

those two active minds—those two useful lives, were so soon to be removed and ended.

My heart is very sad, and feels so drawn towards you, my own dearest niece.

May God bless you ever.

> Yours most affectionately,
>
> G. FULLERTON.

On their return to England in 1868, Lady Georgiana and Mr. Fullerton went to Slindon, which still belonged to them, though they had determined to part with it. The summer was passed pleasantly in this charming residence, rendered more charming by the neighbourhood of Arundel Castle, where the Duchess of Norfolk was living. Her nieces came in turn to stay with her, and enjoy the rest which her tenderness supplied. Miss Pitt speaks of the care taken by their aunt and uncle to provide them with every pleasure within reach of their peaceful refuge, such as drives to Arundel Castle and other places in the neighbourhood. She mentions also a visit paid to Mr. and Lady Georgiana Fullerton by the Duc de Nemours, the Duc and Duchesse de Chartres, and the Princess Marguerite. They spent several hours at Slindon, and lost no opportunity of showing to her uncle and aunt the regard which they bore to them. We extract the following passage from the memoranda of Miss Pitt. We shall take the opportunity of drawing rather more largely than is absolutely necessary on these precious notes.

I used to regret that in my early girlhood she spoke so little of religion to me, but I think she feared that, if she did so, she would insensibly touch upon the points on which we differed, and upon which she would not have thought it right to try and influence me when I was quite young. Afterwards, just before the death of my dear father and mother, she did talk to me on these subjects, and we always continued to do so at intervals up to the time of her death, and she often gave me good advice. But I think one learnt more from her example than her words, and from seeing how religion had moulded her character, subduing a naturally too eager, impulsive nature into perfect resignation and abnegation of her own will in small as well as in grave matters. I think the last time I stayed with her in her own house was in the autumn of 1867, when my sister Margaret (now Mrs. Page Roberts) and I paid her a visit at Slindon of some weeks' duration. She was very busy writing at that time, and I can almost see her now sitting at a table in the little room which she used as her study. Still she found time to arrange pleasant drives and excursions for us, and we drove often with her and with my uncle to Arundel Castle, where she seemed very happy with her great friend, the Duchess of Norfolk. At that time, too, the Duc de Nemours and his family were staying at one of the sea places in the neighbourhood.

Since my marriage, in 1872, my intercourse with my aunt was principally in London or at Bournemouth, when staying there with my sisters. We were at the same hotel in Paris in the autumn of 1882. My aunt suffered very much at times, and her illness was beginning to tell upon her nerves. Yet she was going about much as usual, and enjoying the churches and musical services. I recollect her saying to me that it was so strange that she always heard Paris spoken of as such a very wicked city, but that to her, who saw the other side of it, it appeared such a deeply religious one. She took me about with her a good deal to various churches, where there were fine pictures and sculptures to be seen, remaining in devout prayer while I wandered about quietly by myself. St. Roch was, I think, one of her favourite churches. She had been lately at Tours, which had delighted her, and she was much interested in our going there from Paris, and returning again to Paris on our way back to England. I think she enjoyed pictures more in a religious than in an artistic point of view, and with reference to this, I recollect after a tour we had made in Holland, when I was showing her my photographs, which interested her extremely, because they brought back to her the memories of her childhood at the Hague, her pausing before one I had of our Saviour on the Cross from a picture by Rubens in the museum at Antwerp, and saying, "My dear, what a meditation!" and then adding a few words about the expression of each face.

She spent some time at Boulogne on her way back to England, and soon after that settled at Bournemouth, gradually becoming weaker, and at intervals seeming very near death, but then rallying again. I saw her occasionally, making a point of doing so whenever I was at Stapleton, where my sisters live, and which is not far from Bournemouth, and admired not only her sweet patience, but the way in which she made the best of every little pleasure or solace remaining to her. She enjoyed so much the very restricted view from her window, and watching a particular squirrel at play was, she said, a great amusement to her. I used to think her conversation, at that time, so like a chapter out of *Eugenie de Guerin*. One day I found some flowers on her bed which had been sent to her, but there was a tiger lily among them, and she remarked that this was the only flower she did not like, because it looked so wicked. Her loving sympathy, also, never waned, and she would ask specially about any member of the family who was at all unwell, and send some kind message to those whom she was unable to see. When I saw her in the spring of 1884, we both thought it was for the last time, but it was bad for her to give way to emotion, so we did not trust ourselves to say more than the ordinary farewell, but she put a little parting note into my hand. At that time she asked also to see my husband, who was with her for a few minutes. I did, however, see her again, for we were at Stapleton in August of that year, and I went over from thence for the day.

I do not know whether I have dwelt too much on the graver side of my dear aunt's character. If I have done so, it is because, since my cousin's death, I have seen more of her in sorrow than in joy, for the house of mourning was her special haunt. In fact, when things were particularly prosperous with me, I used to regret seeing so little of her. A friend of hers used to say, "Lady Georgiana only goes to the three S's—the sick, the sorrowful, and the sinful," and to some extent this was true. And yet she always had, I think, the power of enjoying. life, and her religion had nothing in it that was morose. She was always very fond of children, and liked to see their pleasure. I recollect her coming once to see my little nephews and nieces with her pockets full of penny toys, because she said she had observed that expensive toys were quite wasted on children, who much preferred quantity to quality. And in later years her affection for my uncle Granville's children almost amounted to a passion.[8] She was *very* fond of their mother also, and, I think, admired her beauty and charm with something of a poetic feeling. It was also a real pleasure to her to give amusements to poor children, and she seemed so to enter into their little joys and sorrows. I remember her telling me one day, when she had been giving prizes to some school children, that she could hardly bear to see the despair of one poor little girl to whose share a doll did *not* fall, which had evidently been the object of her longing. She seemed so entirely to sympathize with the child. My aunt was always ready to take her part in whatever amusements were in vogue amongst us. She played constantly at whist, and liked chess, I think, even better.

She never set herself up in any way to be different from others, and no one who met her in society would have, I think, suspected her gifts of authorship, or how much her life was given up to good works. She only appeared to betray the latter by the extreme simplicity of her dress. She always wore mourning after the death of her son, and that of the plainest description. Once, on visiting a workhouse, the porter, not recognizing her position in life, I suppose on this account,

---

[8] Lord Granville married a second time, in September, 1865, the younger daughter of V. F. Campbell, Esq., of Islay, and the marriage was the source of great happiness and joy to Lady Georgiana. Her other brother, Mr. F. Leveson Gower, to whom so many of her letters were written, lost his wife, Lady Margaret, hardly three years after his marriage. She left one son, born shortly before her own death in 1858. Mr. Leveson Gower was his sister's constant helper, not only in literary matters, but in other ways.

spoke rudely to her, of which she took no notice, but went up
to visit her poor woman. Meantime, he discovered who she
was, and when she came down greeted her with profuse
apologies, assuring her that he would have treated her quite
differently had he recognized her. She quietly replied that she
thought it would be better in future that he should speak civilly
to every one. But she told me this little anecdote afterwards
with much amusement. I think she had a real love of the poor,
and that she really enjoyed being with them.

Some parts of these most interesting notes are
in anticipation of our history, but the reader will
easily excuse our leaving them where they are,
though we have not yet reached the last stage of
Lady Georgiana's life.

We have now to speak in more detail of the
Religious Institute which was, in some respects,
the most important work of Lady Georgiana's life.
It has long been evident that the single house of
the Sisters of Charity, in London, was altogether
insufficient. Cardinal Wiseman said that nine
others at least were required, if the poor Catholics
of London were to be adequately helped. For this,
as is plain, there were no means. But Lady
Georgiana, as we have seen, had another idea
which could not be accomplished by houses of
Sisters of Charity. She wished to open a home
for a great number of pious girls who had a call to
serve God in religion, without having the necessary
dower which was required in all the houses of Mercy
which then existed in England. She imagined a
Religious Institute which should be supported by
some kind of industrial work, where girls might be
received without dower, and might pay the debt

thus incurred by their labour, and, at the same time, take part in visiting the poor, and other charitable works which were always to accompany any other.

These ideas ripened in her mind for a long time before they could be realized. She thought of the matter whether at Mentone or at San Remo, or during her annual returns to England, whither she came back every spring. She heard of a work of the kind in Poland, the end of which seemed to be like that which she aimed at, and her first idea was to affiliate her own work to that.

Meanwhile, an intimate friend, energetic and devoted like herself, Miss Taylor, who afterwards became, under the name of Mother Magdalene, the first Superior of the new Congregation, told her that, in her absence at San Remo, an excellent priest had come to see her, and, without knowing anything about her project, had spoken to her of the necessity of founding an Order precisely similar to that of which she was thinking. After some conversations they resolved on seeking to know the will of God by a fervent novena of prayers, and determined to accept whatever means offered themselves for the accomplishment of the Divine will, or to give up their plans if nothing came to hand towards its accomplishment. Some new recruits came to present themselves before the end of the novena, and, by the end of the year, their numbers had increased, and some rooms had been taken in the City. There the pious little group knelt down before a statue of the Blessed Virgin, and she was declared the special protector of the work. The prayer then made was one of those prayers which in a special manner consecrate the object of a life. The Congregation is now well founded and flourishing, and the statue is preserved with tender veneration in its principal house.

It was Lady Georgiana's wish that, before they began the work, Miss Taylor should visit the Order called the Little Servants of Mary, in the Grand Duchy of Posen. She preferred following the direction of others to directing herself. But it was found that the affiliation was not practicable, and that the new work must depend upon its own resources. They set seriously to work, and, in a short time, the new community was able to find a kind of work which fell under the design of its institution, and made it almost self-supporting. A large number of girls were soon received of the class to whom Lady Georgiana had intended to offer an asylum, and many of these became by their zeal, their exemplary life, and their piety, the source of the greatest consolation to the foundress. We have not space to go into details on the progress of this work, the fruit of her charity, and which she guided and sustained by her wisdom and zeal as long as her life lasted. Her husband has carried on its support since her death; as if his life here below had been prolonged only that he might complete what he had seen her begin. Her blessed influence seems to have remained continually present, almost visibly, to further it. The community has taken the name of the Poor Servants of the Mother of God Incarnate. Since her death it has been approved and blessed by the Sovereign Pontiff, and been encouraged to found its central house in Rome itself. It is needless to name the generous benefactor through whose means it has been able to accomplish this desire almost as soon as it was formed.

It is easy to imagine that as soon as Lady Georgiana had begun the foundation, she followed its advancing steps and successive development with an extreme interest. Its success has been such as she could never anticipate. She had intended it for London, and wished it to gather together the girls of the poorer classes, who were to be actively employed in visiting the neighbouring poor in their dwellings. But this activity soon spread to other kinds of labour. She had the happiness to see it spread to Ireland, and its numbers greatly augmented, and the Sisters called in to direct schools, orphanages, and hospitals. She was especially interested in the Providence Hospital, at St. Helens, Lancashire. The industrial labour which at first served mainly to support the whole was washing, but since her time printing has been added, and this new work seems likely to succeed as the other. If she did not live to see her work in all its expansion, she at all events saw it extend beyond all her own expectations. She said, towards the end of her life, that God had His own designs. When we try sincerely to accomplish these, we often find ourselves departing from the plans with which we began. We wished one thing. We find in the course of our work that He wished something else, perhaps something which far surpasses our expectations and our hopes. All that we have to do is to accept everything from Him, and in what we do for Him cling to His will and not to our own.

In 1865, Lord Granville had been named Lord Warden of the Cinque Ports, an office which entitled him to the residence of Walmer Castle, near Dover. The Duke of Wellington had been one of his predecessors, and had become very fond of this abode, where he spent a good deal of his time, and where he ended his glorious life. Lord Granville also liked it very much, and from the first Lady Georgiana loved it, as the place where she could find her brother at home, and enjoy with him and for his sake the cloudless happiness in the midst of which he lived, and which reflected itself upon her own life. Later on it was remarked how her countenance would light up when she spoke of her young sister-in-law, her affection for whom was the brightest and keenest of her joys during her last twenty years of life. She had the happiness to see the children of her brother grow up around her, and it is needless to describe the floods of motherly tenderness which she had in her heart for them. They were a last brightness spread over her declining years, the memory of their dear aunt remains ever present to them, and her prayers protect them continually.

CHAPTER XVIII.

It will easily be understood that the war of 1870, and the misfortunes which it brought upon France, awakened the liveliest sympathy in Lady Georgiana for the country of her childhood and youth, which she had learnt to love almost as her own. She followed every phase of that terrible struggle with inconceivable anguish, and when, even before the final disasters were over, her first thought was to find what her sympathetic charity could do to alleviate some at least of those cruel sufferings, her zeal must have failed of its object, great as that zeal was, if she had been alone. But she was but one of a large number of ladies like herself, who were ready to devote themselves to the aid of the French fugitives who were landing every day in England, old men, women, and children, in the greatest state of destitution, flying from the invasion as it passed on from one part of France to another. We must give some short account of this phase of the work of charity, if only that it may be a specimen of a new kind of devotion on the part of herself and others like her.

Lady Lothian was the first, and one of the most

Y

generous of all these ladies, whose name must remain for ever engraven on the French heart. This incomparable friend of Lady Georgiana was, as long as she lived, her most intimate associate in every charitable and religious work. She was made President of the Ladies' Committee, which was organized for the relief of the refugees, by collections, subscriptions, and succours of every kind. Lady Lothian began by selling her carriage, that she might have at once some money wherewith to meet the first needs. Then, at the sacrifice of every other care and of her personal comfort, she turned her house in Bruton Street into a kind of central office, where applications might be made, information received, succour distributed, and the like. The ground floor was given up to the work of administration, while the drawing-rooms were devoted to the reception of contributions of every kind, from persons of all ranks, from the highest to the lowest. A great number of artisans and workmen sent their offerings, carefully labelled, *For the French.* It is well known that the working men of London gave at that time each one day's wages, and the magnificent collection, organized by the Lord Mayor, amounted to £40,000.

It would be impossible to name all the assistants in the good work. We may mention Lady Londonderry, the Duchess of Buccleuch, Lady Newburgh, Lady Denbigh, Lady O'Hagan, and her sister, Lady Alexander Lennox, Mrs. Pollen, Miss Langdale, and last of all, Lady Herbert of Lea, who was one of those whose charity at this crisis went beyond all ordinary sacrifices. Among the refugees from France it was not always the poorest who were the most difficult to relieve. A certain number had been taken by surprise by the invading armies, and obliged to fly, so as to be for the time entirely without resources, and who were either unable or unwilling to make their state of distress known. The good ladies who devoted themselves to the aid of France made it their business to find out these refugees. They opened their own doors to them, and these shipwrecked outcasts of the war found in them hospitality which could not be refused, and which many of them availed themselves of for the whole time during which the storm lasted. Lady Herbert was the first to set the example of this kind charity. From the first days of the exile she received under her roof an old gentleman of a very honourable and distinguished family, who remained her guest for two months, and found there all the care and attention which he would have had in his own home. Poor young girls were received by others. The mothers of families with others who found refuge for them till the time of their return to their country. Alms and help were distributed to others whose condition required, or was such that they could not refuse to accept them. The French could not have met with more cordial and delicate charity from their own fellow-countrymen, and we must add to this, the large succours in kind that were sent to France by means of the same organization.

While every care was taken to provide the

fugitives with shelter, profuse supplies were sent to France of everything that could be of comfort to the sick and wounded. Private charity was of incalculable service in this respect, besides the immense convoys sent by the city of London. Protestant ladies joined with Catholics in the good work, Irish and Scotch with English. It was a noble movement of sympathy, worthy alike of the great country from which the aid came, and of that which received it.

Lady Lothian, it may well be supposed, had no more efficient auxiliary during all these months than Lady Georgiana. Her intelligence and her devotion were unrivalled, and besides this, she was particularly fitted to receive the strangers, whose language and country she knew better than any one else. At the end of the war, M. Thiers wished to send to the English ladies some mark of the gratitude of France, and it was received in the name of all, and most deservedly, by Lady Lothian. Lady Georgiana gave herself no repose during this period of activity and agitation, except a short visit from time to time to Walmer Castle, where she could breathe the sea air, and enjoy the society of her sister-in-law, for Lord Granville, then Foreign Secretary, could rarely leave London and snatch a few moments at Walmer. His younger brother was in Parliament, dividing his time between politics and the care of his son's education, whom Lady Georgiana loved with a redoubled interest on account of the sad loss which had fallen on him as a child. The correspondence between Lady

Georgiana and Mr. Leveson Gower was always active, and we can only give at length a portion of the letters between them.

To the Hon. F. Leveson Gower.

Walmer Castle, *September* 15, 1870.

DEAREST FREDDY,—We are quite alone here with Cas,[1] which is enjoyable and great rest, but it does not give me much to say. G. saw you a moment, I hear, yesterday, so you will have heard of his interview with Thiers. He wrote to Cas that he thought there was a gleam of a hope of peace, but really the news from France is so bad, that when peace is made with Prussia, I fear there will immediately follow civil war. The language in the ultra-Republican papers is atrocious.

---

[1] Lady Granville, whose name is "Castalia," was thus called in the family. Lady Georgiana addressed her in the following stanzas :

> Bright as the crystal stream which flows
>   From thine own fountain's source,
> Or as the sparkling rays which play
>   Upon its rippling course,—
> Fair as the morning beams which gild
>   Its waters, sweet and clear,
> Castalia ! thy strange sounding name
>   Familiar grows and dear.
> Oh, may a likeness in thy life
>   To that sweet name be found—
> A spring of hope and peace and joy
>   Refreshing all around !
> And if as time goes on, its stream
>   Grows deeper and more wide,
> Embracing duties, cares, and aims
>   Which in strong hearts abide ;
> When life's increasing trials prove
>   The metal of thy heart,
> When called upon to bear and act
>   A woman's lofty part—
> Then may the current be as pure,
>   The ripple not less bright,
> And on the surging water shine
>   A ray of heaven's light !

They have at Lyons the red flag and a government independent of the Paris one. Nice and Mentone proclaim the Italian Republic. It grieves me so to see that at Mentone the *soi disant* National Guards have murdered the *Commissaire de Police, à coups de bayonettes.* I suppose it is in the hands of the Garibaldians. It is the old story over again, tyranny under the name of freedom. Knowing all the people so well there, it seems to come home to me so painfully.

G. will not come home, Cas thinks, till Saturday. That day Lord Ebury and Sir James Lacaita (I do not know if I spell the name right) are expected.

Vita[2] is in great force and the greatest of darlings. Lady Lothian begs me to thank you very gratefully for your kind donation.

My best love to darling George.

Ever your affectionate

G. F., *E. de M.*

[2] "Vita," a short name for Lord Granville's daughter, Lady Victoria, then aged three years. Lady Georgiana wrote of her thus :

O little Vita, I had deem'd
  My heart had grown too old,
Something so young, something so bright,
  Thus warmly to enfold.

A calm regard, a fervent prayer,
  Perchance some silent tears,
Were all that heart had thought to give
  In its declining years.

But thou hast touch'd some latent chords
  That seldom now resound,
And moved the secret springs that still
  In its lone depths are found.

O little life ! I love thee for
  The present and the past ;
I love thee for the mould in which
  Thy childish form is cast.

I love thee for thy voice, for all
  Thy graceful winning ways,
And each resemblance that awakes
  The thought of other days.

To the same.

Walmer Castle.

... It *must* be anxious work to have any power of action or no action at such a crisis. We are expecting eagerly the result of the interview. G. has no hope of peace at once, and thinks that if Jules Favre was to propose to agree at this moment to the best terms that could by any possibility be offered, he would run the risk of his life, and the Government be overthrown, but still he thinks it may be an opening when the situation becomes still more desperate. Mr. Forster[3] is of opinion that if the French are absolutely determined to continue the struggle, and to make every sacrifice, they must end by beating the Prussians, that a nation like France cannot be conquered, but he does not believe they are *de cette force ou à cette hauteur.* He did not say this in French.

The destruction of the village of Bazeilles is the most horrible thing ever heard of, if the details of it are true. ...

I am glad to see that it was a band of Garibaldian bandits that invaded Mentone, killed a man, and pillaged its public offices—not the inhabitants, who proclaimed the Italian Republic.

Ever affectionately,

G. FULLERTON.

During the following years Mr. Fullerton and Lady Georgiana continued to spend their winters abroad, either at Mentone or at San Remo, stopping on their way home at Paris, to pass a few days with Madame de Salvo. They often thought of going again to Rome, but a series of obstacles which seemed quite fortuitous continually hindered them. It was a trial to Lady Georgiana, accustomed as she was to resignation in small matters as well as great, to give up those pilgrimages which she most desired to accomplish. This was particularly the case as

---

[3] Chief Secretary for Ireland under Mr. Gladstone.

to Rome, where so many important and sorrowful events had happened since their last sojourn there. It would, indeed, have been sweet to her to lay at the feet of Pius IX. her devout and filial homage, all the more on account of his sufferings, and of the need that she felt of making some reparation for all the outrages by which the last years of his Pontificate had been embittered. Her husband shared her desire, but the project could never be realized. The journey to Rome was often begun, but some cause always intervened to prevent it. It was the same later on with the pilgrimage to Lourdes. She made use of all these contradictions to acquire fresh merit by her joyful obedience to God's will. It was another occasion of merit to her to have to part, in 1875, finally from the pleasant, much loved abode at Slindon. After this Mr. Fullerton and Lady Georgiana spent their winters at Bournemouth, where the climate is wonderfully mild and the air pure. They had no residence of their own till the year 1877, when they bought what became their permanent home till the end of her life. Ayrfield proved a calm and happy retreat, to which Lady Georgiana became much attached, all the more because here, for the first time, she had the great privilege of a chapel in the house, in which the Blessed Sacrament was kept. Those who knew her love the spot all the more, because it was where she breathed her last.

To return now to her correspondence with her brother. The letter which follows has relation to a discussion between them on the subject of the effects which noble birth and station practically had on those who possessed them. Lady Georgiana seems to have thought more highly of this effect than her brother, and the question was whether it was more practically true that, with such persons, *Noblesse oblige,* or *Noblesse dispense.*

To the Hon. F. Leveson Gower.

Slindon Cottage, Arundel, *Sept.* 8, 1872.

DEAREST FREDDY,—I was not angry, though a little provoked, I own, at the assertion that a feeling, which was universal till lately amongst the highly educated persons in all countries, could be a *vulgar* one. The term seems to me so entirely misapplied.

If you had called it old-fashioned, mischievous, unreasonable, and objectionable, I could have understood it better, though I might not have agreed with you. What struck me as preposterous, was the idea that what has been, rightly or wrongly, the feeling from generation to generation of the most high-bred and chivalrous persons, held by some of the best and noblest of men, which I have seen myself, in persons of the greatest refinement of mind and manners, our father included, could be vulgar. I remember how much annoyed he was when the ancient title of his family was merged in the new dukedom of Sutherland. This seems to me exactly to illustrate the difference between a vulgar love of rank and a respect for ancestry. I am speaking all along of the feeling that makes a person value an ancient and honourable descent. Family pride means one or other of two things—either it is *bona fide pride,* which produces arrogant assumption and contempt of others, and then, whether it is vulgar or not, it is something worse—a sin—or else it is used in the sense in which people use it when they say, " I take a pride in bringing up my children well, or in making my garden pretty." That is, they derive satisfaction from it. Now, I consider that this satisfaction or this pleasure taken in looking back to a long line of ancestry, more or less distinguished in their day, would be a source of faults in a proud and arrogant nature, would show itself in a thousand vulgar ways in a low-bred person, but in one humble of heart. and refined in mind, would conduce to courtesy of manner and generosity of conduct. In France, whatever you may think of the politics of the Legitimist party, you cannot refuse to admit that they are the most high-bred. The respect for birth, independent of fortune, whether it is right or just, seems to me the most *un*vulgar of all feelings. Where it does not exist, the worship of wealth, to my mind the most vulgar of worships, generally takes its place.

I will not enter upon the wide subject of the influence which this order of ideas has on society. I am not positive as to my own opinions on the subject. Our argument was only as to their being vulgar or the reverse.

I was delighted with one thing you said, and thought it very clever. *Noblesse dispense* has, indeed, been too often the counterpart of *Noblesse oblige.*

God bless you. Holmbury will be the best consolation for leaving Slindon.

Yours ever affectionately,

G.F.

P.S.—What would Lady Marian say on the question we are arguing? I do not take into account the feelings of the Catholic gentry of England. They are so mixed up with reverence for their ancestors as martyrs to the faith, that they can scarcely come into the same category.

Mr. Leveson Gower replied that he did not intend to apply the epithet *vulgar* to any but those who founded the good opinion they had of themselves and others excusively on rank or birth, and considered these accidents as dispensing them from acquiring merit on other grounds. Thus the brother and sister were entirely of one mind. Not long after the date of this, Lady Georgiana learnt that a lady friend of hers who was in mourning for the recent loss of a passionately loved husband, had

just lost also her only son. She wrote to her as
follows :

To the Hon. Lady Simeon.

Bournemouth, *Feb.* 23, 1873.

MY DEAR LADY SIMEON,—None but those who have known
a sorrow like unto yours could almost venture to write to you at
this moment. *I have,* and you can well believe how deeply
I feel for you, and pray that our Lord will enable you to bear
this *immense* grief with courage.

Though full of supernatural consolation, and, I have no
doubt, acquiesced in as one of the special mercies of a loving
God to your beloved child, yet the anguish is so sharp that it is
difficult to you, I am sure, to press the cross as devoutly as you
would wish on your bruised heart on the unhealed wound of a
previous great affliction. Our Blessed Lord takes from you the
joys, and leaves you the duties of life. May He draw you so
near to Himself that, after a time, you may know, even on earth,
the strange happiness He can give to the broken-hearted.

God bless you, dear Lady Simeon.

Believe me, yours always affectionately,

GEORGIANA FULLERTON, *E. de M.*

The allusion here made to her own loss is
reserved, indeed, but we know how rare such
references are in her letters. It shows us how
deep and incurable was the wound, and what a
distance there is between the most perfect resignation and forgetfulness or even the slightest break
in continual remembrance of the sorrow. We find
the following list of dates in one of the books of
prayer most constantly in use with her.

July 15. Day of his birth.

September 14 (1846). Day of his conditional
Baptism.

October 2. Day of his first Confession.

All Saints.   Day of his first Communion.
May 5.   Day of his last Communion.
May 29.   Day of his death.
June 2.   Day of his burial.

The years during which Mr. Fullerton and Lady
Georgiana spent the winter at San Remo, or at
Mentone, or at Cannes, were just those when the
active work begun by her in London would have
made her wish to return and live there.   Not only
did the work which was now her principal care
develope less rapidly in consequence of her absence,
but there were others in existence or founded continually which she might have helped on.   Lady
Lothian in particular did not know what to do
without her.   These two friends never wanted so
much to be together.[4]

Sometimes, after Lady Georgiana's permanent
return to England, she desired to go abroad, notwithstanding all the affections and duties which
retained her at home.   She may have gazed from
the walls of Walmer Castle on the French coast,
and felt what the Germans express by their untrans-
lateable word *Sehnsucht*, at once the desire to see
again persons and places we have loved, and that
other deeper and larger yearning which is the
product of our previsions, more vague but more

---

[4] Lady Georgiana, though she always found and made work for herself
everywhere, was still most glad when it was in her own country.   In one of
her private notes we find the following : "April 18.   Arrived at Dover, *Deo
gratias!* Breathed again the dear English air, went to pray in the poor
little chapel.   O my God, I thank Thee for all Thy mercies, with an
ardently grateful heart.   I commend to Thee the time I am about to spend
in my own dear country.   Give me grace to work hard for Thee !"

insatiable, concerning that other country for which alone we are made and which we cannot yet possess. These yearnings, like all the feelings of her heart, were deep and intense. But they passed and re-passed on the surface of her soul, and she had long learnt to pay little attention to them. She was well content to give herself entirely to the occupations which her former absence from England had inter-rupted. She took them up again with ardour, not only when at London but at Bournemouth, where she soon found many ways of doing good.

Enough has already been said of this side of her life. Her journal may show us something of the interior spirit of recollection which was, as it were, the soul of her active exterior existence. It need only be said that from the date of her last return to England, we find all the virtues of which we have spoken developing more and more in her soul. It was her daily prayer, taught by the saints and the masters of the spiritual life, that she might reach that degree of holiness for which God intended her when He called her into existence, and this prayer, we may venture to think, was graciously heard.

Her charity, always so intense, became more tender, more ardent, more evenly distributed among those who came to her for alms, for advice, for support, and for sympathy. She had always felt for sufferings of others, had always listened to their tales with attention, interest, and patience. But as she advanced in life her patience became more tender, more penetrating, more wise in counselling, more intelligent in understanding, more powerful in consoling. It may almost be said, that those large hearts which are so closely united to Him Who is love itself, obtain from Him a share of His power, and have a right to say with Him to the burthened and labouring, Come unto me and I will refresh you.

Her humility, as may well be imagined, kept pace with her charity. Her renouncement of everything was so complete, and had been so for many years, that it seemed impossible to go further, yet she managed to do so as the time went on, in the poverty and simplicity of her dress. She might have seemed to exceed in this, but it was a kind of excess at which the angels smile. She went every day to Mass on foot, even when, less from age than from illness, which already had fastened on her, she began to stoop, with her black cloak on her, and wearing an old bonnet, and no gloves generally, for she reserved them for the occasions when she was to make an appearance. It seemed as if she found them too troublesome to take off when giving alms. In the church at Farm Street she was seen so many years following, kneeling in the same place, to which so many eyes have since been sorrowfully turned to seek her in vain.[5]

If we ask ourselves whether the cordiality and affectionateness of her social relations suffered in

---

[5] The story that was once circulated about Lady Georgiana's having taken the place of a crossing-sweeper near Farm Street, that the poor woman might go and hear Mass one Sunday morning, has no foundation but the imagination of some person who thought it *likely* to have happened. Lady Georgiana herself heard of it, and denied it most positively. Nor is it at all like her great humility, as she would have been seen at the crossing by many who knew her. She would rather have given the woman an alms to compensate for any loss which her absence might have entailed upon her.

any degree from these exceptional features in her life, her correspondence will supply the answer. There we find always the same simplicity, the same warmth of heart, the same lively and noble imagination, the same absence of all tendency to set herself up in any way as a critic or a model. The letters from which the following extracts are made, were written about this period. Mr. Leveson Gower was travelling in Italy with his son, then about twenty years of age. She writes to him:

To the Hon. F. Leveson Gower.

DEAREST FREDDY,—Though your letter told me that you have the gout, I received it with much pleasure. It is true that you are immoveable, but you can enjoy everything through George. You can see and hear with and by him. That is a great enjoyment, and by this time I hope you are well again, and that you have good weather. It is so with us, in spite of the difference of climate. I am told to address to you at Naples.

Oh! it makes my mouth water to read the names of the places you have been at. Umbria is unlike anything else. In my eyes it is the *beau ideal* of beauty beyond any other country.

I can hardly hold in my desire to see those lovely parts again, but I know this will never be. It would seem sad, except for that passage in the Bible: "Eye has not seen, ear has not heard," &c. Heaven will give us the perfection of everything here below.

As for Rome, the desire to go there again was in past times still more intense, but now it would not be a joy. It would be like going into a profaned church.

The sister of her intimate friend, the Marquise de Salvo, had just lost her daughter. It was a kind of loss which always found an echo in Lady

Georgiana's heart.　She writes thus almost without knowing her :

To Mrs. Nunn.

Ayrfield, Bournemouth, *January* 8.

DEAR MRS. NUNN,—Thank you very much for your kind note.　Indeed, I feel that those who love dearly the same person cannot be as strangers to each other, and your beloved sister being my dearest and kindest friend, my heart warmed towards you.　There is another between us in the similarity of the trials God has sent us.

Twenty-five years have passed since my crushing sorrow made me feel as if life was over, and every possibility of joy gone out of it.　But it is not so.　There is a dreary waste to be travelled through, but light shines upon it after a time, and grief softens as we advance towards the end.　I have ventured to say this because of the deep sympathy I feel with one so blest as to have had such a child as yours, and so heart-broken at her early removal from your side.

Believe me, yours very sincerely,

GEORGIANA FULLERTON.

This is a letter of thanks for the present of the Life of the young Dauphin Louis XVII. :

To the same.

Tunbridge Wells, *August* 30.

MY DEAR MRS. NUNN,—Many thanks for the little book you sent me.　It interested me much to look at the history of the martyred child, though some parts of it I *could not read*. It is, to my mind, by far the most painful incident I know in history.　Other children may, *perhaps*, have suffered as much, but none the mental torture of this poor boy—and never with so bitter a contrast with the past.　It is much the worst blot on the fearful page of the French Revolution.　Other cruelties may be accounted for by delusions and fanaticisms, but this has neither parallel or cause.

Your dear sister's imaginings during her hours of work at

the Trianon must have been very vivid. I have just published a tale of the time of the Reign of Terror,[1] so my own thoughts have run in that direction.

Yours, dear Mrs. Nunn, most sincerely,

G. FULLERTON.

It is impossible not to be struck with the number of the chords, so to speak, which vibrated in Lady Georgiana's heart. All was in harmony there—a harmony of truth, sweetness, and force. Her profound humility, her boundless charity, her perfect abandonment of self to the will of God, strike us no less than the vigour and vivacity of her intelligence, which seemed to grow instead of to become enfeebled by years. Such is the manner in which the servants of God find themselves strengthened by His grace in so many different forms. Lady Georgiana may remind us of what was said of St. Teresa by the Franciscan nun, sister of St. Francis Borgia, that "she ate, and slept, and talked, and conducted herself like the rest of the world, and yet she was a saint." Her spirit seemed, like that of her Lord, humble, simple, earnest, sincere. She lived among us after His example, never troubling any one, and, at the same time, the consolation of all hearts.

[1] *A Will and a Way.*

Z

CHAPTER XIX.

1873.

THE charity and zeal of Lady Georgiana were not limited to the works which she had contributed to found, or which sprang up before her every day. Her character and mind were such as to make her disposed to look beyond the things amidst which she lived, and she had grown up among influences which favoured this disposition. From her youth she had taken interest in a variety of subjects, even the most distant from her own occupations. We have never seen her lose her interest in politics— her love for her brothers was too tender, and the life of each of them was too closely mingled with public affairs, in which, moreover, Lord Granville occupied too eminent a post, for her to remain indifferent to what so closely concerned him. Her own feelings, and the tendencies of the Liberal party, which was that of her family, led her to give her sympathies readily to the oppressed, wherever they were to be found. These sympathies could not remain inactive in the case in which conscience was the subject of oppression. In that case she was ready to take up her pen, and to wield it with vigour. She could appeal to public opinion, and this not only with reference to what might pass in England, but also when the complaints to be made and the miseries to be alleviated were to be found at a distance. It is well to give one instance out of many of this side of her character. It was said of the great Burke, that an iniquity committed at the other end of the world roused the indignation of his soul as much as if he had seen it perpetrated under his own eye. Justice, for him, did not know the limits of time or space. It was much the same with the charity of Lady Georgiana. An example may be found in the following correspondence with Mrs. Monsell, now Lady Emly, relating to the atrocities committed in Annam. Mrs. Monsell seems to have appealed to her for aid in this matter.

To Mrs. Monsell.

27, Chapel Street, Park Lane, W.

DEAR MRS. MONSELL,—By Lady Lothian's desire, I return you the paper about Annam and the poor kidnapped Christian women. I have written the enclosed letter, in case you like to send it to the Catholic newspapers.

They require that every letter of the nature of an appeal should be accompanied by a paid advertisement, it may be very short, so as not to cost more than two or three shillings. In this case it might be, "Subscriptions in behalf of the Captive Christian women of Annam, will be gratefully received by the Dowager Marchioness of Lothian, 15, Bruton Street, Lady Georgiana Fullerton, and Mrs. Monsell, Tervoe, Limerick" (with the addresses). You might, if you wished it, open a list of subscribers, but this might be reserved for the following week. My husband and I will each give £1, which I will send you. Would to God we could do much more in such a case, but if many would give a little—something—much would be achieved.

I send you on the side of the page the directions of the five Catholic newspapers.

Yours, dear Mrs. Monsell, always affectionately,

G. FULLERTON, *E. de M.*

(You present your compliments to the Editor, and would be much obliged to him if he would insert the enclosed letter, as well as the accompanying advertisement.)

The letter contained the following eloquent appeal to the Catholic Editors in London :

27, Chapel Street, Park Lane, *July* 18, 1873.

SIR,—The work of the *Sainte Enfance* for the rescue of Chinese infants, doomed to death in countless numbers, has long been known amongst us. Through its agency thousands of these innocent souls have been baptized, and many of them brought up as Christians.

Important and consoling as this work of mercy has proved, there comes, at this moment, from the same part of the world, a yet more imperative and heart-rending cry for help. The pirates who infest the coast of the kingdom of Annam have been for years in the habit of kidnapping the unfortunate and defenceless inhabitants of that country (whom a jealous and tyrannical Government prohibits from keeping arms in their houses) and carrying them off to China, the men to be exported as coolies, and the women to be sold to a still more dreadful captivity, for this nefarious traffic consigns them to houses of infamy, and to a fate worse than death. Pac Hoï, a Chinese town north of the Gulf of Tonquin, is the chief seat of this abominable trade. Many of these unfortunate women are Christians, and it is in their behalf that the Catholic missionaries make an earnest appeal. A little money goes a great way under these circumstances ; and the deliverance of the poor victims, our sisters in the faith, can be often secured àt a trifling cost. Measures are being taken by European Governments to stop this terrible evil, but whilst negotiations are going on, the poor creatures are liable to a fate which can only be averted by the Christians on the spot offering to purchase their freedom. Out of their poverty they found means to liberate sixteen of these prisoners, but can do no more. The Committee in Paris, acting in behalf of the *Œuvre des Missions Catholiques*, appeals to English Catholics, and especially to women, to come forward and help in this urgent, and, we may hope, temporary emergency. In the list of advertisements will be found the names of the ladies in London who will gladly receive subscriptions for this object.

I remain, Sir, faithfully yours,

GEORGIANA FULLERTON.

Is it too much to hope that we might raise £50 for this purpose?

We have quoted the whole of this letter as a specimen of the ardour with which Lady Georgiana took up the cause of the oppressed at a distance as well as at home, and also of the clearness and simplicity with which she could plead it. These qualities were frequently called into operation, for she pleaded publicly for a great number of phases of distress, both to Catholics and Protestants, and she seldom appealed in vain. But if the sufferers in the distant land of Annam could so move her compassion, it may easily be imagined how much she felt for others who were far more near home, and whose only crime was that they were faithful in their allegiance to the Holy See. This was the case with the Polish subjects of Russia, which Power, at the time at which the following was written, was persecuting them, at the same moment that it was assuming the defence of the Christian subjects of Turkey.

To the Hon. F. Leveson Gower.

Stewart's Hotel, Bournemouth.

We are both, of course, intensely interested about the politics, with different *shades* of feeling, about the Eastern question. I am more anti-Russian than Fullerton is. Peace for this country I ardently desire, almost at any price. And there we agree. But he does not dread as much as I do the extension of Russian sway. Cruelty in Christians is worse than in Turks, and it is a disgusting hypocrisy to be humane and sympathetic about the subjects of the Sultan, and to treat Poland in precisely the same manner itself. No, not *precisely.* *Some* of the Turkish atrocities are not committed, but much of the treatment is precisely similar. However, there is this great difference, Russia *could*, at any moment, improve and change its course, Turkey *cannot*, and, therefore, though with regret that humanity has no better champion, I must wish Russia to succeed against her. As to our going to war, it seems perfect madness without an ally, and with America and Ireland watching their opportunities.

On this subject, however, she did not think herself called on to appeal to public opinion. Nevertheless, the cause seemed to her so just that she strove to secure for it defenders and influence. Although, since becoming a Catholic, she had almost lost sight of Mr. Gladstone, she now addressed herself to him as to the most illustrious as well as the most powerful of English statesmen.

To the Right Hon. W. E. Gladstone.

December 18, 1876.

DEAR MR. GLADSTONE,—May I ask you to read the *brochure* I send by this post? Grieved and pained as I have been at the line you have adopted of late years with regard to our Church, I do not forget your kindness to me in past days, and I own that I felt pleasure in being able recently to sympathize with you on one subject, and to join in the wishes you so eloquently expressed on the Turkish question. I may venture to say that I have had those thoughts and feelings longer than yourself, for, at the time of the Crimean War, I could not reconcile myself to the idea of England's waging war to uphold an Empire you justly stigmatized as a disgrace to humanity.

I wish Turkish misrule at any cost to be suppressed, and with every reason to dread and dislike the sway of Russia, and knowing it to be the most cruelly persecuting power in existence, I had rather see it, for a time, prevail, rather than that Christians should indefinitely continue to be trodden under foot by the Turks. *They cannot* change or improve, whereas Russia *might,* at any moment, recognize the glaring inconsistency between her attacks on the Turks and her efforts in behalf of their victims, and her own equally horrible treatment of her Polish Catholic subjects, and repent of her misdeeds.

Therefore I wish, even át the price of her temporary ascendancy, that if no other means succeed, she may be God's instrument in the deliverance of the Christians under the Turkish yoke. But will you let me go on to say with what an aching heart and with what deep disappointment I have vainly watched for a single word of sympathy from your lips, or those of any one of the Liberal party, for the victims of Russian despotism, or the expression of a hope that, whilst acting the part of a liberator towards the Christians of Turkey, the Czar would change his line of conduct towards the United Greeks of his own dominions? My heart throbbed with painful excitement when I read those beautiful words of yours as to the traditionary policy of England towards the weak and suffering, and contrasted them with this cold dead silence as to the sufferings of the unfortunate populations of Lithuania and Poland. If you doubt that the cruelties mentioned in the little work I send you are, in a measure, going on at this moment, I can furnish you with evidence on that point.

I remain, dear Mr. Gladstone, sincerely yours,
GEORGIANA FULLERTON.

Mr. Gladstone answered this ardent appeal as follows :

Hawarden Castle, *December* 21, 1876.
MY DEAR LADY G. FULLERTON,—I have begun the book you have been kind enough to send me ; but I shall not be able to finish it to-day, and I am unwilling to let a single post pass without thanking you for your letter.

I rejoice in your generous view of the Eastern question ;

for generous I must think it on your part, to entertain sentiments unhappily very different from those which alone, at this
great crisis, have received public countenance from the Court
of Rome with respect to Eastern affairs. And, even had there
been no utterance from that high quarter, it would still have
been very generous in you to write as you do write, with the
convictions you entertain (and I have no opposite convictions)
respecting the conduct of the Russians in and to Poland.

I am truly sorry that you should have been disappointed by
noticing an absence of sympathetic expressions on that subject.
So far as this concerns me, let me plead my cause at your bar.

I have never (I believe) given strong expression to any
feelings about the conduct of the Russians to the Poles, simply
because I have no adequate acquaintance with the case, and
because my brain and mind are so heavily charged, that I
cannot go on to speak, out of my way; but am indeed in
perpetual arrear, notwithstanding every effort, with what seem
my immediate duties.

It would have been one of my immediate duties to acquaint
myself with the proceedings of the Russians to the Poles, had
I, with reference to the Eastern question, been preaching confidence in Russia. This confidence I could not preach; for,
except as to the personal character and intentions of the
Emperor, I do not feel it. Indeed, there are very few Governments indeed that at all command it from me. The action of
Governments, in matters international, does not, I think, exhibit
a very bright side of human nature.

Perhaps you think that I, who have not scrupled to assail
to the best of my ability the Governments of Naples and of
Turkey, need not be so squeamish about Russia. But, in my
own view, I was very squeamish about both those Governments.
This year I was silent for seven months, from February to
September, about Turkish crime, and only spoke when the
"smouldering scandal broke and blazed" in the face of the
whole world. When I had collected accusations, of necessity
ex parte, against the Government of Naples (not without sifting
them as well as I could), I took measures to bring the whole of
them before the accused Government itself, through the friendly
Government of Austria, and only when despairing of any satisfaction, gave them, five months later, to the world.

I feel profoundly the responsibility of all false accusation for all men; and I think this responsibility to be multiplied tenfold in the case of one who, like myself, has spent a long life in public and often in conspicuous functions. For the words of such men are not without echoes; and they are responsible for the echoes as well as for the words.

I trust I have made clear the reasons, from my point of view, of the silence which has disappointed you.

Do not suppose I mean to imply that the subject is one unfit for investigation. Quite the contrary. The Latin Church has a legitimate interest in the matter, and might, I suppose, properly employ its powerful and highly organized Press for the purpose. If this were to be done, I would venture on one suggestion. I do not think so grave a controversy can with advantage be conducted anonymously; however needful it may be that in many cases the names of original witnesses might have to be covered. Secondly, it is surely right that whatever pointed charge is made, exact *references* should be given. Without the observance of these two conditions, I do not think there would be any powerful action on the general mind, which is what you would desire to move.

There are other points of your grieved but kind letter, on which I should have been prompted to say a word; but perhaps neither your time nor my own permit it; yet I beg you to believe this—there does not live the man more anxious than I am to spend, far away from the sight and voices of contention, the space, be it longer or shorter, that lies between his past labours and his grave.

Believe me always, sincerely yours,
W. E. GLADSTONE.

P.S.—Not even on the simple question of the Russians in Turkestan have I been bold enough to give a general judgment. I venture to enclose a hymn for your acceptance.

This characteristic and interesting letter contained some passages which Lady Georgiana felt impossible to leave unanswered.

Lady Georgiana to Mr. Gladstone.

Bournemouth, *December* 29.

DEAR MR. GLADSTONE,—Let me begin by thanking you most sincerely for your letter, for the kind spirit in which you write, and for the very beautiful hymn you have sent me, and then, as briefly as I can, for I am anxious not to trespass on your time, say a few words in reply. With regard to the sentiments of the Court of Rome on the Eastern question, I think the Holy Father has not himself given utterance to any opinion on the subject. Cardinal Franchi said to me three months ago : "We abominate the Turkish misrule, but we dread still more the systematic tyranny of Russia and her deadly hatred of the Catholic Church." This is the view which the Catholic newspapers have, generally speaking, adopted, though the *Univers*, one of the most influential, has not followed that line. The great majority of Catholics hold it, and I can quite understand their reasoning, though, for my own part, events and their consequences seem to me so uncertain that I had rather see one grievous evil suppressed, and take the chance of what Providence may ordain as the result.

I quite admit that no attack should be made upon nations or Governments without an adequate acquaintance with the state of the case, and that because you have attacked what you considered to be bad Governments, it would be unreasonable to call upon you to take a similar course with respect to every Government accused even of worse misdeeds than those you alleged in other instances. But, when you say that you cannot go out of your way to investigate a question such as that of Russia's conduct to Poland, I cannot admit that it would be going *out of your way*. It seems to me so closely connected with the question which has engaged and must long engage them, and you allow that it is so. May I venture to say that it seems to me an imperative duty in one whose words and whose influence have so much power, to examine it? You have thrown the whole weight of your eloquence and have led others to follow you on the side of Russia in the contest about, alas ! to begin, this awful contest of which we cannot guess what will be the end. You have praised her publicly for her humane sympathy with the Christian subjects of the Porte, with emphasis and all earnestness; you could hardly have done so had you believed that she was herself cruelly persecuting her own subjects, such cruelties as those mentioned in the pamphlet I sent you, and, therefore, your praise on the one side and your silence on the other, are a sort of acquittal from your lips in the face of Europe. Therefore I cannot but think that you are bound to examine if these statements contained in the book I sent you *are* true or not. The work of the Père Lescœur, called *L'Eglise Catholique en Pologne*, "does not only relate," as the *Correspondant* observes in a recent article, "but it proves by a variety of documents, by the writings of American Diplomatists, the protestations of English Ministers, the official acts of the Russian Government, and reports of its agents," the nature of the persecution which has been carried on in Poland. If you would like to look at it I could send it to you. I enclose two letters from the *Univers*, which, I think, will interest you. They incidentally seem to show what Poland has suffered, but they confirm in me the hope I have felt ever since this Eastern question has arisen, that Russia may be herself beneficially affected.

I should have thought that the ill-treatment of Poland had been notorious enough in past years, since it drew the strongest remonstrances from the English Government itself, to give a probability to the truth of the statement in question.

With regard to the suggestion that the Catholic Press should take up the subject, indeed, dear Mr. Gladstone, it has done so already in the strongest and most urgent manner. But our papers are not read in this country, and when the Ministerial portion of the Press, to serve their own interests at this moment, began to speak of the Polish and Lithuanian persecutions, there was an absolute silence on the subject in all the Protestant newspapers.

Some more letters were exchanged on the subject, in which the same arguments were repeated on both sides. The result which Lady Georgiana had aimed at was not obtained. The eloquent voice of Mr. Gladstone was not raised, as all know, in favour of the Uniates who were persecuted by Russia, and did not plead the cause of the Catholics of Poland. This Lady Georgiana regretted, no doubt, but without any bitterness, as we may judge from the following letter to her brother, written after meeting Mr. Gladstone at Walmer some years later (1881).

To the Hon. F. Leveson Gower.

Walmer Castle, Deal.

. . . Mr. Gladstone went away on Wednesday, Mrs. and Miss G. yesterday. I had not enjoyed such an intellectual pleasure for a long time as his conversation. He is a most extraordinary man. I used to take to him a great deal in 1844 and 1845.

After I became a Catholic he all but cut me, and, of late years, I had no opportunity of ever meeting him. I have, at different times, painfully resented some of his acts and words ; but the Land Bill, and his courageous and patient perseverance in carrying it through, I could not but strongly admire. His cordiality, the charm of his conversation, his candour in argument even on those points on which he is most strongly prejudiced, sympathy on many points, his undoubted earnestness and honesty of purpose, won me back to some of my old feelings about him. There is a French saying that one must not see one's enemies, because then one can no longer hate them. This applies, in a measure, to friends one has been estranged from. Coldness vanishes in personal intercourse.

We have seen the interest which Lady Georgiana could take in distant miseries, and this may show us the ardour which she felt when the matters concerned were before her eyes and within reach of her own efforts. She wrote to Lady Herbert about a Bill, before Parliament in 1866, which dealt with the position of the Catholic children who were collected in the workhouses.[1]

[1] See Chapter xv.

Chapel Street, *May* 17, 1866.

I wish you had been in London to-day—we have a meeting of ladies at Lady Lothian's, to concert all possible means, spiritual and temporal, of furthering the passing of the Bill for the workhouse children. I mean any means in our own power. Father Gallwey will be present to help us in this, and it has the Archbishop's warmest approval. I saw him (the Archbishop) last night. He recommends a union of prayers, and that we should endeavour to procure one thousand Masses to be said with this object, each associate promising to procure a certain number. Then the temporal means will be concerting to write, speak, and send papers containing a statement of our grievances to Members of Parliament we are acquainted with. You could do more in this way than all of us put together. I shall take a list of the persons suggested as most important to persuade or enlighten, and will write to you again.

This letter about the Sisters in the Holy Land belongs to a far later date.

To Lady Herbert.

27, Chapel Street, *July* 26.

DEAREST LADY HERBERT,—I enclose the letter I have just received from Madame de Salvo (she is a cousin of our Archbishop), as it will interest you to see what she says of the Sisters in the East. You can destroy it and so need not take the trouble of answering this note.

I have received this week between £13 and £14 for the Beyrouth Sisters, and so hope to be able to make a second *envoi* of 250 francs. But what misery there is all over the world and at our own doors !

We do indeed want such a Saint as St. Vincent of Paul.

Yours ever affectionately,

G. FULLERTON, *E. de M.*

But quotations such as this might be multiplied indefinitely, if they were to show all the objects of her charity. What has been given must suffice to convey some idea of the truth. In the midst of all these charitable works she found time, especially when she went to rest at Walmer, for reading books other than those which directly related to the daily occupations and varied interests of her own life. To one such book, in which she was profoundly interested, the letters mentioned in the next paragraph allude. Our readers will, perhaps, not have forgotten a letter of Miss Martineau's on the first publication of *Ellen Middleton*, expressing her satisfaction at Lady Georgiana's first work, and the flattering terms in which that remarkable woman had expressed herself. The years that had passed since that time had never brought them together. Their moral separation was as great as their material distance. Miss Martineau had died since, and her autobiography was published in 1877.

There are two letters to Mr. Leveson Gower on the subject of this autobiography, of which it is better to speak in a few words than to insert them at length. Lady Georgiana approached the book with much interest, on account of the circumstances which we have already mentioned. But the interest soon became very painful, and she was unable to continue reading the book to the end. She says that there were many things in her own childhood of which she was reminded by what Miss Martineau said of her own. It is not surprising to find her saying that she might have ended as Miss Martineau did, if she had not found her way to the Church, and that, under different circumstances, Miss Martineau might have become a Catholic. For there is truth in the common saying, that there are only two quite logical alternatives that are presented for choice to educated minds, though there are but comparatively few such minds to whom either of those alternatives is actually presented without much that is foreign to the simple logical issue, to give a colour to the eye which considers it. Lady Georgiana started from a different point of view from any that was familiar to Miss Martineau, and the circumstances of the latter lady, her education and surroundings, could hardly be considered propitious to the tone of mind, especially the docility and humility, without which all the opportunities of which Lady Georgiana was enabled to avail herself might have been thrown away.

The year 1877 brought to Lady Georgiana a sorrow as unforeseen as it was keen, perhaps the last great trial of her life. Lady Lothian, the friend who was so dear to her, whom she delighted to name as her model, as well as her companion, was suddenly (on May 13) torn away from her children, her friends, and the Church. She was taking part in the deputation sent to Rome to present to Pius IX. the offerings of the English Catholics, on the occasion of his episcopal jubilee.[2]

It was there, after some days which she passed, as she said, " in a joy too great for this world," that a rapid illness, ended in a few days by a blessed death, transferred her to her true country of which she seemed to be enjoying a foretaste. What those days of desolation which followed this thunderstroke

[2] He was consecrated Archbishop of Spoleto in 1827.

were to Lady Georgiana, we must not attempt to tell. Like other days of sorrow which had marked her life, she passed them in silence. The remains of Lady Lothian were brought from Rome by her sons, to find their resting-place in Scotland. They remained for twenty-four hours in London. Lady Herbert, her devoted friend, obtained leave that they might be placed in her private chapel. The whole of that day and night her friends gathered round the bier. Masses were offered in continual succession, and those whom Lady Lothian had helped, those who loved her and who loved to walk in her footsteps, rich and poor, young and old, all were eager to be present, and the greater number to receive Communion. Thus passed the morning, and at last those who had heard or said Mass left the chapel, and Lady Herbert had provided a meal for those who did not wish to leave the house.

When all were assembled, Lady Georgiana was not to be seen. She was found in the chapel, prostrate before the coffin of her friend and giving full vent to her sorrow now that she was entirely alone.

Her tears were flowing in floods, and prayers interrupted by sobs broke from her lips. Her friend who thus surprised her in her sorrow, knew how to respect it. She left the chapel in silence, and without disturbing the free course of her tears and prayers.

Lady Georgiana's life had been full of trials. But we only find three occasions when the impetuosity of her heart seems to have overpowered the almost absolute control which she had gained over herself. One of these, as our readers remember, was when she heard of the death of her sister, another was when we have seen her by the bier of her friend. The third was by another grave, even more dear and more sacred, which she always visited with no one to witness her grief, except one only time when she consented to have a companion. Among all the persons with whom her life was mingled, there was one whom we should have named earlier. Her zeal, her piety, her marvellous talent for organization, won her at once the admiration and the confidence of Lady Georgiana. Mdlle. Teulière, whose name is dear and well known to many friends both in Paris and in London, belonged to that phalanx of souls literally vowed to do good, who make the poor their great and their only family. It is a body to which France in the day of misery and affliction gave birth, and which owes its continued power of existence, of action, of increase and extension, to the same great country. Lady Georgiana may have had other friends as intimate as Mdlle. Teulière. There were none whom she saw more often, whose company and whose assistance day by day were more necessary and more precious.

One day Lady Georgiana consented to take Mdlle. Teulière to the grave of her son. It was the greatest proof of friendship and confidence that she could have given. Perhaps she thought herself strong enough to remain calm, or perhaps she wished to gain the power of mastering herself there as elsewhere, and

AA

to make trial of her courage. However this may be, Mdlle. Teulière saw her completely struck down with anguish. She could not control her sobs and cries of sorrow. Her friend endeavoured to calm her, pressed her hands, embraced her, and shed tears herself with her. Poor Lady Georgiana reproached herself with her weakness, and begged her companion not to think that it meant any revolt against the will of God. For such an ardent and tender a heart to have broken down three times in her life, seems to us rather a proof of her heroic strength than of her weakness.

Lady Lothian's life had been more than edifying. It had been full of interest, she had not, like Lady Georgiana, watched the great Oxford movement without personally sharing in it. She had known all its various phases and been more directly under its influence. She had entered ardently into the excitement and shocks which we find traced in many letters of that period, of which the history remains to be written. If her correspondence ever sees the light, it will have a place of its own among the records of our time. No one could help being charmed by her—her high spirit, her grace, her gay charity, and something of that gift of humour which, when it is found in company with seriousness and strength, gives to them an attraction of their own. Her children inherit much of her character, it is divided among them all. It is not surprising that they should have desired, from the first, to see that character traced for them. It was a task which required at once great tenderness and great talent, and they could find these qualities nowhere so well united as in Lady Georgiana. In fact, she was at once pointed out by every one for this great task.

She was then at the end of her literary career, and it was thought well that she should not over-burthen herself with original composition, though she undertook some translations, which cost her, perhaps, quite as much labour. She could have no task to perform that she could love better, none that could be more worthy of her pen than this *Life of Lady Lothian*. But it was not till too late that she resolved to do nothing else till she had accomplished this. She took it up as the will of God for the time, and she left behind her a part of the work more or less completed, the beginning and the end. It is hoped that the intermediate part may be supplied by another hand, though it can never be done with the grace and beauty with which she would have adorned it.

CHAPTER XX.

TOWARDS the end of 1881, Lady Georgiana was attacked by a malady which tried her endurance seriously, and led to a long course of suffering and of merit which ended only with her life. The gravity of the evil was not revealed at once, but from that time her health was undermined. The disease was painful and active, and a keener air than that of Bournemouth was thought necessary to restore her. She was accordingly taken to Tunbridge Wells, where she slowly recovered her strength. She was too weak to be told the news of the murder of her cousin, Lord Frederic Cavendish, at Dublin, which took place early in May, soon after her journey had been made. She learnt it with immense grief some weeks later. The tragic end of Lord Frederic was more than a family affliction. He had gone to Ireland as Chief Secretary, his heart full of sympathy for her children, and his life had been taken by Irishmen. It was an immense calamity for their country and for all who loved it.

Lady Georgiana's stay at Tunbridge Wells, however, was most beneficial to her health, and

about the beginning of the autumn she was fairly
recovered. Her husband and herself had long
desired to make the pilgrimage to Lourdes, and it
was thought well that the pious attempt should be
made. Once more, therefore, they crossed the
Channel, and after an absence of seven years, once
more they visited Paris. They no longer found
there the brilliant and numerous circle of friends
of old days, but there were there two or three dear
intimate friends, especially the Marquise de Salvo
and the Duchesse de Galliera. The first of these
lived an active and busy life, regulated like that of
a cloister. She never left Paris, except to go as
far as Versailles, and so was always to be found.
Although the Duchesse de Galliera lived at Paris
ordinarily, where she spent her time in acts of
beneficence, a good part of her year was passed in
Italy, where she had other duties and was occupied
in other good works. This time, however, the
friends met, and it was for the last time, not at
Paris but at Tours, where Mr. and Lady Georgiana
Fullerton spent a fortnight on the road towards
Lourdes. The Duchesse was then in the neighbourhood, at Rochecotte, the property of the Marquise
de Castellane. Mrs. Craven was there also. Both
hastened to Tours to meet their English friends,
and they were charged by the hospitable owner
of that charming château to invite them to share
its hospitality. Madame de Castellane and Lady
Georgiana had not met since 1843, when the latter
had seen the former take part in amateur theatricals
at Nice, and had been seen by her on her knees in

the Church of the Gesù at Rome. Since then, both had known the severe trials of life, and their souls had been drawn together by the bond of a common faith. They probably knew each other better than in those early days, but to the deep regret of both the meeting could not take place.

It was while they were staying for these few days at Tours that Mrs. Craven passed two days with her friend, and went with her to visit the Convent of Marmoutier, occupied by the religious of the Sacré Cœur. Madame de Montalembert was at that time the Superior. Lady Georgiana expressed the singular joy which she always felt on finding herself in France. The gaiety and serenity of her countenance told little of the suffering she underwent from time to time, for her disease was rather hidden than inactive. But she never complained or spoke of her health. The only thing she mentioned was the failing of her eyesight, for she found it increasingly difficult to read or write. She did not say what a terrible blow the loss of eyesight would be to her, although the fear must often have been in her mind.

Madame de Montalembert is described to us as "a radiant personification of the religious life." Those who speak thus, have no intention of saddening her humility by misplaced compliments. Joy is one of the fruits of the Holy Spirit, produced by His presence in the Christian heart, and it is good, it is useful, and it is consoling to find this fruit shining forth in the countenance, the language, and the whole demeanour of those who have chosen as their lot to find it nowhere in the things of this world. Those who have found themselves unable to choose this austere lot may do well to compare from time to time their own joys, gathered in the common paths of the world, with those which they sometimes see reflected in the faces, or of which they catch the notes in the voices, of such persons as the lady of whom we speak. Lady Georgiana soon found herself at ease with this valiant and joyous soul, and it was charming to hear them converse together. Returning from Marmoutier they were joined by Mr. Fullerton, and they went to pray together at the tomb of St. Martin. They found their way also for Benediction to another spot redolent of piety and prayer, the spot consecrated to the memory of one who is only not yet called a saint, because the sole authority on earth which can give him that title has not yet conferred it. It was the spot, now transformed into a chapel, where the venerable M. Dupont lived and prayed before the picture of the adorable Face of our Lord, for which he had the tenderest devotion, and where his ardent petitions were so often heard and granted. The faithful who were wont to commend themselves and their wants to his prayers while he was alive, continue to come and do so, now that he is no more, and a large number of daily graces attest that their prayers are not made in vain.

Lady Georgiana and her husband continued, every day while at Tours, to visit this sanctuary, edifying the people by their exactitude, their piety, and profound recollection. She did not think of her own health, but she thought a great deal of that of her husband, which was then often precarious. Her care of him was unremitting. It was a care to which everything gave way, all her desires, tastes, and to which she would willingly have sacrificed even her occupations of charity and piety, if he himself would ever have consented to it. In the sanctuary of which we speak, one of the special devotions of the people is to beg that the sign of the Cross may be made on their foreheads with the oil of the lamp that burns before the sacred picture. Lady Georgiana asked that they might kneel side by side to receive this holy unction on their foreheads and on their eyes. Her thought was certainly more for him than for herself, and no one can tell what graces of courage and strength he may have received there, for the persevering constancy with which so many good works, left unfinished by her, have since been carried out. But for herself, she certainly received, then and there, a kind of pledge that her prayers were to be efficacious. Her own eyes were cured by the touch of the holy oil. She had come to Tours prepared and resigned to be unable for the future to read or write. But she was at once delivered from this fear, and she felt no difficulty in this respect for the rest of her life. She never forgot "the Holy Face," and she introduced the devotion to the church at Bournemouth on her return. A lamp always burnt before it, also, in her private chapel at Ayrfield.

Graces and favours spring from prayer, and the faith which has inspired and given its efficacy to

prayer, is itself fostered and fortified by the sight
of places where God has shown His gracious powers
in any visible or tangible manner. It is this that
gives birth to pilgrimages, and it cannot be denied
that the impulse which draws to such places so
many among those who suffer and desire and hope
for relief, is natural, as well as the gratitude which
brings back to the same spots those who have
obtained by prayer the deliverance from this or that
misery of their lives. We have only now to do with
those who can understand and share in the feelings
which brought Lady Georgiana and her husband to
the sanctuary of the Holy Face, and which were
about to guide their steps as they thought to that
of Lourdes also.

Lady Georgiana Fullerton had ardently desired
to pay this visit for years. Perhaps her desires had
been even too ardent, as she herself said, of her
longing to go again to Rome, that it had been too
passionate. However this may be, she had to give
up this scheme just at the moment when she seemed
to be about to accomplish it. The night before the
day fixed for their departure, Mr. Fullerton fell ill,
and it was judged prudent not to continue the
journey. Mrs. Craven had come to Tours to take
leave of them, and was able to witness the sweetness
and serenity with which Lady Georgiana accepted
this disappointment. She could not help showing
the tears in her eyes, but there was no word of
regret or complaint. All was for the best, she saw
now that the journey would have been imprudent—
if they had gone further, they would certainly have

repented it. She was quite convinced that the best thing for them was to retrace their steps. Her only thought seemed to be to prevent her husband from thinking it was a sacrifice to her. They went back to Paris, where she herself fell ill, and where they had to remain for several months. During this stay she wrote the following letter to Miss Langdale, who has been already mentioned in these pages as one of her faithful friends and companions in her life of active charity.

To Miss Langdale.

Hôtel Wagram, Rue de Rivoli, *November* 6, 1882.

MY DEAR FANNY,—I ought to have thanked you sooner for your kind letter, but, for a fortnight, I was laid up in a sort of way, though not uninterruptedly, by an attack of gout in eyes, ears, and mouth, which made me utterly good for nothing. I am, thank God, much better now, and able to get about during these my last days, for, unless the weather is tempestuous to-morrow, we mean to go to Boulogne on Wednesday, and watch for a smooth passage. So I hope before the end of the week to be in London on our way to Ayrfield. This attack of gout has confirmed my belief that climate has little, if anything, to do with my ailments, and I hope my kind friends will leave off crying out against Bournemouth for me. This hotel is so sunny, so quiet, so comfortable, the aspect so charming, that we are quite sorry to come away, but we must get over our journey before the winter sets in. On the whole the weather has been, though rainy, very pleasant here, always fine intervals, and singularly mild. My husband is much in his usual state of health now, so I have much tö be thankful for. I could not help smiling, however, at your expression about my earthly bliss in being at Paris again. I have, indeed, enjoyed seeing old friends and the churches, and I like France, I own. But, my dear Fanny, what with anxiety at first, then suffering, and sometimes the depression with which, at the age of seventy, one looks at old familiar scenes, recalling vividly the past, there is nothing joyful in the heart, saving the gratitude of having reached the port of safety midway in life. Hoping to see you before many days have elapsed, I will write no more. . . .

A few days after this, the travellers took their departure for Boulogne, intending to cross the water at once, according to the expectation expressed in the letter just quoted. Bad weather at first prevented the crossing, but it was put off from time to time without any definite cause, and Lady Georgiana, who was never to see France again, was not sorry to linger. Weeks passed away, and the beginning of the new year found them still at Boulogne. Lady Georgiana's health improved by the stay, and she found many sources of enjoyment in the religious opportunities afforded by a city in which Catholic life is so fervent and so active. She had visited the house of the Sisters of Charity some years before, and, as soon as her strength permitted, she went to inform herself about the names and dwellings of the poorest people in the town, that she might herself, as she did always and everywhere, take them some needful succours. The Sister to whom she addressed herself did not know her, although she had been the same to whom Lady Georgiana had applied before. She gave her, however, all the information which she wanted, and Lady Georgiana was returning home when she found the door of the school open, went in, and waited for the end of the class. She then asked if she might be allowed to give the children a dinner and a dessert. It was allowed, and then she proceeded to enumerate all the dishes that she required, adding that she wished the Sister to take *carte blanche*, for she desired the children to have a sumptuous banquet. The good Sister looked at her with some hesitation, her modest dress sug gesting the suspicion which she expressed by saying that she would be delighted to meet her views, but that it was fair to tell her that such a feast as she had ordered might, perhaps, exceed her means. Lady Georgiana laughed, and then told the Sister who she was, and reminded her of her former visit. The good Sister excused herself in confusion, and found no further difficulty in obeying her entirely. It was a brilliant feast, and was followed in the course of a month by another, at Christmas, at which Lady Georgiana presided, and which became, in fact, an institution, for her example was followed every year from that time, and her visit thus procured the poor children a yearly feast.

The poor of Boulogne, even more than the children, had reason to bless the presence of Lady Georgiana. Her bountiful alms are still remembered there. At Christmas she distributed a large quantity of coals and food. She paid their rents, and on the day of the feast she would take to them herself what they wanted to make a good dinner. Her strength seemed to return in these works of charity, and she spoke in great gratitude to the Sister that she had been allowed the joy of helping these poor people, especially as what she had given them was really necessary. This was her last visit to France.

Mr. and Lady Georgiana Fullerton returned at last to England about the end of January, 1883. The improvement in her strength continued with occasional fluctuations till the end of that year, which was passed partly in their house in London, or with her brothers at Walmer Castle or Holmbury. At the end of the year she returned to Bournemouth, which, after that time, she never quitted. She spent her time, amid other occupations, in writing as usual. The work in which she took most interest was the *Life of Lady Lothian*, in which her heart was greatly occupied. She had intended writing her Life in succession to that of Lady Falkland and Lady Buckingham. These three Lives had a resemblance one to another, though they were passed in different epochs of our history. The first of them was the mother of the famous Lord Falkland of the days of Charles I. This was finished and published in 1883. • The biography of Lady Buckingham was postponed in order that Lady Georgiana might write the Life of Lady Lothian, whose death we have mentioned, but this she was not able to accomplish. She wrote, however, the first and the last parts, that is, the Life of Lady Lothian to within a few years of her conversion, and all the account of her last journey, and death at Rome. She spoke of this to Mrs. Craven during a visit which she was able to pay to her at Ayrfield in the closing months of the same year, 1883.

[In the following pages Mrs. Craven speaks in the first person. Her narrative of this last visit gives an insight into the ordinary life of the

Fullertons at Ayrfield.]   " Lady Georgiana's sufferings, of which she never complained, were not so
great as to forbid her taking long drives in an open
carriage, and we thus saw with her the beautiful
neighbourhood of Bournemouth. She took me to
all her favourite spots, most frequently to the pine
woods which look out on the sea, and which clothe
with a perpetual green that smiling and picturesque
coast.   The weather was exceptionally beautiful.
In no northern climate can I remember to have
seen so bright and pure a sky. Nowhere out of
Italy have I ever felt in so soft and genial an air.
Many will remember, too, the marvellous splendours
to be seen that year at the time of sunset and in the
earlier moments of twilight. We enjoyed it all as
if we had been young, in spite of her illness which
we could never forget, in spite of the age of both of
us, and a secret disquiet which hung like a cloud
over my own life, and at times seemed to stifle my
heart. We enjoyed all our surroundings, as if the
future was lit up by the wonderful hues of that
luminous sky, and had for us hopes in this world
which could by possibility be fulfilled. It was an
illusion quickly and sadly dissipated. We were
both already old, and the future had for one of us
suffering and death before long, for the other, the
greatest of the pains and bereavements that life can
know.   It was true, but there were other things
true also, such as no one has understood better
than that noble and holy soul whose language has
more than once been cited in these pages, and her
words may well be echoed by all those who live on

the same faith and in the same hope. 'We speak,' says Madame Swetchine, ' of the decline of age, but in beings such as we are, to decline is also to ascend. Body and soul are in an almost perpetual contradiction. Nature fails, and while it does so, it is not simply destruction that is hastening on, but liberty, glory, the perfection of the soul always increasing in radiance as the spiritual principle within us gradually absorbs all that is not spiritual. The weakness of the body increases, the soul gains new vigour. David was old when he invoked the God of his youth, and it was not the God of the past on Whom he called, but the God of the present, the God of that youth the budding vigour of which he felt within himself. The children of light have the day with them in the midst of darkness, and the children of immortality keep their youth amidst the snows and frosts of old age.'

" At the end of our drives we stopped, sometimes. at the convent of some French nuns who had charge of the Catholic poor school, or more often at the Convalescent Home which Lady Georgiana had founded at Bournemouth, the last such place where she was to practice her favourite work of charity for the poor, the young, and the sick, whom she here found united together. The evenings were passed in quiet conversation, or a game of cards, over which we often laughed in a manner which it now brings tears into my eyes to think of. At ten o'clock the whole household met in the chapel, to end in united prayer the day that had begun in the same place with Mass. A few visitors broke in from

time to time on this uniform and calm life, one of
whom was Count Albert de Mun, and another was
Père du Lac. Lady Georgiana remembered this
visit in the last days of her life.

"A few words only that I can remember, about
the finishing of her Life of Lady Lothian, fell from
Lady Georgiana's lips at this time, to show her
consciousness of her declining strength, though
there was reason enough to be gravely apprehensive.
On the day on which we did not visit either the
school or the Convalescent Home, the drive ended
by a call on some of the friends and neighbours of
whom she saw the most. Among these I may name
Baroness von Hügel, who possessed a charming
home at Bournemouth, and whose conversation was
brilliant and original in the highest degree. Another
friend was Lady Victoria Kirwan, aunt of the young
Duchess of Norfolk, who was then staying with
her. Another was the octogenarian poet, Sir Henry
Taylor, author of *Philip van Artevelde*. He lived
with his family in a house called *The Roost*, and much
pleasant time was often passed with him. His home
was full of intelligence, cleverness, and brilliancy.
Lady Georgiana was highly appreciated by him. It
was a circle in which individual opinions were
expressed with the utmost freedom, and the conversation was thereby rendered more genial instead of
more bitter, for every one there was permitted to set
forth his or her thoughts to the full without encoun-
tering systematic opposition, and the mind was thus
prepared to listen to the other side in turn without
impatience. There was no violence in these dis-

cussions—there was divergence enough, but an air of calm and good faith which would have given the truest argument the best chance of prevailing, if, even by a fireside, it had not been as difficult to acknowledge oneself defeated as on a field of battle.

"In discussions of this kind Lady Georgiana, who was generally silent from reserve, indifference, or humility, would often let herself out with unusual freedom. I can hear still her sonorous and pleasant voice, when she became animated on such subjects. I can see the fine face of Sir Henry Taylor listening to her or answering her, his long white beard, his noble features, and the red dressing-gown in which he wrapped himself up. It was a picturesque sight. This is one of my last recollections of Lady Georgiana. She was at the end of her life, and the aspirations of her soul were already far from this world, in which she still used her social charms, though with some reserve and unwillingness."

"One day," adds Mrs. Craven, "there was a mention of the poems of Tennyson, on whom a peerage had just been conferred. She asked me if I liked his poetry, and on my answering that I preferred the poets of my youth, but that I admired some of his works extremely, especially the _Idylls of the King_, she took up a volume from the table, and read me the scene between Arthur and Guenevere after her repentance, asking whether there could be anything in the world finer. Her voice seemed more harmonious and sweet than usual, and it sounded to me like beautiful music.

"Christmas Eve came soon after, and that night

BB

the colours in the sky, of which I have spoken, were more beautiful than ever. As my husband and myself watched the lights from the road which runs along the cliff, it seemed to us that we were under the heaven of Naples. Memories of our distant youth and the south where it had been passed, came back in our old age, and we said we should never forget that Christmas Eve. It was to be my last Christmas with him. At night, the little chapel at Ayrfield, with garlands of flowers and the red berries of the holly. There was no Midnight Mass, but we sang after prayers the *Adeste Fideles*, before a crib beautifully lighted up. The service next day was finely celebrated in the church, with music such as is not often heard outside the great towns, and a congregation of striking devotion, as is nearly always the case in England. The crib, after the Italian custom, was the great centre of devotion. Nothing was wanting but the sound of the bagpipers to revive my Neapolitan recollections.

" It was to be her last Christmas there, and the preparations for it may have cost her some exertion. She had determined that year to give a real treat to the young persons of the Convalescent Home, a treat such as they had never had there, as if she felt beforehand that it would be her last. It was a small pleasant house in a little garden. It was under the charge of one who was at once an experienced manager, an indefatigable servant, and a person capable of ruling a household. Miss Shea kept everything in neat and good order, and possessed an inexhaustible fund of good-humour and gaiety. She made herself literally all to all, and seemed never to be in a hurry or pressed for time. Without missing time to read for herself she was at every one's service. Lady Newburgh once declared that 'without any exaggeration she was the best woman in the world.' It may be well imagined that Lady Georgiana's charities were well served in such hands. There were no lugubrious previsions there, though the home was not long to survive its foundress. The day after Christmas was fixed for this happy family gathering. Lady Georgiana took her place in Miss Shea's apartment, surrounded by packages and bundles of all shapes and sizes, full of presents for the young people, which she insisted on giving to them with her own hands, for the sake of being able to accompany them with kind words and friendly advice. The scene then changed to the work-room, brilliantly lighted up, where she had had a piano placed. An improvised concert followed, which was enjoyed by the poor audience as much as if they had been persons of education and culti-vated taste. Then followed tea. Lady Georgiana and Miss Shea distributed the cakes, which disap-peared with a rapidity rather alarming for the good health of the young convalescents. Miss Shea undertook to answer for the consequences. They must all enjoy themselves, and have a merry, happy Christmas.

" I would fain stop here. Those who are to reap in the joys of an eternal brightness, must have sown here in tears. And the days of sorrow, when sufferings seem to come with more force and in greater measure, because the time for their accomplishment is short, are hard to pass through, but yet more hard to write of. For we have light and force at the time—light that shines through the darkest clouds, force at which we wonder ourselves, and which enables us to pass the abyss which seems beyond our powers. But this light and this force remain no longer with us when the day which required them has passed away, and when we have only to remember what has been." ·

CHAPTER XXI.

THE last year of Lady Georgiana's life was that of a confirmed invalid. Mrs. Craven, whose narrative was followed in the last chapter, tells us how she and her husband took their leave of their kind hosts at Ayrfield, on January 7, 1884. The day before they left, she wrote thus to Miss Langdale:

To Miss Langdale.

Jan. 1884.

. . . I am certainly better than I was, and my pains much less severe and constant, sometimes for two or three days none at all. But there is always the tendency, and any over-exertion or derangement brings on a bad fit of it. I rather think it will remain so until, in the summer, I go to some bracing place in England or abroad. I am very thankful to be as well as I am on the whole. The Cravens leave us to-morrow, I am sorry to say. These six weeks of their society have been to me a very rare enjoyment, and I shall miss her very much. There is sadness too in a separation without any idea when or where to meet again.

Later in the same letter she speaks of a sermon of Father Gallwey's on the late Lady Herries (preached at Everingham, Dec. 4, 1883).

I like it immensely, Mrs. Craven is in great admiration too. We agreed that, whereas that on Lady Lothian described a saint of this century, this one seems to be the description of one of the ages of faith. When it has had its course and is out of print, I wish so much that a volume could be published of Father G.'s funeral sermons. They ought not to be lost to posterity, but remain as biographies of our time. If I could hope that it would be done, it would be better than, as I had meant to ask for, reprinting Lady Lothian's in the Appendix to her *Life*. . . .

Lady Georgiana asked her friends on their departure to promise to return in the spring, when the rhododendrons, for which the neighbourhood of Bournemouth is famous, would be in bloom. Mr. Craven assented, with an assurance that the month he had passed there had been the happiest for a long time that he could remember. After a fervent "God bless you!" they set out. But, a week after, Mr. Craven had a second stroke of paralysis, from which he recovered, but which naturally left behind it, in the anxious heart of his wife, forebodings of the saddest kind. It was settled that the Cravens should return as soon as possible to their ordinary home in Paris. They had not finished their preparations for the journey, when they learnt that a new and sharp attack had fallen on Lady Georgiana, and that she had been in imminent danger. This danger passed away for a time, and there were hopes that she might even move from Bournemouth later in the spring. These hopes are mentioned in the following letter to her dear friend, Miss Langdale.

To Miss Langdale.

DEAREST FANNY,—I am going on very satisfactorily, though I have not yet left my two rooms, and I think I shall soon be, in some respects, in the same state as I was previous to this attack. But there will always be a liability, or rather certainty, of its return, with more or less intensity, and this must greatly modify my mode of life. Henceforward, it must be that of a complete invalid. There are many compensations to this, and I am surrounded with blessings. It will be some time before it will be thought right for me to travel. I do not expect to be in London, except for a few days on my way later on to Tunbridge Wells. Dear Lady Henry Kerr is now lying by the side of her husband and Lady Lothian at Dalkeith,[1] three holy occupants of the same vault! Give my best love to dear Constance.

January 24.

Three weeks later, February 18th, she writes to her brother Frederic.

To the Hon. F. Leveson Gower.

DEAREST FREDDY,—It is so good of you to have twice written to me, and still more good to talk of coming soon again. I have no doubt it will be convenient. There seems to be a possibility of the Granvilles coming to-morrow, not for more, I suppose, than a very short visit, but you will know. You must not be impatient for better accounts of me. My ailings are chronic; for the most part just now the state of the liver is troublesome, but that may improve any day. There are great blessings in my state, for one bad night I have generally two or three good ones, and several hours in the day often without pain. The balcony of my window, on which I can step out, is delightful. Yesterday was a most lovely day. I sat there for an hour. I pray with all my heart for General Gordon and his mission. I have been reading to-day the penny sketch of his life. It is a beautiful character, and his history does not seem to belong to our days. He has shown throughout the greatest kindness to our missionaries and men, so in every way my heart warms towards him.

The history of the year, with her, was that of a succession of these crises, during some of which she seemed to be almost on the brink of the grave.

[1] Lady Henry Kerr died Jan. 18, 1884.

In the intervals she rallied, and some of these intervals were of considerable length, so that many months of the year passed in comparative ease and absence of suffering. But she never again left Bournemouth, and it was only at the beginning of the year that she was able to go out for the shortest time. We have a succession of letters written by her to Mrs. Craven, which furnish a sort of chronicle on which it will be pleasant to draw. The first letter is written on the 2nd of March, and after the attack which we have spoken of had passed away.

You will be glad to hear that I have had two good days, with really little pain. This morning was a beautiful Bournemouth day, and during the course of my drive I took a first walk of five minutes in a fir-wood. February over, it seems as if a corner of the winter was turned, and Lent will soon be over. Not that I rejoice in the lapse of time. No, each little bit of it is so precious, when so little is left. However, I hope I have had of late a little more feeling that death may be sweet when it comes, and pray that this may increase. . . .

Then she mentions some news from Egypt, where fighting was going on :

General Graham's victory is a great relief, and how brave our troops have been ! Imagine Colonel Baker going on giving directions, with his face shattered by a bullet ! But the poor Arabs were brave too, and how dreadful it is to read of the horrible slaughter. When I was young, and after it, for awhile, military exploits, and glory, and victory, used to give me an exulting feeling that has entirely vanished. I can think of nothing but the agonies and the horrors. But I do thank God that the impending dangers thickening in Africa have had a check. We are so glad to hear Mr. Craven is better. The Granvilles came to us on Saturday. . . .

Ten days later she writes again :

On Sunday I could not write, it was a bad day with me as to pain, and the Granvilles were here, so I gave to them every moment of ease. The doctor does not admit that I am worse than I was, and I suppose that one's own impressions are not reliable. Dearest Lady Londonderry I hear of also, very pale, suffering, and coughing incessantly. Is it not strange that we are all struck down, as it were, at once?[2] I like to think, my dearest, that you are comparatively the strong one amongst my friends now, though you will smile at the word strong. We are having the most beautiful weather here, but I believe too fine for me in some respects, a bit of real winter would have done me good. We shall see if the change of air after Easter brings improvement. You wanted to know what Father G.'s impression is as to *Ellen Middleton.* He sees no objection to its being reprinted. He says he supposes novels have a different effect on different persons, but that as to himself (it was the only one he had read for thirty years), it helped him to write a sermon.[3] . . .

A severe attack came on towards the end of March, and the danger was serious. She writes after it had passed away:

To Mrs. Craven.

I know you will be glad to have had a few lines from what was so near being my death-bed. I am going on as favourably as possible, though I must not move, even to the sofa, for a few days. My life must always be a most precarious one, but there seems plenty of strength. . . . Father Gallwey came to me, and left on Thursday, and now his doctor sends him out of London with orders to rest for some time in pure air. So he returns to-day for an indefinite time. Imagine what a consolation for me! I am overwhelmed with gratitude for the

[2] Lady Herbert was ill at the same time.

[3] *Ellen Middleton* had long been out of print, and it was a matter of debate among Lady Georgiana and her friends whether it should be republished. The Preface to the new edition was dated the 31st of May of this year.

innumerable blessings of every kind I am surrounded with. Surely on no one have so many been lavished. My dearest husband was wonderfully supported during the night, when all was nearly over. God is so good to us.

A week later she had another attack, which also passed off:

March 29.

Saturday and Sunday a crisis occurred, which, though each was far less serious than the previous one, made me feel I should not get through a recurrence on the following day. None came, and I am already recovering satisfactorily. It is a strange thing to be brought in this way face to face with death, so completely in God's hands. And what good hands they are! The doctor says the crises may diminish, and then I may live on. Of course if they increased the end must come. I feel very calm, and full of gratitude, convinced that all is for the best for me and others. My husband is so good, and supported, and well in health. Father G. has been with us nearly a fortnight.

This note was written on the blank leaf of a little poem called the *School for Sorrow.* She says to Mrs. Craven: "You have had more of the School of Sorrow than I have, and I have not known spiritual desolation. But it might come any day."

It was about this time that she began to write a few lines, which were never finished, about her last view of the sea. The window of her room at Ayrfield was so placed that, although it did not command the sea, on account of the trees and roofs which shut it out, still a slender line of blue was perceptible from it, as long as the trees were in their winter state. As spring advanced, the foliage shut out this streak of the sea. Lady Georgiana was moved to tears at the thought that she might never see it again, and she bade the blue line adieu, to which her eyes were closed by the hand of God. The lines are dated April 30th.

Things were better with Lady Georgiana towards the end of that month, and she was encouraged to seek a fresh outburst of intercession for the beginning of May, in hopes of something more considerable in the way of amendment. In truth, the prayers made for her were incessant. She writes on the 13th of May:

A few words to tell you that though for three or four days I was more suffering and ill than usual, and was obliged to put off the dear Granvilles' visit on Saturday, perfect quiet having been ordered me, it has turned out favourably. The doctor is so well satisfied that he says he will perhaps let me, in a few days, get from my bed to a sofa, and be rolled into my sitting-room. I cannot but attribute these favourable circumstances to the prayers so numerously and charitably made for me during this month of blessings. The spring is in all its beauty, and I am not without my share of its enjoyments. I can see from my bed a bright green sycamore mixing its fresh foliage with that of a fir-tree. My husband and Miss Doggett[4] drove to Heron's Court yesterday, and brought me back an abundance of hawthorn (*le buisson blanc* don't your peasants call it?), and lilac from the cottage gardens. I am glad you and Mr. Craven are well, and able to enjoy this lovely time of the year, nowhere so lovely as in Paris. How pretty the view must now be from the window near which you write!

. . . I tell my husband he need not write to you so often, that no news will be good news. The doctor says to-day that he thinks to-morrow I may go to my sitting-room.

The next letter, written a month later, is most characteristic :

[4] A very old friend of the family.

To the same.

A few lines in answer to your letter of the 2nd. I am going on essentially satisfactorily, though I have not yet left my bed, nor is it possible to foresee when I shall do so. It is such a strange illness. The doctor says I am really not weak, and that, if it was prudent for me to get up, after the first moment of giddiness from change of position, I should walk about and be able to do all I did twelve months ago, provided a crisis, such as twice endangered my life—was not provoked. There are still symptoms that moving might cause it, and he does not venture to risk that. I smiled at your idea that in a few weeks I might be going to Tunbridge Wells! However well I might seem, or however long been without a crisis, I can hardly fancy my ever having courage to take a journey, and brave what is so sudden, dangerous, and unspeakably distressing as these attacks. You must make up your mind, dearest friend, to what I firmly expect, if my life is ever so much prolonged, and that is, that whether I leave my bed or my rooms, I shall never leave this place. . . .

But still, my health and strength, in spite of all drawbacks, are astonishing. It took some time to resign myself to the thought of never seeing again places and persons who cannot come to me, such as the Duchess of Norfolk, Lady Londonderry—the idea of Walmer, Holmbury, London, Farm Street Church, made me, up to three weeks ago, shed many tears. I do not speak of places and friends abroad, for hopes with regard to them had been too vague and faint to make much difference. The words, "Never again," have always had a strange effect on me. They have made me burst into tears at parting with persons not particularly dear to me, and, in travelling, used often to sadden me in leaving places there seemed no chance of ever revisiting, and thus I suffered much during the time that followed the clear consciousness of my precarious condition, and my abiding conviction of nothing like a cure. Ten days before the feast of Our Lady Help of Christians, I received from Don Bosco a picture of her, and these words written at the back, *O Maria! ajuto dei Christiani, portate una speciale benedizione alla vostra figlia inferma, e ottenete del vostro Figlio tutta la sanita che non e contraria al bene dell'*

anima sua, noi pregheremo. We made a novena, apart from
the prayers of the month of Mary, to Our Lady Help of
Christians, which ended on the day of the feast, the 24th of
May. Till that day nothing particular had struck me in Don
Bosco's prayer, but on it, it struck me with irresistible force,
that this illness has been sent me as the means of making,
with glad and ready acceptance, the sacrifices which would
have cost me most had I been free, and called to religious life
—to cease to pray in the churches I love, to see only at rare
intervals my spiritual father, not to see my brother's children
growing up in his house, to have friends who will never be able
to come and see me—some of my greatest—not to look on the
varied beauties of earth and sky. These would have been the
pangs I should have felt in becoming a nun. These pangs I
could now turn into offerings gladly, readily ; made—my bed,
my cell ; my sitting-room, the parlour ; the house, my religious
home. Everything assumed a new aspect, when any of these
"never agains" make my heart ache, the pain is superseded by
the joy and the conviction that, according to Don Bosco's
prayer, that kind of health is granted me which will be the
best for my soul. There is a dependence, and many resulting
humiliations in my illness, which, if turned to account, may
answer to those found in the religious life. Can you conceive
how much happier I have been since that day? These thoughts
seemed the answer from our Blessed Lady on the feast of Help
of Christians. I cannot now pray for a cure. Should it come,
it will be God's will, and grace will be given for a return to a
comparatively active life, but I do not expect it. At the same
time that I feel life and strength enough in me to last some
time. . . .

The letter ends by a postscript :

P.S.—You are not one of those I feel sure I shall not see
again. God may bring us together.

A little earlier than this, she wrote a note to her
highly valued friend, Mdlle. Teulière, in which she
again speaks of her feelings on the approach of
death :

To Mdlle. Tulière.

When I came to know my state, I had a moment of tears and emotion, as I thought that I might never again see France and my friends on the Continent, and perhaps even never go again to be with my brothers, but it lasted only a short time. The life that I shall have to lead will be the best and most tranquil stage of my existence. I have always prayed much to God that I might become holy before I die. This is the answer, and I bless Him for it. When I think on all the blessings with which I am overwhelmed, I don't know how to thank God enough. My sufferings are useful to me, and the kind of life which they necessitate is a help to recollection and prayer. St. Alphonsus Liguori said, "My God, you make me suffer much, and you do right," and I may well say, "My God, you make me suffer a little, and you do right."

The next of these notes is dated August 11th, when her state was not quite so good. "I am still in bed and whatever the doctor may say of future possibilities of improvement, I do not think I shall ever leave it." Then she mentions some of her bad symptoms. "The great heat tells upon me no doubt, though here it is very bearable. There is always a breeze from the sea. My husband keeps wonderfully well. We must rejoice in this hot summer. The harvest will be marvellous, apparently." Then she mentions the attacks on religion in the French Assembly: "How sickening the scenes at Versailles are! if only France can be sickened with them. When I think of your nephew (M. de Mun), with his noble mien and beautiful countenance addressing that *tas des miserables*, it makes me think of an archangel facing the satanic hordes. I have nearly finished the *Life of the Bishop of Orleans*, it has in-

terested and edified me more than I can say." She
mentions what was a great joy to her at the time,
the conversion of her niece, Miss Emily Fullerton.
" We are expecting her to-day. . . Her hard work at
the children's hospital, joined to the emotions and
fatigues she has gone through these late weeks,
have tired her very much and she is coming to rest
with us."

About this time shadows gathered around the
friends, which were forerunners of sorrows. Towards
the end of August, when his state seemed to promise
a suspense, if not a cessation, to all the anxieties
of which he had been the object, Mr. Augustus
Craven had a fresh attack of paralysis, which
deprived him of all use of his right side. It was
six weeks still before the final blow fell, but it
will easily be supposed that they were weeks of
terrible trial. Here is Lady Georgiana's letter of
September 23rd.

DEAREST DEAR FRIEND,—You know how I feel for you,
how intensely I pray for you that you may be supported under
this heavy trial. The sad news has been no surprise to me.
I thought your dear husband very feeble even when he was
comparatively so well here. Oh, dear Pauline, ever since his
attack in London I felt you had only a reprieve. God may
grant you another. Let us have frequent accounts. His piety,
his resignation, the material and spiritual blessings with which
you are surrounded, the friendship and tenderness of your
excellent friend,[5] are proofs that He never suffers you to be
tried more severely than you can bear. It is not His way with
His poor children. He mitigates the heaviest griefs. Dearest
friend, we closed our old lives with the weeks we spent together,
they were His gifts. Now, we both have done in different

[5] Madame de Salvo.

ways with all but the more or less gradual preparation for departure. Speak of us to your dear husband, tell him how we pray for him, and ask his prayers. Take care of yourself for his sake. I am much the same—days of great suffering, intervals of ease, no question of leaving my bed. Father Gallwey has been a week with us, left us yesterday, he will pray for you. Lady Londonderry will not linger long. She suffers much.

In fact, Lady Londonderry died at her house in Upper Brook Street at the beginning of October, having borne a long and most painful illness with great resignation and sweetness.

About this time, Lady Georgiana wrote the following letter to Mr. Aubrey de Vere, who visited occasionally his relative, Sir Henry Taylor, at Bournemouth, and whom Lady Georgiana was able to see from time to time even in her last illness. The occasion of the letter connects it with the Oratory of the Sacred Heart at Bournemouth. A well known friend of Lady Georgiana, the late Count Torre Diaz, had presented a beautiful and valuable copy of Murillo's Immaculate Conception, and Mr. de Vere had written a poem on the subject which he had given to Lady Georgiana. The verses were acknowledged in the following note:

To Mr. Aubrey de Vere.

Ayrfield, Bournemouth, *Sept.* 27, 1884.

MY DEAR MR. DE VERE,—I should have written yesterday, had it not been a bad day for me, and I wanted to write myself to thank you for sending me the verses which so truly and vividly describe our Blessed Mother's beautiful picture, and suggest new thoughts concerning her. A Christian poet alone could write of her what a Christian painter delineated. The words our Lord said to St. Thomas of Aquin, "Thou hast well written of Me," our holy Mother must, I think, be saying to you. You have added another flower to those which compose her chaplet. Your visits were a great pleasure to me. It is one of the great mitigations which God in His love allows me, that there are days in which I can thoroughly enjoy the society of those I care for. At this moment I am rather fatigued by the sufferings of yesterday, but can look forward now, I hope, to a good interval. . . ."[6]

Early in the year of which we are speaking, another friend of Lady Georgiana's (as is mentioned

---

[6] The poem will be found in *The Month* for October, 1884. It is unhappily too long to be inserted here, but we may extract a few lines describing the picture :

> She stands in Heaven :
> Not yet the utmost mountain-peaks of earth,
> Forth from the hoary deep unlifted still,
> Have felt her foot's pure touch.   A cloud from God,
> On streaming like a tide, thus far hath borne her
> To the threshold only of the house of man ;
> Angelic heads and wings beneath her gleam,
> And lily, and rose, and palm.   Her knee is bent ;
> Her moon-like face is tearful with great awe :
> Her universe is God, and other none ;
> Piercing all worlds her gaze is fixed on Him ;
> She waits His Will supreme. . . .
>   The painter's hand
> Wrought well !   Yon robe glitters, a pearl of dawn ;
> Yon purple scarf blown back by her advance
> Is dark with dews and shades of vanquished night ;
> The raised hands upward pointing from that breast
> Are matutinal with some heavenlier beam
> Than streaks our East.   That sunless mist behind her
> Wins but from her its glow.
>   O young fair face !—
> For though that form to maiden graciousness
> Hath reached, the face is maiden less than child,
> Or both in one, an earlier mystery
> Precursor of that Maiden Motherhood
> Which blends two gifts divine.

CC

in a former letter), Lady Henry Kerr, had died, and in December her daughter Henrietta, after a long period of suffering, against which she strove heroically for the sake of continuing as long as possible her duties in the school at Roehampton Convent, went to join her mother in the next world. The news of her death was kept for a few days from Lady Georgiana, who was very weak, but she wrote on December 12th to the Superior of the convent:

To Madame Digby.

DEAR REV. MOTHER,—I have only just heard that the angel of your dear house has gone to pray for you there, where her prayers will be more powerful than in this poor sad world, where she suffered and worked so much to the last. Just at that moment it was desired that I should not be at all excited, and for that reason it is that I was kept some days in ignorance that the blow so long expected had come. Within a year how many of her dear ones have preceded her to Heaven, and will greet there the flower of the family, the "child of the Sacred Heart." . . . I could never have hoped to see her again, and when that is the case, the next world seems nearer than the place of pilgrimage. Oh, poor Rev. Mother, I do feel for you! If a notice is drawn up of her holy devoted life, will you let me see it? My contemporaries are fast disappearing, but we thought of her as still young, and became accustomed to the miracle of her prolonged life. I am so glad my convert niece saw her. It must have been an effort. May God give her a special reward for it. I cannot write much at a time, so this note must end with an earnest prayer that God may support and console you.

Mr. Craven died on the 4th of October, and his wife was not able to write that day to Lady Georgiana. The latter could not answer the mournful announcement till the 9th.

... At last I can write a few lines which I have been longing to do. You know how constantly I have been thinking of you. It was no surprise to me to hear that the crushing blow had fallen, and having since you left us constantly expected it, that is, after the attack in London, I can but bless God that the time and place have been well chosen for you by God's mercy, and that this great affliction is attended by so much religious consolation. I long very much to hear from you, but if it is too great an effort to write, do ask our dear kind friend to let me know how you are and all about you. An overwhelming grief simplifies many things, and your life will be sadder, indeed, but calmer than heretofore. I call to mind vividly your dear husband's words when he took leave of me, his saying that he had not been so happy for many years as he had been with us here. It was for all of us the last bit of one kind of happiness. I have very suffering days, but others of comfort and freedom from pains—but I am getting weaker.

The letter ends by a kind message of condolence from Lord Granville to Mrs. Craven.

The next letter shows a still further decline in strength, it is dated the 9th of November.

Your letter was indeed a proof that the first days of deep sorrow are, oh, far from being the saddest and the most heart-breaking. . . . Yesterday was, I think, the anniversary of your arrival here last year. Oh, dear friend, how little we thought that you would be that day year plunged in all the anguish of bereavement, and I, after several months, in bed with increasing sufferings, saying to my poor husband, when he spoke of Christmas, "Oh, my dearest, I shall not be with you then!" I feel so ill, but I think life will last still some time. But now there are not many days when I can write letters, and only an hour or two in the day when freedom from suffering allows it. . . . May God bless, strengthen, support you! may He inspire us both to make the best use we can of the sufferings of our closing lives. . . .

In December, Lady Georgiana heard of the death in London of Madame de Paiva, one of the Pereira family, noted for her simple and earnest piety and activity in good works. She wrote as follows to the sister with whom she had lived for a great portion of her life.

To Miss Pereira.

Dec. 11, 1884.

It is only just now, my dear friend, that I have heard that God has taken to Himself that dear and holy sister of yours, leaving you in loneliness and desolation, but in the full sense that she has gone to Him and that your separation will be short. How many this year have left us for Heaven! are missed from their accustomed places in church, and draw our thoughts onward or rather upward. Some favoured ones, like your beloved sister, so well prepared, so constantly united with God, that the transition scarcely seems to us abrupt. Others are nearing, others have reached their end, slowly and amidst much pain and suffering. He knows what is best for each. Literally she had no care, no thought, but for the Church of God. All was done for it and through it. What a large number of relations will welcome her, and you have indeed, dear friend, in every sense treasures laid up in Heaven. God bless you. Pray for me that the few days that remain may be more like hers than they have been.

Yours always affectionately,

GEORGIANA FULLERTON.

The next letter to Mrs. Craven reflects somewhat of despondency as to the turn affairs were taking in France. It is dated the 12th of December.

. . . You said in the letter which crossed mine that you would write again in a few days. Soon afterwards an increase of my sufferings took place, and in the short intervals of illness I had no energy to write. For three days I have been better, and must, dearest, inquire how and where you are. This month of December keeps you constantly in my thoughts, and I long for an intercourse with you, and to know if you have yet been able to form to yourself any idea for the future. I have seen in the *Univers* to-day the announcement of the death of the Comte de la Ferte Mun, and am so afraid that he may be your brother-in-law, and that sorrow is encompassing you on every side. In the same paper I read an enthusiastic burst of admiration and sympathy elicited by your nephew's eloquent protest against the iniquities of the Chamber. Everything seems as gloomy as possible, but though our Lord seems asleep and unmindful of His children's trials, so that we are inclined to say, "Dost Thou not care that we perish?" we must hope, and trust, and offer up our sufferings for the tempest-tossed Church, in this her hour of anguish. . . .

The next letter is the last of the series, written on January 2, 1885.

. . . I meant and wished to write to you on New Year's Day, but was too much prostrated, and feeling a little stronger to-day, I must do so, not, alas! to wish you a happy New Year, that is not God's will for you or for me—not that kind of innocent happiness which, thanks to His mercy, we enjoyed during those days that were drawing to their close. The difficulty of conquering my inordinate love of life clings to me, and regrets, natural to youth and middle age, but inconceivable when existence in any case must have ended very soon. This is what I pray for now, to begin to love our Lord with a love which swallows up all other loves, and makes those who have it long for death. The canonization of our English Martyrs will soon be brought to a conclusive decision. A wonderful miracle has taken place in favour of a poor man who invoked them. This made Father Gallwey urge us to devote this Christmas time to prayers for my recovery through their intercession. I do not believe, in my case, in a miraculous cure, but I do hope they will obtain for me that supernaturalized grace I pray for. No particular prayers are enjoined, but those I enclose are very beautiful, the Psalm applies in their case in a remarkable manner. And now what are my thoughts, my hopes, dear friend, for you? I am satisfied with the immediate ones, *e poi*, God will point out the path you will have to follow, the evening rays will illuminate it. . . . I am ashamed of this dreadful scribble, but my hand has become very unsteady and my thoughts also. It pleases me to picture you now with those whom you most love, amidst your French friends. What a tie it is between those who have loved and appreciated our departed ones! God bless you my dearest friend. . . .

The traces of increasing suffering and weakness which may be perceived in these last letters are enough to prepare the reader for the approach of the end. Lady Georgiana was to survive the Christmas Day which was spoken of, indeed the last note to Mrs. Craven was written after that date. But she was not able to spend it as the last had been spent. Still it was a day which those about her will remember, and she was careful to provide every one with a little souvenir, even writing with her own hand to one of her servants who was keeping the house in Chapel Street a few words of farewell. We must not lift the veil from the last scene of her partings. We have seen how she had prayed that she might come to love our Lord with a love that swallowed up all others, and might make her long to die, and we may be sure that there was nothing excited or passionate about her farewells to earth, tenderly as she loved those whom she had to leave behind. Her state grew worse about the 15th of January, but nothing tempted the calm and peace of her soul, and the clearness of her mind. It was on the 19th of January that the end came. Her eyes were fixed tenderly on her crucifix, her husband,

and brothers, and her faithful servants, were by her side, along with the Father who for so many years had been the guide of her spiritual life. She passed away so quietly that all the careful attention of those who stood around her, could not detect the exact moment, at which her soul exchanged the miseries of this life for the endless possession of the Eternal Truth and Light to Whom she had been so faithfully and entirely devoted.

APPENDIX.

Some mention has been made in the Preface of the notes and memoranda of her religious life, left behind her by Lady Georgiana, and, as these have been more sparingly used in the text of the present volume than in the French *Life* by Mrs. Craven, it may be well to give some account of them in general. The time has hardly come for the publication of all that Lady Georgiana has left behind her of this kind.

The earliest of the notes now available are not dated, but they seem to belong to the time soon after her great blow in the loss of her son.[1]

The earliest in date seem to be those which will be found in the fourteenth chapter.

These notes were made before Lady Georgiana's return to England in 1857, which seems to be the date at which she determined to give herself more systematically and seriously than ever to a life of religious devotion and charity. It would seem also that in the course of that and the following year, she became a more constant attendant at the church in Farm Street near which she lived, and placed herself under the

[1] See p. 340.

direction to which she adhered during the rest of her life, and which she spoke of as one of the greatest blessings she had ever received from God.

The next set of notes is dated 1859. They appear to have been made while she was following the Spiritual Exercises, as they are usually given in public in the church at Farm Street, beginning on Passion Sunday. Some of the thoughts which she notes down might have been suggested by some of the meditations. The date corresponds to one of the early days of Passion Week in that year.

The resolutions of this year include an hour's meditation every day, daily Communion, and confession twice a week, daily practice of bodily mortification, and something special on Wednesdays and Fridays. Her resolution for particular examen is, " To do everything as perfectly as I possibly can, not, of course, as perfectly as it can be done, but as well as by application and earnest good will I can do it." She also seems to have made a resolution about this time to make a vow, if she can obtain permission, to give herself to any work to which God shall call her, and which is judged by her director to be His will for her, and to keep herself ready to obey any person whom He shall point out to her as her Superior and directress, in anything that may not interfere with the duties of her state of life.

Then follow some remarks on the question of her employments, whether they should be literary or simply charitable works, of which something has already been said. She goes into details about the amount of her income from works of fiction, and the like.[2] On July 1, 1859, she makes an offering of herself to labour for poor

² See p. 342.

children, "to honour and serve our Lord in the persons of those little ones whose angels always see the face of His Father in Heaven." She prays that this may be no momentary resolution, but the firm and steadfast purpose of her soul. (This offering was afterwards enlarged so as to include working for the conversion of souls.)

In the next year, 1860, there are some notes on meditation made in a retreat which began, apparently, on September 1st.

From the Meditation on Sin.

In the application to myself I thought of the dreadful ingratitude of not having done my utmost to serve God, and not taking real earnest pains to conquer my faults and correspond with His grace. The great grace of conversion has been granted me, repeated and pressing calls to a perfect life have been vouchsafed to me, and a very clear understanding of what that perfect life ought to be, and all the time I fall short of it through lack of a really firm will. I am in exactly the state now about perfection that I was many years about the most common duties of religion. I now spend one day, imperfectly indeed, but in the best way I can, and then weeks, perhaps, not doing my best, and this is wilfully offending God, though it does not seem to me so at the moment.

In the next Meditation (also on Sin).

The best way of awakening in ourselves contrition, is by thinking still more of God's goodness and of His great mercies to us than of our sins. Whilst thinking over the sins of my childhood and youth, I did not feel much moved, nor when I thought of all those rooms in the Embassy where I spent those years and so much offended God; but when I thought of the little room within our school-room, where I had knelt down one day, when I was thirteen years old, and asked the Blessed Virgin to pray for me, then the "dull hard stone" melted within my heart, and I was moved to tears of contrition.

A little later.

God's unbounded marvellous goodness and patience, waiting, as He does, for every one of us! He waited for me in my worst and most careless days. He has now been waiting for these many years, since I have been a Catholic, for a thorough conversion of heart to Him. Such a grace bestowed! Such a miserable, poor return for it! Being able to do better, and really practically not caring to do better! Not caring enough to pray well, to make the little effort of always preparing my meditation over-night, though I know by experience it makes all the difference, not overcoming languor and fatigue in the morning, and so omitting my meditation, for fear, forsooth, of knocking myself up for the day, as if my work were so very valuable and laborious! resolving over and over again that instead of feeling impatient with those who beg of me when I cannot help them, and irritable, almost, with Almighty God, for not giving me always the means to do so, that I would lay their case and my own inability before Him, and ask Him to help and console them when I cannot do it, and then, from mere laziness, not doing it. Resolving to pray, to read, and to meditate as I walk and drive about, which I *can* do, for worldly sights and sounds do not really much distract me, and from laziness, not doing it! Resolving to lift up my

mind to God and ask His blessing on each employment,
and each occupation, and not doing it, simply, if the
truth be spoken, because I do not feel it worth while
to take the trouble to serve God more perfectly. Let it
be so no more, O my God! Give me grace to correspond with Thy grace.

These are followed by some resolutions as to matters
of daily life. After these some small faults are constantly noted down. She seems to have had the
practice of reading in the New Testament daily on her
knees, probably as a preparation for meditation on it,
and some specimen may be given of the thoughts which
afterwards occurred to her.

"Father ——— told me to repeat often in God's
presence the acknowledgment of His great goodness
and my own misery and ingratitude. He said it was
good to put the thought into words and use them often.
He told me to make a constant practice of reading
the New Testament on my knees, getting thoroughly
acquainted with it, weighing every little circumstance,
every word, to make it a subject of special prayer
that by so doing I might get to know Christ more, and
become more like Him and our Blessed Lady, to do
things because they would have done them, and in the
manner they would have done them. I will try, besides
preparation at night and meditation in the morning, to
spend ten minutes in this way immediately before or
after luncheon, and a quarter of an hour whilst before
the Blessed Sacrament."

In 1862, she seems to have made a retreat at Roehampton, in August, or, at all events, to have spent
some time there in retirement. It seems to have been

with the object of preparing herself to join the Congregation of the *Enfants de Marie du Sacré Cœur*, which is connected with the Convent at Roehampton, that this retreat was made. At all events, it was on August 9 of that year that she became a Member. Lady Georgiana and Lady Lothian were successively " Presidents " of the Congregation up to the time of the death of the latter, and, after that, Lady Georgiana held the office up to her own decease.

During this retreat it was suggested to her to devote herself more than she had yet done to an Apostolate of zeal and prayer for the conversion of persons in the higher ranks of life. She does not seem to have been led by her own inclination to this, for reasons which have been already mentioned. " I will keep a list of persons for whom I will constantly pray and get prayers, and I will be on the watch for every opportunity of winning them to the Faith, and offer up alms and little mortifications for that purpose." Her remarks on this suggestion have been already quoted. She feared it would interfere with her recollection and spirit of prayer. We have already spoken of this.

We find, soon after this, a form of general examination of conscience, and some ejaculations she was in the habit of using constantly, while performing the most ordinary actions.

In 1863, there are some resolutions dated from the Convent of the Sacré Cœur, Rue de Varennes, Paris, July 24th.

We read among them the following :

" St. Francis of Assisi thought the greatest joy on earth would be to be called a thief and an impostor; to be beaten and to be ignominiously thrust out of his monastery, and I cannot bear to be told, but not at all unkindly, that my sufferings and infirmities are in great part fancy, and have it said that a doctor said so! I will resolve never again to deny it—when it is said, to smile good-humouredly and to say nothing."

There is another book of retreat notes undated, which seems to have been written about this time. Among other resolutions is this, " To study to make my life in every respect as nearly as possible the life of a religious accidentally obliged to live in the world— a *Fille de Marie*, for instance. I must consider whether I can practice a greater degree of mortification without making myself less active and capable of work.

" To take as the subject of my particular examen, and be very faithful to it, humiliation, outward and inward, according to the eight points specified in Rodriguez, the third of which includes doing every action very well, as doing it in the sight of God." She had before, as we have seen, made this last point the subject of this examen.

In 1865 there are some notes on August 1st, perhaps in retreat. She then resolves to begin again to practice what Madame de Chantal vowed and kept for so many years, " that is, always to do what will seem to me to be most perfect." And she writes in her little book of particular examen, " Resolution for the year, to do whatever will seem to me most perfect. Subject for particular examen—faults against this resolution."

> Da me posso nullo,
> Con Dio, posso tutto.

Some resolutions of this retreat refer to her keeping faithfully or improving upon the rules of the Congregation of the *Enfants de Marie.* Some rules for penances and the like are added.

She lays before her spiritual guide the doubt as to the matter of writing books of fiction, of which something has been already said. Before this, she suggests the following to her director:

" To fight against the love of praise as regards my writings, would it be good and in accordance with that resolution to determine not to read, unless compelled to do so, anything about them in the newspapers and reviews, unless I hear it is unfavourable? It has hitherto been an intense pleasure to look out for those notices. It is sometimes useful to read them, but I am inclined to think that for a year at least it will be best to forego the advantage, and gain that of practising a good sensible mortification."

This proposal was approved. We have already said something on the question of continuing her works of fiction.

Then follow a series of simple and beautiful resolutions as to practical matters, and ejaculatory prayers, and the like. There is one about her monthly retreat, on which day she resolves to hear an additional Mass, to make one hour more of prayer, to visit the Blessed Sacrament for a longer time in the afternoon, but not to attempt to shut herself up for the whole day and keep silence, and finally to make a review of her conscience for the month, and show her resolutions to her confessor.

The following are some of her " ejaculations."

Going out of my house.
Angele Dei
Qui custos es mei,

Me tibi commissam pietate superna
Illumina, custodi, rege et guberna.

Coming home.

Glòry be to the Father, &c.

Going into a house.

Refrain my tongue from evil, and my lips that they speak no guile.

Coming out of a house.

Have mercy on me, O Lord, according to Thy great mercy, and according to the multitude of Thy tender mercies, blot out all my offences.

Going into a room.

O Sacred Heart of Jesus, I implore the grace to love Thee daily more and more.

Coming out of a room.

O Mary, conceived without sin, pray for me who have recourse to thee.

Going into a church.

Blessed be Jesus in the Most Holy Sacrament of the Altar.

Going out of a church.

Lord, now lettest Thou Thy servant depart in peace.

Beginning to read.

Deus in adjutorium meum intende.

Closing the book.

Domine ad adjuvandum me festina.

Closing a letter for a charitable object.

Propter te, Deus meus.

DD

If it is a refusal of help—

A Hail Mary. Also a Hail Mary for every beggar or petitioner I refuse, or, God be merciful to me, a sinner.

From this date, August, 1865, there are daily notes of points of meditation, sometimes interrupted for several months, generally followed by a list of faults noted during the day.

Some few specimens of these points may be given.

On the marriage in Cana.

1. They have no wine.
2. My hour is not yet come.
3. Whatsoever He shall say to you, do ye.

Before the feast of the Holy Cross.

1. O crux Ave spes unica.
2. Adoramus te Christe et benedicimus tibi, quia per sanctam Crucem tuam redemisti mundum.

On the Parable of the Sower.

1. "In a good, in a very good heart"—Make my heart, O Lord, not only good, but very good.
2. "Keep the word"—how to hear with profit. Keep it—how to keep it, as the Blessed Virgin kept all those words in her heart.
3. "And bring forth fruit"—To let no listening to or reading of the word fail to bring forth fruit.
4. "In patience."

The leper and the centurion's servant (St. Matt. vii. 3).

1. Lord, if Thou wilt, Thou canst make me clean.
2. I will; be thou made clean.
3. I will come and heal him.

4. Lord, I am not worthy that Thou shouldst enter under my roof, but only say the word, and my servant shall be healed.

5. I have not found so great faith in Israel.

6. Go, and as thou hast believed, so be it done to thee.

Conversion of St. Paul (Acts ix.).

1. Suddenly a light from heaven shined round about him.

2. Lord, what wilt Thou have me to do?

3. For behold he prayeth.

4. The grace of God in me hath not been void.

5. Who are they who will receive a hundred-fold?

6. To me Thy friends, O God, are made exceedingly honourable.

On Colossians iii. 12—17.

1. Holy and beloved, what are we to put on?

2. Mercy, benignity, humility, modesty, patience.

3. Have charity, which is the bond of perfection.

4. Let the peace of Christ rejoice in your hearts.

5. All whatsoever you do in word or in work, all things do ye in the Name of our Lord Jesus Christ; giving thanks to God and the Father through Jesus Christ our Lord.

Our Lord and Nicodemus (St. John ii. 23—25; iii.).

1. Jesus knows all men; He knows what is in them; He knows what is in me.

2. We know that He is come a teacher from God. His miracles prove it.

3. Unless a man be born again of water and the Holy Ghost, he cannot enter into the Kingdom of God.

4. And as Moses lifted up the serpent in the

desert, so must the Son of Man be lifted up, that whosoever believeth in Him may not perish, but may have life everlasting.

5. Men have loved darkness rather than light.

6. He that loves truth comes to the light.

Asking, seeking, knocking (St. Luke ix. 9—13).

1. My God, I ask, give me grace to be a Saint.

2. My God, I seek, let me find out what You would have me to do.

3. My God, I knock, open to me the door of Your Sacred Heart.

4. My God, I ask of Thee Thy good Spirit, give it me.

The Beatitudes.

1. Oh, my Lord Jesus, make me poor in spirit, and give me the Kingdom of Heaven.

2. Make me mourn for my sins and those of others, and then comfort me.

3. Make me meek like Thyself, and then unite my heart to Thine.

4. Give me grace to hunger and thirst after righteousness, and then fill me with it.

5. Make my heart pure, that I may see Thee.

6. Make me merciful, that I may obtain mercy.

7. Make me a peacemaker, that I may become Thy child.

St. Andrew and St. Peter coming to our Lord (St. John i. 42).

1. Jesus is our end. How God leads each of us to Him.

2. In what unlikely ways He leads unlikely people.

3. Who so unlikely as us?

4. Who so far off through sin, ignorance, coldness, relapses ?

5. Everything in life, stars of Bethlehem—sorrows, joys, &c.

Zaccheus (St. Luke xix. 3).

1. He sought to see Jesus.

2. This day I must abide in thy house.

3. To-day if you shall hear His voice exciting you to greater perfection and imitation of Himself, harden not your hearts.

4. Open the door of your heart as soon as you hear Him knock.

Our Lord at the well (St. John iv.).

1. Our Lord sitting at the well.

2. His weariness.

3. Our consolation.

4. Looking down in our hearts, and asking for love.

Opening of St. John's Gospel (St. John i.).

1. In the beginning was the Word, and the Word was with God, and the Word was God.

2. The same was in the beginning with God.

3. All things were made by Him, and without Him was made nothing that was made.

Charity (1 Cor. xiii.).

Charity is :
> Patient,
> Kind,
> Envies not,
> Deals not perversely,
> Is not puffed up.

The same.

Charity is not ambitious,
> Seeketh not her own,
> Is not provoked to evil,
> Rejoiceth not in iniquity, but rejoiceth in the
> truth.

The same.

Charity
> Beareth all things,
> Believeth all things,
> Hopeth all things,
> Endureth all things,
> And never falls away.

The widow's mite (St. Luke xxi.).

She has cast in all she had, and do I give all?
What can I give more?
What shall I give more?

Watch and pray (St. Matt. xxvi. 41).

Watch ye and pray,
That you enter not into temptation.
The spirit is willing,
But the flesh is weak.
He prayed, saying the same words.

Commission of the Apostles (St. John xv. 16).

1. I have appointed you that you should go and
should bring forth fruit.

2. And your fruit should remain.

3. That whatsoever you shall ask of the Father in
My Name, He may give it you.

The Christian Vocation.

I beseech you that you walk worthy of the vocation to which you are called.

1. What is my vocation?
2. Do I walk worthy of it? Humility, mildness, patience, charity.

Love of God (St. Matt. xxii. 37—40).

Thou shalt love the Lord thy God with,

1. Thy whole heart.
2. Thy whole soul.
3. Thy whole mind, and thy neighbour as thyself.

Eternal Life (St. John xvii. 3).

1. Now this is eternal life that they may know Thee, the only true God, and Jesus Christ Whom Thou hast sent.
2. I have glorified Thee on the earth.
3. I have finished the work which Thou givest Me to do.

The same.

1. I pray not that Thou shouldst take them out of the world, but that Thou shouldst keep them from evil.
2. Sanctify them in truth. Thy word is truth.
3. As Thou hast sent Me into the world, I also have sent them into the world.

The Hæmorhoissa.

1. Cut, burn, spare not, so Thou showest me mercy.
2. If I can but touch the hem of His garment I shall be healed.
3. Go in peace, thy faith hath made thee whole.

Magdalene, Thomas, and Peter.

1. Rabboni—Master.
2. Tarry with us for the day is far spent.
3. My Lord and my God !
4. My God, Thou knowest that I love Thee !

The Annunciation.

1. There is no word impossible to Thee, my God.
2. Behold the handmaid of the Lord.
3. Be it done unto me according to Thy word.

The Epiphany.

1. We have seen His star in the East and are come to adore Him.
2. Go and diligently inquire after the Child.
3. And they offered Him—gold, frankincense, and myrrh.

Our Lord's Power.

1. Lord, if Thou wilt, Thou canst make me clean.
2. There is no word impossible with Thee.
3. Lord, what wilt Thou have me to do ?

These specimens will suffice, and perhaps more than suffice. They are given here for the use and encouragement of persons who will be resolute and constant enough to follow Lady Georgiana's habit of choosing the points, or heads, of their meditations for themselves, instead of taking them from meditation-books. Indeed, after 1863, her notes consist chiefly of records of the meditations she had prepared for herself day after day. These are often found continuous for months together, but often also they are interrupted, whether from sickness or some other cause. There are occasional notes of other matters. One time she says she should wish to make a vow to make it the object of her life to cooperate, in whatever way God may put it in her power, with the design of establishing in London a convent where the Blessed Sacrament may be adored day and night. Such a convent was established in 1863 at Harley House, and Lady Georgiana was one of the first to welcome the religious with great cordiality, as the records of the convent show. We find further on such remarks as these.

From St. Teresa: "All we have to do is to lay our will on the altar, not suffering it, as far as in us lies, to be defiled by anything of earth.

"One day spent in humility and self-knowledge, though at the cost of so many afflictions and labours, I account to be a greater favour from our Lord than many days spent in prayer.

"Our spiritual progress does not depend on the length of time we spend in prayer, for when we fulfil with greater perfection the duties to which we are called by charity or obedience, we advance more in the love of God in a few moments thus employed than in many long hours of consideration."

A manuscript book, begun November 23, 1865, is devoted to inscribing the promises obtained in answer to the widely circulated appeals for prayers on behalf of her nephew, whose cure she hoped to obtain through the Blessed Sacrament. The miracle that had lately taken place at Metz, in which Mdlle. de Clery had been cured of the same incurable paralysis as that from which her nephew was suffering, was an encouragement and incentive to prayer, and the appeal was warmly responded to in every direction. Special devotions and Masses were offered at the great sanctuaries in France,

D D

Spain, and Italy, and innumerable communities were enlisted in the good work. At the end of many pages devoted to the list of prayers, Lady Georgiana writes, May 17, 1866:

" Many more prayers than these have been put up. The requests for them have circulated since November last, in English, French, Spanish, and Portuguese. They are going on in many places even now. God's ways are not as our ways, but the extraordinary dispensation which has answered this great union of supplications is doubtless the pledge, and, perhaps, the forerunner of extraordinary mercies." [1]

As our readers know, Lord and Lady Rivers died, one on the 28th, the other on the 30th of April, 1866. Their son Henry, the last of their male children, succeeded his father, only to die in the following May.

In 1868, there are some notes written before returning to England, and amongst them is the passage quoted above, in which she rejoices and gives thanks in returning " to the dear English air." [2] This return took place in April—it was the year in which she had lost her nephew, the last of the sons of her sister, and in which her nieces had had to give up their home at Rushmore. There are entries made daily during the summer, except one or two intervals.

In the August of this year she made a retreat at the Convent of Notre Dame de Sion, Worthing, of which there are considerable records in her papers. She was beset all through with much weakness and fatigue, but struggled bravely against them. We give some extracts. .

" Aug. 3rd. No joy on entering the retreat, different

---

[1] See chapter xviL   [2] P. 428.

from anything I ever felt before—dull, indifferent, hard, irritable feeling; only when in the opening discourse the Father said that Father Segneri had gone into retreat an ordinary man and had come out a Saint, I felt an ardent desire that such a change might come over me this time; and the words : ' Man was created to *praise*,' made the tears come into my eyes. My soul does find joy in magnifying the Lord, and my spirit generally rejoices in God my Saviour.

"Aug. 4th. Could not think much; my head is weak, but I sat at the window with tears and joy of heart praising God for everything I saw, the sky, the clouds, the harvest, the sea, the birds, the horse that came to drink with eagerness at a trough in the field. It all made me think of the Psalms, and my heart burned within me.

"' The use of creatures.' I examined myself on this point, and found that though my actions are not generally speaking inordinate, my wishes are. I am anxious indeed to do God's will, but I too ardently desire that His will should be mine. I wish to be well, especially under certain circumstances. I am very anxious not to die abroad. I dread suffering. I wish my books to succeed, and wish for a great deal of money to do good with. I wish to live to be as old as my mother was, to do good of course, but what folly! Does not God know best? Does the servant fret because his Master calls him away from the work he is doing only for Him?"

In the succeeding meditations there seems to have been a constant struggle against weakness and fatigue, but perseverance throughout, and varying success. On the last day:

". . . I have suffered a little in mind and body during

this retreat, but I feel it has been nevertheless a useful and a blessed one. I believe, too, that whereas before I felt much better during the retreat than my usual state, this time I felt worse, and I think this is not altogether unsatisfactory. It is humbling, but gives me more hope of the effect of what I have heard, and probing of the weakness of my soul, being lasting.

" The two last meditations were on the manner of obtaining Divine love. They were beautiful, but such an aching of the heart came over me, like a presenti-ment of some great sorrow, or danger, or evil. ' Fiat,' with all my heart. I turn to my Father and say: ' Thy will be done.' The retreat is over now, and I will make my vow to-morrow morning after my medi-tation. Resolutions much as before.

" To make this year subject of particular examen: Preparation or recollection before speaking to God or other, or sitting down to write."

In September she is again at Walmer Castle. " During the last three weeks what a change has seemed to come over my spiritual life! I am more fully resolved than ever to correspond to God's grace to the uttermost of my power. I have more hope of doing so than I ever had before. May God help me."

On November 12th, she is on the eve of leaving for the winter. She writes at Dover : " I want to try to make these five months' absence a sort of retreat, a preparation for the other part of the year in which any improvement that may have been made can be tested."

On New Year's Eve she writes a resolution: " To take for the subject of the particular examen this year the sense of the presence of God in this way,—to notice as a fault anything said or done when alone or with others which I should not have said or done if the person, whose approval I value most in the world, was present."

In the following years there are several interruptions in the notes from illness. About 1872 there is the draft of a statement in French about her poverty, by which she means that the writing works of imagination having been forbidden her as too wearying to her head, and all her jewels having been sold, she was without her usual amount of resources for her good works and charities. She says also that her husband had just given her a large sum, as well as other sums before. " I think I took too great a pleasure in disposing of rather large sums, and now our Lord makes me feel a true poverty, for sometimes I do not know how to meet demands." She mentions also, about the same time, that her particular examen had been for some time the imitation of our Blessed Lady in all her actions, words, and the like.

The notes on the points of meditation cease after 1874, though there are short notes at intervals feebly written.

In her prayer-book, just before the list of days of particular devotion connected with her son, p. 427, is written on the same page an extract from Father Faber: " From that moment till the moment of death the sorrow abode with them, a wonderful, deep, and fixed sorrow. It put itself in harmony with every kind of feeling. It adapted itself to all circumstances. It never darkened into gloom. It never melted into light. It lived on in the present, and the clear view of the future was part of its present and it never let go its hold of the past. The characteristics of this sorrow were, that it was lifelong, quiet, supernatural, and a fountain of love."

Her papers also contain some unpolished verses which she must have written without meaning them for any eye but her own, for she does not care for rhyme or metre, and passes from English to French in the same stanzas. Some of these are dated at Aldenham, September 8, 1846, and therefore not long after her conversion to Catholicism. The date is the feast of the Nativity of our Blessed Lady, and the first verses seem like a thanksgiving for Holy Communion, for they speak of the "blessing she this day receives." Then they pass on to speak of her son.[3]

> Mon enfant Dieu-donné,
>   C'est le nom que mon cœur,
> Te donne bien souvent
>   Dans les jours de ses pleurs
> Aujourd'hui dans ma joie
>   Au comble de bonheur. . . .

There the lines break off, and they are continued on the same page, July, 1856, that is, soon after the loss of her son :

> Aujourd'hui, dans les larmes
>   Au fort de mon douleur
> Je le repete encore,
>   Mon enfant Dieu-donné
> Dieu reprend son trésor.

And then she adds: "*Mon Dieu, je vous adore, mais mon cœur est brisé !*"

May we be forgiven if we have lifted too much the veil which ought to conceal such a sorrow, for the sake of showing how soon after her great affliction she was enabled to think of it with resignation as coming from the good hand of her Heavenly Father !

---

[3] Her son was conditionally baptized, September 14, 1846.

II.

NOTES BY LADY VICTORIA KIRWAN.

WE may here add some notes by the late Lady
Victoria Kirwan—who has lately joined her friend in
the next world—giving some traits of Lady Georgiana's
character, as shown in her work at Bournemouth.

My first recollections of Lady Georgiana Fullerton
are many years ago now—before my conversion. I had
read her books and felt such an attraction towards her
that I could not keep from seeking her society. She
was, at that time, much interested in a young girl,
Mary Shaw, who was dying of consumption in a
lodging under the care of a kind Catholic lady, herself
an invalid. Lady Georgiana went constantly to Mary,
and I met her there, as I visited the poor girl too. I
recollect one of the many kind things she did there.
One afternoon I was with Mary and Lady Georgiana
came in, and, seeing I was tired (I had walked there),
she said, "Now I am going to stay with Mary, and you
shall take my fly home, and I can wait here for it,"
and so she did. I remember, when she first met me
after being received, the bright way in which she welcomed me with, "Ah, my dear, I know you are like
a fish out of water." When she settled at Bournemouth, her one idea was how much good she could do
to every one. She begged in all directions till she got
money enough to start the little house, St. Joseph's,
which now, alas! has to be closed for want of funds.
That little home was a great interest to her. She

carefully provided a treat for the patients every great feast, and she would come herself and play a round game with them, staying till near her dinner-hour often, and entering into everything. She would join in the games of those patients well enough to be in the sitting-room, and then she would go and sit with those too ill to be downstairs. One Lent she was laid up, and she sent for me and said, " My dear, I should like you to go every day in Passion and Holy Week and read Anne Catharine Emmerich's *Dolorous Passion* to the patients at St. Joseph's." At the sale for Invalids' Work here, she always went herself and bought a great deal of the St. Joseph's patients' work. She always helped to pay for those who could not pay for themselves. When there was any feast more than an ordinary one she always sent money for a fly for the patients to go to church. With all her correspondence and busy life, her thought and kindness for those patients was wonderful.

Then she originated, with the Fathers' sanction and approval, a guild or confraternity for young women, and it was placed under the patronage of St. Walburga, and constantly she would go to the monthly meetings and sit amongst the girls and tell them some interesting account of a pilgrimage or some such thing. She always provided their Christmas treat, and also she gave them, every summer, an excursion, paying for everything and planning it all with the greatest care and forethought. Then she took the kindest interest in the schools, and always gave their Christmas-tree, coming and distributing the prizes herself with kind words to every child. Then she started a work meeting every fortnight at the convent. She always sent money for the postal cards to announce the meeting, and money to put in the nuns' box. She regularly remembered to do this up to nearly the end of her illness. Through all her worst sufferings she always came to the work meetings, and would sit and work first at a flannel petticoat and then, as she became ill, she used to knit stockings. She always filled the three spare places in her fly with those to whom the walk would have been fatiguing. When she was ill or unable to come, she constantly sent the money for a fly to be used by those whom it would tire to walk. She nearly always bought the flannel, calico, &c., for the poor clothes, and on my suggesting that we should all subscribe one shilling, she would not hear of it and said, " No, my dear, I don't think I like it, a shilling is very important to some people." Long after she was completely laid up she would, on the work meeting day, send interesting bits of Catholic news to be read out, passages in some of the Catholic magazines, and always listened to the details of the meetings with the greatest interest. No one ever asked her help here in vain. She always gave to every case of want that came to her knowledge, and many a time I know she had only a few shillings left in her purse.

Of her many acts of high spirituality and virtue, I could never say enough. I only pray God may give me grace to follow in her steps, though, indeed, so far behind her, to my life's end. Once, I remember a friend of mine telling me she drove on a very hot day along a dusty road with Lady Georgiana, who sat all the time in the heat of the sun without parasol or gloves on her hands. In the coldest weather she would only wear her thin black shawl till a friend bought for her, and insisted on her wearing, a Shetland thick one. I recollect once the inside of her mouth and tongue was very painful, being ulcerated, and I began to pity her and she stopped me at once saying, " My dear, it's a very good thing, I've often been greedy, I dare say." Once we were both coming back very tired from the work meeting, and she said suddenly, " My dear, this is the very moment to pay a visit to——" (mentioning a poor woman who was certainly a trial to her friends). And she accordingly gave orders to drive at once to her cottage, which we did, and our Lord was good to us,— for she was out.

Once something very trying, very annoying, happened, and Lady Georgiana was asked as the person in authority to interfere. She said, " Yes, I will, but just wait a little while—I must first go into the chapel."

She had all the bright gaiety of youth, and enjoyed everything like a child would. I brought her a tin flask, a large quart one of water from St. Winefrid's Well, and she sent for me and said, " Now, my dear, we must decant this," which we did. I found her with an array of bottles, a lighted candle, and sealing-wax, and when she had finished, she said, " Now we must have a little drink, and will say a Hail Mary first." So we knelt down and said a Hail Mary, and then she poured out the water for her and me, and we drank it, she saying, with her bright smile, " Is not it refreshing, how I have enjoyed it ! "

Of the last two years of this beautiful life, I can say but little, for her illness was so severe, and her sufferings so great that I did not often see her, but when I did, it seemed like going to see an angel. She would sit up to receive me with her own bright smile, and begin to ask at once after the sick people in the place and any case of distress she knew of. She never spoke of her own sufferings except to say how kind every one was to her. She was always bright when the pain was gone, and once she said, laughing, to her doctor, "I am sure you are thinking what a deal of killing this old woman takes." She told me she made the Stations every day on some little picture Stations she had. The last Christmas she was alive she remembered many of us, sending us each a little picture. One of the last notes I ever received from her was a few pencil lines to say she was praying so much for the canonization of the English Martyrs. Two days before she died she was going to send for me, and then the end came and our Lord called her home. She looked like an angel in her coffin, with a kind of surprised smile on her face, from which every line had gone, and she looked quite young.

All who knew her as I did must feel she can never be replaced. Her loss is irreparable, but we can thank God Who sent us such an example of charity and holiness, to be our dearest memory and consolation, and for His everlasting glory.

www.ingramcontent.com/pod-product-compliance
Lightning Source LLC
Chambersburg PA
CBHW032021110726
47901CB00004B/1153